Own the Eights Maybe Baby

Own the Eights: Book Three

Krista Sandor

Candy Castle Books

Chapter One
Georgie

Georgiana Jensen-Marks stared at a window.

A tiny plastic window barely the size of a Tic Tac, her heart beating like a drum.

She narrowed her gaze, as if by sheer force of will, she could alter the outcome and stop another set of faint pink lines from materializing.

"Georgie? Are you okay in there?" her husband asked from the other side of the bathroom door.

Husband.

Jordan Marks, CrossFit trainer extraordinaire, Emperor of Asshattery, reigning Sovereign of Scat, and her partner in lifestyle blogging, was her husband.

After a breakneck-speed romance, where at times, she was damn near ready to break his perfect neck and a whirlwind wedding, she and Jordan had promised to love and honor each other for the rest of their lives. In front of their closest friends and family and a little over two hundred of her mother's high society country club confidants, the acclaimed event planning guru, the Denver Wedding Frau, had given them the wedding of their dreams and the knowledge that their love was the kind that could last a lifetime.

With the changes they'd endured over such a short period, it was a miracle they didn't have whiplash!

She'd met Jordan only five months ago when they were forced to team up for the CityBeat Battle of the Blogs. Her Own the Eights philosophy, preaching the merits of dating a solid, dependable eight over a self-obsessed ten, had been the polar opposite of Jordan's Perfect Ten Mindset. But over a few weeks, the man she'd dubbed the Emperor of Asshattery because that's exactly who he was when they'd met, had become the one person she couldn't live without.

Together, they'd created the More Than Just a Number blog, marrying the best of each of their blogs and creating one hell of a bang in the blogosphere.

She'd never dreamed Jordan would pop the question on live TV so soon after they'd moved in together. But that's what happened a couple of months ago. In only a few weeks from that unconventional proposal, and with more ups and downs than she could count, they'd made it to the altar—stronger and more in love than ever.

With the wedding behind them, this time was supposed to be about them. They'd spent the last fifteen days on their honeymoon, breathing in the salty-sweet Fiji air while indulging in the naughtiest teachings of the Kama Sutra.

Eat. Sleep. Sex. Repeat.

Their time in the beach bungalow had been a welcome reprieve from their publicized romance and newsworthy nuptials. Thanks to their status as CityBeat's top-rated bloggers, coauthoring their More Than Just a Number lifestyle blog with millions of followers across the globe, the world had watched them fall in love and get married.

It was everything she'd ever wanted.

And everyone wanted a piece of the CityBeat sweethearts.

Opportunities were rolling in by the dozen. Companies were lining up, asking for endorsements. Publishers were dangling book deals, and conferences wanted them as keynote speakers.

She and Jordan had dreamed of this—dreamed of helping people find happiness and reach their true potential. They wanted to be household names associated with living your best life by taking care of yourself, your community, and the world.

Day after day, their blog garnered more likes, more followers, and more people who wrote in, sharing how their posts had inspired them to lead a better life and often, find love in the process.

They were now back in Denver—back in their eclectic Tennyson neighborhood, where her cozy bookstore sat next door to her husband's CrossFit gym. Now was the time to jump head-on into their roles as business owners and superbloggers.

Charging ahead at light speed, they were living the dream.

Nothing could stop them.

That's what she'd thought until a pair of pink lines begged to differ.

She opened the bathroom door and handed Jordan the positive pregnancy test. With slow, deliberate movements akin to that of a crisis negotiator, he regarded her as one would treat a ticking time bomb.

It wasn't that far off the mark. Once they'd landed in Denver after their long flight from Fiji, Jordan had dropped an actual bomb.

A pregnancy bomb!

You might be knocked up is not what she'd expected her husband to say while they stood next to the baggage claim carousel, waiting for their luggage.

"I need another test and a giant glass of water. No, make that pineapple juice," she said with as much dignity as one can muster when seated on the toilet with her underwear pooled around her ankles.

She'd been in the bathroom, peeing on pregnancy tests, for the better part of the morning. This was not even close to what she thought she'd be doing the day after they'd returned from their honeymoon. She met her husband's gaze, then glanced down to see their dog, Mr. Tuesday. Concern welled in his doggy eyes with one ear poised and alert, looking at her in much the same way as Jordan.

"Georgie, babe, that was the twelfth positive test," Jordan said, maintaining his calm demeanor. However, he couldn't completely hide the hint of trepidation when he and Mr. Tuesday shared a knowing glance.

Even her literary trifecta—Lizzy Bennet, Jane Eyre, and Hermione Granger, the three imaginary characters she'd consulted and confided in since she was a girl, were ready to throw in the testing towel and accept what was right in front of them.

She craned her neck and maintained her perch on the potty, trying to see if any pink and white boxes were left on the bathroom counter.

This was not an easy feat.

"There should be one more, right?" she asked.

Jordan and Mr. Tuesday shared another knowing look.

Men!

Once her husband had made the *baby-in-the-oven* baggage claim proclamation, she did what any woman in her situation would do.

4

Shop.

Despite being exhausted from their long flight, she'd insisted they stop at the drugstore on the way home. She'd slid an entire row of pregnancy tests into their basket along with several packs of Winterfresh gum, a carton of pineapple juice, a deck of playing cards, a travel-sized bottle of hand sanitizer, and eight grab-and-go Slim Jims to draw the clerk's attention away from the more sensitive items— like how she always bought a handful of ChapSticks when purchasing tampons.

Stealthy, huh?

Georgie's shoulders slumped.

Who did she think she was? A possibly pregnant Houdini?

In her defense, Winterfresh breath was never a bad thing.

Jordan looked over his shoulder. "Yep, there's one test left."

One test.

One more shot at putting this pregnancy scare behind them.

It wasn't like she didn't want children...someday. She loved children. Well, she loved having them come into her bookshop, enjoyed suggesting picture books to their parents, and adored introducing older kids to the classics.

But she was an only child, and her extent of child-rearing knowledge revolved around fiction.

She didn't have a clue about the non-fiction nuts and bolts of what to do with a child, let alone a baby.

A baby?

A wave of anxiety, thick with unease, welled in her chest. But she'd be lying if she said there wasn't a thread of excitement woven through the fabric of frayed nerves. As she sat on the toilet seat, it was as if she were strapped into a roller coaster, the cars clicking up the track, then coming to a halt, motionless for barely a breath, dangling inches away from the first terrifying drop.

"I'll need that test and some pineapple juice STAT!" she blurted—a touch more forcefully than she'd expected.

Why was she talking like a soap opera doctor?

She held out her hand, waiting for Jordan to pass her the test, when the man pulled the travel-sized hand sanitizer she'd purchased from the drugstore from his pocket and squirted a glop into her palm.

"You've been handling a lot of pee covered plastic."

There's a sentence she'd never expected to fall from her husband's lips.

She rubbed her hands together. The man wasn't wrong. Peeing on twelve pregnancy test sticks did take a level of finesse she hadn't quite mastered.

He shared another look with the dog. "I called your gynecologist's office. They can get us in for an appointment later this morning."

And...another sentence she hadn't expected to hear from him.

"How'd you get the number for my gynecologist?"

"It's in your phone contacts under gynecologist," he answered with a bemused grin.

Why wasn't he freaking out? In situations like these— and in every chick flick she'd ever laughed, sighed, and swooned over—the guy always freaked out!

"We've got an appointment with Hector and Bobby at the CityBeat building," she answered, brushing past the gyno appointment comment.

Today, they were scheduled to meet with CityBeat's founders and their good friends, Hector Garcia and Bobby

Chen, to chart a grand path for their More Than Just a Number blog and brand. The CityBeat marketing team and PR crew would also be in attendance to help set the course for the next twelve months, regarding the direction of their wildly popular blog.

They needed to capitalize on their success and strike while the iron was hot.

"The meeting is this afternoon. We can make both appointments work," he replied, all crisis negotiator cool.

She shifted her hips. Right about now, a padded toilet seat cover sounded like heaven.

"Do you think we need to go see my doctor?"

He crouched down to her level. "I think it would give us a definitive answer. Twelve tests seem pretty conclusive, but a professional opinion is always a good thing to get."

Maybe he had a point. But she wasn't ready to be *definitive* about anything yet.

She held out her sanitized hand. "I'll take number thirteen, please."

He met her gaze, and she tried to read him. Once upon a time, her husband had completely lost it over having to interact with baby goats and an alpaca named Fred. And while he'd conquered his fear of goats, they'd both agreed alpacas, with their ability to spew green gunk from their bellies like mammal cannons, could be real assholes when they wanted. Still, knowing how her husband behaved when something freaked him out, she couldn't tell how he felt about their pregnancy purgatory. He'd gone all CrossFit trainer cool. A trait she'd admired in him. But what did he think of all this?

And how could *this* have happened?

Just as the thought crossed her mind, she filed it under *duh*.

She wasn't an idiot.

She knew exactly how this happened.

Any kid who's sat through sex ed knows *how* it happened.

But she was on the pill. Granted, the two weeks before their wedding, life had gotten pretty crazy with their less than stellar performance at a wilderness boot camp and then a giant fight that had Jordan bunking at his dad's place. She'd wondered if they would make it to the altar. It was like living in some bizarre space-time continuum where the days were both excruciatingly long while also racing by in the blink of an eye.

She'd missed a few birth control pills here and there. More like here and there and there and there again. Surely, a little pill snafu couldn't mean the complete loss of protection, could it?

She swallowed past the lump in her throat, her mouth growing dry. Perhaps it was the dependence on tropical juice she'd acquired, ingesting so much pineapple over the last few weeks. She'd detested the fruit her entire life until they landed in Fiji, and she became a pineapple power-eater.

A pineapple power-eater?

Holy pineapple pregnancy craving!

But that could be a fluke.

They'd been in a tropical paradise. When in Rome, one ate pasta. When in Fiji, one ate pineapple. Or, was it just her, ordering bowl after bowl of pineapple salsa to go along with her grilled steak, pineapple, and avocado salad, and then, for dessert, a slice—or four—of pineapple upside-down cake?

There was no denying she'd ingested a hell of a lot of pineapple over the last two weeks.

"It's November, right?"

He nodded. "Yeah, today's the first Monday in November."

She'd known that they were meeting with Hector and Bobby the day after they returned from their honeymoon. But she hadn't fully grasped the date had fallen in November because, while October passed with their wedding celebration and their honeymoon, one significant event never occurred.

Good old Aunt Flo hadn't stopped by for a visit.

Yep, she'd missed her last period.

Still, she was a little irregular, like back when she was sixteen. Maybe her cycle was recalibrating.

That had to be it! Her whole body was recalibrating. It probably happened to all women in their late twenties. She'd google it—possibly write an entire blog post about it. She could collaborate with experts in the field to construct an in-depth examination of the subject.

The Great Recalibration of the Female Body!

A jolt of euphoria surged through her, which was quickly tamped down by the blaring bullshit alarm going off inside her brain.

"Are you sure you want to take another test, babe? They'll probably have you do one at the doctor's office."

She'd swiped thirteen boxes into the basket. She might as well make use of all of them.

"Yeah, I'm sure," she answered, that mix of fear and excitement back, percolating in her chest.

Jordan tucked a lock of hair behind her ear. "Coming right up, messy bun girl," he answered, then reached for the pregnancy test when her phone, laying on the counter next to it, pinged.

Jordan grabbed the test with one hand and her cell with the other, then sucked in a tight breath.

"It's your mom."

Georgie groaned. That was what she needed at this very moment—not!

Dear Universe, you've got one heck of a sense of humor!

She slumped forward as her left foot started to go numb from all the toilet sitting.

"I better answer it. If I don't, she'll keep calling. She knows we got back late last night."

He handed her the phone and the box, and she swiped to accept the call before it headed to voicemail.

"Pumpkin, where are you? Is that your cheek?"

Lorraine Vanderdinkle's voice rang out. But it wasn't just her mother's honeyed, moneyed voice coming from her phone. Nope, the woman's Botox smooth face stared at her from the other side of the screen.

Sweet baby, Jesus! This was not the time for a video call with her mother—while she sat on the toilet, clutching a pregnancy test.

She held the phone in front of her face and plastered on a grin. "I'm right here, Mom. I didn't realize we were doing a video chat."

"Look at that tan! Pumpkin, you are glowing! How was Fiji? Anything exciting to report?" the woman purred.

Georgie shared a look with her husband. "It was fantastic—lots of fun in the sun! Your standard beach honeymoon—no more, no less," she added, then immediately wanted to stuff her mouth with all the Slim Jims she'd bought at the drugstore to block the deluge of game show hostess gobbledygook flowing from her mouth.

Between stuffing her face with pineapple prepared in every way, shape, and form, their time in Fiji was about as

X-rated as a honeymoon could get, but she wasn't about to go there. Nor was she about to drop the bomb that she was possibly pregnant.

"And Jordan? Where's that husband of yours?" Lorraine pressed.

"He's right here," she answered, her plastic grin smashed to her face.

"Well, let me say hello to my son-in-law!"

"Now?"

"Of course, now! What could you be doing other than relaxing after that long flight back to Denver?"

What was she supposed to do? Stand up and reveal her location or stay put and hope her mother didn't notice the back of the toilet seat? She tapped the object in her hand against her chin.

"Georgie, the box!" Jordan whisper-shouted.

"What's that in your hand, pumpkin?" Her mother's image zoomed in as if she were trying to get a closer look through the phone.

Without thinking, Georgie flung the pregnancy test out of the bathroom.

"Ouch!"

And right into the face of her husband.

"Is that Jordan?" her mother chimed.

"Hold on, Mom," she said, covering the camera with her hand, then mouthing an apology to the poor man who just got whacked in the face with the corner of a pregnancy test box.

Jordan rubbed his cheek, but there was no time to address the damage. He needed to take one for the team and get on this video call. She waved him over, and he wedged his large body next to her in the snug space between the toilet and the wall.

"I'm here, Lorraine. How are you?"

"Look at that gorgeous face! Who would have thought Georgiana could have snagged such a handsome man? The universe did you a favor, pumpkin."

Georgie parted her lips to reply, but nothing came out. Luckily, her mother wasn't expecting an answer and pulled the phone back to reveal her stepfather, Howard Vanderdinkle, seated by her side.

Her mother turned to the man. "Howard, don't they look wonderful?"

Her stepfather narrowed his gaze. "Are you sitting on the toilet, Georgie?"

"We're cleaning the bathroom. You guys caught us mid-chore," Jordan replied, swooping in like a champ.

"We've been spending a lot of time here...cleaning," she added, then got a better look at her mother and Howard's surroundings in the camera frame.

It was dark, and colorful silk banners infused with twinkling lights illuminated her parents as an elephant lumbered by behind them.

Now, it was her turn to pull the phone in close to try to get a better look at the background.

"Where are you guys?"

"India!" her mother exclaimed.

"The country?" Georgie shot back.

Her mother's tinkling laughter carried over the phone's speaker. "Yes, the country, pumpkin!"

"Why are you there?" Jordan asked.

"Because of Buddha," the woman replied, then handed Howard the phone so she could do a little mid-call Namaste move.

Lorraine Vanderdinkle had transformed. To keep the busybody socialite out of their hair before their nuptials, the wedding planner had put her mother in touch with a psychic energist, who told her she possessed a gift for reading the spiritual energy emitted from wedding favors. As cockeyed as it sounds, her mother embraced her new *ability* and dove head-first into communing with the universe as well as measuring the psychic energy of scented candles and imported chocolates—which, in all honesty, turned out to be quite lovely wedding favors.

The Chanel-clad woman who had dragged her all over the country to compete in beauty pageants when she was growing up, now donned flowing tunics and jangly necklaces with giant crystals.

But it was one thing for her mother and Howard to jet off to their bungalow in Fiji, their place in Aspen, or a chalet in Switzerland. Her business-minded stepfather owned a successful venture capitalist firm, and money wasn't an issue for them. But India seemed way out of the collective wheelhouse for her workaholic stepfather.

Thanks to him spending long hours at the office and her rigorous pageant schedule, she and Howard hadn't spent much time together while she was growing up. Her parents divorced when she was a girl, and when she wasn't with her mother, she'd spent half of her time with her literature-loving mechanic father. She'd straddled two worlds: one of opulence and many, many beauty pageants with her mother and a simpler life, spending hours browsing the shelves of the public library with her father. When he passed away suddenly, she'd told herself that despite the money and connections her mother and stepfather could offer, she'd make her way in this world on her own, just like her father.

She'd worked hard and had earned her success. In the process, she'd also learned more about her mother's motivations, which may seem a little nutty but always came from a good place, as well as uncovering her stepfather's hidden devotion to her and her mother.

Still, while Howard seemed to get a kick out of her mom, cruising the high-end shops of Denver's Cherry Creek neighborhood in a Prius instead of being driven around in a Bentley, she hadn't expected the pragmatic man to jump on the psychic energy bandwagon.

"The Buddha told you to go to India?" she asked, needing some clarification.

"The Buddha came to me in a dream and instructed me to come here with Howard."

Georgie pursed her lips. "You dreamed about the Buddha?"

Her mother's expression grew pensive. "I dreamed about a turtle, but he had a message for me from Buddha."

Georgie stifled a chuckle as Jordan cleared his throat to most likely abstain from laughing as well. But maybe turtle Buddha was doing her a favor. If she were pregnant—not that she believed she was—her mother would insist she partake in some kind of prenatal psychic seminar.

"How long will you be visiting India?" Jordan asked, blessedly shifting gears.

"Twelve months," her mother answered.

"A year?" she questioned, her voice going up an octave.

"Yes, pumpkin." Her mother sighed. "I wish your father hadn't insisted we send you to public school. Maybe you'd have learned that."

That yearlong break wasn't looking so bad.

"I'm fully aware twelve months equals a year, Mom."

"Because I told you so," Lorraine Vanderdinkle replied, then sighed again as she turned to her husband, her many crystals clapping together. "You see, Howard, a mother's job is never done."

"What will you be doing for a year?" Jordan asked.

"Beginning the journey to enlightenment and harnessing our chi at an exclusive five-star retreat cut off from civilization," she answered.

Howard leaned forward. "And I've invested in a few companies near the retreat, so if you need anything, you can always contact my office. They'll know how to get ahold of me."

Her mother raised her index finger. "But only for something very important. Howard and I are committed to pursuing complete spiritual awakening, and my energist felt I needed to continue developing my psychic energy reading abilities."

The hint of a grin pulled at the corners of her stepfather's mouth. How he fell madly in love with her crazy train of a mother was something she'd never fully understand.

Still, the man she'd remembered from her childhood, who always seemed to be working, looked at ease. Lorraine Vanderdinkle truly was the yin to his yang.

Her mother's forehead produced a slight spasm—the Botox equivalent of her surprised face. "I almost forgot, pumpkin! You and Jordan will need to take over a few of our charity duties while we're gone. A gala here, a benefit there, maybe a planning meeting or two. I'll have my assistant Nicolette get you the details."

Benefits, galas, and planning meetings? Georgie swallowed hard. They had a lot on their plate already, but how could she say no?

"I thought you fired Nicolette because she was a Sagittarius?" she queried.

"I have a new Nicolette! She's a Libra!" her mother answered, as if hiring someone based on their horoscope made complete sense.

Jordan leaned in. "Howard, Lorraine, we should probably tell you that—"

Without missing a beat, Georgie angled the phone away from her husband and filled the frame with her face. She was not about to allow him to disclose the possibility of a bun in the oven—not when they weren't one hundred percent sure.

And with the way she knew her mother would fuss over a pregnancy, it was in everyone's best interest to keep this under wraps as long as possible.

"Jordan was going to say that India sounds magical!" she announced, cutting him off in game show hostess mode. "We wish you all the best. Don't worry! We've got everything under control."

"All right, then! Kiss, kiss! Namaste!" her mother trilled as Howard waved goodbye, and the screen went blank.

Jordan raised an eyebrow. "You don't want to tell them?"

She sat back against the hard, plastic seat, now wishing the whole damn toilet was padded. "Tell them what?"

Jordan cocked his head to the side. He was no fool. She knew what he was thinking but feigned naive.

"We don't know anything yet."

His expression softened. "Georgie."

She still couldn't understand how he was so calm.

If she were pregnant, what then? Yes, a baby! She'd picked that up in sex ed. But what did it mean for their lives and their marriage? They hadn't even known each other for six months. Their love story had unfolded in record time. She hadn't even begun to wrap her mind around becoming a mother.

And what kind of mother would she be?

She steadied herself. "Let's take this one step at a time, okay?"

"We've already taken twelve pee-covered steps," he countered with a sweet smile.

She sat up straight as if she were the Princess of Potties. "For all we know, those tests could be defective—"

"Georgiana!" Jordan shot back.

She raised her hand. "Let me finish. And Howard pretty much said if we needed to get a message to them, we could go through his office. Let's not put the cart before the horse. Like I told my mother, we've got everything under control."

Jordan gave her his best *I-call-bullshit* face, but it didn't work on her.

"We do!" she said, but the roller-coaster anxiety pangs in her chest begged to differ.

He glanced at his watch. "We need to leave for the doctor's appointment soon. Can you be ready to go in twenty minutes?"

Twenty minutes to get ready. A fifteen-minute drive to the office. In under an hour, they might be taking their seats on the Babyland express.

Her heart jumped into her throat, but she swallowed back the emotion. "Absolutely, I'm totally in control."

Chapter Two
Jordan

"This is it," Georgie said, pointing to a pair of frosted glass doors.

Jordan glanced down the beige hallway, taking in the nondescript interior of the medical building. It seemed as good as any other—not that he frequented ob-gyn offices. In fact, this constituted his first visit.

But he wasn't in the dark when it came to human reproduction.

Thanks to majoring in kinesiology, he understood not only the mechanics of human movement but had in-depth training in anatomy and nutrition. As a CrossFit trainer, he'd maintained his professional knowledge on the subject with numerous continuing education classes. Not to mention, all the research he'd done himself, staying up-to-date with the latest exercise science findings and crafting fitness routines for people of all ability levels.

He knew bodies.

Men's bodies.

Women's bodies.

And even pregnant women's bodies. His coursework

demanded it. Movement was a critical element in pregnancy health. Moderate exercise reduced the risk of delivering a low birth weight baby. It improved the mother's mood, increased her energy, aided in sleep, and could reduce aches and pains. The list went on and on, and as a fitness professional, he was obligated to remain informed.

After consulting with pregnant clients and collecting the necessary medical information, he could whip up a prenatal workout plan in no time flat.

But today wasn't a casual appointment to set up a fitness regimen for just anyone.

He was ninety-nine-point-nine percent sure this appointment would confirm what had hit him like a Mack truck in Fiji.

His pineapple-loving sex machine of a wife was most likely with child.

When did it happen? Hell if he knew!

They had less than a three-week window between the date he proposed in late September and their wedding on the third Saturday in October. Their wham, bam, thank you, ma'am light-speed of an engagement ebbed and flowed with emotional highs and lows that had put their relationship to the test.

But that didn't mean they'd scrimped on the hanky-panky.

The moment he'd put together all the signs and realized the love of his life could be carrying actual life, he'd gone into health researcher mode, counting up all the times they'd been intimate since his wife's last period in September.

Yeah, her period! He wasn't one of those boyfriends, now, a husband, who got embarrassed by all that. In his opinion, it was a badge of honor. He had no qualms standing in line at the market with a box of jumbo organic cotton tampons in one hand and a couple of tubes of vegan chocolate chip cookie dough in the other.

During that short window of time, their sexcapades sessions had been just as crazy as everything else.

They'd done it in the car, in a tent, and in the wilderness, accidentally, in front of an alpaca—something he'd never recommend. If they ever decided to knock boots in the great outdoors again, he'd be doing a broad alpaca perimeter sweep first. That's for damn sure!

And it wasn't like they weren't careful.

Georgie was on the pill. But throughout that handful of weeks, and especially during their stint at a godforsaken wilderness boot camp, he'd had no idea if she'd taken it. And it wasn't like he was in the right headspace to remind her. To say things had gone sideways during that time, was the understatement of the century.

Not only had they gone sideways, but they'd also gone upside down, inside out, outside in, and any other twisted, discombobulated comparison one could imagine. All he could do was be grateful they'd made it out in one piece as husband and wife.

Georgie squeezed his hand. "We need to go inside. I don't remember ever seeing doctors examining patients in the hallway."

He gazed down at his beautiful wife. Tendrils of her chestnut-colored hair framed her face. She met his gaze with her blue-green eyes. The same eyes that had seared into his soul from the first awkward moment their lives collided.

She smiled up at him, trying to keep it light. But he knew his Georgiana. He'd caught glimpses of her through the half-closed bedroom door while she was getting ready for the appointment. It had taken her four tries to twist her hair into her signature messy bun. Then there were the wardrobe changes. She'd gone from jeans to leggings to yoga pants, to some strange one-piece contraption of pants already attached to the shirt. She'd switched outfits at Mach speed before pausing in front of the mirror and pressing a trembling hand to her abdomen.

She was worried—and so was he. They hadn't discussed having children. Their lives revolved around each other, their blog, and their businesses.

Where did a baby fit into all that? He didn't have the foggiest notion.

One thing he did know, however, was that biology didn't care about your plans.

Life always found a way, and it didn't concede to your agenda. It didn't agree to return at a more convenient date. It didn't compromise. It didn't have to. They may have slipped up and given biology the upper hand. But from this moment on, he'd willed himself to be smarter and to be steady. If a baby were coming, he'd be prepared to do whatever it took to make sure this child had every advantage he never had.

This child would never be bullied.

Never teased or ridiculed.

In his dusty Colorado Plains hometown, he'd grown up a skinny kid on the proverbial wrong side of the tracks. They'd always had food on the table, and when his mother was still alive, she'd kept their home bright and tidy. But his father's mechanic's salary could only stretch so far. While his dad had done his best after his mother passed away, the man's heart had hardened from grief, and a rift had formed between father and son. A vast chasm only breached thanks in large part to Georgie. He and his father had grown close again, but he wanted a different upbringing for his child.

"Hey, Sovereign of Scat! This was your idea. I was fine staying home and tearing into those Slim Jims. And I just thought of something!" she added.

He reached for the handle, chuckling at the moniker she'd given him during their stint at the bridal wilderness boot camp. "What's that?"

"I could wrap pineapple slices around the beef jerky. Doesn't that sound amazing?" she answered as he held the door for her.

His ninety-nine-point-nine percent pregnant prediction notched up to ninety-nine-point-nine-*nine* until they entered the waiting room, and thoughts of numbers and percentages vanished from his thoughts as his jaw nearly hit the floor. He figured ob-gyn offices were like any other doctor's office. Quiet, orderly places where patients sat, sedately waiting to be called for their appointment.

But not this place!

This place looked like a toy shop that swallowed a tiny library.

Children's board books littered the floor while blocks lay strewn everywhere. The real kicker? Nobody seemed concerned about the noise level. Toddlers crashed toy trucks together with the gusto of deranged demolition operators. Parents holding tiny bundles sat together, talking like two-year-olds, cooing and producing animated expressions. Interspersed with the insanity, pregnant women rested, rubbing their ample bellies. A few outliers sat in chairs on the other side of baby ground zero, staring at their phones or leafing through magazines.

He glanced at the clock near the check-in desk. It was

like pregnancy on steroids in here, and it wasn't even eleven o'clock in the morning.

"Name, please?" the receptionist inquired.

"Jordan Marks," he answered, trying to get his bearing as a LEGO whizzed past his face.

The woman at the desk gave him a placating smile. "No, sir. Unless you've got a uterus, I probably need her name."

Georgie stepped forward. "I'm Georgiana Jensen-Marks, but you probably still have me as Georgiana Jensen. I recently got married and changed my name."

"Congratulations! And you're here for..." the woman trailed off, typing away on her computer. "Ah, here it is! A pregnancy check."

Georgie's body went rigid. "Yes, but it's probably a mistake. You know how those home tests can be."

The woman nodded. "Accurate."

Georgie glanced at him. "See, I'm accurate."

"No, dear," the receptionist said, leaning forward with a distinct crinkle to her brow. "Those home pregnancy tests are quite accurate. How many have you taken?"

"Twelve."

"Twelve!" the woman echoed, nearly knocking her glasses clean off her face.

Georgie lowered her voice. "Could the results be skewed if you'd ingested a lot of pineapple?"

The receptionist's crinkle deepened. "How much pineapple?"

"An obscene amount," Georgie answered, looking from side to side as if she were expecting the pineapple police to bust in.

The woman sat back and gave them the once-over. "You'll have to ask the doctor about the pineapple. But right now, you need you to go back and give us a urine sample, and then it looks like a blood draw as well. Head over to the nurses' desk on that side of the office," she said, gesturing past the preschool pandemonium portion of the space. "And sir, you can wait over there with the other dads and dads-to-be."

He observed the men. Most appeared as shell-shocked as a group of WWII soldiers in a foxhole.

And what was this *other dads* business?

Was he already lumped in with them?

Panic welled in Georgie's eyes.

"I'll sit here," he offered, gesturing to the farthest chair from the group of men. "In the adults-only section."

Adults-only?

What was wrong with him?

The secretary shook her head. "No, sir, the nurse will be calling for you to come to join your wife from that side of the practice."

A hallway ran past the check-in desk, connecting two sides of the office with the waiting room situated in the center. He glanced at the women, sitting quietly, checking their phones—far, far away from the mayhem on the other side. He wanted this—the adult section or whatever you wanted to call it. He scanned the dad zone to find a half-naked toddler twirling in a sea of toys.

"What happens on the quiet side of the office?" he asked.

"Our non-pregnancy related appointments," the receptionist answered.

He glanced at the carnival gone off the rails section of the waiting room.

"We're not one hundred percent sure Georgie's pregnant. That's why we're here. We're very close to sure, but that should be enough to get me into the quiet zone, at least for today, don't you think?"

The receptionist's placating expression was back. "Here's the receptacle for your urine sample, dear," she said, ignoring his plea and handing Georgie a plastic cup.

His wife stared down at it, her name and date of birth printed along the side. This was it—the moment of truth.

She squeaked a nervous laugh. "Well, we conquered shit shovels. What's a little pee in a cup?"

Before he could reply, the maddening hum of the office went dead quiet. Not even a baby farted.

Georgie's eyes went wide, and her cheeks grew crimson. "I dropped the s-word in front of a bunch of children, didn't I?"

The entire waiting room stared at them. Even the receptionist sat motionless, her hand pressed to her chest.

He needed to handle this—and fast.

"My wife didn't say a bad word. She said *ship shovel*. Ship with a *p*. You know, the shovel you'd use when you need one on a ship. Ship with a *p*—definitely, not a *t*."

Had crickets not been smart enough to avoid this place, they'd be chirping.

"I'm going to go pee in the cup and have my blood drawn," Georgie said, going from beet-red to dishwater gray as the noise returned to the level of heavy metal concert meets *Sesame Street*.

He pressed a kiss to the crown of her head. "You should do great with the pee part. You've had plenty of practice this morning."

She frowned up at him. "Jordan, why don't you sit down. I'm sure they'll call you back when they get me into an examination room."

Sit down and shut up, asshat!

He knew that's what his wife wanted to say—or would have said—if she weren't freaking out about the possibility of gestating a human on top of making sure she didn't drop another bad word in front of the baby brigade.

What was wrong with him?

Actually, he could answer that.

This place!

On TV, couples went into a tastefully decorated doctor's office where pregnancy advice was dispensed over a mahogany desk without a chorus of wailing children or crashing toy cars.

Then, the penny dropped.

He was pregnancy book smart.

He understood the biology and the physiology of a pregnant woman's body. Still, when it came to having hands-on experience with an actual pregnancy or understanding the intricacies of fetal development, he was as clueless as the dad chasing his half-naked kid around in circles.

He tried to block out the noise and steadied himself. He needed to stay calm. He might not know anything about growing a baby, but they could learn. They'd figure it out.

"We've got this, Georgie," he said, drawing his thumb down her jawline as his heart fluttered, freaking fluttered in his chest.

How he loved this woman—his true north. If someone had asked him a year ago where he'd be at this time, never in a million years would he have thought it would be here, married to the love of his life, most likely preparing for a baby.

Not just a baby, their baby.

"Okay," she answered on a shaky breath.

He held her misty gaze. "Messy bun girl, no matter what they tell us today, we're in this together. You and me."

He leaned in and lowered his voice. "You know the Emperor of Asshattery would be nothing without his Empress to call him out whenever he acted like—"

"A giant asshat," she whispered lovingly, finishing his sentence as the corners of her lips curled into the hint of a grin.

"Ms. Jensen-Marks?"

They turned to see a stone-faced nurse, standing near the entrance to the pregnancy side of the office.

Georgie blew out a slow breath. "I'll see you in a little bit," she said, then nodded to the woman and followed her back.

He watched her go, wishing he could join her. There wasn't much he could do. He could hold the pee cup for her. But it might look weird if they tag-teamed the urine sample portion of the visit. Like a warrior accepting defeat, he scanned the alien world of the ob-gyn waiting room, looking for the safest place to sit. Carefully, he navigated his way through a Lincoln Log minefield, passed a child banging his fist on a toy steering wheel's horn as if he were training for a baby road rage competition, then took a seat across from a trio of men.

"Look, fellas! Fresh meat!" a red-cheeked, heavy-set man said with a wide grin.

Jordan stared at him. "Excuse me?"

"Don't take offense," the guy said, wrangling a toddler. "From the way you were talking to your wife, we could tell this is your first trip to the pregnancy rodeo."

Jordan cleared his throat. "We're not sure she's pregnant. There's a good chance I should be over there," he replied, gesturing with his chin toward the quiet zone.

"Did she do the pee test at home?" a man with a shock of red hair asked.

"Yes," he answered, wondering why the hell he didn't tell this guy to mind his own business.

What was it with this place? Did everyone know everybody's business around here? Was there some unspoken rule that once one was relegated to this side of the office, all privacy disappeared?

"And you got the plus or the two lines?" came the third man with a little girl sitting on his lap, sucking her thumb.

"Or did you get one of those fancy tests with a little computer screen that says *pregnant*? Joanie loves those," piped the dad, chasing a half-naked toddler.

"She used the kind with two lines," he answered.

"And both lines showed up?" the redheaded man asked.

"Yeah."

The jovial man slapped his leg. "She's pregnant."

Jordan looked from man to man before settling his gaze on the proclaimer of pregnancy. "Are you a doctor?"

"A dentist," he answered with a shrug.

Jordan nodded, not sure if that counted.

"Do you want a natural birth or will you guys opt for an epidural?" the man chasing the child asked.

This twenty-questions was worse than listening to that kid bang out "Mary Had a Little Lamb" on the toy steering wheel's horn.

"I'm not sure yet," he answered.

"And preschools—you need to get on the wait-list for the good ones," the dad with the little girl offered, then blew a raspberry on her belly.

"We don't even know if we're pregnant," he stammered.

The redheaded man waved him off. "It doesn't matter if you're pregnant. My wife and I got our name on the wait-list for the advanced toddler baseball clinic before we'd even conceived."

"You had no kid but put a fake kid on the wait-list?" he asked, trying to keep the cynicism out of his voice.

The man leaned forward. "That's how the game is played."

"You're kidding!" he whisper-shouted back.

"No, sir! I am not! You need to act now. How far along is your wife?"

Jordan closed his eyes, his mind spinning, trying to calculate the date. His pregnant clients simply told him how far along they were in their pregnancy. But to calculate the due date, he vaguely remembered that you had to measure the duration starting on the first day of the woman's last period—or something like that. He'd have to pull out his physiology manuals when they got home and brush up.

He rubbed his temples. "Six weeks, maybe a little more?"

The dentist dad's eyes went wide. "Six weeks! That's an eternity, man!"

Jordan's gaze ping-ponged between the men as a shock of anxiety hit his system. "How can forty-two days be an eternity?"

He didn't know all that much about fetal development, but he couldn't imagine the kid was more than the size of a gumball.

The man chasing his kid plopped down next to him, holding the child upside-down by his ankles as the boy giggled with delight. "You need to get on it. You're a big guy. Do you play sports? Do you want your kid to play first base, or how about the NFL?"

"The National Football League?" Jordan repeated. This was getting ludicrous!

The man set the child right-side up. "No, the other NFL. Newborn fitness lessons. They're classes to work on baby hand-eye coordination to get your kid ready to try out for the club teams."

Jordan's mouth hung open. He'd spent the last decade of his life immersed in the fitness world, but he'd never heard of these kinds of classes or that you needed to get on the wait-list pre-baby.

"You start training your baby to be a professional athlete during infancy?" he asked, incredulity lacing the question.

Had he heard the guy wrong? He was trying to hold it together and play it cool for Georgie, but his nerves were starting to get the better of him.

The guy shook his head. "You should start before that! I began prepping Dewey to play quarterback, explaining football plays to my wife's belly once the doc said our little bun in the oven was able to hear."

"You did that while your wife was still pregnant?" Jordan pressed.

"Yep! And look at him now! That kid is going places," the man answered.

Jordan glanced down to find this Dewey, who was *apparently* going places, sitting on the floor, cross-legged with both his index fingers jammed up his nose.

The dentist clucked his tongue at Dewey's dad. "You're blowing his mind."

"Let's move on. How about a musical instrument?" another dad asked.

He didn't know which dad because his damn head was spinning thanks to the waiting room interrogation.

He tried to think, then imagined a little boy or girl, bowing away on a violin or fingertips fluttering down black and white piano keys.

"Music is great. I'm sure we'd consider it," he answered cautiously.

"Then you're really late," the man with the little girl said.

"I am?" he shot back.

"Yeah, the best teachers in Denver are booked way before six weeks."

"Like five weeks?" he queried, unable to believe the insane timeline parents needed to follow to give a kid a hobby these days.

How much *pre*-prenatal prep was required?

The man lowered his voice. "Try, four."

Jordan reared back, bumping a flurry of board books off an end table. "Holy sh—"

"Whoa!" the dads said in unison, graciously cutting off his expletive.

Oh, f!

He and Georgie would have to crack down on their language, too, or else they might have a kid whose first word would be asshat or douche canoe.

Douche canoe was two words—but he and Georgie were relatively smart people. They'd probably have a smart kid who could manage it.

Jesus! Wait...*goodness!* What was wrong with him? He had to weed these words out of his vocabulary.

He reached down to pick up the books when the nose-picker kid—*who was going places*—grabbed the book in his hand.

"Hey, buddy! I was cleaning those up." He released the book and allowed the child to take it.

The little cherub stared at him with wide blue eyes. What color eyes would their baby have? His were sage green, and Georgie's were a gorgeous shade of bluish-green. There was a chance their baby would look up at him with inquisitive blue eyes like this. He cocked his head to the side and stared at the boy, all rosy cheeks and dark curls. When the toddler wasn't digging for gold up his nostrils, the kid was kind of cute. He smiled at the child, feeling damned, no, *darned* good about this father business when the boy held the book above his head.

"Are you going to show me the book?" he asked, channeling Mr. Rogers.

He could do this. Kids liked him. This kid liked him. That had to mean something.

The little boy grinned up at him, then shook his head as a maniacal twinkle glinted in his baby-blues.

"You're not?" he asked as a thread of trepidation wove its way through his chest.

With a grin akin to that of a mad scientist, the child reared back, then used every ounce of NFL baby training to whack him clean in the eye, wielding the board book with the agility of a tiny major league baseball player, swinging for the fences.

"Holy hard as hell board book!" he blurted, unable to stop himself, but not before losing his balance and falling to the floor. Thankfully, he was able to keep himself from clobbering the little boy by twisting his torso and tweaking his back in the process.

He pushed up onto his knees, then massaged a sharp kink in his neck as his eyeball throbbed. His half-blurry gaze darted between the now crying blue-eyed toddler, afraid of the giant man almost flattening him into a pancake as the dads sat motionless, staring at him with expressions of horror.

"Sorry, I didn't expect—" he began when a woman's stern voice cut him off.

"I'm looking for Mr. Marks."

He glanced up to find a nurse with a deep crease

between her eyebrows and thin, pursed lips. Swap out the scrubs for a corset and a Victorian gown with a high, lace-trimmed neckline, and this lady would be a dead ringer for a harsh headmistress in a period piece.

He'd have to tell Georgie about her—once they were far, far away from this place.

He raised his hand like a kindergartener. "That's me. I'm Jordan Marks."

"I'm here to bring you back. Are you ready?" she asked with a disapproving gaze, taking in the crying child and the look of shock on every face in the waiting room.

Was he ready?

Now, that was the question.

He thought he was ready—figured a few physiology classes in college and a working knowledge of pregnancy had put him ahead of the curve when it came to this baby business. He let out a tight breath, then glanced up and caught a glimpse of the little girl, no longer sucking her thumb. Instead, the child stuck her tongue out at him, giving him the toddler equivalent of go fuck yourself.

With his back aching and his eye pounding, he rose to his feet like a defeated gladiator.

What the hell had he and Georgie gotten themselves into?

He stepped over the crying child, nodded to the speechless fathers, then hobbled toward the nurse.

"I'm as ready as I'll ever be," he said, praying that this would be his lowest moment of the whole pregnancy journey. Unfortunately, a nagging little voice in his head told him this was just the beginning.

Chapter Three
Georgie

Georgie shifted her weight in the chair, then crossed and uncrossed her legs. This wasn't her first time rocking the gown you tie in the front for your annual lady parts examination. She'd been going to the gynecologist since she was a teenager. But for this visit, the nurse had told her she only needed to remove her clothes from the waist down.

Not an easy feat. Scratch that. Not possible when wearing a one-piece romper. Yes, that fashion-forward pants connected to the shirt ensemble, which meant, if the bottom had to go, so did the top.

Her mother had sent it to her ages ago with a Lorraine Vanderdinkle special passively aggressive note, explaining the garment was fashionably chic and meant to spruce up her dowdy librarian wardrobe. Why she chose today of all days to wear it, she didn't know.

And to make matters worse, thanks to her brain fog or a possible vitamin C overdose with all the pineapple juice she'd ingested over the last several weeks, she'd chosen a particularly sexy bra. Nobody wore their most seductive underwear to the ob-gyn. If there was an occasion for the demure beige full-support number, it was for the gynecologist!

It had to be the nerves and the anxiety clouding her addled mind that had led her to make this fashion faux pas.

However, aside from the possibility that this could be one of the most momentous days of her life, so far, the visit seemed pretty routine.

She'd peed in the cup, then opened the strange little cabinet door next to the toilet and left her sample beside another cup of pee. This wasn't her first time navigating the whole pee at the doctor's office song and dance, but so far, urine seemed to play quite an important role in the pursuit of pregnancy pronouncements. In all her life, she'd never thought as much about pee as she had in the last few hours.

Jordan was right about her kicking ass with the pee cup. In this case, practice did make perfect. She'd filled that plastic receptacle like a champ, then gave a little fist bump, and instantly felt like an asshat.

Who cheered for pee?

Apparently, Georgiana Jensen-Marks.

The routine blood draw was nothing to write home about. She'd sat there and watched as the tiny vile filled with the substance that would tell them definitively if there was a bun or, in her case, a pineapple upside-down cake in the oven.

Truth be told, it was starting to sink in.

As the phlebotomist pricked her vein, she'd stared at the tasteful display of happy women cradling their bellies plastered on pastel-colored pamphlets. Until this visit, she'd never paid much attention to them. Pregnancy seemed so far off—something that happened to other people. Especially because, before she'd met Jordan, she'd spent the last couple of years dwelling in a sexual desert.

At her last annual appointment, there wasn't a snowball's chance in hell she could be pregnant.

In a bout of cleverness during that appointment, she'd written something cheeky about her lack of sexual partners on the health intake form. The nurse, a lovely young woman named Gina, had chuckled when she'd read it. Then, they'd enjoyed some girl talk, dishing about the pitfalls of dating and the difficulties in trying to find a good guy. She'd even recommended her Own the Eights blog to the bubbly woman. It was too bad she wasn't here today. The nurse who'd met her at the dreaded doctor scale had the warmth of a wet blanket.

With a scowl, the woman begrudgingly introduced herself as Joyce.

If anyone could take the joy out of Joyce, it was this lady. Still, she appeared competent, and hopefully, the all-smiles Nurse Gina would be back when she was due for her next visit.

Next visit?

This used to be a place she'd breeze in and out of once a year.

If Jordan and twelve pregnancy tests were correct, there was a good chance they'd be here quite a bit.

She crossed her fingers, hoping her favorite nurse would return when the door to the exam room opened. Joyless Joyce entered the snug space with Jordan trailing behind; his shoulders slumped like a kid who'd been caught stealing from the cookie jar.

Georgie adjusted the oversized gown and attempted to muster up as much dignity as one could in a hospital-issued frock and a sexy bra.

Jordan gasped. "Why are you naked?"

"Because she wore a onesie to the obstetrician," the nurse huffed, scribbling something onto a chart.

"I'm not naked. I'm in a hospital gown, so the doctor can do an exam," she answered, then smiled at Joyce. "And it's a romper, not a onesie. Onesies are for babies. I know that much."

"What's a romper?" Jordan asked.

"What I wore here! It's a *fashionably chic* one-piece shirt and pants outfit," she answered, regurgitating her mother's words.

"One piece, like a onesie," Nurse Joyce countered under her breath as she attended to the chart.

"Why'd you wear that? Are there special clothes you're supposed to wear here?" Jordan asked in a hushed voice, confusion marring his handsome face. Except something was different.

When she'd left him, the man looked ready to conquer the world. Calm and collected, he'd stayed right outside the door as she'd peed on pregnancy test after pregnancy test this morning. He'd held her hand in the car ride over, gently brushing his thumb across her knuckles. Even once they'd arrived, despite being surprised by the kid factor in the waiting room, he'd been steady—her solid supporter.

He deflated into the seat next to her, and the giant CrossFit trainer looked as if he'd completed ten Ironman competitions in a row, then got plowed over by a steamroller.

She touched a long scratch on his cheek below his left eye.

"What happened?"

"A nose-picking toddler attacked me with a book. He got me good, Georgie," her husband answered with absolutely no sarcasm or humor infused into his ridiculous statement.

"You got into a fight with a child?" She had to have misunderstood.

"No, not a fight."

"Then, what happened?"

Jordan sighed a deep contemplative sound. "The dads out there were telling me about the baby NFL and all the wait-lists we needed to get on to make sure we have a normal kid. I was so blown away that I accidentally knocked a bunch of those board books off a little table."

"A baby NFL?" she questioned. He wasn't making any sense.

Jordan's eyes went mad-professor wide. "Yeah, crazy, huh?"

Oh yes! Somebody seemed crazy! A certain six-foot-four behemoth of a man seated beside her.

"Okay, but I'm not sure how that leads to a baby assaulting you," she pressed gently.

He leaned in. "It was a toddler, Georgie. They're a different beast. He faked me out. Kids are smart. They're deceptively cute. They draw you in and then, whack! You find yourself nearly smashing them like a pancake."

In the fifteen minutes she'd been separated from her husband, the man had gone from Mr. Positivity to sounding like a war vet, recalling days on the battlefield.

"You tried to smash a toddler?" She had to piece this out. Something had to be missing.

"Not on purpose! It happened when I fell out of the chair."

"You fell onto the floor?" she questioned.

"I told you. The kid had NFL training," Jordan answered, exasperation coating the words.

For the love of Pete!

She looked to Joyce, who'd started typing away on the exam room computer. Perhaps Nurse Scowl could help fill in the gaps in her husband's explanation.

"Did you notice anything interesting going on when you went to fetch my husband?" she asked, going for indifferent nonchalance—which wasn't easy when wearing a black sex kitten bra beneath a potato sack.

"He was on the ground next to a crying child. I don't know if I'd call it interesting," Joyce answered, gaze glued to the computer screen.

"Do you see that a lot around here?" she continued with a laugh meant to sound playful but veered closer to psycho.

The woman turned away from the screen. "No," she answered with the pleasantness of a slug.

Wait! That wasn't fair to slugs. There had to be some pleasant ones out there.

"I need to ask you a few questions, Mrs. Jensen-Marks," Nurse Joyce said, squinting at a piece of paper in the chart.

"Go ahead."

Joyce pursed her lips. "A lot has changed for you. Last time you were here, under relationship status, you circled single, then wrote in that the doctor may need to clear the cobwebs because it had been so long since you'd *gotten any*."

Gah! That's what she'd written last year, and Dr. Rosenstein thought it was hilarious.

Georgie smoothed her potato sack gown. "Well, that's certainly not the case now."

Jordan perked up and tossed her a little wink. "I can attest to that. There are no cobwebs in my wife's lady parts, and Georgie's all about getting some these days."

Sweet Jesus! Did he think he was helping?

"And you're married now, I see," Joyce continued.

"Yes, just last month," she confirmed, grateful to move on to a less embarrassing subject.

The nurse raised an eyebrow. "Shotgun wedding, I assume?"

Georgie gasped. "No! Goodness, no! Getting pregnant wasn't even on our radar during that time."

"Were you having sex?" A smirk pulled at the corners of Joyce's lips.

Georgie knew where this was going. Oh, how she needed Nurse Gina! Gina would have been all high fives and sweet giggles upon hearing about her recent wedding, not hardened features and disapproving glares.

A bead of sweat ran down her back. "Yes, we engaged in sexual activity."

There! She'd make it sound clinical—like something you'd read in a nature magazine. Nobody begrudged animals for *getting some*!

"Were you using protection consistently?" Joyce asked in a tone that said she already knew the answer—which was pretty damn clear when one made an appointment for a pregnancy check.

Georgie shifted in the chair as another bead of perspiration slid down her spine. "Define consistently."

The crabby nurse scribbled a note. "I'll take that as a no."

Georgie turned to her husband, who winced. Even he knew this wasn't going well. With her eyes, she asked him to swoop in and say something funny or charming. Anything to make her look less like an irresponsible woman whose wedding ceremony had included firearms.

"Alcohol consumption?" the nurse asked.

"Only a glass of champagne at our wedding," Georgie answered.

Jordan took her hand and tossed her another wink. "And with all the pineapple juice Georgie's been downing, she might just have a piña colada in her belly."

Oh, Jordan!

The nurse frowned. "So, you're binge drinkers?"

"No! Nothing of that sort," Georgie answered.

"My wife's right! On our honeymoon, we didn't touch any alcohol."

She breathed a sigh of relief, but Jordan wasn't done.

"You see, I wouldn't have been able to keep up with my wife's sex drive if I'd ingested alcohol. I needed to be at peak performance. It got pretty wild, if you know what I mean," he added, tossing Joyce a wink.

Did he think he was helping? She looked like a binge-drinking sex maniac!

Georgie adjusted her potato sack. It was time to shift gears.

"Will Gina be back soon?"

"Who?" Joyce grunted.

"Nurse Gina. She usually goes through all the health questions with me," she answered, praying her favorite nurse was in the vicinity.

"Oh, her. She moved to France with her boyfriend, Pierre. She told everybody some blog taught her how to meet a nice guy," Joyce replied flatly.

France?

And a blog that helped her find a good guy?

"How lovely for her," Georgie answered with a pinched grin.

She wanted to be happy for the woman. It was most likely

her advice that helped the kind Gina find love. But now, she detested this Pierre for taking the compassionate nurse and leaving her with this grouchy sourpuss. She wanted to kick herself for suggesting Gina check out the blog in the first place.

Was this a little selfish?

She glanced at the scowling Joyce.

Nope, she was all for selfish at the moment.

"It's poppycock!" the crabby nurse remarked.

"What's poppycock?" she asked, treading lightly. And who still used the word poppycock?

Joyce turned toward them. "All that internet mumbo jumbo! All those talking heads, filling the void with nonsense."

"Not all of it is nonsense. There are places with helpful information, like CityBeat," Jordan offered.

Joyce reared back. "Did you say city *freak*? Is that a porn site?"

Jordan waved his hands. "No, no! Not freak! Beat. Beat with a *b*. Like, 'Beat It.'"

The poor man was zero for two in the spell-it-out department.

"Beat it?" the woman gasped in horror.

"It's a song—an old popular pop song," her husband stammered, his crimson cheeks matching his red scratch.

Joyce looked ready to call the cops and report a pervert in the building when somebody tapped out a cheery knock on the door. Before the addled nurse could request backup, a man with glossy blond hair and cheekbones for miles entered the room. He flashed a smile that glinted in the light like a toothpaste commercial.

Who the heck was this made-for-TV doctor?

"Joyce, you delightful creature, I'll take it from here,"

the man purred, sending another dazzling smile toward the grouch.

He was like *Baywatch* meets *ER* with a dash of *General Hospital* flare thrown in.

"That's your gynecologist?" Jordan asked under his breath.

"I don't know who this is," she whispered back.

The TV doctor flashed his pearly whites. "Let me help you out with that. I'm Chad Beaver, MD. And you two must be Georgiana and Jordan—or else I'm in the wrong exam room. Wouldn't be the first time that happened, would it, Joyce?"

The nurse replied with a surly harrumph.

"Forgive me for asking," the doctor continued, oblivious to Joyce's discontent. "But aren't you the More Than Just a Number CityBeat couple?"

"That's us," Jordan answered with a grin.

"Joyce, we've got internet royalty in our office. Isn't that exciting?" the doctor remarked.

The nurse's eyes went wide, likely thinking they were part of the internet porn industry.

One thing was for damn sure—they weren't winning any points with Joyce today.

Georgie glanced around the tiny room, hoping Nurse Gina and Dr. Rosenstein would materialize. Could she be hallucinating? Could an overabundance of pineapple cause delusions? She shook her head, trying to clear the gynecological mirage, but Dr. Beaver and Nurse Scowl were still there.

"Where's Dr. Christine Rosenstein? I always see her," Georgie stammered.

"Dr. Rosenstein got married about six months ago," the man answered.

"She did?"

"Yes, some blog helped her meet her soul mate, and they moved to Australia," the doctor answered over his shoulder as he washed his hands in the tiny sink.

Georgie blinked vacantly at the backside of the shiny doctor.

Every health professional she trusted with her vagina had left the continent thanks to her blog!

"Did you ask to make an appointment with Dr. Rosenstein when you called?" she asked her husband through a plastic grin.

"I called the office and said you needed to be seen today. I didn't ask for a specific doctor," he answered through a wide, fake grin of his own.

"I'm the new doc at the practice, and I've taken on all her patients. It looks like we'll be seeing a lot of each other because someone is close to eight weeks pregnant," the man answered, drying his hands with a paper towel.

"What?" she blurted.

If she'd had coffee in her mouth, she would have spewed it all over the room like an angry, spitting alpaca.

"It's the number between seven and nine," Joyce mumbled under her breath, then logged off the computer and left the exam room.

"Isn't she the best?" Dr. Beaver remarked, watching the crotchety nurse leave.

Georgie couldn't think about joyless Joyce or the fact that her obstetrician was named Dr. Beaver. Yes, it was the humor of a twelve-year-old to laugh at something as childish as that. But holy freaking semi-aquatic rodent! Her obstetrician's last name was Beaver, and he just dropped that she was two months along in this pregnancy!

She stared at the doctor, her mind spinning. "How can I be eight weeks pregnant?"

The man sat down on a stool and leaned in. "Well, Georgiana, it all starts with a happy little egg who's hoping to meet an eager little sperm."

Georgie shared a look with her husband, who appeared as gobsmacked as a happy little sperm running into a hopeful little egg.

"Dr. Beaver, I know how it happens. I just didn't expect to be so far along," she offered.

The shiny ob-gyn pulled a sheet of paper from his pocket. "I picked up your labs, and the blood doesn't lie. According to what you reported as the first day of your last period and taking into account the amount of hCG hormone detected in your blood sample, I'd put your due date around the twenty-second of June."

"You're kidding," Jordan breathed.

Dr. Beaver's features grew pensive. "No, I'm science-*ing*."

Her husband squeezed her hand. "Georgie, that was the date of the Denver Trot last year. What are the chances we'd have a baby due the same day a year later?"

"Fairly high if you're not practicing safe sex," the doctor answered, glancing at Joyce's notes in the chart.

It didn't seem real!

Last June, she'd met Jordan. They'd fallen in love while competing in the CityBeat Battle of the Blogs. They'd gotten engaged on live TV only a couple of months later, and now, they would be welcoming a child all in a year!

Talk about hitting life's significant milestones like a speed racer!

"How accurate are those blood tests? Is there a chance it could be a false positive? Or could it be my cycle *recali-*

brating?" she asked, throwing out the equivalent of a pregnancy Hail Mary.

Dr. Beaver frowned. "There's basically no chance that you're not pregnant."

"But how are you so sure?" she queried, like a spunky, prenatal Nancy Drew.

Her husband squeezed her hand. "He's science-*ing*, Georgie. That's how he knows."

"Yep, a whole lotta science," the doctor replied, raising his fist and getting a little bump from her husband.

Were these two bro-ing out over science?

"We're not *bro-ing* out. We're *science-ing* out," Jordan replied.

She glanced between the men. "Did I just say what I was thinking out loud?"

"Many patients mention baby brain can put them in a bit of a fog. I suggest light exercise to stay regulated. For me, it's tennis. I just won the men's singles tournament at my country club. It keeps me sharp," the shiny doctor added.

Georgie stared down at her abdomen. The man could have disclosed he'd won Wimbledon with one hand tied behind his back, and she wouldn't have cared.

This was real. She was pregnant.

Not only was she pregnant—she was eight weeks pregnant. What she'd labeled as a little pineapple overload bloat in her belly turned out to be a little human living inside her for nearly two months. Her mind went to her trifecta, but they were of no help. Their fictional mouths hung open, none of them offering up even a lick of advice.

The doctor's brow creased. "Who are Lizzy, Jane, and Hermione? And what are they supposed to lick?"

"Did I do it again?" she asked.

Jordan nodded with a bemused grin.

She had to stop this. Just because she was pregnant, it didn't mean she had to lose her ever-lovin' mind.

She snapped into librarian mode. "What happens now? Should I start taking prenatal vitamins? Should I refrain from horseback riding?"

"Georgie, when was the last time you rode a horse?" Jordan asked.

"Probably twenty years ago, but you never know when a horse could cross your path."

It was a valid concern!

"And sex?" she asked.

"That's a good question," Jordan agreed.

"Yes, on those prenatal vitamins, hold off on the horses or any extreme sports, and yes to continued sexual activity. These pamphlets can guide you on pregnancy do's and don'ts," the doctor added as he plucked pastel booklet after pastel booklet and set them on the counter.

"Georgie, it's real. We're having a baby," Jordan said with tears in his eyes.

Her mouth grew dry. Holy diaper pail! She was going to be a mother!

"Are you okay, babe?" her husband asked gently.

She stared at a smiling woman, cradling a baby on a petal-pink leaflet. Was she okay?

Was anyone okay when implanted with a human?

Was she supposed to feel like a mother now?

Would she be like her mother?

A shiver danced down her spine.

"It's a lot to take in."

"Like a gallon of pineapple juice?" her husband teased with a misty grin.

She wanted to laugh, but her thoughts morphed into a

frenzied tornado of worry, excitement, and doubt, draining the humor right out of her.

How would they grow their brand, manage their businesses, and have a baby?

"Let's take a look. The baby should have a heartbeat by now," Dr. Beaver said, then patted the exam table.

In a zombie-state, she rose to her feet, settled herself on the exam table, and covered her bottom half with the papery towel as the doctor rolled over the portable ultrasound.

"This happens with me in here?" Jordan asked, looking in horror as she planted her heels in the stirrups.

"Absolutely," the doctor answered, then removed the vaginal probe from the stand and beckoned him over with it.

"What in God's name is that?" her husband exclaimed.

"A transducer. But I like to think of it as a magic wand," Dr. Beaver said, wielding the device like a handsome gynecological wizard, to which Hermione gave a thumbs-up.

"Why a magic wand?" Jordan asked.

"Because this is how we get to see your baby."

"Where's the outside thing that goes on the stomach— like the ones they use on TV?" Jordan pressed.

"We'll use that when Georgiana's further along."

Her husband eyed the transducer warily. "You're going to put that wand inside my wife?"

Dr. Beaver flashed his TV doctor smile. "That's where the magic happens!"

She reached out, and Jordan came to stand beside her and took her hand. She needed this whole wizard and wand talk to be over. Would she ever be able to reread the *Harry Potter Series* without thinking of that giant medical dildo?

Her husband's features grew pensive as he observed the

probe, then turned to her. "You should be good with that size wand. Especially after the honeymoon and all the—"

She gave his hand a sharp squeeze. "Jordan, everyone here knows we've done it. We don't need to rehash the antics of our honeymoon."

"Don't you worry about me! Sex machines are my bread and butter," the doctor chimed.

That's certainly not something one would expect to hear from a doctor, but she was having that kind of day. She leaned onto the crinkly paper lining the exam table.

Dr. Beaver held up the probe, then busted open a condom and rolled it down the shaft.

"What the hell is that for?" Jordan exclaimed like a nun who accidentally sauntered into a whore house—or an ob-gyn exam room.

"It's for your wife's protection. This fellow's been around," Dr. Beaver added, glopping a dollop of lubricant on top of the device.

This wasn't her idea of fun either, but he wasn't the one about to have Mr. *Been Around* shoved where the sun don't shine.

"Jordan, it'll be all right, and it's not like Dr. Beaver is about to stick that thing inside you."

"Jesus! I should hope not!" He glanced down at her. "Sorry, babe, I thought I knew about pregnancy, but this is all blowing my mind."

"Aren't you a CrossFit trainer?" the obstetrician asked, wheeling himself between her legs on the little doctor stool.

"Yeah, and my degree is in kinesiology. I learned how to advise women on how to exercise safely during pregnancy, but they never whipped out a giant vagina magic wand when I was in college."

"Looks like you missed out!" the doctor replied with a made-for-TV laugh.

Should she ask to see his credentials?

"Do you have children of your own, Dr. Beaver?" she asked instead.

"I do. A boy and a girl," he answered, donning a head-lamp and turning on the vagina illumination light.

Okay, he was a father. He could sympathize.

"Did your wife allow you to deliver them?"

Dr. Beaver folded back the paper towel cover-up. "No, my husband and I adopted our children."

"Oh! I assumed..." she trailed off, feeling like an asshat.

"No worries! The only vaginas I see are the ones at work. And, Georgiana?"

"Yes?"

"Yours looks great," he answered, from between her thighs.

Again, not something one would expect your baby doctor to throw out casually, but before she could think of how to possibly respond, a cold tap to her lady area said this magical baby-finding probe session was a go.

"Watch the screen. I'm going to look around, take some measurements, then snap a few pictures," the doctor said, beginning the ultrasound.

"Does it hurt?" Jordan whispered.

She shook her head. "It's just weird."

"You're telling me," he said under his breath.

"You didn't expect to watch a doctor stick a giant medical magic wand in your wife this morning?" she teased —which was a pretty big accomplishment in her situation. Humor, while being probed, did not come easy.

"That's some cervix you've got there!" the doctor remarked.

"Um...thank you?" she answered. Dr. Rosenstein had never complimented her lady parts, and she wasn't quite sure how to respond.

"I've never seen Georgie's cervix, but everything else down there is pretty great and up to code," Jordan replied, then cringed. "Sorry, words are coming out of my mouth, but they seem to be bypassing my brain."

She smiled up at him and squeezed his hand. At least, he was as nervous as she was. Between the magical probe and up to code vagina, today was going down as not only the day she learned she and Jordan would be parents, but the day she realized she didn't have a clue about any of it. She stared at a framed picture hanging on the wall of a mother and baby in a state of maternal bliss.

That woman looked like she had it all under control.

Would she be able to do it?

"How about some music?" the doctor asked, cutting into her thoughts.

"Seems like a good time for some Michael Bolton," Jordan answered, perking up. "I can pull it up on my phone."

"That's a great call," she agreed.

There was nothing like his soothing voice and moving ballads. The man was a lyrical genius.

"Not that kind of music," the doctor said with a chuckle, then pushed a button.

A quick whooshing sound engulfed the room.

"Techno?" Jordan asked the man, currently directing a probe in her lady parts.

"No, that would be your baby's heartbeat."

Whoosh, whoosh, whoosh.

Each punctuated splash of sound washed over her.

That was their baby—a real little person with a tiny baby heart.

Jordan crouched, so his head was even with hers, and wrapped his arm around her. They stared at the screen as the grainy image stilled, and a form came into focus.

"Is that alien peanut-looking thing our baby?" he asked.

"It sure is and measuring about the size of a blueberry. Everything looks great," Dr. Beaver replied.

She stared at the alien peanut. Her alien peanut. Their alien peanut.

"Wow," she whispered, emotion clogging her throat as pure joy—not the Joyce kind—the real thing, like opening your eyes on an extraterrestrial planet and experiencing an entirely new spectrum of color. An unexplored wonderland. A vast terrain of what-ifs. A million questions bubbling to the surface.

Jordan tightened his grip. "Wow, is right."

"I'll take a few pictures for you to put up on the fridge," the doctor said, continuing the exam.

She nodded, but she wasn't paying attention to the male model obstetrician between her thighs. This was a new chapter for them. As much as her life had changed in the past five months, finding Jordan, falling in love and getting married, it had been about the two of them. This chapter introduced a whole new plot twist—a plot twist with a little person, half her and half Jordan.

Dr. Beaver removed the probe, and she slid up to sit on the table.

"Oh my!" Dr. Beaver remarked.

Her gaze bounced from the probe to the ultrasound display to the doctor. "Is something wrong?"

"Babe, your gown is open, and you went with a fancy bra!" Jordan said, eyes wide.

She pulled the potato sack around her.

"We mostly see beige around here! Thanks for spicing up my day," the doc added with a sparkling smile.

This appointment may go down as the most embarrassing day of her life, and perhaps, if she and Jordan could figure out this parenting business, also, as one of the best.

"Here you go," the doctor said, handing Jordan the printed images. "Take your time and stop by the front desk before you leave. The receptionist will have a bag of pregnancy essentials along with the list of scheduled visits. Again, it's such a pleasure meeting you both, and Georgiana?"

"Yes?" she answered, starting to think Dr. Beaver was a pretty great guy.

"You've got one of the top ten cervixes I've ever seen. And I've seen a lot."

Maybe great was too strong a word.

Dr. Beaver left the room, and she sank onto the exam table. She stared up at the ceiling, then startled when a warm sensation overtook her belly.

She glanced down and found her husband caressing her abdomen.

"Georgie Jensen-Marks has a perfect ten cervix," he said with a cocky twist to his lips.

"Stop it," she said, but there was no bite to her words. It was pretty funny.

"And my super sperm put a baby inside you," he added.

"How do you know it wasn't my super egg that gobbled up your sperm?" she countered, unleashing a smirk of her own.

He chuckled as his devilish grin faded. "I love you, messy knocked-up bun girl."

That sure didn't roll off the tongue, but she didn't care.

She slid her hand on top of his. "I guess if you have to gestate a baby, a little Asshattery heir is the way to go."

"And nice call on the lingerie. I think it earned us some points with the doctor. You know, it's like wearing your Sunday best, except the underwear version."

She shook her head and released a long sigh.

"We'll figure this out. We will," Jordan said, staring into her eyes.

She observed this man as a pregnant pause, pun intended, allowed them to take in the moment.

"I really thought you were an asshat when we first met," she said, stroking his cheek just below his toddler battle scar, then noticed the little mark next to it that had to be from when she pegged him with the pregnancy test box.

What a day!

"And you know how much I hated your Birkenstock sandals," he replied, but his expression said the opposite.

She brushed her thumb across his baby combat injuries. "That seems like ages ago, doesn't it?"

"It does," he answered, staring down at her belly.

What was their next step? Did they tell people about the pregnancy? Should they keep it to themselves? And God help her, what would she do about her mother? Her mind was about to start a new spin cycle when their phones chimed the appointment alert for their meeting with Hector and Bobby.

"How are we going to play this with CityBeat?" he asked.

She blew out a tight breath. "I have no idea."

The one thing she did know was that they needed to come up with a strategy—and fast.

Chapter Four
Jordan

Jordan glanced at his watch, then listened as his wife hummed her delight.

"We've got a little over twenty minutes before we should leave to make it to CityBeat on time," he cautioned, but it was no use.

She'd fallen in love.

"I'll be finished way before then. I promise. I just want to savor each bite," Georgie answered through her third slice of pineapple cheesecake.

This eating for two was no joke!

After the appointment with Dr. Beaver, which, holy hell, was quite a name for an obstetrician, they needed some time to decompress and regroup before heading over to meet with Bobby and Hector. He'd searched the internet for a place with pineapple desserts and found this coffee shop a block away from the CityBeat building.

And bingo! He was the baby daddy of the year. Okay, more like the baby daddy of the quarter-hour, but he'd take it.

It almost didn't seem real that their child—an actual living creature—was due in June! Freaking June! He was a number's guy. And he couldn't help but calculate that by this time next year, they'd have an almost five-month-old baby!

He'd been thrown for a loop in the waiting room from hell. But the moment their alien peanut baby, who was probably ninety percent pineapple at this point, materialized through the fuzzy gray and black lines on the ultrasound, he forgot about the baby NFL and the fact that they should have gotten this kid on a wait-list to play cello, viola, or harpsichord before he and Georgie had even met.

He was going to be a father. He didn't think his heart could hold any more love than he had for his wife, but when that alien peanut appeared, he was done for. A goner. Like the Grinch, his heart expanded in his chest.

A boy or a girl, it didn't matter to him.

What did matter was giving this baby everything.

Unfortunately, he didn't know where the hell to start. He should have asked those dads to give him the number for the baby NFL.

"Did you babysit growing up?" he asked as his wife enjoyed the final bite of cheesecake.

He wanted her in a state of complete pineapple bliss. After what she'd endured with that insane magic probe, he'd need to get this place on speed-dial to ensure they always had plenty of the pineapple deliciousness on hand.

He knew Georgie had fallen in love with the baby the minute its little alien form came to life on the screen—just like he had. It was as if a tidal wave of emotion overtook the exam room and washed over them. But that didn't mean their concerns about what life would look like now had vanished. He wasn't sure how they would balance this pregnancy with all their commitments. Luckily, between her second and third slice of cheesecake, he'd gotten an idea.

They'd approach this pregnancy scientifically. And that required a baseline. When he worked with clients, it was his job to assess their current fitness level and work from that point. He and Georgie needed a pregnancy knowledge baseline. Only then could they measure the impact that impending parenthood would have on their lives.

While she *oohed* and *aahed* through her dessert, he'd gone over his actual knowledge of what to do with an infant, which wasn't much.

A decade ago, when he'd met his former fitness mentor, Deacon Perry, his daughters were babies. He'd held them and watched as Deacon's now ex-wife and his father's current girlfriend, Maureen, cared for the twin girls. But he didn't pay all that much attention to the day-to-day *how-to-keep-your-baby-alive* routine.

These actions happened. They had to have—the girls were still living, thriving eleven-year-olds. But he didn't know the logistics and mechanics of how this *keeping-baby-alive* process worked.

Georgie set down her fork and glanced over at the pastry display. "It looks like I got the last slice of pineapple cheesecake."

She'd inhaled the last three slices, but he was a smart enough husband to *not* mention that part.

She took a sip of pineapple juice. "To answer your question, no, I never babysat growing up. I was too busy being dragged from pageant to pageant. What about you?"

He shook his head, about to answer when an infant wailed a few tables over. Like baby detectives, they observed as the mother popped a pacifier into the infant's mouth, and the child calmed instantly.

"We should order a few cases of those," he said as the woman deftly strapped her little one into a stroller and left the shop.

"We could make it a recurring order, so they arrive every month without us having to think about it. Like what I did with the pineapple-scented dryer sheets."

"No more lemon-verbena dryer sheets?" He'd grown quite attached to the smell.

She shook her head. "While I was waiting to have my blood drawn, I googled pineapple scent, and they popped up. I couldn't help but order them. This pregnant body thing is so weird. Everything I used to like now sounds awful."

He reached across the table and took her hand. "I think pineapple-scented dryer sheets are a great choice."

She held his gaze. "You do?"

"Sure! Who wouldn't want to smell like fruit cocktail all day?"

She chuckled, and her sweet laugh washed over him. After the craziness of their doctor's appointment, it was good to see her relaxed.

"We do have one thing going for us on the baby front," he offered.

Georgie leaned in. "What's that?"

"You have a whole children's section in your bookstore."

Why hadn't he thought of this earlier? Children of all ages attended story time at the bookshop. Parents and their little ones perused the picture books section, and Georgie was a whiz at recommending new series and popular children's book authors to her customers.

His wife chewed her lip. "It's one thing to read a book to

a group of parents and their babies. It's another to know what to do after the story ends."

Dammit! Maybe she had a point. She was pregnancy book smart about children's literature in the same way that he was pregnancy book smart with his knowledge of kinesiology.

He glanced at a young couple seated by the window, each staring at their phone.

"That's it!" he said, snapping his fingers.

"What? Did they add more pineapple cheesecake to the display?" Georgie asked, craning her neck.

"No, not cheesecake—the internet! We can search the hell out of it. Anytime we need to know how to do something, we google it."

Georgie beamed at him. "Okay, let's try it."

He pulled out his phone. "What topic?"

She drummed her fingers on the table. "Let's look up how to soothe a crying baby. We already know a pacifier works, so we're already ahead."

Look at this! Barely a few hours in as expectant parents, and they were killing it. No, not killing it. Their main goal for the next eighteen years was to make sure this little pineapple peanut growing in Georgie's belly remained very much alive. They were rocking it! That's more like it! The internet, where they reigned as CityBeat's sweethearts, would be their salvation.

"Let's do this on three," he said, adrenaline pumping.

Georgie held his gaze, her thumb hovering over her phone's keyboard. "Is this a challenge?" she asked with a twinkle in her eyes.

From the Battle of the Blogs to their wedding wilderness boot camp, every facet of their relationship had hinged on some sort of challenge.

He bit back a grin. Why not this one? He could be creative.

"Why yes, it is, little lady. We're in Colorado, the Wild West. This here is what you'd call a Western Wi-Fi show-down," he answered, throwing in a little twang because he didn't half-ass anything—not even this strangely erotic cowboy internet banter.

"I hope you came prepared, buckaroo. This isn't my first time at the Western Wi-Fi rodeo," she answered.

And God help him! This was damn hot! He made a mental note to suggest their next Western Wi-Fi search be for finding the location of the closest store selling cowgirl boots.

They'd never dipped their toe into adult role-play. He used to think the whole dress-up to rip each other's clothes off made no sense, but he'd be on board with investing in some Western wear. Georgie in fire engine red boots and nothing else would be a sight to see. But it wasn't only the crackle of excitement between them. They needed this tiny respite to remember who they were to each other. That thread that connected his heart to hers from the first moment they'd met.

They may have thought they'd despised each other—believed that the other was their complete opposite. But it was there from the start, that déjà vu meets serendipitous spark. That magnetic force, drawing them together, letting them know they'd make it through whatever challenges life threw their way.

"Three, two," Georgie counted, then paused and gazed at him like he was a piece of pineapple cheesecake.

"Did they restock the pastry case?" he asked.

She shook her head. "No. I'm picturing you as a cowboy," she answered with a naughty smirk.

He shifted in his seat as his blood supply headed straight to his hard length.

He stroked his thumb across her knuckles. "I may have to find someplace private to have my way with the rancher's daughter," he replied, getting way too turned on by this conversation.

"The rancher's daughter! That's good," she said in a low rasp, not helping calm the raging hard-on in his pants.

She licked her lips. "One."

He stared at her delectable mouth. He'd already started in on his ravaging the rancher's daughter fantasy.

"One what?"

"Remember, the countdown? The one about researching how to soothe a crying baby," she replied with a sexy as hell purr.

Damn her powers of seduction!

"That's right!" he exclaimed.

He went to work, typing in the search bar, then clicked on an interesting result.

Georgie held out her phone. "This website says, let them cry. They'll learn to self-soothe."

He skimmed his article. "The one I clicked on says you're not supposed to do that. Crying is a child's way of expressing distress. Leaving them to cry it out could be trau-matizing."

Georgie glanced at her phone with a creased brow. "Oh."

"Yeah," he said, not at all pleased with the internet. "This has to be an anomaly. We'll figure out which one is right later."

He checked his watch, then stole a glance at his worried wife. He needed to shift the mood.

"We still have twelve minutes before our meeting.

Could the lonely rancher's daughter use a little cowboy comfort?"

The uneasiness drained from her face, and her seductive smirk returned.

She looked around the coffee shop. "Unfortunately, there doesn't seem to be a haystack for miles."

He could do better than a haystack.

"Come on. I have an idea."

He took her hand as they left the coffee shop and headed toward the CityBeat building. While they were on their honeymoon, Bobby and Hector had messaged him with pics of their new workspace. The men had decided to renovate a bank of unused offices. And that meant an empty room for them to act out whatever fantasy they wanted in ten minutes or less.

They breezed into the CityBeat building. He waved to security, then guided his wife into an elevator. There was no need for them to provide ID. Their images were plastered all over the lobby.

Some days, it didn't hurt to be quasi-famous.

"You seem quite determined," Georgie said, eyeing him carefully.

"It happens to be your lucky day, ma'am. When I was out corralling the cattle, I came upon a secret spot."

Look at him, talking the talk!

"Did you now?" she asked, gazing up at him through her lashes.

The elevator pinged their arrival.

"Are we going to Bobby and Hector's new office?" Georgie asked as they headed down the hall.

"Yep."

"The still empty offices?" she probed—in a very non-medical way.

"That's right," he twanged.

"You are one clever cowboy, Jordan Marks."

He tipped a pretend hat. "I aim to please, ma'am."

"That's what I'm hoping for," she replied with that damn sexy rasp.

They were cleared for sex by a medical professional, and he'd be ordering her a complete cowgirl ensemble and himself a pair of chaps and a Stetson hat when he got back to his laptop.

He opened the door to the newly renovated office and flicked on the light, revealing a sprawling high-tech room with monitors fixed to the walls and modern furniture.

And toys!

Bobby and Hector's old office was jam-packed with recreational items sure to spark creativity. And this office took that sentiment to the next level. A ping-pong table sat in the center of a cluster of old Arcade games with a trio of Skee-Ball alleys, a mini putting green, and a trampoline built into the floor.

But they weren't here to master Ms. Pac-Man or to work on their table tennis serve.

Nope, he'd remembered seeing one very suitable item in the photos Hector had sent, sure to complement their carnal cowboy reenactment.

On the far side of the room, roped off like a main attraction, sat the perfect item for a randy ranch gal.

"Is that what I think it is?" Georgie asked, wide-eyed.

"How are your bull wrangling skills, little lady?"

Seductively, she ran her index finger down the length of his torso. "We'll have to find out."

She dropped her purse onto the ground and sauntered over to a giant mechanical bull. He locked the door to the office, then turned to find Georgie sitting atop the headless beast.

She undid a button on her blouse, revealing the hint of her sexy bra. "You know what they say. Save a bull. Ride a cowboy."

"I think you mean, save a horse, ride a cowboy, little lady," he countered as his gaze raked over her body.

"I'm not allowed to ride a horse and probably not a bull either. So, that leaves me with one alternative."

"Good thing there's an available cowboy in the building," he replied with a low twang.

He climbed onto the mechanical torso, facing his wife, and guided her body onto his lap. She straddled him and wrapped her arms around his neck as he palmed the globes of her ass. This never got old. Everything about Georgie, from her petite frame to the glint in her mischievous eyes, set him ablaze with desire.

With their lives balanced on the precipice of change, they needed to lose themselves in each other—if only for a few minutes, and then they'd worry about what to tell everyone at CityBeat.

He pressed a kiss to the corner of her mouth.

"It's too bad we can't turn it on," she said on a sexy sigh.

"I don't think we'll need to," he answered, rocking his hips.

His wife moaned as his hard length strained through his pants. He set a slow, delicious pace as the friction between them intensified. Georgie parted her lips on another breathy sigh, and he captured her mouth in a slow, sensual kiss.

He wanted her, but the drive to take her hard and fast had morphed into something deeper. Passion burned within him, but his need had taken on a protective edge. Her body didn't only belong to him anymore. His wife was as sassy, smart, and as tough as they came, but she was also with child.

"We're getting one of these for the house," she said, grinding into him.

"It feels okay? Nothing hurts?" he asked. He had to check.

She twisted her fingers into the hair at the nape of his neck. "Jordan, two days ago, I rode you like the dirtiest rancher's daughter in all of Fiji. I don't think that much has changed with my body in forty-eight hours."

A fresh surge of lust tore through him. "We didn't even make it out of the bungalow that day."

"Let's see if you can put this bronco to shame, buckaroo," she teased.

Hot cowboy sex on a stationary mechanical bull? Yeehaw, hell yes!

He dialed up his pace, rocking his hips while he held her close.

"Let's lose the pants, cowgirl," he groaned, his cock weeping with the need to meet her sweet center.

"That'll be tricky in a romper, but I'm keen to see you crazy kids try and pull it off," came a voice that didn't belong to his wife.

They stilled, then glanced down at the mechanical bull. This thing didn't talk, did it?

"Who is that?" Georgie asked.

"Not the headless bull," came the amused voice.

He shared a look with his wife, who's expression screamed extreme mortification.

"Welcome home, newlyweds! It's Bobby and me," Hector said, his voice booming.

"Where are you guys?" Georgie asked, looking around.

"We're right next door," Bobby answered.

Georgie frowned, still searching for the location of the speakers. "How'd you know we were in here?"

"You tripped a motion sensor and security started monitoring. They called to let us know two sexual deviants had broken into the new office," Hector replied as if getting the call regarding sexual deviants had broken into the building was cause for celebration.

"Sexual deviants?" Georgie echoed.

"You are making out on a mechanical bull. Very *Urban Cowboy* of you," Hector answered.

Georgie's cheeks flushed a deep pink. "You can see us? Like totally see us?"

"Of course! We're an internet tech company. We have cameras everywhere," Bobby answered.

Jordan frowned. "Why didn't you say something sooner?"

"It couldn't go that far. Georgie's in a romper. Don't get me wrong, it's a gorgeous garment, but I just read one of our fashion blogger's post about it being the equivalent of a naughty no-no if you're hoping to knock out a quickie. Did your mother send it to you?" Hector finished.

Georgie dropped her head to rest on his shoulder. "This cannot be happening."

"At least it's only Hector and Bobby," he said, running his hand down her back.

"No, it's the entire CityBeat PR and Marketing team," Hector corrected.

Georgie gasped. "All of you are watching us?"

"Like I said, we wanted to see how you handled the romper situation," Hector answered.

"I had five bucks on you, Jordan," came another voice.

"Barry? Is that you?" he asked.

"Yeah! It's good to see you guys. How was Fiji?" the

man replied jovially, as if there was nothing weird about engaging in high-tech peeping Tom-ery.

"Hold on! What do you mean you had five bucks on Jordan?" Georgie asked with an incensed crinkle to her brow.

"No offense, Georgie. I figured he'd use his super strength and rip your romper," Barry replied.

Georgie gasped. "Rip my romper!"

"You guys had a whole sexy Western vibe going. I said Jordan would go all macho cowboy, but the Belgian Waffle Princess said you'd put the kibosh on that," Barry added with a hint of trepidation.

"Where did the Belgian Waffle Princess come from? I thought she was in Belgium," Georgie replied as this conversation went from weird to Bonkersville.

Throughout their stint as CityBeat contributors, they'd interacted with a few of the other CityBeat bloggers. While they'd never met the Belgian Waffle Princess blogger, she'd always sent them kind messages.

Barry cleared his throat. "No, she's in Sheboygan, Wisconsin. She only blogs about Belgian waffles. We were having a video conference with her when the alarm tripped," Barry added.

Romper ripping bets and a Sheboygan Waffle Princess?

This crazy train had gone far enough.

"Okay, everyone," he said, addressing the empty room. "The romper is intact. Barry, you owe the princess five bucks. Do you want us to come to you, or do you guys want to join us in here?"

An electric hum cut through the room.

"What is that?" Georgie asked, looking from side to side.

"Surprise, surprise!" Hector crooned as the far wall retracted, exposing a crowd of CityBeat employees.

Jordan slid off the bull, then helped Georgie down.

"You put in a moving wall?" she exclaimed.

"Electric retractable dividers! Aren't they fabulous?" Hector added with a charismatic wave of his hands.

"My husband decided that instead of moving offices, we double the size of our workspace and use both," Bobby said with a hint of amusement.

Hector rubbed his hands together like a flamboyant mad scientist. "We also needed more room for the bull. Do you want me to turn it on? We can test if a romper holds up to ten seconds on Tank."

"Tank?" Georgie repeated, her complexion growing pale.

"Hector named the bull," Bobby answered.

Hector clapped the ass of the mechanical beast. "Then, after the romper research, we can share all the amazing things we want to have you lovebirds involved with to promote the More Than Just a Number blog and brand. Colorado loves you two, and our team has big ideas about incorporating a whole *explore the great outdoors* angle. What are your thoughts on free-climbing and paragliding?" Hector added with a wicked glint in his eyes.

Oh shit! This was not good.

Georgie's gaze bounced from Hector to the bull. "Could Jordan and I have a word with you and Bobby, privately?"

He looked at his wife. Thanks to the naughty cowboy ravages the rancher's daughter role-play, they hadn't played out what they'd wanted to accomplish in this meeting.

Was she about to drop the pregnancy bomb?

What impact would that have on their standing with CityBeat?

Would they have to hit the pause button?

There was no way in hell he was about to watch his pregnant wife strap into a glider and swoop off a cliff or dangle from a rope thousands of feet above the ground.

He took Georgie's hand, looked from Hector to Bobby, then held his wife's gaze.

The moment of truth had arrived.

Chapter Five
Georgie

"I s everything okay?" Bobby asked, pushing his glasses to the bridge of his nose.

Georgie tightened her grip on Jordan's hand. "Yes, everything is...fine."

As fine as one can be after discovering an eight-week-old blueberry-sized human had set up camp in your uterus and learned that a hoard of people had just watched them perform act one of the first act of the *Naughty Rancher's Daughter*.

Concern marred Hector's expression as he lowered his voice and spoke to the marketing and PR employees. The group headed back to the other side of the office when Barry looked over his shoulder and caught her gaze.

"Barry, would you mind staying as well?" she asked.

Barry had been with them from the beginning. The easygoing producer had been by their side during the Battle of the Blogs, and like Hector and Bobby, he'd become like family.

"Sure, Georgie," the man said, pressing a button on the wall that activated the retractable divider to close.

Hector paced in front of them. "It's the whole outdoors angle, isn't it? You think it will be like that awful boot camp the Denver Wedding Frau made you attend before you got married where you had to bring your own pooper scooper."

"Shit shovel," she and Jordan said in unison as a chill traveled down her spine.

That implement from hell would haunt them forever.

Bobby gave them a sympathetic grin. "We promise that there won't be any camping involved. The team thought it would be great for you to branch out and highlight some of the attractions the state has to offer, and the Colorado office of tourism also reached out to us. They'd love to have you as ambassadors. And it's not all extreme sports. They'd mentioned having you visit some of the city's small breweries, and they even suggested a trip to the Western slope to check out Colorado's vineyards and budding wine industry. The sky's the limit!"

While partaking in wine tastings and extreme sports to showcase the state would be an incredible opportunity, it didn't exactly fit into the parameters of a safe pregnancy.

"That all sounds great," she answered warily, sharing a look with her husband.

"Interesting ideas," he added, but the concern in his eyes signaled his unease.

Hector gestured to a pair of sofas, and they settled themselves.

"I feel a *but* coming on," the man said, catching Bobby's eye.

This was the moment she'd been dreading since the first pair of pink lines appeared on the pregnancy test this morning. The moment she'd realized the plans she and Jordan had made had to be scrapped.

It wasn't as if she didn't want her baby. She did. Sweet blueberry pineapple surprise, she did!

The minute that alien peanut showed up on the screen, she knew it was meant to be. What she didn't have the answer to was what happens next, followed quickly by a sense of panic, not knowing the first thing about raising a child.

She loved her mom, but the woman had her quirks when it came to parenting. When she was a girl, Lorraine Vanderdinkle's idea of mother-daughter bonding had been to spend the weekend in a hotel ballroom, wearing enough rouge to make a newscaster cringe and jamming high heels onto her little feet so she could parade on stage in a beauty pageant.

She didn't want to be that kind of mother. She wanted to shower her child with books and days spent staring at the sky, searching for cloud-shaped animals. She wanted to sing songs and finger paint. With Jordan on one side and her on the other, she'd imagined swinging their little one between them as they enjoyed a meandering walk.

But what if her child wanted to be in beauty pageants?

Would she be like her mother and deny the wish because it wasn't in line with her taste?

While they were on their honeymoon, between bouts of mind-blowing sex, they'd planned their future.

Their love story unfolded over a handful of months. Their honeymoon in Fiji had been their first real vacation. Lying in the shade of a cluster of leafy palm trees, they'd listened to the ocean's calming melody as they'd laughed and dreamed, talking of the future and the adventures to come.

A future that included growing their brand and their

businesses. Jordan wanted to branch out and open gyms in other parts of the city, and she had dreams of doing the same with her bookstore. They wanted to travel and share their More Than Just a Number philosophy all over the world. Yes, it would be a lot of work, but they'd be in it together. CityBeat's sweethearts. Partners. A team. A perfect pair.

The idea of turning their duet into a trio hadn't even popped up.

Like some abstract concept, she'd wanted to become a mother—someday.

That someday, however, happened to be the day after they'd returned from their honeymoon.

She fixed her beauty queen smile to her face and turned to the men sitting across from them. "Jordan and I have some news."

"What kind of news?" Hector asked, his knee bouncing like a kid ready for recess.

It was now or never. Whatever plans CityBeat had in the works, they'd either be put on hold indefinitely or go down the drain.

"The kind of news that wets diapers," she answered, waiting for Bobby, Hector, and Barry to go nuts.

"Is my Aunt Gertrude coming to town? And if she was, how would you know that, Georgie?" Barry asked wide-eyed.

"No, I don't know anything about your Aunt Gertrude. I'm trying to tell you all that I'm pregnant."

The men sat there, as still as statues, until Bobby and Barry's shoulder's slumped, and Hector broke out into an ear to ear grin.

"Two somebodies owe me a hot fudge sundae," Hector chimed, snapping his fingers in a triumphant set of clicks.

"What do hot fudge sundaes have to do with us having a baby?" Jordan asked.

"It has to do with a bet I won," Hector answered with another smart snap.

She stared at the men. This could not be a pregnancy fog or mirage or whatever Dr. Beaver said women with child experienced. She was eighty-five percent sure this was not how people usually responded to a pregnancy announcement.

"A bet about what?" She needed some damn clarification.

Hector leaned forward. "You, Georgie! I bet Barry and Bobby a hot fudge sundae that you were knocked up."

"When?" she said with as much indignance as she could muster.

"At your wedding."

She reared back, her mouth hanging open.

"You thought Georgie was pregnant at our wedding?" Jordan sputtered. "I didn't put it together until the end of our honeymoon."

"How far along are you, honey?" Hector asked.

"Almost eight weeks," she answered, unable to believe how many people got a pregnancy vibe off her when she'd been oblivious—and all of them *uterus-less* men!

Hector clapped his hands. "I was right! I'm the pregnancy whisperer!"

Barry stared at his cell phone. "Sorry, boss. Somebody already claimed that title."

Hector's knee was back to bouncing. "Fine! I'm the... *baby sleuther*," he said with a dramatic baby sleuthing edge.

"You're safe with that one, and if you don't mind, I'm going to send a quick email to my aunt while she's on my mind—just to make sure she doesn't have any trips planned to come to Denver. She snores, too," Barry replied, gaze fixed to his phone.

Georgie shared a look with her husband, who shrugged. What do you say to a guy who disclosed that his aunt wets herself and snores? Hallmark sure as hell didn't have a sympathy card for it, and her trifecta had nothing, her fictional friends cringing at the thought.

Luckily, they didn't have to address the afflicted aunt.

"Bobby! We're going to be fairy godfathers!" Hector exclaimed and hugged his husband.

Diaper-wearing aunts, fairy godfathers, baby sleuthing, and hot fudge sundaes?

Georgie leaned in toward Jordan. "Am I having a pregnancy delusion?"

"No, babe. They seem genuinely happy. I don't get it either."

"You're not upset or disappointed?" she asked the men.

"Are you kidding! Under the circumstances, this is the best news!" Bobby answered.

The circumstances?

"You understand that means Georgie and I can't jump off of cliffs while holding hands or guzzle local ale in matching beer steins," Jordan said, sharing a perplexed look with her.

"All the plans and sponsorships will have to be canceled. I'm due in June," she added.

"Not canceled, amended," Hector replied with a devious little glint in his eyes.

"Amended to what?" Jordan asked.

Hector steepled his fingers as a contemplative crease formed on his brow. "Barry, have they arrived?"

They?

What was Hector talking about?

The CityBeat producer checked his phone. "Yep, they're here."

"Tell them what's going on and ask them to join us."

"Will do!" Barry replied, hammering out a text.

Georgie looked around. Were there more people watching them?

"Who are you talking about?" she shot back.

Barry pocketed his phone and stood, but Hector raised his hand, ushering him to sit.

"Hold on, one hot knocked-up second!" Hector said, doing a yoga-thing with his hands, drawing his index finger and thumb together in a mystical okay gesture.

"Now, Georgie, you know the psychic energist shared that I have a gift. I know things. Spiritual things. Energetic things," he whispered into the air.

Sweet Jesus!

She'd been grateful to have her mother, Hector, and Bobby occupied and out of her hair when their wedding planner sent them to a psychic energist, who deemed them enlightened, then assigned the trio the important job of reading the spiritual energy of wedding favors.

But she'd never considered the ramifications or ripple effect of their newfound skill set.

At least Bobby seemed to have realized their psychic abilities mounted up to supernatural silliness. Unfortunately, that insight hadn't dawned on his husband.

Hector looked ready to continue talking of otherworldly things when his eyebrows jumped to his hairline. "Wait! Have you told your mother and Howard about the baby?"

Oh, crap!

"Not yet. We just confirmed the pregnancy with the doctor this morning," Jordan answered.

And there it was—again, the question of when they would tell her mother.

How would she handle spilling the beans? The minute her mom found out she was going to be a grandmother, she'd visit the dermatologist for a few Botox hits and then, depending on which Lorraine Vanderdinkle personality showed up, it would either be Mrs. Namaste Vanderdinkle, let's chant and light some candles, or socialite Lorraine, who'd be all about designer baby this and designer baby that.

Either version, she wasn't up for it. Not yet. Not when she hadn't fully wrapped her mind around becoming a mother.

No, she'd hold off telling her parents. People did that. They waited, didn't they? Plus, her mother and Howard were probably very busy meditating and measuring the psychic energy of mini Buddhas and elephant figurines. When she and Jordan were ready, they'd call her stepfather's office and send word. It bought them a little time.

Georgie swallowed hard. "My mother and Howard are in India, honing their psychic skills at a retreat for the next several months, but we wanted to wait before we told them."

"We did?" Jordan asked under his breath.

Damn those wanton pregnancy hormones! Instead of planning and strategizing their next steps with her family and CityBeat, they'd gone all sexy cowboy scenario instead. She'd never thought of her CrossFit husband donning Western wear, but with a body like his and abs that literally brought her to her knees, this man in chaps would be a Texas-sized panty-melter.

And rope! Cowboys used rope, lots of rope. They were always lassoing animals in cowboy movies. Jordan in chaps, tying her wrists together, then taking her like a wild stallion. That would be—

"Georgie?" her husband said gently.

"Yes?"

"You spaced out and started salivating," he answered, concern woven into the words.

"I did?" She wiped the back of her wrist across her lips. Yep, full-on drool. Leave it to her to not only suffer from pregnancy fog but a sex-fueled pregnancy haze.

"You were saying you wanted to wait on telling your mother," Bobby offered, getting her back on track.

"Yes, that's right," she answered, hoping she didn't look like someone who'd blanked out for an imaginary quickie with a cowboy. "We want my mom to harness her chi and balance her yang before dropping such psychically exciting news," she added, throwing together one heck of a word salad.

"I see," Hector answered, tapping his chin.

"Yes, that's it," she reiterated, glancing at her husband who, bless him, nodded like what she said had made complete sense.

Hector stilled. "Your mother is quite gifted, Georgie. She knew before we opened the box that the first batch of wedding favor chocolate from Switzerland had an adverse aura."

"Yeah, that's some expert psychic maneuvering," she replied as if they were discussing something gravely serious and not the perceived ominous vibes emitted from a box of candy.

"Have you ever had psychically unbalanced chocolate?" Hector asked, lowering his voice.

She pressed her hand to her belly. The thought of chocolate, balanced or unbalanced, made her want to hurl.

"I'm sure it would have ruined everything. It was a good catch," she replied as the faint hint of an acoustic guitar drifted into the room.

"What's that?" Jordan asked.

"That's how we're amending your situation. The universe works in mysterious ways. Open the door, Barry!" Hector said, that glint back in his eyes.

Barry bolted from his spot on the couch. "You guys will love this!" he said, almost as wild-eyed as Hector.

With a dramatic flair, the CityBeat producer threw open the door, and the guitar music grew louder. And it wasn't just a guitar. There was singing. And it wasn't only one person. No, two distinctly male voices wafted into the room.

"My name's Lenny, and this is Stu, we love little babies, it's what we do!"

Two smiling men entered the room. Looking to be in their mid-fifties with hipster beards, one man was tall and thin while the other was short and plump. Wearing newsboy caps and jaunty scarves tied around their necks, they looked like the kindergarten version of vagabonds—the tall one playing the guitar while the shorter man shimmied around with a tambourine.

"We should call Dr. Beaver and ask if men can suffer from pregnancy delusions," Jordan whispered, narrowing his gaze at the singing manifestation.

"We love to learn! We love to sing! When it comes to babies, we know everything," the men continued.

"Do you see two guys standing in front of us singing about babies?" she asked, unable to look away from the crooning odd couple.

"Yeah," he answered, staring slack-jawed at the men.

She cocked her head to the side. "Then, we're either

having the same pregnancy delusion, or this is really happening."

"What the f—" Jordan began, coming to his feet.

She sprang up and clapped her hand over his mouth.

"Who are these people, and why are they singing?" she asked the CityBeat founders.

"This is the next frontier, Georgie," Hector offered, which told her nothing.

"The next frontier is grown men dressed up as put together hobos who sing about babies? No offense," she said to the men, who'd stopped singing.

"None taken. That's what we were going for," the taller of the two replied with a friendly strum.

Hector raised his hands like a carnival barker. "City-Beat Rattle. We're getting into the baby business," he said, piling on the drama.

The stout man slung the tambourine under his arm, then plucked a trio of baby rattles from his pocket like a gypsy Mary Poppins and started juggling.

"Meet Lenny and Stu. They're the hottest thing on the baby music circuit," Barry added.

"And toddlers and preschoolers. Our chant, 'The Clean-up Chicken Dance,' is used in early childhood education classes across the globe," the tall man with the guitar replied.

"That is quite an accomplishment," she offered, still not sure this was happening.

She reached over and pinched her husband as the short rattle juggler slid the baby toys back into his pockets.

"Ouch! What was that for?" Jordan exclaimed with a startle.

"A reality check," she answered.

"Good call," he whispered back, rubbing his arm.

Georgie's thoughts went to her literary trifecta. But the girl wizard and Georgian-era ladies sat stupefied with no advice to dispense on the topic of internet baby sites.

These three were no help today!

"You're starting a new company?" Jordan asked.

"Not a new company—an offshoot," Bobby replied.

"And now we've got CityBeat's sweethearts, welcoming their own bundle of joy, to bridge the gap from our main site to our parent-friendly domain," Hector added as a topsy-turvy wave washed over her.

No, no, no, no, no, no!

She plastered on her beauty queen smile, which she only used in dire situations. "But Hector, we don't want to make anything public yet. Remember, I haven't told my mother."

The man waved her off. "That's not a problem. The site won't be up and running until late July. You'll have delivered by then—and hopefully, told your mother," he answered with a chastising lift of his eyebrow.

"And all the content we put together will be archived until then," Bobby supplied.

"And the timing couldn't be better," Barry added.

Jordan crossed his arms. "For what?"

"Lenny and Stu are leading the first-ever CityBeat Rattle Battle of the Births," Hector answered, in circus ringmaster mode.

For Pete's sake!

"The what?" her husband exclaimed.

"We tested Battle of the Babies, but people thought it was a *Hunger Games-type* contest with infants, and they didn't seem to like it," the CityBeat producer replied.

She cringed. "Well, yeah! Who would want to see babies fight each other?"

"Surprisingly, men aged fifty-two to fifty-eight and women seventy-seven to seventy-nine. But they're not the age group we're targeting with CityBeat Rattle," Barry answered with a grin that seemed very misplaced, even if he were proud of the data and stats.

Battling babies shouldn't be palatable to anyone!

"We've been in the child development game for the better part of the last twenty years," the short man offered.

"Sorry, which one are you?" she asked, pivoting from the CityBeat crew to the singing baby vagabonds.

"I'm Stu," the man replied.

"Then that would make you, Lenny," Jordan said to the tall man, but instead of answering, the musical duo started singing.

"Good job! Good job! You did a good job! Good job! Good job! You used your brain!" the men belted as Stu broke out the tambourine, and Lenny strummed a catchy tune.

"Holy f—" she began before Jordan stifled the curse by cupping his hand over her mouth.

"Naughty words, naughty words. No, no, naughty words," the men chanted, not missing a beat.

But Jordan raised his hands in surrender. "No more singing until someone explains what the *heck* Battle of the Births is."

"Nice job with the *h, e, double l* substitution," she said under her breath.

"As long as we keep this PG, I think we can stop them from busting out into song," he whispered back.

"Deal," she murmured.

"How much do you two know about caring for a baby?" Stu asked with a warm Disney-esque grin.

"We know that they need to eat," she answered.

"And they need to have their diapers changed," Jordan supplied.

She lifted her chin in a triumphant little movement. Maybe they knew more than she thought.

"Do you know how often newborns need to be fed?" Lenny pressed.

"And have you decided if you're going to use cloth or disposable diapers?" Stu added.

"Cloth diapers? Non-pioneer parents choose cloth?" Jordan asked with a bewildered expression.

She was thinking the same thing.

"It's quite a debate, and some are very passionate about the subject," Lenny replied.

"What about nutrition? Do you think you'll breastfeed or use formula or a combination?" Stu continued.

She turned to her husband, who gave her man-eyes for, *fuck-if-I-know*. No, not fuck, *heck*. *Heck-if-I-know* eyes.

"We just found out we were expecting this morning," Jordan sputtered, this reply quickly becoming their trademark response when asked about anything pregnancy-related.

"When are you due?" the stout Stu asked.

"June twenty-second," she answered, unable to hold back a grin. This whole situation may be insane, but the thought of her alien blueberry pineapple peanut sent a dizzying wave of warmth through her body.

"See, they're right on track," Hector added, losing the carnival edge and sliding into tech mogul.

She frowned. "On track for what?"

"The other expectant contestants," Stu answered.

"The name Battle of the Births has a fierce ring to it, but it's not as cutthroat as it sounds. We're working with a few other couples all due in June. It's more parent education than an actual competition," Lenny assured them.

She turned to Hector and Bobby. "You're asking us to do another competition?"

"Every phase of your relationship has had one. What's one more?" Bobby answered with a teasing twist to his lips.

He wasn't wrong, but this wasn't just about them anymore. They had a baby to consider.

Lenny shifted the guitar to his back. "Maybe this will help. Both Stu and I have degrees in child development, and over the years, we've helped many couples prepare to become parents."

"Do you always dress like cheerful vagrants?" she asked warily.

"No, we're in costume to film a few promo spots for CityBeat Rattle with a few parent-training items that just arrived."

Hector pressed his hands together meditatively. "See, my psychic intuition brought you all here today. It's meant to be!"

Georgie chewed her lip. "I'm not sure about this."

They had a lot on their plate—with their blog and businesses—and God only knows what they'd have to take on for her mother's charity activities.

"Can we have a minute?" Jordan asked.

"Of course! Lenny and Stu's packages arrived. We'll be over on the far side of the room checking out the delivery," Hector answered.

The men migrated toward a stack of boxes, and the room started to spin.

She sank into the couch and stared up at the ceiling. "I've lost count of all the people without ovaries who know more about this baby business than I do," she said, waiting for Jordan to laugh, but he remained quiet. She sat up and found him sitting beside her, staring at one of the ultrasound pictures.

She leaned into him and traced the outline of their peanut baby. "It's pretty wild, isn't it?"

"I think we do it, Georgie," he said, gaze trained on the black and gray image.

"You do?"

He nodded. "Hector and Bobby wouldn't allow a bunch of quacks to spearhead a site for expectant parents and childhood development blogs. And I don't know about you, but I didn't know the answer to any of the questions Lenny and Stu asked. Sure, we could google it, but what if we kept getting conflicting opinions? And they did say they had degrees in child development."

All that was true, but was it smart to pile on another task and be roped into another CityBeat contest?

Then again, would it be smart to accept? This Battle of the Births could provide them with the information and training they needed.

And how competitive could it be?

She gazed down at her wrist and stared at the charm bracelet Jordan had given her. She ran her finger over the delicate silver eight and ten, then gazed at the tiny computer mouse and trowel charms tucked between a silver sandal, a book, a barbell, and a miniature cookie. These were the reminders of their love and their past challenges. But something was off with the cookie! Just the sight of it made her belly go sour.

"Okay, let's do it," she said, looking away from the cookie charm.

"Yeah?" he asked.

She gave him the hint of a grin. "You're right. It sounds like these guys could get us on track."

Jordan slid the ultrasound photo back into his pocket. "We're in," he called across the room.

"That's excellent news! This is going to be such an adventure!" Hector crooned as she and Jordan made their way toward the group.

"And you can take this with you today," Stu said, holding out a lumpy sack a little larger than a shoebox.

Presents already? Maybe this wasn't so bad.

"What is it?" she asked, accepting the gift.

"A baby," Lenny said with a jovial expression.

"What!" she exclaimed, panic flooding her system.

Why was this man okay with a baby being stuffed into a bag?

She opened the cinched cloth wrapping and found...

"Thank goodness! It's not a real baby," she cried, removing the mannequin infant from the wrapping.

"You're giving us a fake baby? A *faby*?" Jordan questioned as they stared at the remarkably lifelike figure.

"It's an infant care simulation doll. Stu and I designed them. We'll be using them later in the Battle of the Births. But for now, take it home, and get used to having it around," Lenny explained.

She stared at the little thing. Dressed in only a white cotton diaper, its painted eyes gazed up at her.

"You want us to hang out with a fake baby?" Jordan pressed.

Stu nodded. "Yes! Carry it around the house. Take it on a walk. It'll help you ease into becoming parents."

"Does it need anything?" she asked, touching the mannequin's chin.

"That's what this is for," Stu replied, then handed Jordan a giant bag.

"The fake baby needs all this?" he exclaimed, his large frame slumping as he secured the strap of the bag over his shoulder.

"Like I said. Get used to it. We'll be in touch with the details, but plan on a challenge or two during each trimester," Lenny replied.

Her gaze bounced between the diaper bag and the fake baby—*Faby*...whatever.

This was it.

In for a penny, in for a pound.

She cradled the infant care simulation doll in her arms as the walls seemed to cave in on them; the air growing stagnant.

She inhaled a steadying breath. "Hector, I have to ask. What made you think I was pregnant in the first place?"

"It was what you were eating at your wedding reception. Well, more like what you *were* and what you *weren't* eating," the man answered.

But that didn't make any sense.

She shifted the fake baby in her arms. "I hardly ate anything at all. It was such a whirlwind of an evening."

"Then perhaps you don't remember when you honored me with a dance."

Her brows knit together. "Of course, I remember our dance."

"Do you also remember the part where I twirled you around, and you plucked a piece of pineapple off the dessert table?"

She thought back to their dance. They'd laughed and talked, but she had no recollection of fruit being a part of it.

"I remember the twirl but not eating any pineapple."

"You certainly did. I was surprised to see you do that after what your mother told us."

"What did she say?" Georgie asked, but she already had a good idea.

Hector leaned in. "One afternoon after we'd read the psychic energy of three hundred citrus-scented votive candles for your wedding, a tiring task, your mother told us the story of how you cleared out a Ritz-Carlton ballroom, losing your lunch all over the beauty pageant judges after you ate a pineapple fruit cup," he replied.

"It was the pineapple that tipped you off?" she pressed.

"That, and you didn't even glance at the tiny tubes of vegan chocolate chip cookie dough we had made especially for your wedding day. We all know how you feel about those."

"That reminds me," Barry piped up. "We've got some here! Hold on! I'll get you one!" the man offered and headed for the office's kitchenette.

Her stomach did a flip-flop at the mention of the vegan treat.

Jordan stroked her arm. "Georgie, are you okay? You look a little green."

"Have you had any bouts of morning sickness yet?" Stu asked.

She blinked as the thought of tiny tubes of vegan chocolate chip cookie dough, once her go-to stress reliever and the tasty treat that never let her down, now turned her stomach.

"Um, I haven't experienced morning sickness yet... but..." she rasped as the taste of bile flooded her mouth.

Barry jogged toward them, his hands teeming with the pocket-sized tubes of vegan dough.

"Look, Georgie! We've got a ton of them! You can take a bunch home with you!"

She tried to wave him off, but in the blink of an eye, her mild belly flip-flops morphed into a heavy-duty, high-speed tumble that would put an industrial clothes dryer to shame.

Her stomach spasmed.

This was not good!

There was no time to hightail it to the restroom. She tossed the fake baby...*faby*...whatever, to her husband and lunged for a trash can.

But she was too late.

Just as she'd done years ago in a child-sized evening dress and five-inch heels, she lost her three delectable slices of pineapple cheesecake all over poor Barry's feet.

"Whoa!" the man exclaimed.

"Thank God we installed tile instead of carpet!" Hector murmured to Bobby, leaping out of the way.

"There it is. A telltale sign," Stu replied calmly as if it were standard practice for women to lose their lunch, or in her case a trifecta of cheesecake, in his presence.

"There's a pack of ginger lozenges in the diaper bag. They can help ease the nausea," Lenny added.

She wiped the back of her hand across her lips.

Perfect! More advice from Team No Uterus.

Jordan leaned over and rubbed her back with the fake baby tucked under his arm, its little head inches from hers. The doll seemed to have a mischievous curve to its fake baby lips. Were they always like that? Was she having another pregnancy delusion?

"I'm sure the nausea will end soon, and we'll figure everything out," Jordan said, trying to reassure her.

She held the doll's gaze and knew instantly that her husband was wrong.

It was just the beginning of this pregnancy roller coaster —and they were locked in for the entire ride.

Chapter Six
Jordan

J ordan steadied himself. "We've got something to share with you."

"Some very important news," Georgie added, squeezing his hand like a vice.

Who knew librarians had such a grip?

He glanced at his wife. She'd whipped out her beauty queen grin—the giveaway she was nervous.

She wasn't the only one.

"But we want you to know that we love you very much and always will. That will never change," his wife continued.

Mr. Tuesday, their black and white beloved mixed-breed pup, cocked his head to the side.

Georgie lowered her voice. "This is a lot for him. We've only been living together for six months and with the wedding, and then with us being gone the last couple of weeks for our honeymoon, I think he's confused."

Who wouldn't be confused? It was as if the universe decided they were on the relationship Autobahn.

"I think you should tell him, Jordan," his wife said with a crease between her brows.

"Why me?" he asked through a smile, talking like a ventriloquist. Why? Because he didn't want to upset the dog. This would have made no sense to him before falling in love with Georgie and her crazy canine. But now, he was a dog dad. And that's what dog dads do.

"You did do this to me," she said with a covert gesture to her belly. "You know, planted the seed. Fertilized the garden," she whispered as Mr. Tuesday's head cocked to the other side.

"You seemed onboard with the *gardening*," he replied cautiously.

"True. I couldn't get enough of it—the gardening, that is," she added quickly, her cheeks growing pink with embarrassment.

Did she think Mr. Tuesday had an opinion on their sex life?

Did she not want their dog to know that they'd done the dirty a bazillion times in a tropical paradise and, not to mention, this morning in the shower? They all lived in the same house. In some doggy way, he had to know.

Jesus, this was getting weird.

Let's get real. The dog had no idea what they were talking about. There was a good chance that the only reason he'd humored them for this long was that he still smelled the four Slim Jims Georgie ate before they'd left for the doctor's office this morning.

He scratched between the pup's ears. "All right, Mr. Tuesday, here's the big news. You're going to be a big brother."

"We're having a baby, and it will look a little bit like

this," Georgie said, holding out the doll Lenny and Stu had given them.

"This is Faby," he went on, introducing a dog to a doll—something he'd never expected to be doing, but life with Georgie was chock-full of these moments.

"Faby?" his wife questioned.

He tapped the doll's rubbery nose. "It's a fake baby—so, Faby. That makes sense, don't you think?"

Both Georgie and Mr. Tuesday's heads cocked to the same side.

"Is that a boy name or a girl name?" she asked.

He glanced at the fake baby's diaper. "Should we look?"

The doll itself appeared quite lifelike with chubby cheeks, a cute button nose, and a cooing little mouth, but looked gender neutral—at least, to him.

"Would that be creepy? What if it's got a tiny penis," Georgie said, whispering the p-word part.

"Then, it's a boy," he answered.

Georgie pursed her lips. "I get that, but wouldn't it still be a little strange?"

"I would think a boy with no penis would be stranger," he offered.

Were they debating a baby doll's anatomy?

She stared at the diaper. "You're probably right."

Probably? But he wasn't about to go there.

"Let's just look," he added, gingerly taking the doll from his wife.

He placed Faby on the coffee table and tried to pull the cloth diaper down like a pair of trousers.

"Am I doing it wrong?"

Georgie pointed to the side of the diaper. "I think there's Velcro. Try that."

"Good call," he replied, peeling back the tiny strips of adhesive to reveal...

Now, he was the one cocking his head to the side. "There's nothing."

Georgie leaned in. "Is it a girl?"

He frowned and inspected the fake baby. "It's like a Barbie or a Ken doll. Nothing downstairs."

A mischievous grin pulled at the corners of his wife's mouth. "How do you know what Ken and Barbie look like naked?"

"Hey, I had a very progressive mother. It wasn't just race cars and robots lining my toy box," he answered with mock incredulity before his chest tightened with emotion.

What would his mother think about how his life had turned out if she were still here?

His gaze traveled from the genderless toy doll to his wife. His mother would have loved Georgie. She would have adored Jensen's Bookshop. The two would have talked classics until late into the night, debating the finer points of *Pride and Prejudice*. It was his mother's love of reading that had led him to comic books after she'd passed away.

And those stories had become his escape after her death.

He'd find an isolated corner of the library and lose himself in the lives of Peter Parker and Clark Kent. In those moments, he wasn't a scrawny, picked-on kid with a father wracked by grief. No, he'd become those superheroes, over-coming hardships, beating the villains, and saving the day.

"Look, Jordan," Georgie said, pulling him from the past.

He pressed a kiss to the back of her hand as they watched Mr. Tuesday sniff and prod the mannequin infant with his nose.

"It looks like he approves of Faby, our no-sex baby," Georgie remarked, patting the pup's head.

"It's got to be a good sign," he answered, feeling pretty damn proud.

Look at them, introducing their beloved pet to a plastic model infant!

They were excellent dog parents. Sure, human babies were probably more work, but they'd get there. Granted, they didn't have a clue about the baby NFL or fencing for toddlers—which, after everything he'd learned from the waiting room dads today, probably was a thing. But Lenny and Stu seemed well-connected in this new universe, baby-verse, whatever you want to call the phase of life they were about to enter. And despite their outfits, the men seemed as if they'd be able to provide them with everything they needed to know.

Baby 101, here they come!

He was about to tell his wife they should google toddler fencing to see if it existed when she gasped.

"What is it? Is it the baby? Do you need to hurl again? Should I get a bucket?" he blurted, morphing into a high-alert expectant father.

Georgie waved him off. "It's nothing like that! I remembered that Irene said that Mr. Tuesday loved cuddling into her pregnant belly while we were in Fiji."

"You're sure you're okay?" he pressed, not wanting a repeat of what happened in Hector and Bobby's new office.

Georgie sat back into the cushions and chuckled, relief written all over her face. "I'm fine. I can't believe I totally spaced that Irene and Will can help us field any pregnancy questions. They're due in March."

That's right! In all the pregnancy hoopla, he'd forgotten their friends were already living the expectant parent life.

"With the Battle of the Births and our friends able to help us fill in our pregnancy knowledge gaps, I think we've got this, babe. But are you sure you don't want me to set a trash can next to the couch? You know, just in case," he said, then gave her his best vomit face.

Georgie plucked a small decorative pillow off the couch and went to whack him with it when a knock at the door caught their attention and stopped her mid-swing.

"Are you expecting anyone?" he asked.

She shook her head. "No. We're meeting everyone at the bookshop in a little while to catch up and tell them about our honeymoon." She picked up her phone and glanced at it. "No one messaged me that they were going to stop by."

He checked his cell. No texts or new messages, either.

"It's Nicolette. Lorraine Vanderdinkle's executive assistant," came a woman's voice from the other side of the door.

"I'll get it," he said, leaving the couch and opening the front door to a rush of chilly November air.

"Hello," he said, taking in the new Nicolette.

The petite woman had on sunglasses as big as dinner plates and a straw hat—pretty strange for fall in Colorado, but what did he know about fashion. He'd just learned what a lady romper was today.

"I have something for you and Miss Georgiana," she said in a thick French accent.

The woman rooted around in her bag. She pulled out her passport, then plucked an envelope from the tote, crammed with magazines and a bottle of sunscreen.

"Are you going on a trip?" he asked as she handed over the envelope.

She stiffened. "No."

He tapped the envelope to the doorframe. "Well, thanks for bringing this by."

Nicolette glanced at her watch. "I better be going. Everything you need to know is in the letter," she said, then ran down the path and jumped into a waiting car.

That was weird, but you'd have to be weird to work for Georgie's mom.

"What did Nicolette want?" Georgie called.

"She dropped off a letter," he answered, closing the door only to have it pop open.

"It does that from time to time when the weather gets cooler. Jiggle the handle, and then it should close," Georgie instructed.

He gave the knob a little shake but stilled when he read the letter's return address.

"It's from the office of Lorraine Vanderdinkle," he said, sauntering over to the couch as Georgie leaned forward to get a better look at the special delivery.

"Your mom has an office?" he asked, handing her the envelope.

"Who knows these days," Georgie answered, opening the letter, then scanning the page.

He looked over her shoulder. "What does it say?"

"The gist is that many of my mother's charity duties are mainly ceremonial in nature."

"Okay," he answered, wrapping his arm around her shoulders.

"I think the only thing we have to do is host a Western-themed charity event for literacy education in May."

"Are you sure that's it? I thought she did a ton of socialite stuff?" he asked, glancing at the page.

She angled the letter so he could skim the message. And his wife was right. While Lorraine sat on many boards and supported several charities, there appeared to be very little to do.

"I think the bulk of her work is a decent amount of bluster and flowery titles," Georgie added.

He finished reading the message and twisted a lock of her hair around his finger. "That's good, right? One less thing to worry about?"

"I agree," she said with a wide grin. "And we could host a Western-themed literacy charity event in our sleep!"

"Western, huh?" he said as the rancher's daughter scenario flashed through his mind.

Georgie's expression grew wicked. "Speaking of Western, I want you to close your eyes."

"Why?" he asked, meeting her naughty grin with one of his own.

She glanced at her phone. "Because we have a little time before we have to meet everyone at the bookstore, and I remembered something that I think you might like."

"You've got a giant mechanical bull hidden in the closet?" he teased.

She stood up and glanced over her shoulder. "Not a bull. Now, close your eyes," she directed.

"Are you going all naughty librarian?" he continued, hearing her footsteps disappear toward the back of the bungalow.

He'd never tire of his dirty little bookseller.

Georgie in those grandma glasses, a messy bun, and nothing else was about as hot as it gets.

He closed his eyes and listened as a clunk caught his attention. It had to be either Georgie doing God knows what or Mr. Tuesday playing with one of his slobbery tennis balls.

"Are you ready?" Georgie purred.

"That was fast!" he answered, his eyes still closed.

"When you're a beauty pageant veteran, you know how to rock a quick outfit change."

"No more onesie," he said, riling her up.

"It's a chic, fashion-forward romper, if you've forgotten. But you're right. The romper is off," she answered with a hint of playful irritation.

"I hope you kept on the sexy bra you wore for Dr. Beaver and Nurse Joyce."

Hey, he had no issues with his wife wearing sexy lingerie period—even if it were to see her gynecologist.

"I'm still wearing the bra," she answered, moving closer as a small gust of air whooshed over his face.

"Did you pack a palm leaf from Fiji in your bag so you could fan me and feed me grapes like a Greek god?" he asked, getting into the idea of role-play.

Bad cop/good cop, rock star and groupie, sexy spies, and of course, his rancher's daughter fantasy shot to the top of the list, thanks to their hot make-out session.

Honestly, the make-believe possibilities were endless.

"No," she answered as another puff of air kissed his cheeks. "This is more in line with the rancher's daughter."

Hell to the yes!

He sucked in a tight breath as his blood supply headed south.

"You can look now," Georgie said on a sultry rasp.

Slowly, he opened his eyes. "Winner, winner, cowboy dinner!" he exclaimed, unable to stop himself.

Standing in front of him and twirling a baton in a jean skirt barely covering her ass, Georgie wore a checkered shirt tied in the front like a modern-day Daisy Duke in red— that's right—red cowgirl boots.

A naughty rancher's daughter!

His gaze raked over her body. "How did I not know you had those boots?"

"This was my costume for the Miss Rootin' Tootin' Pageant in Wyoming. My mom wanted to go with a Western theme."

Under normal circumstances, had his wife uttered the words *rootin'* and *tootin'*, he would have laughed his ass off. But in that outfit, looking like a cowboy's super-fantasy, all he could do was drink her in.

"Again," he said, coming to his feet and gripping the baton mid-twirl. "Where have you been hiding this?"

"I have a box of pageant outfits. I haven't opened it in years, but I remembered this outfit when we got home. Last time I wore it, I hopped off the pageant stage in the middle of my baton routine and ran all the way to a donut shop. Nobody in Wyoming blinked an eye at a girl dressed like this running down the street. It was a little looser and a little longer back then. I didn't look like—"

"A ranch hand's wet dream," he answered.

"Something like that," she replied, drawing her index finger between her ample cleavage.

"Who needs a mechanical bull when you've got the rancher's daughter version of Georgiana Jensen-Marks in boots and a jean skirt," he said and dropped the baton to the floor.

"How about Georgiana Jensen-Marks in boots, a jean skirt, and no panties?"

Jesus, how he loved this woman!

"You look like you've had a hard, hard day rounding up the cattle," she said, falling into character.

Two could play at this.

"It's a lot of work being a cowboy, but I think I could

handle one more ride," he answered, throwing in some twang.

She pressed her hand to his chest, walked him back to the couch, then guided him to sit.

"You're not riding anything, cowboy. That's my job," she answered, then straddled him and went to work, unbuttoning his fly.

All this sexy cowboy dirty talk had him ready to explode. Georgie gripped his hard length as he palmed her ass then slid his other hand between her thighs, finding her sweet center hot and wet.

"I hope you don't think I do this with all the ranch hands," she said, working his cock in slow, delicious strokes.

He matched her pace as he caressed her most sensitive place. She might know how to drive him wild with that sexy outfit and cowgirl dirty talk, but this ranch hand had some tricks up his sleeve.

He dialed up his pace, stroking her tight bundle of nerves with his thumb while teasing her slick entrance with two fingers. "I know you like it like this. When you're in the barn, and you think no one can see you, I like to watch you touch yourself."

He could totally get into the role of the randy cowboy peeping Tom.

"Do you like watching me?" she said, then closed her eyes, losing herself to his touch.

"I'd rather be inside of you," he growled. He was damn close, but he wasn't about to go over the edge without Miss Rootin' Tootin'.

She released his hard length, and he lined up his cock, brushing the glistening head of his shaft across her delicate folds. Georgie ran her tongue across her top lip before she arched into him and welcomed his penetration with a breathy moan.

"Georgiana, you're so wet for me, you dirty cowgirl," he said against her lips, then captured her mouth in a breathtaking kiss.

As their bodies moved together, their tongues met, licking and caressing in a sensual dance. After today's life-changing revelations, they needed a release, a respite, a moment to lose themselves in one another.

And while they'd done it on just about every surface of the bungalow, here on the couch with Georgie's hands pressed to his chest as she rode his cock would always bring him back to their first time. It seemed like eons, not months ago, that they'd given in to their mutual disdain and opted for a little sexual stress relief.

He'd never been more drawn, more furious, more frustrated, or more attracted to another person until his life collided with hers.

He rolled his hips and set a heated pace as Georgie's faint gasps of pleasure bloomed into moans of ecstasy. The friction between them grew into a fiery inferno as he kissed her neck and gripped her ass, ready to take them over the edge.

"Yes," she panted and raked her nails across his shoulders.

He had the rancher's daughter right where he wanted her.

Without missing a beat, he worked her body, changing the angle of penetration. And then, they were there, hovering in that space between this world and the next, teetering on the edge of complete carnal gratification. Georgie cried out as they met their frenzied release, rocking and clinging to one another, drawing out each rippling wave of their climax.

"It looks like the rancher's daughter likes it quick and dirty," he said, then pressed a kiss to the corner of her mouth.

"Oh, she likes it other ways, too."

"This cowboy could use some details," he replied, lowering his voice as the thought of round two sent a fresh jolt of lust straight to his cock.

Georgie sighed, coming back from wanton bliss. "The rancher's daughter likes it...dog!" she finished, her warm body going stiff.

"You want it doggy style, cowgirl?" he asked, but something was off.

She gazed past his shoulder. "No, not doggy style. It's our dog."

"What about him?" he asked as a cool rush of air sent goose bumps prickling up his arms.

Georgie gasped. "He ran out the door with our Faby!"

Chapter Seven
Georgie

Georgie blinked.

Had she just watched Mr. Tuesday swipe the half-diapered doll and run out the front door?

And had she and Jordan had dirty-girl cowboy sex in front of Faby, their fake baby?

"Georgie, we need to go after him," Jordan cried, jolting her from her stupefied state.

"Hold on! I need to do a quick clean-up," she said, maneuvering her body off her husband's cock, then grabbed a few tissues from the box on the end table. It was one thing to chase after a runaway dog dressed like a slutty farmhand. It was an entirely different bale of hay doing it with you-know-what running down your thighs.

Jordan adjusted his clothing, then plucked his jacket and her cardigan from the wall hooks.

"Here, babe! We need to hurry!" he said, tossing her the garment.

They started for the door when she spotted the diaper bag.

"Do you think we should bring Faby's stuff?" she asked.

Jordan ran his hands through his hair. "I don't know. Do you think there's something in there that Faby will need?"

"I'm not sure what to bring on a mission to save a fake baby from a real dog," she replied, worry starting to get the best of her.

Her husband paced the length of the living room. "I bet Mr. Tuesday thinks Faby is another chew toy," he said, then froze.

Wide-eyed, his jaw dropped, and she knew they both just happened upon the same chilling revelation.

They could not show up to the Battle of the Births with a mauled fake baby—or worse than that—no fake baby at all!

What kind of parents lost their fake baby hours after they'd been entrusted with its care?

"We have to save Faby!" she exclaimed.

"We have to!" he repeated, slinging the diaper bag's strap across his body before taking her hand as they made a mad dash out the front door.

After barely a block, Jordan was ahead with her lagging behind like a tortoise tethered to a cheetah.

Sweet baby chaser! Her husband could run!

She released his hand as they rounded the corner, headed toward the Tennyson neighborhood's business district.

She gasped for breath and pointed down the street. "Keep running, Jordan! You're faster! There's a good chance Mr. Tuesday is headed for the park. You can corner him there."

Jordan shook his head. "I am not leaving you behind. We'll run at your pace. It's safe for you to continue to exercise at the same level you're used to."

She stared up at the sky. Streaked in heavenly shades of

orange and blue, the dusk Denver nightscape was a sight to see. But soon, this masterpiece of majestic colors would fade into black. Then, not only would they still be searching for a dog and a doll, they'd be doing it in the dark of night.

She shook her head. "No, you have to go! We'll be losing the light soon, and God knows where he'll go if we can't find him and Faby soon. You're stronger and faster. You need to get to Mr. Tuesday and rescue our fake baby."

Jordan ran his hands through his hair again, leaving his perfect dark waves curling out this way and that like a toddler with bedhead.

He took her hand, his green eyes brimming with apprehension. "Georgie, please don't make me choose between my pregnant wife and my fake baby!"

This was complete insanity.

"Okay, we'll jog together. I'll try to pick up the pace a bit. Keep an eye out for Mr. Tuesday and Faby!"

They continued, weaving their way past couples and families strolling down the sidewalk when a chorus of shrieks and squeals caught their attention.

"Is that dog eating a baby?" trilled a distraught woman with a scrap of white material in her hand.

Oh no! She had Faby's diaper!

"There he is!" Jordan exclaimed as a blur of black and white fur shot down the street, leaving a slew of horrified people in his wake.

They took off running, and Jordan gestured to the woman.

"Grab it, babe!" he said as the chase shifted into high gear.

Passing the shocked Tennyson Street patrons, she snagged the diaper out of the woman's pinched grip. "Thank you! And don't worry. It's not a real baby!" she called over her shoulder to the slack-jawed lady as they closed in on their targets.

The diaper bag jostled up and down, bumping Jordan's elbow, then her arm, then Jordan's elbow, then her arm again in a bizarre pre-parental masochistic motion. Could they stop and reposition the bag? Sure, if they wanted to spend the rest of the night searching for a dog and a doll. But they were losing daylight by the second, and there was no time to hesitate. Jordan glanced over, and she met his gaze, then nodded.

Like Zen-master mind readers, without a word spoken between them, the choice had been made.

They'd endure the punishing blows from the devil of a diaper bag to capture their dog and save their fake baby.

"This baby stuff weighs a ton, and that's saying something. I spend my days in a CrossFit gym flipping tractor tires, and that's nothing compared to this," Jordan said through tight breaths as the wrecking ball of a diaper bag pinballed between them.

"We can't stop! We have to endure the pain," she answered, suddenly craving a tall glass of pineapple juice and a slice of pineapple cheesecake.

Damn these pregnancy cravings, popping up at the worst possible moment!

"It looks like he's headed to your bookshop," Jordan bit out as the diaper bag continued its bumpy assault.

The dog showed no signs of slowing when the door to Jensen's Books opened, and a surprised customer exiting the establishment shrieked as she held the door for the runaway fake baby-snatcher.

"It's not a real baby!" Georgie cried as they crossed the street and barreled inside the shop to find over a dozen pairs of eyes bouncing between them and Mr. Tuesday.

Her longtime family friends Gene and Marjory Gilbert, along with Irene and her husband, Will, sat on barstools that wrapped around the café portion of the shop. Jordan's father, Denny, and Maureen, their accountant and also Denny's girlfriend, had settled themselves nearby in a cozy seating area along with Maureen's eleven-year-old twins Mya and Mia. Their high school volunteers, Simon and Talya, turned teenagers in love, cuddled across from them in an oversized chair. Even the blue-haired brigade, the octogenarians who enjoyed frequenting her store under the guise of enjoying a place to do their needlework when all they wanted was to get a good look at Jordan running past the shop shirtless—and honestly, who could blame them—were in attendance, their knitting projects halted by the canine kerfuffle.

Everyone was there—all assembled to get together to hear about their honeymoon.

Becca, her sassy friend who managed the bookstore, came out from behind the counter and scratched between the dog's ears.

"What's Mr. Tuesday doing with a naked baby doll?"

"Yeah, that's a freaky chew toy, son," Denny offered, sharing a look with Maureen.

Jordan leaned forward and pressed his hands to his thighs, working to catch his breath.

"It's not a chew toy. It's Faby. Our fake baby. Georgie and I have to keep it in one piece so we can prove that we'll be able to take care of our baby when he or she arrives in June," the man bit out between deep, punctuated breaths.

Running while carrying a diaper bag was clearly not for the faint of heart.

Gene Gilbert reached behind the counter and grabbed

a bottle of water. "Coming at you, Jordan," the man said, tossing the bottle across the shop.

At the sight of a thrown object, Mr. Tuesday dropped the doll and followed the bottle's trajectory. But he wasn't quick enough. Like a hydration-deprived gladiator, her husband swiped the bottle out of the air, ripped off the cap, and downed the liquid as Mr. Tuesday pranced around him in circles.

Quickly, she rescued Faby from the hardwood floor, cradled the doll in her arms, and checked for punctures before counting to make sure the doll's plastic fingers and toes were intact.

"Faby's okay—just a little slobbery," she said as Jordan came to her side.

Her husband cradled Faby's head in his massive hand, doing his own scan. "Thank God! We should get Faby's diaper back on and see if there are any clothes in the diaper bag."

Relief washed over her. Despite the wild baby doll goose chase, Faby was no worse for wear. Even better? Mr. Tuesday was safely corralled in the bookshop, and at least for the moment, they weren't the worst fake parents on the planet.

She set Faby on a table and diapered the doll.

"Look! Clothes and wipey-things," Jordan exclaimed, pulling the items from the diaper bag. He removed a moist tissue, then cleaned the slobber marks off Faby's arm as she took the clothes and proceeded to dress the doll in a full-body onesie that zippered up the front.

With Faby safe, cleaned up, and dressed, she handed the doll to Jordan, then crouched down to be eye to eye with Mr. Tuesday.

"There will be no chewing the fake baby, mister. I'm

serious! No table scraps for a week if we catch you pulling another stunt like that."

Mr. Tuesday released a sad doggy sigh, and her heart nearly broke. But they had to lay down the law. It was for his own good.

"Your mom is right, big guy. We have to be careful with Faby," Jordan continued.

Their pup went all puppy-dog eyes, and she pressed a kiss to the top of her dog's head.

"We still love you and always will," she whispered into the dog's soft fur.

"We're all fine, and that's what matters," Jordan added as the dog's ears perked up, and his sad bad-dog expression disappeared into a throaty yawn.

And suddenly, she felt like a nap herself—and maybe some pineapple upside-down cake.

What a day!

Crisis averted. Faby rescued. And thanks to one heck of a mad dash, Mr. Tuesday would probably conk out for the rest of the night.

They'd triumphed over their first parenting trial—sort of. But a win was a win.

She reached for Faby, and Jordan gently handed her the doll. Dressed in a one-piece outfit with little ducks peppering the fabric, she stared at the small mannequin's mischievous painted eyes and the quirk of its cooed lips. If dolls had actual thoughts, she was sure this one quite enjoyed that treacherous romp.

"Um…Georgie, Jordan? Everything all right?" Becca asked.

Georgie looked up to find the entire group staring at them. She and Jordan stood as Mr. Tuesday made his way to his dog bed situated behind the counter. And then she realized what these people had observed: two grown adults fawning over a doll.

"We're fine! Completely fine," she answered, resurrecting her beauty queen grin.

"Did you come from a square dance?" Irene asked, narrowing her gaze.

Georgie glanced down at her outfit, aka cowgirl-slutty couture.

She tried to pull the cardigan down past her scrap of a jean skirt, but you could only stretch a cardigan so far.

"I'm wearing this because..." she began.

"Because Georgie and I have been asked to host a children's literacy event with a Western theme in May," Jordan finished, like a white knight, swooping in to save a damsel, tangled up in a clothing catastrophe.

"And I was trying on different outfits," she added, giving up on covering her legs and pulled the cardigan around her body to hide her visible midriff and the black bra, peeking out, highlighting her cleavage.

Gene frowned. "I'm no expert on women's clothing, but I don't think that's an outfit you want to go with for a children's event."

"Yes, dear, perhaps, something a little less..." Marjory trailed off.

"Slutty!" piped one of the blue-haired brigade, gazes back on their knitting.

Those Michael Bolton-loving ladies were feisty old broads!

"I couldn't agree more. Remind me to mark this choice as a no," she said to Jordan, feeling her beauty queen grin veering off into deranged clown territory.

Her husband leaned in and lowered his voice. "You'll keep the boots, right?"

My God! This man!

"Yes, I'll keep it all. But this is strictly an indoor outfit for adult dress-up only," she whispered back.

"Gotcha," he replied with that handsome ranch hand grin that almost had her melting into a pool of enamored pineapple until another voice caught her attention.

"Hey, Georgie?" Becca chimed.

"Yeah, what is it?" she answered, in the headspace somewhere between riding her cowboy and wolfing down more pineapple cheesecake.

Becca crossed her arms and cocked her head to the side. "Are you pregnant?"

Oh no! Lengthening her grin another painful millimeter, she remembered what Jordan had said after they'd burst into the bookshop.

"How do you mean?" she asked, instantly knowing this was not the correct response.

Becca glanced at the wall of spectators, then tapped her chin theatrically. "Well, I don't think there are many variations of being pregnant. I've never been pregnant, but I'm pretty sure that when someone asks if you're pregnant, it's a yes or no answer."

"I can back you up, Becca. It's a one hundred percent yes or no situation," Maureen said as her twins giggled on the couch.

Irene rubbed her belly. "Yep, there's no gray area on this one."

"Not to mention, Jordan blurted out that you were expecting a baby in June," Simon added.

"I said that?" her husband asked with a bewildered expression.

Their family and friends nodded.

Georgie glanced at Faby, and then to Jordan, who was

giving her *oh-shit* eyes. No, not oh-shit-eyes—oh-*shoot*-eyes. There was the hint of a difference.

Expletive version or not, he was right.

What were they supposed to say? Again, they'd chosen to get it on before deciding what—or even if—they wanted to tell everyone.

She chewed her lip. From this moment on, they'd talk first and get their ducks in a row before starting the naughty rodeo antics.

"Am I going to be a grandfather?" Denny asked, his eyes shining with tears.

Jordan wrapped his arm around her shoulder. She glanced up and found him smiling the sweetest smile.

The smile of a proud expectant father, and her beauty queen facade melted away.

"Yes, you are. Jordan and I are expecting a baby," she answered.

The big man stood and ushered her to the couch.

"Sit, Georgie! Let's get you off your feet. You can take my seat. And Jordan, let's get you settled next to your wife," the man said, wiping a tear from his cheek.

"When did you find out?" Maureen asked.

"This morning," Jordan answered.

Irene and Will sat down on a loveseat across from them, and while their friends appeared happy, worry flashed in Irene's eyes.

"How far along are you?" Maureen pressed.

"Eight weeks," she answered with a nervous cringe.

"That would mean..." Maureen began, but the twins cut her off.

"That Georgie was pregnant when she got married!" the girls exclaimed.

"How do you know that?" Jordan asked, raising an eyebrow.

The twins shared a look.

"Math!" the girls giggled in unison.

"How about Talya and I take Mia and Mya to get some ice cream down the block," Simon offered.

"It's on me," Maureen said, rapidly plucking a few bills from her purse and handing them to the teen.

"Who's ready for a triple scoop?" Talya asked as the twins bounced from their seats and followed the teens out the door as the adults crowded in.

"This is incredible news! How are you feeling?" Maureen asked.

Georgie glanced around the group. This was not how she'd envisioned telling their friends and family—and there was still the issue of telling her mother—but there was no turning back now.

"I'm doing pretty well. I want to eat pineapple all the time, and I threw up on a guy's shoes this morning," she answered.

"That sounds about right," Irene said with a bemused twist to her lips.

"For me, it was cottage cheese with olives and potato chips mixed in," Maureen offered with a grimace. "I can't even look at cottage cheese now."

Denny patted Jordan's leg. "When your mother was pregnant with you, all she wanted was scrambled eggs. She ate them morning, noon, and night."

"Was this planned?" Marjory asked.

Georgie sighed. "No, not at all. I could hardly believe it was true until we saw the baby on the ultrasound."

Jordan pulled the grainy photo from his pocket and passed it to his dad and Maureen.

"Your mother must be over the moon. Will she and Howard be joining us tonight?" Maureen asked, handing the photo to the Gilberts.

Georgie swallowed past the lump in her throat. "My mom's not in Denver. She's in India with Howard at a spiritual retreat."

"Are they coming home soon?" Gene Gilbert asked, handing the photo to Irene and Will.

"Not yet. We wanted to wait to tell them," she said, going for pregnancy-casual but sounding more pregnancy-asshat.

"Oh," Maureen replied with a crease to her brow.

Oh, was right. Was she the worst daughter in the world? Possibly? Absolutely?

No, she couldn't be *the worst.*

After they had a handle on the pregnancy thing, they would tell her mother.

"We're still trying to wrap our heads around it. Georgie's not that far along, and we still have so much to learn. Fortunately, we're involved in a project to help us get there," Jordan answered, white knighting it again and blessedly, turning the talk away from her mother.

"A project?" Denny repeated.

"With CityBeat. They're launching a site for pregnancy and child development blogs called CityBeat Rattle," Jordan replied.

Gene narrowed his gaze. "What's your part in all that?"

Georgie recycled her beauty queen grin. "We're competing in the Battle of the Births."

"The what?" the entire group exclaimed, shock gracing their faces.

Imagine if they'd kept it the Battle of the Babies!

Jordan raised his hands defensively. "It's not as brutal as it sounds. Hector and Bobby assured us that it's a friendly competition and more of a learning experience. They're going to gather footage now before launching the site in July."

Georgie turned to her pregnant friend and her husband. "That's why we're so grateful to have you both. You guys are a trimester ahead of us and can help us out along the way."

"And let me tell you, we need all the help we can get. That's why we've got this fake baby. It's all part of the Battle of the Births," Jordan added, gesturing to the doll.

"And I thought you two were a bunch of superfreaks playing with a doll," Becca teased.

Georgie chuckled and shifted Faby in her arms, but the reality of their situation was starting to sink in. By this time next year, she and Irene would each have a little one of their own. And until then, they'd be gestating partners in crime, supporting each other through the thick and thin of their pregnancies.

She beamed at her friend, but the wattage on her grin dimmed as she watched Irene and Becca share a pensive glance.

It was probably nothing—a weird sister thing. But her trifecta shook their heads. No, something was up. Lizzy, Jane, and Hermione were never wrong.

Georgie turned up the wattage on her smile and tried to discount her literary trio. "It'll be great, Irene. We can exercise together and eat all sorts of weird foods. I'm so happy not to be in this pregnancy boat alone."

Now, Irene shared a look with her husband—the same serious look she'd exchanged with her sister.

Irene stroked her belly. "We can do all that. It'll just have to be over the phone or video chat."

Georgie frowned. "Why would we need video chat? We live in the same neighborhood, and you run the bistro a few blocks away? Your little sister manages my bookshop. We hardly ever go a day without seeing each other."

Irene's gaze grew misty. "Will and I are moving to Iceland."

Georgie's mouth fell open. "Iceland? Like the country?"

Irene gave a teary chuckle. "Yes, that Iceland."

"Why?" she threw back, wide-eyed as her literary trio matched her expression.

Even her imaginary trifecta was thrown by that info drop.

A warm grin stretched across Irene's face. "A few months back, my old graduate advisor reached out to me. Funding had run out on a renewable energy research project we were working on back when I was in school, going for my masters in bioenergy. After things dried up with the research, I started taking more shifts at the bistro. One thing led to another, and years passed. I never thought I'd get the chance to finish my degree. But that's all changed. Now, my advisor's connected with a university in Iceland and has funding for the next five years. I didn't want to say anything until I knew it was going to happen. I got the call last week. The project is good to go."

"You'll be in Iceland for five years," Georgie said on a stunned exhale.

Will took his wife's hand. "I knew this was huge for Irene, so I asked my boss if I could work remotely, and he agreed."

"What about your baby? You're due in March," Georgie pressed.

This was ridiculous, right? Who picked up and moved to Iceland mid-pregnancy?

Irene gave her belly another loving pat. "People have babies in Iceland, Georgie."

"I'm..." she began, then paused, taking in her friend's joyful expression.

Of course, she wanted Irene to follow her dreams and earn her degree.

Would she miss her terribly?

Yes.

Could they make it work with calls and video chats?

They'd have to.

Georgie pushed aside her hopes of double pregnancy bliss with her BFF and reached across the table and squeezed Irene's hand.

"I'm so happy for you. This is a huge opportunity."

"And Will and I have you to thank," Irene added.

Georgie cocked her head to the side. "You do?"

Irene gazed lovingly at her husband. "If it weren't for your Own the Eights blog, I wouldn't have met my husband. And, without Will's encouragement, I don't know if I would have taken the leap and agreed to move across the Atlantic."

"We owe you big. We do," Will answered, then pressed a kiss to his wife's temple.

"That's great news! We're so happy for you both," Jordan said, shaking Will's hand, then leaning over to kiss Irene's cheek.

Everyone turned their attention to the Iceland-bound couple, but Georgie felt a pregnancy haze coming on as the group's conversation faded into the background.

She was happy for Irene, but now she was three for three.

First, sweet nurse Gina. Then, her gynecologist, Dr. Rosenstein. And now, Irene.

One, two, three.

Uno, dos, and gone without a *tres!*

Her blog—her words—had helped these women find love. They'd also taken them thousands of miles away when she needed them the most.

"What's going on?" came a man's voice from behind.

It was most likely a bookshop patron chatting with a companion, but as she watched the landscape of her life shift yet again, she blew out a tight breath.

"Irene is moving to Iceland, my gynecologist is kicking it in Australia, and I'm pregnant," she replied, answering the question aloud to herself, even though it wasn't meant for her.

"You're pregnant?" came the same voice. A voice she could not believe she hadn't recognized.

She whipped around to find Brice Casey—the man who seemed to pop up in every phase of her life—standing behind her, donning his Casey Pest Control T-shirt.

She pinched herself, testing to see if this was a pregnancy mirage. But he was still there, smiling that goofy grin with his perfect hair. Granted, she'd softened on Brice—even liked the guy. He did get them to their wedding on time, thanks to his penchant for showing up at key moments in her life. He'd even stayed for the nuptials, and they did the Chicken Dance together. More than that, she couldn't forget that her disastrous date with him years ago had been the catalyst for starting the Own the Eights blog. Without this well-meaning, half-witted asshat, who knows where she'd be!

"What are you doing here, Brice?" she asked.

He held up a sheet of paper. "Making sure you don't have any creepy crawlies in the bookstore."

Georgie froze. "Are there spiders in my shop?"

The thought of those eight-legged mini-monsters made her want to head for the spider-less hills.

"No, but Becca mentioned you guys never had a pest control check the other night when we were..."

"Discussing bookshop maintenance. Let me look over the invoice," her friend interjected, rushing to Brice's side and plucking the sheet of paper from his grasp.

Was this another possible pregnancy hallucination?

"Are you and Brice..." she trailed off, staring at her friend.

Becca scoffed and waved her off. "As the manager, I've got a little bookstore business to deal with," she answered, then took the pest control prince by the arm and led him toward the office.

That was certainly odd.

She was about to mention her hunch about Becca and Brice to Jordan when his phone pinged, and like one of Pavlov's dogs, instantly, she knew what was coming.

"Is that a CityBeat alert?" she asked.

In the flurry to get out the door, she'd left her cell at home, but she'd bet two slices of pineapple cheesecake that her phone just pinged the alert as well.

It was like the Battle of the Blogs. She could feel it in her bones—another challenge, calling their name.

"Yeah," he answered, checking his phone.

"What does it say?"

Jordan pocketed his cell. "They sent us the date for the first challenge."

"And Faby?" she asked.

"Faby's coming with us."

She glanced at the doll in her arms, staring up at her with that playful glint.

Game on.

Ready or not, here they go again.

Chapter Eight
Jordan

"Are you doing all right in there, messy bun girl?" Jordan gave a soft knock from the other side of the door. This had become a common arrangement—him, on one side, while Georgie lost her breakfast, lunch, dinner, or even a snack in the restroom on the other side.

Whatever asshat named morning sickness, *morning sickness*, didn't seem to take into account that nausea could hit at any time of the day.

"I was able to buy some pineapple lollipops and a bottle of pineapple juice," he said, glancing into the paper bag.

"What about pineapple squares? Do we still have any left in the car?" his wife asked from the other side of the restroom door.

They'd been driving when Georgie turned the telltale shade of green. Fortunately, he was able to pull over at a coffee shop and rush her inside before she lost *her* insides.

"I think we've got a few left in the car." He glanced over his shoulder. "And there are a couple of nice people out in the hall, waiting for the restroom." He smiled at the patrons, then lowered his voice. "My wife's almost twelve weeks pregnant. The doctor says her morning sickness should ease up soon."

"And that?" one of the women asked, pointing to the lifelike Faby, nestled into the crook of his arm.

"This is our fake baby," he answered without missing a beat.

Each lady gave him a placating smile, then they turned and headed back into the coffee shop.

"Never mind. No rush, messy bun girl," he called to Georgie.

If he'd learned one thing over the last month, it was how to clear out a restaurant or coffee shop. He wasn't sure if it was his vomiting wife or the fact that he usually had a doll with him while he stood near the entrance to the ladies' room.

Either way, it gave them a little privacy, and no one had called the cops on them yet.

Even with an infant simulation doll in tow and the bouts of anytime-of-day sickness, which is what it should be called, they'd fallen into a rhythm. Georgie still craved pineapple like a citrus maniac, but they'd gotten back into the groove of writing for their More Than Just a Number blog and running their businesses. Granted, Faby was always close by. But their fake baby didn't make a sound or wet its diaper. So, despite having to keep an eye on Mr. Tuesday to head off another runaway Faby incident, their fake infant had blended into their lives like an innocuous, incredibly lifelike Elf on a Shelf. Except, it was Faby, Georgie and Jordan's fake baby, which had a certain ring to it he'd liked.

Or he was losing it. Either way, they'd come to like the hunk of plastic and silicon, and life moved on.

Georgie and Irene had weekly video chats to talk about all things human gestation. And, on the growing a person front, their alien peanut was chugging right along. Truth be told, the science geek in him was fascinated with Georgie's changing body.

Always an early riser, he'd gather his sleeping wife into his arms and run his hands down her abdomen. Dressed in her signature cardigan and leggings, one wouldn't know she was carrying precious cargo. But in those moments when her naked body was warm and snuggled into his, he'd caress the slight hint of a bump and marvel at the miracle of the human body.

And then there was the sex.

When Georgie wasn't losing her lunch, she was positively ravenous—and not only for pineapple cheesecake—but for all kinds of naughtiness.

A little pregnancy tidbit he'd never heard about.

Sure, he could rattle off facts about a pregnant woman's loosening ligaments, but he'd never read about a revved up libido.

Perhaps that was just his Georgie.

Not that he was complaining.

He didn't need a reason to get down and dirty with his beautiful wife—especially when she had a box full of costumes.

Cheerleader. Mermaid. Even a Nutcracker number from some holiday pageant.

But the rancher's daughter remained in the top spot. All she had to do was slide on those boots to get him rock-hard, and instantly, he was ready for a roll in the hay, or bed, or floor, or kitchen table, or sofa. You name it, they could figure out a way to procreate on it.

He leaned against the wall, thinking back to last night's

reverse cowgirl naughtiness when the sound of running water coming from the restroom pulled him from his walk down sexytimes cowboy lane.

"I'd like to splash a little water on my face, and then I'll be out," she called to him.

"Faby and I'll be waiting right here," he answered as his belly did a flip-flop.

Today was a big day.

The big day.

Their first Battle of the Births challenge.

It was no wonder Georgie got sick. He was jittery as hell. It was a wonder he hadn't lost his lunch, too.

He'd tried telling himself that this contest was ceremonial at most and not a real competition like the Battle of the Blogs or the wilderness boot camp torment they'd endured before their wedding. No, this would be similar to a class or a seminar. A learning experience they desperately needed because, thanks to their busy schedules, all the baby knowledge they'd garnered over the last month had come from a toy baby.

No burping or feedings. Nope, just a onesie change, here and there, whenever the mood struck.

Honestly, they had the fake baby care down to an art, but he had a suspicion that real babies took a heck of a lot more work.

"I'm coming out," Georgie said, opening the door.

He cupped her face in his hand and stroked her cheek with his thumb. "It looks like you've got some color back."

She sighed and closed her eyes. "Yeah, I feel much better, but remind me to go easy on those pineapple squares."

He nodded, but it was no use. She was like a mama bear with those squares, and he was a smart enough husband not to get between his wife and whatever pineapple delight she'd happened upon that week.

"And how is Faby?" she asked.

"Just chilling and rocking at being the best fake baby in Denver," he said, switching the doll to his other arm as he followed his wife out of the shop and back to the car.

Georgie settled herself into the passenger seat, and he passed her the doll. She gently set Faby between her feet on the car's floorboards. It wasn't that they didn't want Faby up with them, but it distressed other drivers to see an infant, even a fake infant, riding shotgun. So, they'd switched to the *what-you-can't-see-won't-hurt-you* option.

And, then again, Faby was a fake baby.

Still, who needs the hassle of getting pulled over and explaining why two seemingly ordinary adults are toting around a doll. Yep, that happened. Twice.

He started the car and maneuvered the BMW into traffic as they headed toward an industrial section of the city.

"I feel like we've been here before," Georgie said, staring at warehouse after warehouse.

He gasped, hardly able to believe his eyes. "You're right! We have."

A giant nondescript building loomed in front of them with a weathered porcelain doll head painted on the crumbling exterior.

"We're in the same location as the Denver wedding underground! We're not headed to the same building, are we? They can't be one and the same!" Georgie whisper-shouted.

He glanced at the GPS. "No, the address Lenny and Stu sent for the first Battle of the Births challenge is for the warehouse across the street."

"What are the chances? That's crazy," she said, shaking her head.

It was about to get crazier.

"Georgie, there's a limo pulling up to the Denver wedding underground!" he whisper-shouted back.

He had no idea why they were whisper-shouting, but it seemed like the right thing to do.

He turned into the parking lot for the Battle of the Births location, which gave them a perfect perch to watch as a doe-eyed couple emerged from the car along with Cornelia Lieblingsschatz, the Denver Wedding Frau and the city's premier wedding planner.

"That was us not so long ago," Georgie recalled as Cornelia glanced at their car.

Clad in her signature black with her silvery asymmetrical bob, the formidable woman stilled, then drew her Jackie-O sunglasses down, and gave them a tiny twist of a grin.

"I'm sure glad she likes us. She is one scary lady," he said, watching the intimidating wedding planner usher the bewildered couple into the building.

"She sure is, but we owe her and Hans," Georgie answered as another couple entered the warehouse.

He reached across the console, took his wife's hand into his, then gazed down at her wedding and engagement rings. They shared matching titanium wedding bands, and his chest tightened remembering when Hans shared the story of how, in a marriage, you lived within the confines of the ring. Sometimes, on opposite sides when you disagree, but always able to reunite in the center. He ran his thumb across her knuckles, grateful that Cornelia and her husband had given them the gift of knowing they were meant to be together, despite their rocky ride to the altar.

"I wonder how the dildo guy is doing?" Georgie said with a teasing glint in her eyes.

"Why don't you pop over and ask," he threw back.

Georgie shook her head. "Oh no! When Cornelia is in Denver Wedding Frau mode, nobody is safe."

He pressed a kiss to her palm as a pair of cars turned into the parking lot. There were already at least a half dozen vehicles parked haphazardly in the large lot. But, with all the industrial buildings, it was hard to tell if every car was here for the Battle of the Births. However, when couples emerged from the vehicles, each carrying a fake baby and a diaper bag, then entered the building, they knew this was the right place.

"It looks like it's now or never," Georgie said with the hint of trepidation as she lifted Faby onto her lap.

His wife was right. It was go-time. He swallowed hard, his mouth going dry. But he needed to keep this light and upbeat.

He tucked a lock of hair behind her ear. "We're going to crush this challenge!"

Georgie held his gaze. "Do you think we're ready?"

He nodded, forcing his features to remain neutral. "I bet it'll be like school or Baby 101. I don't think we have anything to worry about. Sit tight," he said, even though he wasn't sure what baby secrets the warehouse held.

He exited the SUV, grabbed the baby bag from the back, then helped his wife out of the car.

"No matter what's in there, we're good," he said, going for the strategy of repeating himself.

Georgie glanced down at Faby.

"Hey, we conquered shit shovels and wilderness boot camp. We can do this," he added, reaching into his fitness motivation trainer toolbox.

Georgie winced. "I don't know if *conquered* is the right word."

"Okay, endured. We endured shit shovels and wilderness boot camp," he said, amending his statement.

As two decidedly non-outdoorsy types, they'd put up with a hell of a lot more wilderness bullshit than most people experience in a lifetime.

And here's the thing. They'd only been together for six months. But it was six months jam-packed with just about every emotion on the spectrum. In love years, if those existed like dog years, which they should, they'd be at least a decade in—maybe two—especially after what happened with that alpaca in the middle of freaking nowhere Colorado.

Georgie leaned into him as they walked up to the entrance. "You might also be pushing it with *endured*, but it'll have to do."

Good. She was getting her sense of humor back, and the nervous pageant expression was nowhere to be seen.

"Are you ready?" he asked, reaching for the doorknob.

"I think so. It's..." She released an audible breath as the hint of the anxious beauty queen expression stretched across her face. "I'm worried about my mom."

He understood this. Georgie's mom was great. He loved Lorraine. But she was also a lot.

A hell of a lot.

The errant lock of hair he'd tucked behind her ear had broken free, and he smoothed her chestnut wisps into place. "You know you can tell her at any time, babe."

"I know. I'm just not ready."

He tilted her chin and held her gaze. "That's okay. We only told everyone at the bookshop because I screwed up and blurted it out."

Georgie stared at the door. "Are we sure about this? The whole Battle of the Births?"

"How about I make a deal with you? If a guy greets us at the door with a tub full of rubber cocks, we head for the hills and never look back," he offered, straight-faced.

Georgie smiled her real smile, the one she gave him each time he stepped foot in her bookshop.

She pushed up onto her tiptoes and kissed his cheek. "Deal. Rubber cocks at a baby challenge will be a hard no in our playbook."

"Look at us! We've got standards and everything," he said, feeling pretty damn good. Then, he opened the door and found...

Nothing.

Well, not nothing.

"Isn't this place great?"

They turned to find Barry, their trusty CityBeat producer.

"What's going on here?" Georgie asked.

The enormous space stretched out before them with individual rooms divided by clear plexiglass. Couples stood in each sectioned off area, waving their hands and moving around while wearing a head covering.

"Those are top of the line virtual reality headsets. This place is a tech junkies dream," Barry explained, pointing to several couples engaged in God knows what.

"I don't see a whole lot going on," Georgie said, staring at a man who cradled nothing but air and rocked from side to side.

Barry held out his phone. "Everything in here can be viewed via the Battle of the Births app."

Jordan looked on with his wife. "There's an app?"

Barry shrugged. "There's an app for everything. Here,

give me your phones. My job is to get you all uploaded and Battle of the Births ready—at least, with the tech side."

"Is this a virtual reality parent training center?" Jordan asked, glancing at the vast space as a cameraman in a CityBeat T-shirt hung back and filmed their entrance.

"That's right," Lenny said, emerging from behind a frosted glass door in non-hobo attire.

"We're not only the hottest musical duo on the toddler scene. We're also making the baby prep experience high-tech," Stu offered, following close behind, and also not dressed like a hobo.

Jordan almost didn't recognize them.

"Take a look. We have access to everyone's feed," Lenny said, holding out an iPad.

It all made sense now. That man rocking side to side was holding a virtual baby. A woman who looked like she was kneading imaginary dough was changing a diaper.

"That's amazing," Georgie said, her gaze bouncing from the screen to the actual humans moving awkwardly in clear boxes.

"And I see you've got your infant care simulation doll. Good, good!" Stu said.

"Yep, and Faby is safe and sound and in one piece," Jordan answered, grateful Mr. Tuesday hadn't chewed the fake kid's arm off.

"That's right! No baby shenanigans with Faby," Georgie added with a toothpaste commercial smile.

Did they sound like used infant care simulation doll salespeople? Most likely, but it was better than having to explain that their dog had taken the doll on a wild romp through Denver.

"Who's Faby?" Barry asked.

Jordan tapped the doll's button nose. "This is Faby. It's a fake baby, so, Faby."

Lenny and Stu pursed their lips.

Were they not supposed to name the baby? Were they supposed to simply call it *doll* or *plastic infant* or *child simulation*? Those sounded clinical and drab. Faby had a nice ring to it.

"Most expectant parents name their infant care simulation doll," Lenny supplied with a crease between his brows.

"That's what we did," Georgie answered.

The man's crease deepened. "Usually, a real name like Tony or Claire."

He and Georgie stared at Faby, who looked nothing like a Tony or a Claire.

"But Faby works," the good-natured Stu offered, sharing a quick glance with his partner.

"And the app works," Barry added, handing them their phones. "The app will show you your standing in the competition. You earn points for all your correct choices in the simulator. It's like a video game."

"The app also integrates with your infant care simulation doll. It's slick baby tech, that's for sure," Lenny added.

Now it was his wife with a crease between her brows. "There's an app for fake babies?"

He met Georgie's gaze and shrugged. He was lost, too.

"It's a lot to take in. Do your best. I'll take Faby, and Lenny will get you situated in a simulation cubicle," Stu explained.

"Where will you put Faby?" Georgie asked, eyeing the man.

"In the infant care simulation nursery," Stu said, then opened the frosted glass door to reveal a child's playroom filled with dolls.

Jordan leaned in and lowered his voice. "That's a little creepy, right?"

"It's better than putting Faby back in the bag," she countered.

True.

"Come with me. We're going to put you through a simulation to test your parenting abilities," Lenny said, leading them down a hallway.

"Are all these people competing in the Battle of the Births?" Georgie asked.

"They sure are. We've got eleven couples taking part in the challenge."

"What does the winner get?" Jordan asked, working to keep his nerves in check. This was not the Baby 101, sit down and listen to a lecture he was expecting.

Lenny paused. "A baby...and bragging rights, I suppose."

Bragging rights?

That revelation brought out the competitive streak in him, and his face must have shown it because his wife immediately flashed *simmer-down-asshat* eyes at him.

She'd crowned him the Emperor of Asshattery, and sometimes, his royal jackass-ed-ness reared its regal head.

"If I'm hearing you right, the scores will indicate if we're complete parenting nightmares," he replied, half-joking, but Lenny didn't laugh.

The baby expert opened the glass door and gestured for them to enter the room. "Do your best, and we'll go from there."

"No singing vagabonds today?" Georgie asked, her voice rising an octave.

"We don't sing on simulation days," Lenny replied, stone-cold serious.

"Sure, that makes sense," his wife answered, her voice still lingering in anxious octave land.

Clearly, these men did not mess around when it came to baby prep.

Note to self: Lenny and Stu dressed as jaunty drifters were all bright smiles and singing in the rain.

Lenny and Stu in button-ups and khakis were no bull-shit baby busters.

"Put on the VR headsets. The system will count you down before the simulation begins. Good luck," the man directed before shutting the door.

Georgie looked from side to side at the couples talking and moving around their clear boxes.

"This must be what it's like for lab rats."

"Yeah, kind of weird, but also pretty cool." He picked up the headset. "VR is becoming popular in fitness. They've got virtual reality workout regimens. And one of my clients in construction told me the other day that they use it for figuring out plumbing on large-scale projects."

Georgie eyed the headset. "Let's not flush a VR baby down a virtual toilet."

Or allow a virtual dog to take it on a virtual jaunt about town.

His wife put on the headset and gasped. "Wow! You've got to see this," she said, waving her hands.

He followed suit and blinked as a virtual Georgie stood in front of him.

He looked around. "Are we in a grocery store?"

"It sure seems like it," virtual Georgie answered when a woman's robotic voice piped in.

"Five, four, three, two, one. Commence simulation."

Ping.

He damn near fell over when Faby appeared out of nowhere and floated between them.

"Holy—" he began, about to drop a string of expletives when the VR version of his wife pressed her hand to his virtual mouth, and strangely, it silenced him.

"It's a video game. I think we grab the baby," Georgie said, pointing to the levitating child.

"Here goes." He reached out, and while his fingers grasped nothing but air, he now held a cooing Faby in the simulation.

"Hello, Faby, the best fake baby around!" he said to the VR infant, then turned to Georgie. "This isn't so bad," he added, but he'd spoken too soon.

Just as the words left his mouth, the Faby's content expression disappeared, and the infant released a piercing wail, booming into his ears through the headset's speakers.

"Grocery Store Simulation. You must purchase all the groceries on your list while also meeting your child's needs," came the robot lady's voice over the howling Faby.

"We've got to figure out how to calm down this video game Faby," he exclaimed.

"Bounce or sway. Move around. See if that helps," VR Georgie suggested.

He danced around, springing from foot to foot, but the baby wasn't having it.

"It's not working, Georgie!"

VR Georgie grabbed a shopping cart, and a virtual list popped up.

Okay! This had to be a good sign. They were making progress.

"We're supposed to shop. Try putting Faby in the cart," she suggested.

He attempted to place the infant in the kiddie seat of

the shopping cart, but the program kept resetting and dangling the crying infant in the air.

"Why won't they let us put the baby in the cart?" he asked, frustration mounting.

Virtual Georgie shrugged. "I don't know. Do you think we're supposed to carry the baby?"

He plucked the hovering Faby and tried to move forward, but with every step, the simulation sent him back to the beginning.

"I don't know what I'm doing wrong, Georgie," he said, anxiety coursing through his body as the child's unrelenting cry threatened to burst his eardrums.

"Sanitizer!" VR Georgie called out, plucking a wipe from a dispenser and virtually cleaning the cart's handle and the baby seatbelt buckle.

Jesus! This had to work otherwise—high-tech dream equipment or not—he was ready to chuck this VR headset into next week.

"Try now," she said.

He walked over to the VR cart and gingerly slipped the baby into the seat and buckled the little belt.

"Bingo!" he cried as the wailing Faby digitally switched to happy Faby.

"That was intense!" Georgie said as they pushed the cart down the virtual aisle, and very non-virtual sweat trailed down his back.

Holy Faby wails! It was one thing to hear a kid cry at the store. But when it's your own kid—even your own virtual kid—it flipped a switch inside that had adrenaline drilling through his veins.

"Let's get our bearing's, and then we can work on the grocery list," Georgie said when a timer appeared in his line of vision.

"Are you seeing this?" he asked.

"The clock? Yeah, it's set to five minutes."

"Is that how long we have to shop?" he asked.

"Five minutes to diaper blowout," came the robot lady's monotone voice.

"A diaper blowout?" he repeated.

They stared at VR Faby, who had stopped crying, but now looked as if it were contemplating Einstein's theory of relativity.

Oh shit! Literally, oh shit!

"I'm pretty sure this baby is going to take a massive dump in." He glanced at the countdown. "In less than four minutes."

"We have less than four minutes to shop for ten items, or else the baby will poop all over?" Georgie replied, her voice back in the freak-out octave.

"That's my best guess, babe. Look at Faby's face."

The VR baby scrunched into a pruny expression as it stared into space.

"What's the first item?" Georgie pressed.

"Milk."

"Almond, soy, cow, or oat?" his wife rattled off.

"I don't think it matters." He looked around and spotted a dairy case. "There, to the right."

They booked it through the virtual store, and VR Georgie touched a jug labeled milk.

Ping.

"Objective met. Proceed to the next item," chimed the eerily calm robot.

"We need bread," he answered, checking the virtual list.

"White, wheat, rye, pumpernickel, potato, or raisin?" his wife listed off like she was the spokesperson for the world of bread.

"Just like the milk, I don't think it matters," he said as they steered the cart toward the virtual bakery.

Georgie swatted a loaf on a high shelf.

Ping.

"Objective met. Proceed to the next item."

"Gherkins?" he said, staring at the weird word.

What the hell was a gherkin?

"It's a fancy pickle!" Georgie exclaimed, reading his mind.

"Pickles should be with condiments," he replied, then did a quick Faby check. The kid was still contemplating the meaning of life.

Okay! They could do this!

"But it doesn't say pickle. It says gherkin. Maybe they're back in the produce section in a refrigerated case," Georgie replied.

He shook his head. "Everything in this store is pretty cut and dry. Bread, milk..."

"But the list says gherkin," VR Georgie interjected, waving her digital arms.

She was right, but it didn't matter.

"Three, two, one. Diaper blowout," came the robot lady's calm voice.

They stared at the digital Faby, who seemed quite content.

"I think we should keep shopping. The kid seems okay," he said when three distinct pings pulsed through his headset and...

Sweet Montezuma!

Like a breached dam, a brown substance burst from Faby's diaper, flowing like a roaring river.

"Faby! No!" Georgie cried, lifting the virtual infant

from the cart, only to have the VR crap shoot out in all directions.

He couldn't move. The virtual Jordan Marks watched in horror as Faby spewed poop like a brown Niagara Falls.

"Twinkle, twinkle..." Virtual Georgie began to sing.

"What are you doing?" he called.

"Trying to stop the blowout!"

"With a song?"

"Do you have a better idea?" she cried, rocking the baby from side to side as an ungodly amount of virtual poop roared out of the VR infant.

"Here, pass me the baby," he cried, reaching through the curtain of brown when everything went black, and a voice called to him from the virtual baby beyond.

"Simulation terminated. Status: failure."

Chapter Nine
Georgie

"**B**abe, say something!"

Georgie stared at her husband—her real husband, not the digital version. He stood in front of her, holding both of their headsets. She looked from side to side, then gazed at her hands. Relief, that wasn't brown or shooting out of a baby with the furious force of a firehose, washed over her.

"Thank God we're not covered in virtual baby diarrhea!" she said, the words tumbling out like...oh, forget it! Enough with the poop talk!

"That was..." her husband began.

"Intense," she finished as Jordan nodded, looking as shell-shocked as she felt.

The plexiglass door swung open, and Lenny and Stu rushed in, then headed toward a tower of servers in the corner of the room.

"Sorry about the diaper glitch. We thought the developers had worked that kink out," the tall Lenny said, opening up a laptop, then plugging it into the server.

Stu nodded. "You're our first couple to do the grocery store simulation, and we sure weren't expecting that."

"Yeah, neither were we," Jordan said, placing the headsets back on their respective hooks.

"Do babies do that?"

Georgie turned to see a white-faced Barry standing in the doorway. Wide-eyed, he stared at his iPad.

"You saw all that?" she asked.

"I don't think I'll ever be able to *un-see* it," the man replied, his gaze locked on the screen.

"That makes two of us," she said under her breath.

But it wasn't the glitch that sent a shiver down her spine. Sure, she may never touch another VR headset for as long as she lived, but all she could hear was that judgmental robotic voice's final word.

Failure.

It echoed. It resonated. Yes, the simulation had glitched, but she and Jordan weren't exactly kicking ass and taking names at the digital market. Quite the opposite. She hadn't even thought to decontaminate the shopping cart. It was dumb luck that she saw the wipe dispenser.

How many other things had she overlooked? How many baby dangers lurked in the light of day or the light of a virtual world that she didn't recognize?

"I'm going to call it a day. I think I've gotten enough footage," Barry said with a shudder.

"And I'd suggest turning off the replay feature," Lenny offered.

The CityBeat producer grimaced, his eyes locked to the screen. "It's like a train wreck. You can't look away. And each time you go back, you see some other freaky part."

"We'll talk to you later, Barry," she called.

The man zombie-walked to the exit as the audio of her shrieking wafted back to them.

She might not know what to do with a pooping baby in a grocery store, but she did know one thing. She sure as hell didn't want to watch their video. It was bad enough living through it. She didn't need the postcard, picture, or the replay.

Stu gestured toward the door. "How about we go somewhere more comfortable and do a debrief."

She'd prefer an appointment with a hypnotherapist to see if the memory of their simulation could be scraped from her brain. However, she had a sneaking suspicion that the little poop nugget of a recollection would be locked in her noggin for life.

Jordan wrapped his arm around her shoulders, and she leaned into her husband as they followed Lenny and Stu out of the simulation area.

"Do you feel all right? That was pretty jarring," he asked, keeping his voice low.

She sighed. "Surprisingly, no nausea after that catastrophe."

He stroked her arm. "Do you think it was a catastrophe?"

She glanced up at him, cocked her head to the side, and gave him wife-eyes.

He gave her a defeated nod. "Yeah, you're right. Even without the crap glitch, it was a catastrophe. We were a mess in there."

They were. Granted, watching a virtual baby levitate in the air probably would have thrown even the most seasoned parent off their game. But she and Jordan had gone into *chicken-with-its-head-cut-off* mode. No plan. No strategy. All panic.

Lenny opened the door to the infant care simulation nursery, and they settled themselves at a table in the center of the room. She was grateful to leave the glass box, but her husband was right. A baby doll daycare was creepy.

They'd grown used to Faby staring at them. But to have ten other pairs of doll eyes boring into them hit somewhere along the lines of a B-level horror movie.

"We always like to start with a couple's strengths and go from there," Stu began, but the look he shared with Lenny wasn't encouraging.

"Stu's correct. It's always good to start with the strengths," Lenny reiterated.

A glimmer of hope flickered in her heart. Perhaps it wasn't as bad as she'd thought.

"What were our strengths?" she asked, ready to glean some knowledge off these child development experts.

"You both did a great job navigating the headset," Lenny answered.

Navigating the headset?

She frowned. "Are you saying that our strength is that we put the headset on our heads?"

"Ding, ding, ding! *Good job, good job! You did a good job!*" Stu sang out, switching to crooning vagabond, which was quite odd when the guy wasn't dressed as a kindly hobo armed with a tambourine.

She shared a worried look with Jordan.

"Just to be clear. You're saying that Georgie and I used the VR headset as prescribed," Jordan questioned with a crease between his brows.

Kudos to the man for trying to make it sound better.

"Yes," Lanny and Stu replied in unison, each donning a grin that would have earned them bonus points in a pageant.

All she wanted to do was *Wicked-Witch-of-the-West-it* out of there and melt into the ground because here's what it boiled down to. Their strength was putting a hunk of plastic on their heads. It didn't get much more bottom of the barrel than that.

"And sorry about breaking into song back there. It's my go-to in challenging situations," Stu replied with a weak grin.

And the punches kept coming! Not only had they failed, but Stu had also labeled them challenging!

Lenny steepled his hands and rested his chin on his fingertips. "Do either of you have siblings?"

"No, Georgie and I are each an only child," Jordan answered.

"And how often do you interact with small children?" Stu queried.

"Here and there. I own a bookshop, and we have a story time," she answered.

Lenny's expression brightened. "That's great! How do you structure it?"

She could feel her beauty queen expression coming on. "Well, I don't exactly structure anything. I have a high school student who volunteers and another employee who leads them. I can recommend books for children of any age, but I work more with the teens, suggesting classics and pertinent series to encourage a lifelong love of reading."

There! That wasn't a half-bad answer.

Lizzy, Jane, and Hermione, her trusty trifecta, nodded their fictional heads. Still, Georgie nearly fell out of her chair when imaginary digital numbers appeared above each member of the trifecta, noting how many times she'd suggested each of their books.

Wowza! That insane VR experience had seeped into her fictional fantasy friend world.

"And you, Jordan, you own a fitness establishment. Do you have any programs for young children?" Stu continued as Jordan's knee bounced beneath the table.

If her tell was a Texas-sized smile stretched across her face, then his was the nervous kid knee bop.

"No, like Georgie, when it comes to kids, I mostly work with teenagers."

"He runs an after-school program for them," she added, gently resting her hand on his leg, that could have given a jackhammer a run for the money. Thankfully, her touch was enough to put the kibosh on his under-the-table tap dance.

"I see," Stu said with a furrowed brow.

"I think this calls for the FBI," Lenny added with a solemn nod.

Her jaw dropped. This debrief sure went to hell in a handbasket quickly!

"You're concerned that we'll be such awful parents that you want to get law enforcement involved? The simulation glitched, and the baby gushed poo like a burst fire hydrant. Maybe we should get a do-over before you take that step," she pleaded.

Jordan raised his hand. "I second a do-over. And, for the record, Georgie and I grocery shop at least once a week, and we've never seen a surge of anything like that come out of a baby."

Lenny sat back. "Yes, the system glitched, but when parenting, one must be ready for *life's* little glitches."

"Especially, when babies and children are involved, a situation can go south in an instant, and you need to be ready to react," Stu added.

"But does it require notifying the Federal Bureau of Investigation?" Jordan pressed.

Lenny and Stu chuckled, and she and her husband stared blankly at the men.

What was so funny?

"Not that FBI. A facilitated baby intervention," Stu explained.

She released the breath she hadn't realized she'd been holding. Between Jordan rattling on about the baby NFL and now a baby FBI, she'd need to start writing down all these acronyms.

"What's a facilitated baby intervention?" she asked as her heart rate slowed.

"Think of it as a Battle of the Births remedial activity," Stu answered.

And her heart rate shot back up. "So, as of right now, we're not even on pre-parenting grade level?"

"Parenting can't be graded, Georgie. It's more of a spectrum of skills," Lenny said, drawing a bell curve into the air with his hand.

She stared at the invisible line. "Where would we be on that spectrum?"

The man pointed into the air at a spot decidedly below and far, far from the top of the curve.

"Yikes!" Jordan exclaimed. "We're not even close to the bell?"

She shook her head. They couldn't be that terrible.

"We've tried to figure out what skills we need. I googled parenting books and got two hundred and sixty-eight million different results."

"And I searched the phrase 'how to be a good parent' and got six hundred and fifteen million results," Jordan added.

She threw up her hands. "Where do you even start? We'd read part of one book only to have another tell you to do the opposite."

Seriously! What did people do?

"The thing is, Georgie and I want to be the best parents we can for our child," Jordan said softly, and his words went right to her heart.

She pressed her hand to her abdomen. She wanted that, too.

Jordan and his father had butted heads after his mom passed, and she'd loathed her mother for parading her around at pageant after pageant for a good chunk of her youth. Sure, they were in a better place with their parents now. Jordan and his dad were doing great, while she and her mom were getting there.

Well, *getting there* might be pushing it. She was, of course, still trying to decide how and when she wanted to spill the beans to her mother about the little bean growing in her belly.

But that unease churning inside wasn't her craving a little pineapple salsa, and it wasn't even her uncertainty on when to share the baby news with her mom. No, what had her chest tightening and her mouth growing dry was that she didn't want their alien blueberry peanut to view them as heavy-handed or insensitive.

There had to be a book or a course or some parent voodoo out there that could teach them how to keep their child alive and make sure they didn't become mega-asshat parents.

The answer had to be there. Except, there was a decent chance it was buried in the internet soup of over sixty gazillion child-rearing results.

Lenny's features softened. "There is a lot of information

out there. That's why we'll implement an FBI. Stu and I will curate a hands-on learning opportunity that will ease you into parenting and also have you interacting with real babies. We'll also put together a list of narrowed down parenting resources so you can educate yourselves on the nuts and bolts of caring for an infant."

"And we can center the FBI activity around your places of business. A gym and a bookshop are great venues for young children—if structured safely," Stu finished.

She nodded. Okay, this is what they needed. Some direction. Some guidance.

Lenny opened a folder and slid out a sheet of paper. "Take this. It's a go-bag checklist. We know that you're only at the end of your first trimester, but it's never too soon to have your hospital bag packed and ready."

"Have you chosen where you're going to deliver?" Stu asked.

If she weren't pregnant, she'd do a cartwheel because she knew the answer to this question!

"Ding, ding, ding! Good job, good job! I did a good job! I know the hospital!" she sang out.

Lenny and Stu cocked their heads to the side while Jordan gave her *what-are-you-doing-superfreak* eyes.

Another note to self: under pressure, only Stu is allowed to break out into song.

In the blink of an eye, she channeled a composed Jane Eyre. "We'll be having our baby at Rose Medical Center," she answered, doing her best not to look insane and really glad she'd read the pamphlet Joyless Joyce had given her with the hospital info.

"Rose is also Georgie's favorite color," Jordan added with the hint of a smirk.

"Pink is your favorite color?" Lenny asked.

Oh no! He did not just equate the color rose to pink.

"Rose isn't pink. It's rose. The color between red and magenta," she answered, biting back a smirk of her own.

The color rose had quite an impact on their wedding, and it appeared to be playing a part in this phase of their lives as well.

"You picked a hospital because it was your favorite color?" Lenny asked, and boom, they were back to looking like inept expectant parents.

"No, no, not at all. Rose Medical Center is where my obstetrician has hospital privileges," she finished, crossing her ankles in a demur little move to appear—again—not insane.

"We'll make sure to add an FBI activity that incorporates Rose Medical Center," Lenny said, taking out a notepad from his pocket and jotting down the information.

Jordan leaned forward. "Can't you guys tell us exactly what we need to know—what we need to do? We're up for the challenge. Our whole relationship is basically built on challenges."

The parenting experts watched them closely.

"And love," she blurted, not wanting Lenny and Stu think they were a pair of lunatics who only wanted a baby as a challenge.

"Yes, absolutely! Tons of love, but also a decent amount of challenges," Jordan said, amending his statement but still managing to step in it.

Lenny chuckled. "You two will be great parents. But every parent is different, and every child is different. You'll have to figure out what works for your family."

Family.

There it was. A family unit. Their own tribe. A party of three.

"You can retrieve Faby now. We've kept you long enough," Lenny said, cutting into her thoughts.

She glanced at the dolls, who all looked like Faby.

"We'll be in touch in the next week or so with a facilitated baby intervention activity," Stu added as he and Lenny stood and pushed in their chairs.

She and Jordan followed suit, coming to their feet, but neither of them moved. She glanced at her husband, who nodded contemplatively at the spread of plastic infants.

He didn't know which one was Faby either!

"Your infant care simulation doll has a band around its ankle with its name," Stu said over his shoulder as the men left the room.

She turned to Jordan, and they stared at each other until the door closed behind the parenting experts, then each released a relieved breath.

"Which one is ours?" he asked with a nervous laugh.

"I don't know," she answered as he gathered her into his arms.

"What do you think?" he asked, resting his chin on her head.

She leaned into him. "I think I could do with a bowl of tortilla chips and an endless supply of pineapple salsa."

He chuckled and rubbed soothing circles between her shoulder blades. "No, about today, Ms. Pineapple Machine."

She gave a slight shrug. "When you're the worst, there's nowhere to go but up. And, at least for today, nobody's reporting us to the real FBI."

He gazed down at her with a sweet boyish grin. "I love you, messy bun girl."

This man. Her Emperor of Asshattery and reigning Sovereign of Scat. They'd figure this out. Jordan wasn't entirely wrong when he'd said their relationship had been built on challenges. She'd challenged his Marks Perfect Ten Mindset philosophy, and he'd challenged her Own the Eights attitude. And look at what happened. They found love and were living the life they'd each dreamed of—with a twist. If the perfect ten and the dependable eight could figure out a way to make it work in the game of love, they had to have a chance at not completely screwing up in their brave new world of pregnancy and parenting.

She held onto this moment, warm and safe in her husband's arms, when her stomach growled as if a ravenous bear had taken up residence in her abdomen.

Jordan's eyes went wide. "Come on! Let's grab our fake baby, and then we can get you a tub of pineapple salsa."

She scanned the bands on the doll's ankles and found their Faby, while her husband retrieved the fake baby's diaper bag. They left the creepy nursery and gave the simulation area one last look before exiting the building. She was about to breathe a sigh of relief when a black limo screeched to a stop in front of them, and the breath caught in her throat.

It couldn't be.

"What time is it in India?" she whispered.

"What does that matter?" Jordan whispered back.

She stared at the car. "I don't know."

"Do you think it's your mom?" he asked, keeping his voice low.

It couldn't be...could it?

She hadn't checked her phone in hours. Could they have texted, and she'd missed it? What if they'd learned of the pregnancy from someone else? What if her mother was here to take her shopping for maternity rompers? Did those even exist?

Her thoughts whirled as question after question fueled a frenzied mind tornado until the tinted window lowered.

Georgie's heart sprang into her throat. She squeezed her eyes shut like a naughty child and waited for her mother's flowery voice to call out. She braced herself for a Lorraine Vanderdinkle tongue-lashing but was met with a husky German accent instead.

"Georgiana! Jordan!" called their former wedding planner from the driver's seat.

"Cornelia, I didn't know you drove this thing," Georgie said—because saying "thank God you're not my mother" seemed somewhat tactless.

"I don't. But when I saw you enter the warehouse with a doll, I put Hans on spy duty."

"Aren't you with clients?" Jordan asked, looking equally relieved.

"We left them with the dildo guy. They'll be fine," Cornelia said with a wave of her hand.

"You two look wonderful! How was Fiji?" the kind Hans asked.

Cornelia whipped off her dark glasses. "Hans! How can you ask about Fiji? Georgiana, are you pregnant?"

Cornelia Lieblingsschatz did not beat around the bush.

"Yes, I am. What tipped you off?" she answered.

Cornelia's gaze dropped to Faby. "I had a hunch there was some baby business near the Denver Wedding Underground."

She glanced at the baby doll in her arms. "Are you thinking of expanding and adding parent training to the Denver Wedding Frau empire?"

Cornelia and Hans looked at each other, then broke out into mad giggles.

Cornelia gasped. "We wouldn't touch parenting prep

with a ten-foot pole. Who's running your classes? The Music Men or Natural Birth Nadine? Those are Denver's hottest pre-baby planners."

"Lenny and Stu, the music men," Jordan answered.

"You're lucky," Cornelia replied.

"What do you mean by that?" Georgie asked.

"A few years back, Hans and I almost worked with an expectant couple who wanted to get married, but they were already with Nadine."

Georgie frowned. "You didn't help plan a couple's wedding because they were expecting?"

"Of course, we plan weddings for expectant clients all the time. Hans and I don't discriminate. We're very modern in our thinking," Cornelia replied.

"Well, then what was wrong with the Natural Nadine couple?" Jordan pressed.

Cornelia shuddered. "Natural Birth Nadine doesn't allow her clients to shave or use deodorant for the duration of their pregnancy. She insists on a complete caveman and cavewoman experience. The smell is atrocious."

Hans grimaced. "We tried working with the couple, but the poor dildo guy fainted from the odor."

Now, there's something you don't hear every day.

"Okay, we'll be sure to steer clear of any Nadine," Jordan replied.

"Your families must be so happy," Hans said, shifting gears.

"Yes, they are. My dad can't wait to become a grandfather," Jordan answered.

"And your mother? I imagine she and Howard are over the moon with joy," Cornelia pressed.

Georgie shifted Faby. "Yeah...well...I'm sure they will be."

The frau pegged her with her sharp wedding planner gaze. "You haven't told them?"

"They're out of the country at a spiritual retreat in India," she replied like a teen making a half-assed excuse after getting caught breaking curfew.

"Really?" Cornelia said with an amused grin. "Looks like you have me to thank for that."

Georgie chuckled. "She takes her psychic gifts seriously."

"You should tell them, Georgie," Hans added gently.

"But not while holding that creepy doll," Cornelia answered when a phone resting in the car's center console pinged.

Hans glanced at the cell. "It's the dildo guy. We need to get back. Congratulations, you two!"

Cornelia lowered her sunglasses. "Tell your mother soon, Georgiana."

"Will do!" she replied with her beauty queen smile stretched across her face, then crossed her fingers behind her back like a disobedient child.

Chapter Ten
Georgie

"Georgiana Jensen-Marks, why haven't you told your mother yet?"

Georgie leaned forward and cradled her head in her hands. "I figured Becca would have mentioned that to you."

Georgie peeked between her fingers at Irene, who scowled at her over video chat.

"One," her friend said, raising her index finger. "My sister is surprisingly hard to connect with these days."

Irene wasn't wrong.

While Becca managed the bookstore, she'd also started her last semester of college this month. But when she wasn't in the shop, she was damn hard to get ahold of. She'd text or call back, eventually, but she'd definitely been preoccupied for the last few months or so.

"I think she's seeing someone, but she won't tell me anything," Irene said, resurrecting her scowl as she rested her hands on her pregnant belly.

"Bec hasn't mentioned anything to me," Georgie

answered, knowing she may not be the best judge of what was going on with the younger Murphy sister.

Life had flown by these last several weeks. This was the first time in over a month that she and Irene were able to connect. Honestly, these days, she was lucky to make it out the door with a pair of matching shoes. Business at the bookstore had doubled last month with holiday shopping, and now, with people setting their January New Years' resolutions, Jordan's gym had picked up even more steam and signed-on an avalanche of new clients. But Irene was right. Something was going on with Becca.

"I'll make sure to play the surrogate big sister and find out what's going on today. Now, tell me everything about your research. Are you leading the way to a world that runs on clean energy alone?"

Irene shook her head. "No, no! You know my project is going well. I'm not letting you off the hook until you tell me what's going on with you and your mom."

"Fine," Georgie said, then took a bite of pineapple cheesecake that her genius of a husband had delivered biweekly to the shop.

"Number two," Irene began. "You're seventeen weeks pregnant. What's holding you back from telling your mom and Howard? Everything is still going well with the pregnancy, right?"

Georgie glanced down at the sway in her abdomen, where the alien blueberry peanut had grown into a mini pineapple surprise. And it wasn't just her belly. Her breasts, once respectable B-cups, had blossomed into *va-va-voom* C-cups. Something that was not lost on her husband, who had become quite a boob man these days.

"These pregnancy breasts are no joke! I had to buy all

new bras last week," she said, gesturing to her ample chest while simultaneously trying to change the subject.

But Irene wasn't having it.

"Seriously, lady! What's holding you back?" Irene pressed.

Georgie shoveled a giant bite of cheesecake into her mouth. "I'm waiting to see what happens today. We've got our FBI meeting in less than an hour."

Irene cocked her head to the side. "Okay, I need you to dial back the cake eating contest and repeat that sentence. All the way in Iceland, it sounded like you said you're meeting with the FBI? You and Jordan haven't decided you've had enough with blogging and decided to dip your toes into the world of prenatal espionage, have you?"

Georgie swallowed her gargantuan bite. "Do you think prenatal espionage is a thing?"

"Georgie," her friend pressed.

She wiped a few crumbs of the cheesecake's delicious graham cracker crust from her lips. "It's not the Federal Bureau of Investigation, FBI. It's the facilitated baby intervention activity that the child development experts set up to give us hands-on baby experience."

Irene pursed her lips. "What are you supposed to do?"

"Some parents are coming to the bookshop with their babies, and Jordan and I are supposed to lead a baby story time movement activity with them."

She'd spent the better part of the day sifting through board books, looking for something that could work with this age group.

"That sounds right up your alley," Irene replied, giving her a thumbs-up.

Georgie twisted the cuff of her sweater. "Maybe."

"Hey, you've got this," Irene said, her expression softening.

Georgie abandoned her sleeve and swiped her finger across the plate, collecting the last morsels of cheesecake, then stuck her finger into her mouth. "I never thought this parenting business would be so complicated."

"Girl! Chill with the pineapple cheesecake!"

Georgie removed her finger from her mouth and sighed. "I want to feel like I've got a handle on my life and on this pregnancy before I bring in my mother's drama and gobbledygook into the mix."

"Gobbledygook?" Irene repeated, biting back a grin.

"I'm a bookshop owner. I use fancy words. And you know what I mean," she replied as her trifecta nodded approvingly.

Irene chuckled. "I think you're making this harder than it actually is. Babies eat, sleep, and poop."

"Oh, I know they poop. Even virtual reality babies poop," she answered with a shudder.

Irene leaned in toward the camera. "Haven't you been practicing with Fabian?"

"Who?"

"That," Irene said, coming in another inch, then pointing toward the bottom of the screen.

Georgie looked down. "You can see that?"

"I see a creepy doll head in your lap like I do on all of our calls."

"Its name is Faby. And yes, the parenting experts sent us some info on diapering, feeding, and bathing."

True to their word, Lenny and Stu had sent them literature that covered the baby basics. She and Jordan could now diaper, bathe, and pretend-feed a doll. It wasn't much, but it was a start.

"Aren't you worried there's something you've missed or some baby fact you still need to learn? Your due date is right around the corner," she said.

Irene released a slow breath. "Sure, I'm nervous. But I'm six years older than Becca. I still remember helping my mom and dad take care of her. It's tiring, but it's not brain surgery."

Georgie gazed down at Faby's little foot. "What about your research? How will you manage caring for a baby and earning your degree?"

There, she'd said it. It was the unknown balancing act lying before her that kept her up at night. How would she run a successful business and a wildly popular blog while caring for her child?

And when it came to her mother, if anyone knew how to knock the earth off its axis, it was Lorraine Vanderdinkle. She loved her mom and understood the woman more today than she ever had. Still, that uncertainty combined with the ambiguity of what motherhood would hold for her made her want to crawl into a hole stocked with pineapple cheesecake and hide out until there was a clear plan and everything made sense. The librarian in her craved a systematic baby blueprint to give her some semblance of control.

"For one thing, I'm not in this alone, and neither are you," Irene said before a warm grin bloomed on her lips. "We've got great husbands, Georgie. Husbands who would move heaven and earth for us. And think of all the support you have in Denver. Jordan's dad, Maureen, the Gilberts, Hector and Bobby—and yes, your mom and Howard, too."

Georgie nodded, knowing her friend was right but still on the fence when it came to her mother.

"Oh, and I almost forgot all those old ladies who pine away for Michael Bolton sitting in your shop, knitting banana hammocks and wool G-strings. You've got an entire grandma brigade at the ready," Irene added with a teasing glint in her eyes.

Georgie broke out into a belly laugh. "I think it's mostly scarves and baby booties, but I hear what you're saying."

"On second thought, you may want to keep a close eye on them. Who knows what naughty things those grannies could be doing," Irene joked as they broke into another round of giggles.

The door to the bookshop office opened, and Jordan entered the snug space.

"It looks like all the fun is in here," he said, setting a giant glass of pineapple juice on her desk, then pressed a kiss to the crown of her head.

She took a gulp as Jordan knelt and waved to Irene.

"It's good to see you, Irene. How are you doing?"

"I'm ready to unload this watermelon," she answered with a pat to her belly.

"You look great to me. And Will? How's he?"

Irene's gaze traveled off camera. "You can ask him now. He just got home."

Jordan glanced at his watch. "Isn't it late in Iceland?"

"It's never too late for *kleina*!"

"*Kleina*?" Georgie repeated.

"Sweetened fried dough. It's a Nordic dessert, and it's all this baby wants," her friend answered as Will appeared on screen and passed his wife the treat.

Irene held the trapezoid-shaped pastry up to the camera, then jammed the whole thing into her mouth.

"Whoa!" Jordan said as Will nodded.

"You are no longer allowed to give me crap for eating while video chatting," she teased.

Irene grinned and said a garbled goodbye as she reached

for another piece of fried dough, then the screen went black.

Jordan leaned against the desk. "They look good."

"They seem to have things under control," she replied, going for breezy, but her husband saw through it.

"Hey, we're getting there. Exhibit A," he replied and lifted Faby from her lap. "Our fake baby is currently rocking the diaper that I expertly put on her."

Defining the diaper job as *expert level* was pushing it. They'd gone through half a dozen disposable diapers, messing up the adhesive tabs before he'd hit the mark. And the cloth diapers? After she'd punctured the poor doll's leg, they decided they were team disposable all the way.

Georgie stared at Faby, then paused.

"Do you think Faby's a *she*?" Georgie asked, eyeing her husband.

Jordan observed the fake baby. "Or he. Faby transcends gender."

"We'll learn the gender of our mini pineapple surprise pretty soon," she said as a crackle of excitement laced with apprehension rippled through her chest.

"Yeah, the big Battle of the Births reveal is only a few weeks away."

She nodded, then glanced at the clock. "But first, we have to get through this story time."

"We've got a few minutes before it starts. Did you pick out a book?" he asked. But before she could answer, the video chat pinged.

She waved off her husband. "I'll tell you in a sec. It's probably Irene calling back to make me watch her eat another *klien*-whatever. I think it's payback for the giant slice of cheesecake I ate during our call. My bet is that she wants to exact a little pastry revenge," she added with a chuckle.

"Georgie, wait—" Jordan exclaimed as she clicked to accept the call.

"Pumpkin?"

Georgie froze, then blinked. This was not Irene. Not even close.

"Is this working?" her mother asked, gaze darting from side to side as she jiggled the phone.

"Yes, it's working. I'm here. Where are you?" she asked, praying that she and her mother still had an ocean between them.

Her mother frowned. "At the spiritual retreat in India. You know that."

Georgie plastered on a grin to mask the relief. Thank goodness her mother was still on the other side of the planet.

"I didn't think you were supposed to use technology. Couldn't it dampen your psychic abilities?" she threw out, grasping for something.

"It was my psychic voice that compelled me to ask to use my phone, so I could reach out to you," she replied.

Holy psychic abilities! Could her mother actually have powers that went beyond gleaning the divine energy of votive candles?

"Did that voice mention why it wanted you to call?" she asked, then glanced at her husband, who remained motionless.

"It must be my maternal instinct," her mother answered.

Jordan gestured to his watch and mouthed *F-B-I*.

Oh no! She needed to get off this call and fast.

"Sure, that's got to be it. Well, everything's all good

here, so we'll let you get back to chanting or whatever psychic fun the retreat has in store for you," she answered when her mother frowned.

"Pumpkin, what's in that glass?"

Georgie's gaze slid to the giant serving of pineapple juice. "Oh, this?" she asked, wishing she had the psychic ability to make it disappear.

The woman leaned in. "It's too light for orange juice."

"Nope, it's not orange juice," she said, making *oh-shit* eyes at her husband.

"Are you drinking pineapple juice?" her mom asked with a troubled expression.

Mayday! Mayday! Mayday!

If anyone knew about her non-pregnant aversion to pineapple, it was Lorraine Vanderdinkle. The woman had had a front-row seat—literally—when she'd spewed a pineapple-laden fruit cup all over a row of judges.

Was this it? Was it time to come clean?

She parted her lips when her husband swooped in and entered the camera frame.

"Hi, Lorraine! It's pee in the cup," Jordan said, grinning into the camera.

"Pee as in urine?" her mother asked, her voice sliding up a few octaves.

The man nodded.

What was Jordan thinking?

"Why on earth would you leave a glass of pee on a desk?" her mother pressed.

Jordan's gaze bounced from the glass to the computer's camera. "I'm trying out the keto diet. With keto, you pee on these strips to learn if your body's in ketosis."

Georgie nodded. There was no turning back now.

Her mother's troubled expression morphed into pure shock. "Shouldn't you be doing that in a bathroom?"

Jordan snapped his fingers. "Gosh, I'm glad you called, Lorraine. That's a great idea!"

"And Jordan," the woman continued.

"Yes," her husband replied, his smile as plastic as hers.

"You may want to see a doctor, dear. That looks like a considerable amount of urine, even for someone as big as you."

Sweet pineapple surprise! This call had gone off the rails fast.

Georgie slid the glass out of the camera's view. "As you can see, we're doing great. Did you need anything else?"

Her mother chewed her lip. "Have you been by the Ritz-Carlton or stopped in at the Country Club?"

Georgie shook her head. "No, those aren't places we usually hang out."

"I drove by your country club the other day," Jordan chimed.

Her mother's face lit up like a Christmas tree. "How did it look? Did you see Gustavo? He always makes sure we have the best table for brunch. I hope he hasn't allowed the Bradfords to sit there. Muffy Bradford has been eyeing our spot for months."

"Sorry, Lorraine, I just drove by."

"So, no Gustavo?" her mother asked with a slight pout.

"No."

Her mother tapped her chin, seemingly lost in thought, which gave her the perfect opportunity to pull the plug on this video chat.

"All righty, then! If that's all, say hi to Howard for us, Mom. Let him know we hope he's doing well."

She moved the cursor to the end call button but stilled when her mother gasped.

"What is it?" she asked.

Her mother leaned in. "I have to tell you about Howard! You'd never believe it. He's completely enamored with the place. He's like a different person. The man, who could barely play a set of tennis without checking his stock portfolio, meditated for four hours yesterday, and he says he wants to start teaching yoga. Yoga!" she exclaimed.

"Isn't that what you guys are supposed to be doing—balancing your chi and centering your energy to bolster your spiritual prowess?" she asked, sharing a look with her husband, who gave her *I'm-not-sure-what-the-hell-you-just-said-but-let's go-with-it* eyes.

Her mother seemed to chew on that before her gaze drifted downward. "Did you go and see Denise?"

"Who?"

"Denise, you know, my personal shopper and bra-fitter at Saks?" her mother explained.

Georgie glanced at her husband, who shrugged.

"Why would you ask that, Mom?"

"Your breasts, Georgiana."

Her mother's expression lost the psychic guru air and morphed into drinks-at-the-club Denver socialite, Mrs. Lorraine Vanderdinkle.

"My breasts?" Georgie threw back.

"Yes, they look amazing. For the first time in years, they're quite perky. You hide your lovely figure in all those ill-fitting cardigans. Oh, and you should have Denise suggest some other pieces! A woman's wardrobe isn't complete without at least one Hermes scarf, a few Ferragamo wrap dresses, and, of course, a chic Chanel blazer to tie it together. You know, Denise was the one who suggested I send you that darling romper."

The room went topsy-turvy. She'd grown used to the psychically empowered version of her mother. This whack in the face of the full-throttle socialite Lorraine was not what she was expecting to encounter. She swallowed hard, her mouth going dry, then reached for her glass of pineapple juice and took a swig.

"Pumpkin! No!" her mother cried, mortification written all over her face.

Georgie looked around the room wildly. "Is something wrong?"

Her mom stared at her, wide-eyed. "You drank from Jordan's glass of urine."

"I did?" she replied, giving her husband SOS eyes.

The man swooped into the camera frame. "The nice thing about urine is that it's sterile, so your daughter should be fine. But we need to go. There's an urgent...blogging event we need to attend to," he added, solidifying his title as the world's worst liar.

"Wait! One more thing!" her mother chimed, not letting them off the call yet. "Have you been in contact with Nicolette?"

Georgie nodded, then positioned the cursor over the end call icon. "Yes, we sure have. We're going to MC a literacy fundraiser in April for you."

"Did they decide on the theme?" her mother asked.

"Western," Jordan answered.

The woman toyed with one of the crystals around her neck. "I love a good Western-themed gala," she replied on a heavy sigh.

Was her mother homesick?

Georgie glanced at the clock. Their FBI activity was set to start in one minute.

"Jordan?" her mother called.

"Yes, Lorraine."

A crease Georgie had never seen appeared on her mother's forehead.

"Why are you holding a doll?" the woman asked, cocking her head to the side.

Georgie glanced at Faby, tucked under her husband's arm. That darn fake baby had become such a part of their lives, she'd forgotten to tell him or at least gesture for him to keep the plastic infant out of the camera's view.

She stared at her mother, who'd raised a suspicious eyebrow. A few months without Botox had allowed the woman's expression to shine through.

"Well, Mom, look at the time. You keep channeling those good vibrations. We've got it all taken care of here in Denver. Love to Howard. Kiss, kiss!" she said, stealing a line from her mother's playbook before signing off and closing her laptop.

She collapsed forward and rested her head on the desk.

"I feel like I just ran a marathon. Do you think my mom's on to us?"

Jordan rubbed the tense muscles between her shoulder blades. "I don't know, babe," he answered as someone knocked on the door.

"It's time for your special story time activity," Talya called from the other side.

"Give us a minute," Jordan replied.

"I don't think you have a minute," Talya answered with a note of concern in her usually cheery voice.

Jordan frowned. "Why not?"

"The toddlers are here for story time. Simon's trying to

corral them now, but they're getting restless. *Really* restless," she finished with a thread of terror woven into the last two words.

"Toddlers?" Georgie exclaimed, then met her husband's gaze as absolute horror flashed in his eyes.

Chapter Eleven
Jordan

"Toddlers," Jordan whispered on a shaky exhale.

Memories of the baby doc's waiting room flashed through his mind. He raised his hand and pressed his fingers to his cheek, remembering the toddler's cherub-like face right before the little devil clocked him below the eye.

"We need to hide all the board books," he said, trailing behind Georgie and Talya as they passed row after row of books, then descended upon the children's area, and he froze.

A handful of years ago, when Maureen's twins were around five or six years old, she'd asked if he could help her out and pick the girls up from a birthday party. The request seemed simple enough, and he was always happy to help. So, of course, he'd said yes.

What Maureen hadn't mentioned when she'd given him the address of the party was that it was being held at a children's pizza and arcade venue.

Noise didn't usually bother him. The gym he'd worked at during that time always had loud music playing, and he'd often have his headphones on, blaring his own tunes. But not even that had prepared him for sound and the fury he'd encountered when he entered the pepperoni scented pandemonium.

Strobe lights flashed wild shades of color while children's music and the maddening hum of video games pulsed as if he'd entered an underground rave. It damn near made him want to scream and run out the door. It was purely dumb luck that the twins had been banging away on a Whack-a-Mole near the entrance when he'd arrived. He was there only for a minute, possibly two, before he'd extricated the children and freed himself from that house of horrors.

But even that nightmare hadn't prepared him for the mayhem that played out before his eyes inside his wife's bookshop.

Unlike the doctor's waiting area, with a sprinkling of noisy and somewhat dangerous tiny humans, the story time area was chock-full of toddlers. He blinked again. Maybe there weren't as many as he thought, but they zoomed around the story time area like bees, massing around a cluster of flowers in a frenzy of motion.

Talya's gaze bounced between them and a gaggle of children climbing on top of Simon, presumably for horse rides—or perhaps that's how the tiny beasts overpowered adults.

"They're kind of riled up," Talya said with a cringe.

"Kind of?" he repeated, then glanced at his wife, whose jaw had nearly hit the floor.

"Where are their parents?" Georgie asked, scanning the space.

"They said they got an email from some guys named Lenny and Stu, telling them that this was a parents' afternoon off activity and that they could leave their toddlers here for a thirty-minute story time. You'd mentioned that babies were coming, but Simon and I figured you guys changed the plans," Talya replied.

Georgie pushed up onto her tiptoes and stared past the rows of books. "Their parents are gone? They're not even in the shop?"

Talya shook her head. "No, they said they wanted to do a little shopping on Tennyson Street. They seemed epically excited to leave their kids here," the teen added with another cringe.

He was sure they were!

He looked around as a trio of pint-sized boys played tug of war with a bean bag chair while a little girl removed her shoes and proceeded to suck on her big toe.

This was not what Lenny and Stu had said would happen. From their last email, the plan was to have a few parents bring their babies in for a thirty-minute music and movement story time. He'd envisioned gentle cooing as four or five human versions of Faby sat on their parents' laps, listening to Georgie read a book and then him, leading the group in some infant-appropriate exercise—not this melee of two-year-olds, ransacking the place like a bunch of blood-thirsty pint-sized Vikings.

His phone buzzed, and he pulled it out to find a text from Stu.

We mixed up your baby story time with a parents' after-noon out event. We know this toddler activity isn't the facili-tated baby intervention we talked about, but Lenny and I agree, it's still a good learning experience. Have fun!

"Who's the text from?" Georgie asked.

"Stu."

"And? Are they coming? Did you tell them what's going on?" Georgie asked with a hopeful lilt.

He shook his head. "Stu said it's a mix-up. They sent the wrong group here. But we still have to go with it."

A crash caught their attention as a pair of little girls with pink bows in their hair pushed over a child-sized table.

"It's getting rough in here," she said, wide-eyed.

"We wish that we could stay and help, but Simon and I have to attend a lecture at the Denver Museum of Nature and Science for school. It starts in fifteen minutes," Talya said apologetically as Simon army-crawled his way out from under the children.

"We're epically sorry," Simon added with a slash of purple marker across his cheek.

Georgie pasted on a grin. "Don't worry. Jordan and I will be fine. But you two need to get moving to make it to the museum in time for the lecture."

He nodded as a puppet soared through the air, followed by a tiny shoe. "Yes, we've got this. You guys better head out."

"Do you want me to get Becca? She's up at the register talking to—" Talya began when a cluster of heat-seeking crayons rained down on them.

"Go! Get out while you can! Things are about to get way past epic," he ordered, using their epic teen verbiage to convey the urgency of the situation.

Not waiting to be told twice, Talya and Simon grabbed their backpacks and made a mad dash for the front of the store.

"At least we got them out relatively unscathed," Georgie said, watching the teens disappear.

He checked his watch. Twenty-four minutes left before the parents would return to claim their hellions. The miniature masters of destruction had already ransacked the art area and the puppet theater. But he could not allow them to discover what was in the far corner. If that area was breached, there was no telling the level of destruction.

"We can't let them open the LEGO bins," Georgie said, reading his mind.

Three large bins teeming with the plastic building materials sat untouched. They couldn't allow them to get scattered all over the floor. If even one of those tubs got tipped over, they'd spend the next decade finding the tiny blocks. And, there was nothing worse than stepping on a LEGO.

But these little humans could smell their fear, and, like a pack of wild dogs, three of them broke off from a group who were pulverizing crayons and headed for the bins.

"I think it's too late," Georgie said as a roaring sound rose from behind them.

"Show me how you move like a tiger!" came a man's pseudo-surfer growly voice.

The toddlers, who were headed for the bins, stopped in their tracks and turned. It was like in those sci-fi movies where evil robots are about to ravage a city, and then, suddenly, the hero intervenes, and their beady robot eyes change from evil red to passive green, halting the destruction that had once seemed imminent.

Jordan turned, ready to greet this toddler whisperer and saw...

"Brice Casey?" he exclaimed.

"Hey, dude!" the man answered with Becca by his side.

"What are you doing here?"

"I'm pretending to be a tiger," the guy answered, crawling into the center of the room as the children gathered around and joined in, all roaring and clawing at the air.

Georgie gasped. "He's like the Pied Piper of *Toddlerville*."

"How did you know what to do with them?" Jordan called.

"Casey Pest control has contracts with a bunch of different childcare locations. Sometimes, they invite me to play along. These little dudes are awesome."

Georgie lowered her voice. "Becca, why is Brice here? Is there a pest control emergency? Oh, my God! We don't have spiders, do we?" Georgie finished, going pale.

"No, he's not here for a pest control appointment," the woman answered, then glanced at Brice, who had sucked in his cheeks, pretending to be a fish while a school of toddlers copied him.

Jordan looked between Becca and the toddler wrangler. "Are you and Brice dating?"

"Yep," Brice answered, able to both entertain toddlers and engage in conversation, which he'd never realized was such a huge accomplishment until today.

Georgie turned to Becca and lowered her voice. "You guys are together?"

"Since we hooked up at your wedding," the man answered before Becca had a chance.

Becca blushed, but she didn't deny it. Unfortunately, Georgie had cocked her head and crossed her arms, going into surrogate big sister mode.

"You guys hooked up at our wedding, and now you're together?" his wife whispered-shouted as if she were cross-examining the woman.

"I didn't know how to tell you or my sister," Becca replied, her cheeks holding the blush.

Back in October, after Brice had picked them up off the side of the road and driven them to their wedding in his pest control van, they'd insisted he stay for the festivities. The event had been a whirlwind. Georgie's mother had invited half of Denver, and his focus hadn't been on keeping an eye on Becca or Brice. No, every time he thought of their wedding day, all he saw was Georgiana—the snarky, beautiful book nerd who had turned his world upside-down.

And he had Brice to thank for it.

Had Georgie not gone on a date with the man years ago and had the guy not acted like such a grade A douche canoe during their brief encounter, she wouldn't have been inspired to start her Own the Eights blog. Would the universe have found another way for their lives to literally collide? Possibly. But, like it or not, Brice Casey was the catalyst for everything that had happened from the moment his wife called him an asshat.

"Why are you smiling like that?" Georgie asked.

He met his wife's gaze. "I think it's great."

"What's great?" she pressed.

He glanced at the man surrounded by kids, prostrate on the ground, and inch-worming-it across the children's area.

"I think it's great that Becca and Brice are a couple."

"You do?" Becca replied.

He nodded. "If it wasn't for Brice, there might not be an us," he said to his wife and watched her features soften.

"That's true," Georgie answered.

He looked down at the plastic Faby in his arms. "Now, if Brice could help Georgie and I get our hands on a real baby to get some actual infant-care experience, I'd call him the perfect boyfriend."

"Dude," Brice called from the carpet, having switched to lying on his back and thrashing his limbs like a flipped turtle.

"Yeah."

"I can be your perfect boyfriend," Brice called, springing to his feet and leading the children in a toddler conga line.

Jordan sucked a breath of air in through his teeth. "Yeah, I'm all good on that front, buddy. I've got Georgie."

"No, dude! What I mean is that I can totally hook you up with a real baby."

"You can?"

"Yeah."

"When?"

Brice grinned. "Today!"

* * *

"Are you nervous?" he asked his wife, who was fiddling with the strap of her purse.

"Why? Are you?" she threw back.

He blew out a slow breath.

Never in a million years did he think he'd be driving to Brice Casey's sister's house. Honestly, he'd never wondered if the guy had a sister, a brother, a dog, or even a stamp collection. He'd never thought that much about the man, besides being grateful that he'd been an asshat to Georgie, which he knew would sound worse if he said that out loud. So, he'd decided to keep that little nugget to himself. But here they were—driving through Denver and headed to the home of the sibling of a guy he'd never expected to like.

"Brice seems to have come a long way," Georgie said.

"Yeah, he has."

"And, Becca's a smart woman. She wouldn't put up with any asshattery," his wife added with a teasing twinkle in her eyes.

He chuckled, thinking of Becca, the ballbuster. "No, I don't believe she would."

After the toddler story time, Georgie and Becca had a little heart-to-heart talk, looping in Irene on a video call. And from what he could hear, between the women giggling and talking over each other, it sounded like Brice was a decent guy. Yes, after several glasses of champagne, they'd hooked up at the wedding. But when Brice had asked to see her again, Becca had laid down an ultimatum. She told the pest control prince she'd only go out with him if he'd read every single Own the Eights blog post. Turns out, he did. She'd even quizzed him on it—and had the emails to prove it.

See...a real ballbuster.

A playful smirk pulled at the corners of his wife's mouth. "And Brice does have awfully good hair."

He laughed. "It's undeniable. Even after playing with the toddlers, not a hair was out of place."

Hey, it was the truth. The guy was blessed with a mop of shiny, shampoo-commercial-ready hair.

But, good hair aside, Brice had come through for them. And as long as he was good to Becca, he wouldn't have to pound the guy into next week.

After Brice had put the toddlers through the make-believe animal paces, he'd led them to the story time carpet. Georgie had read to the brood, and then he'd stepped in and led them in a rousing round of "Head, Shoulders, Knees, and Toes," which was pretty damn fun.

It wasn't the FBI experience they were expecting, but they'd pulled it off.

When the moms and dads arrived to collect their children, it looked like a scene from *Mary Poppins*. The parents gave them a round of applause as they finished off the activity with a little "Row, Row, Row Your Boat," complete with rowing actions.

"Do you remember how old Brice said his nephew was?" Georgie asked.

"Five months. He also mentioned that his sister just went back to work a few weeks ago."

Georgie took out her phone.

"What are you doing?" he asked, stopping at a red light.

"Scouring the web for some info on five-month-old babies."

"Smart! Get in a little research," he said, then raised his hand, and she gave him a high five.

"Okay. Here we go," Georgie began, gaze glued to her cell. "At five months, the baby is starting to sit up for longer periods of time but may need to be propped up to remain upright."

"Faby's got sitting down pat. Who knew Faby was so advanced," he said, glancing down at the baby doll sitting comfortably next to Georgie's feet.

"They're also starting to roll over at this age," Georgie continued.

"Ahh! Sorry, Faby! The real baby has got you there."

"Jordan, stop! You don't want to hurt Faby's feelings," Georgie mock-chided, biting back a grin.

"You're right. Don't feel bad, Faby. You'll always be the best fake baby," he said, reassuring a mannequin infant.

Georgie patted the doll's head. "Faby says thank you and wanted to let you know that you will always be the best Emperor of Asshattery."

He shrugged. "Thanks, Faby. It never hurts to be the best at something."

"And they like peek-a-boo," Georgie added.

He frowned. "Asshats like peek-a-boo?"

"No, silly! Five-month-old babies like peek-a-boo."

He turned down a street lined with tall oaks. "We can totally do peek-a-boo."

Georgie turned toward him, covered her face with her hands, then rocked a peek-a-boo like she was born to do it.

He shook his head and chuckled.

"I guess they do," she said to herself.

"What are you talking about, messy bun girl?"

"Asshats. They also find peek-a-boo amusing."

He parked the car in front of Brice's sister's house, then met his wife's lively gaze. "This peek-a-boo loving asshat sure loves you."

"I should hope so. I'm having this asshat's baby," she purred.

"And you have never been more beautiful or sexier," he said, lowering his voice.

She leaned across the console. "You like a little padding around the middle?"

He cupped her face in his hand, then stroked her cheek with his thumb. "You know, I do. Especially when you put on those cowgirl boots," he whispered against her lips before capturing her mouth in a slow kiss.

Georgie twisted her fingers into the hair at the nape of his neck. He would never tire of kissing this woman. He tilted her head, ready to deepen their kiss when a knock on the passenger side window had them pulling apart as if they were teens caught necking after curfew.

"Hey there! The babysitters aren't supposed to start making out until after the baby falls asleep," Becca said with her signature smart-ass smirk as Brice stood beside her with great hair.

Honestly, it was impossible not to notice.

Okay, that was weird.

He shook off the great hair thought, got out of the car, then went to Georgie's side to help her and Faby out.

"What are you guys doing here?" Georgie asked, shifting Faby to her other arm.

"Since Becca and I aren't watching my nephew, my sister suggested we join her and my brother-in-law for dinner," Brice answered.

"What does your sister do?" Georgie asked as the four-some plus Faby made their way up the path through a mani-cured front yard toward a charming ranch-style home.

"She's a doctor."

"No, I'm serious, Brice," Georgie replied with a chuckle.

"Yeah, so am I. Both my sister and my brother-in-law are doctors."

"Oh, okay," Georgie answered with a sheepish expression.

His wife immediately caught his eye and gave him wife eyes for *can-you-believe-that*. He shrugged and gave her husband eyes for *that's-crazy-I-never-imagined-any-sister-of-Brice-Casey-would-be-allowed-to-prescribe-medicine-for-actual-human-beings*.

It was a lot to convey with eyeballs, but when she gave a slight nod, he knew she'd gotten the gist.

Brice opened the front door. "Hey, Beavers! We're here!" he called.

Beavers?

Well, their family did own a pest control business. He was about to eyeball say this to Georgie when his wife gasped. He followed her gaze and couldn't believe his eyes.

Chapter Twelve
Georgie

"Dr. Beaver?" Georgie exclaimed, wide-eyed.

"Thanks for agreeing to watch Oliver," the man replied, advancing toward them from the back of the house.

"You're married to Brice's sister?" she asked.

"I am."

She stared at her obstetrician. He wasn't in his doctor's coat or wearing a lamp on his head, investigating her lady parts. But here, in Brice Casey's sister's house, stood Dr. Beaver. A man who had told her point-blank that he had a husband and two children.

"Are you leading a double life?" she pressed.

"Georgie," Jordan said under his breath, gesturing to a table dotted with framed photos, but she waved him off.

Dr. Beaver frowned. "I'm not sure that I'm following you."

She shifted Faby to the crook of her arm and pressed her hand to her chest. "Don't you recognize me?"

"Georgie," Jordan tried again, but she shook her head.

She could barely believe that they'd walked in on the type of situation usually reserved for works of fiction.

A man leading a double life.

Two families who never knew the other existed.

She thought of Dr. Beaver's husband—a man she'd never met but was sure he didn't deserve this. And what about the kids! Those poor kids. She didn't know a damn thing about them either, but they sure didn't deserve a two-timing, sneaky gynecologist for a father.

Despite her trifecta holding up signs with the words *stop talking* written in bold fictional letters, Georgie couldn't stop herself.

She narrowed her gaze and lowered her voice. "How do you do it? Do you go back and forth like a thief in the night? Does your wife know? Does your husband know?"

Becca cocked her head to the side. "Georgie, what are you talking about? Are you feeling all right? Is this some weird pregnancy delusion? Because you sound a little cuckoo."

Georgie glanced around the group, then held her doctor's gaze. "I'm Georgiana Jensen-Marks, and this is my husband, Jordan Marks. We saw you a few weeks ago for a check-up. You complimented my lady parts. You said I had a lovely uterus and a splendid cervix. Don't you remember? Or do you have so many secrets to keep that you can't even remember what you tell your patients—even the ones with great cervixes?"

She frowned at the sound of the word. "Or is it *cervi* like the plural of *cactus* is *cacti*?" She shook her head. "I don't know the plural of cervix, but you better believe that I'm going to find out."

She could feel her pregnancy hormones mixing with adrenaline. She was two-parts Wonder Woman and one-part mini pineapple gestater. A pregnant PI! What a discovery! What a baffling coincidence!

She turned to her husband. "How does he not recognize us?"

Jordan bit back a grin. "Because he's not your doctor."

What the hell was going on here? Was this some weird twilight zone pregnancy hallucination?

Just then, a woman holding a baby came toward them, sporting a wide grin. "Honey, you have got to tell your brother about this."

Georgie inspected Dr. Beaver again, taking in his chiseled cheekbones and his camera-ready pearly white smile.

This had to be her doctor.

"You're his wife?" she asked, and instantly, her heart went out to the new mother.

How would she break the news of her husband's betrayal? It was better to tell her, right? Better to rip the bandage off quickly and get it out there. She parted her lips to speak, but Brice's sister spoke first.

"I'm Briana Casey-Beaver, and this is my husband, Thad."

Heat rose to Georgie's cheeks. "Thad. Like *T-H-A-D*?"

"Yes."

"And you're sure it's not Chad. *C-H-A-D*?" she questioned.

"My name is Thad, and the plural or cervix is cervixes," the man—this so-called Thad—answered.

"A-ha!" she cried, pointing at the guy. "See, you are an ob-gyn!"

Thad's brows drew together. "Because I know the plural form of cervix?"

Brice raised his hand. "I know that one, too. *C-E-R-V-I-X-E-S*. Cervixes!" he replied as if he were in a spelling bee.

Georgie's gaze danced between the adults and the baby, all staring at her like she was a lunatic—which, she just might be.

Was she having a moment? Was she losing her mind? And to make matters worse, she was totally craving a giant glass of pineapple juice. The mixed signals coming from her pregnancy brain were enough to make her head explode.

"You must be a patient of my husband's twin brother. He and his husband moved to Denver with their kids recently," Briana said, gesturing to a photo on the foyer table with two remarkably similar-looking men dressed in tennis whites.

Twin brothers.

And then it hit her. While clutching a baby doll inside a stranger's home, she'd accused a man of leading a double life in front of his wife and child. She took a woozy step back.

"Are you all right? Would you like to sit down?" the doctor, who'd never examined her cervix, asked gently.

She steadied herself, then stilled, paralyzed by mortification, and closed her eyes.

Jordan rubbed her back. "Maybe you should sit."

She shook her head. "Give me a second. I'm hoping the ground will swallow me up, but that doesn't seem to be happening," she replied with a wince of a smile before opening her eyes to find that, yes, she'd gone full-on prego-cray-cray in a private residence owned by people she'd never met before.

Her trifecta threw up their hands and shook their fictional heads. She couldn't fault them. They'd tried to stop her.

Georgie turned to the doctors. "I am so sorry. I don't know what came over me."

Briana shared a look with her husband, then chuckled. "You have nothing to worry about. I think an overactive imagination is a symptom of pregnancy. When I was pregnant with Ollie, I had the most vivid dreams."

"And don't forget the grocery store incident," Thad said, tossing his wife a wink.

Briana's cheeks grew rosy. "Oh, yes, the grocery store."

"What happened at the grocery store?" Georgie asked, grateful she wasn't the only one who'd had an embarrassing pregnancy moment.

Briana shifted the baby in her arms. "I thought there was a conspiracy to hide the tapioca pudding. I craved the stuff like a maniac when I was pregnant, and they always seemed to be out when we were there to shop. Well, one afternoon, the store had been sold out one time too many for my liking, and I went toe to toe with the poor dairy manager, accusing him of treacherous tapioca trickery."

Thad nodded. "It's true. My neurosurgeon wife is now known as the treacherous tapioca trickster in the market's dairy department. And her reputation seems to have spread. They watch her like a hawk in the deli. It's only a matter of time before they hear about her in the meat and seafood section," the man teased.

Becca glanced at her watch. "Speaking of time, Brice and I should head over to the restaurant to make sure we don't miss our reservation, especially since we're celebrating Thad's last night."

Georgie's gaze zeroed-in on Thad. "You're leaving?"

He put up his hands in mock-defense. "I am. But I promise. It's not to go visit a secret family. Briana and I both work with Doctors Without Borders. But now that we have Ollie, I'll be going alone this time."

"How long will you be gone?" Jordan asked.

"I'm headed to Central America for eight weeks."

"Putting brains back together. That's my brother-in-law," Brice chimed, slapping the man on the shoulder.

Becca took her boyfriend's hand. "Briana and Thad, we'll meet you at the restaurant. Georgie," her friend added, turning a pointed gaze her way.

"Yes."

"Are you good on the pregnant lady freak-out front? You're not about to accuse the neighbors of running an illegal gambling ring, are you?" her friend asked, but the woman was holding back a grin.

"There will be no more accusations tonight. Cross my heart," she answered, knowing that once Becca mentioned this to her sister, she'd never live it down.

Still, in her defense, how many pregnant women have run into their handsome obstetrician's identical twin brother? It couldn't be that common.

While Brice and Becca said their goodbyes to baby Oliver, she leaned in toward her husband and lowered her voice.

"You should have stopped me from acting like a pregnant police interrogator."

"I tried, babe. You were on quite a tear. If the bookshop and blogging thing ever get boring, you should apply to work for the real FBI. That was quite a shakedown," he whispered back with that cocky smirk of his.

She was about to tell her beloved asshat that he was going to receive quite a shakedown as soon as they got home when Briana closed the door behind Becca and Brice and turned to them.

"Let's head back to the kitchen."

"Thanks for not kicking us out," Jordan said.

Georgie nodded. "Yes, thank you. And I promise. I'm

not a crazy lady. I'm sure that's what crazy people say, but I can tell you, I'm not," she added, then cringed.

Honestly, she needed to travel with a roll of duct tape—or maybe a big can of pineapple chunks. If she were eating, that sure would have stopped her from talking.

Thad waved for them to follow him down the hall. "It's not every day that we get a guest, armed with a doll, accusing me of leading a double life. I can't wait to tell my brother. He'll get such a kick out of this," the man said over his shoulder as they entered the spacious kitchen.

Georgie glanced at Faby and felt her cheeks heat. "For the record, the doll is for a baby prep class Jordan and I are taking. But it's not half as cute as your little one," she added, waving at the child in Briana's arms.

"In all the commotion, I forgot to introduce you to Oliver," Briana replied, then snuggled the sweet boy, who sported quite a lovely head of baby hair.

Good hair must be in the Casey genes.

"He's beautiful," Georgie answered, watching the boy take in the world with inquisitive blue eyes.

She hadn't spent much time with infants—ever. Families with little ones came into her shop, but she couldn't remember the last time she'd held a real baby.

The little boy reached out, and without thinking, she supplied her finger. The baby squealed with delight, then flashed a toothless grin before making raspberry lips at her.

"Look, he already likes you, Georgie," Briana cooed.

"We appreciate you volunteering to watch Ollie. Becca and Brice had offered to babysit. It's so nice that they'll be able to join us tonight," Thad said, pulling out an empty baby bottle from the cabinet.

"We're going to miss Daddy, aren't we, Ollie? But

Grandma and Grandpa and Uncle Brice will help us out," Briana said, making a silly face at the baby.

"That's great that you've got your family close by to help," Jordan replied.

"How about you guys? Do you have relatives in town?" Briana asked as the baby reached for Thad, and she passed the sweet tot over to his father.

"We do," Jordan answered.

"It's a lifesaver when you have a little one. That's for sure. Especially with me going back to work," Briana offered as she took over bottle duty.

Georgie nodded as a pang of guilt settled in her chest. When would she tell her mother? She had no idea. No time ever seemed to be the right time.

"Do you mind me asking how far along you are?" Briana asked.

Georgie caressed her little bump. "A couple days shy of eighteen weeks."

"That's when I was itching to tell everyone I was pregnant and not some wild woman downing pints of tapioca pudding."

Georgie switched Faby to her other arm. "When did you share your pregnancy news?"

"A little after I was twenty-two weeks along. After the ultrasound where we found out the gender and learned this sweet boy was on his way," Briana answered, tapping the tip of her baby's nose.

Georgie shared a glance with her husband. "You did? You waited that long?"

Briana blew out a tight breath. "We did. My family is great, but they can go a little overboard. I'm not sure if you can relate."

"I can," Georgie replied, and the worry she'd been

carrying from the moment the first set of pink lines appeared waned a fraction.

Perhaps she wasn't a terrible person for keeping her mom out of the pregnancy loop.

Briana opened a canister printed with a baby's face, then frowned. "Thad, we'll need to pick up some more formula on the way home tonight. We have just enough to make one more bottle." She turned to them and sighed. "We're constantly forgetting to buy baby formula at the grocery store. With me going back to work, we switched from breast milk a couple of weeks ago," she finished, filling the bottle with water, then adding the last of the formula powder.

"Have you started him on solids yet?" Jordan asked, and Georgie's ears perked up.

Someone has been doing a little late-night baby research.

"We've introduced a little bit of rice cereal," Thad answered.

Jordan nodded, then shifted his weight from foot to foot. "Have you signed Oliver up for the baby NFL?"

Thad and Briana stared at her husband.

"There's a football league for babies?" Thad questioned.

Jordan shook his head. "No, it's not a baby football league. It's something I'd heard a few dads talking about."

The doctors nodded warily, but her husband didn't seem to notice their perplexed expressions and pressed on.

"Have you looked into trumpet lessons or having your son play the viola?" he continued, and ding, ding, ding! Her little double life outburst was starting to look a lot less crazy.

At least she wasn't the only one who would make a fool of themselves tonight.

Thad glanced at his son. "Oliver's not even able to use a spoon. How would he hold a bow or manage a trumpet?"

"Great point!" Jordan replied, clearly going for nonchalance but tanking. "I'd heard a few things, here and there, when it came to raising a well-rounded child."

"We're going to let Ollie be a baby," Thad answered.

Jordan gave an exaggerated nod. "Right! Because he is a baby. He's a real baby. No offense, Faby," he added, addressing the fake baby in her arms—as nutjobs do.

"Will Ollie need to be bathed?" she asked Briana, doing her best to change the subject.

It was that or stuff Faby's head into Jordan's mouth before he asked another wacky child-rearing question.

Briana shook the bottle, then tested a drop of the liquid on the back of her wrist. "No, Thad bathed him before you got here. It's getting close to Ollie's bedtime. All you'll need to do is give him his bottle and rock him a bit. He's a good little sleeper. I don't think he'll give you any trouble. Thad, why don't you pass Ollie to Georgie and let him get used to her."

The man, who was not her obstetrician, glanced at his wife.

"Honey, we're getting a night out," Briana said, raising an eyebrow.

"Right!" the guy replied, springing into action.

"Are you able to put the doll down?" Briana asked.

Georgie startled. "Sorry! Sometimes, I forget I'm holding it. I'm so used to carrying it everywhere," she answered, setting Faby on the kitchen table, then swallowed past the lump in her throat.

This was it. No more mannequin infant—at least, for the next few hours. But they were ready. They'd practiced diapering and feeding. Yes, it was on a doll, but it was better than nothing.

"You're going to spend some time with Georgie and Jordan tonight, big guy," Thad said to his son before placing the child in her arms.

And...*wow*!

The little boy looked up at her with twinkling eyes, pursed his real baby lips, then blew another raspberry.

"You're very good at making that noise," she said, holding the child's gaze and swaying side to side.

The motion came naturally as she adjusted the baby in her arms. Not surprising, Ollie weighed a heck of a lot more than Faby. But it wasn't only his size that had her heart hammering. The warmth of him and the gentle movement of his chest as he breathed sent, not a shiver through her body, but more of a wave—a calming shift, triggering a soothing sensation.

She felt her husband beside her and met his gaze. The mountain of a man patted the baby's head as a look of wonder overtook his features, and she knew he was thinking the exact same thing as she was.

In a matter of months, this would be their life.

"Here's the bottle," Briana said, handing it to Jordan, then retrieving her purse from where it sat on the kitchen island.

Thad's face lit up. "We don't have to take the diaper bag with us tonight."

"Or the stroller or the wearable sling," Briana listed, grinning ear to ear.

"Or the baby booster seat," Thad finished.

Georgie glanced between the parents, who'd grown positively giddy.

"We've got the emergency numbers tacked to the fridge,

and you can't miss Ollie's room. It's the one with the crib. He's already in his pajamas. So, you should be good to go," Briana said over her shoulder as she and Thad high-tailed it down the hall and out the door.

And then, it was the three of them.

Georgie glanced around the kitchen, hardly able to believe that she and Jordan were truly tasked with caring for a human baby.

"I think they wanted a night out," she said, staring at the closed door.

"You'd have to be pretty desperate. I don't know if I would have left my kid. You accused the dad of leading a double life, and I asked them if they'd enrolled their child in an infant football league," he replied, running his hand down his face and shaking his head when little Ollie opened his mouth and belted out quite a yawn.

"I think this fellow is ready for bed," Jordan said softly.

As if on cue, Ollie nuzzled into her and let loose another sleepy yawn.

"He's awfully relaxed," she replied, adjusting her hold on his cherub-chub body.

Jordan looked around. "Where do you think we should give him his bottle? Out here or in his room?"

She scanned the kitchen that led into a cozy living room. "Briana said he liked to be rocked, but I don't see a rocking chair out here."

"Let's try his room," Jordan said, then turned to head toward the other side of the house.

"Wait," she called.

"What is it?"

She grinned up at him. "Why don't you carry the baby."

"Me?" he asked with a stunned expression.

"Yeah, it's amazing. You've got to hold him."

Jordan brushed his finger over the boy's tiny knuckles. "He's so small."

She gazed down at the baby's sweet face. "But he's also a snuggle bug. How about this? I'll do the bottle part. You do the transport."

Jordan blew out a tight breath and did a little boxer jog, prancing back and forth.

She frowned. "What are you doing?"

"Loosening up," he replied, shaking out his arms.

"You'll be carrying a baby, not a five-hundred-pound tractor tire."

"You've got a point," he replied, nixing the pre-conditioning moves.

"Are you ready?" she asked.

Carefully, as if they were orchestrating the handoff of an extremely volatile object, Jordan moved in a step closer. It was like in the movies, where the hero has retrieved something highly explosive, and then must hand it off to the bomb squad.

With exquisite precision, Jordan cradled his arms below hers as they transferred the baby into his strong embrace.

It could have been seconds, minutes, or hours. Time stood still.

Okay, time didn't actually stop. In all fairness, it was probably more like eight seconds. But it was the eight most cautious seconds of their lives.

"I'm doing it, Georgie," he said, grinning like he'd won the lottery as he stared down at Ollie, cradled in his muscled arms.

"Now, you have to carry him to his room," she said, still in hazardous bomb diffusing mode.

He frowned. "Not yet. We need a plan. You should scout out the house and find his room first."

"Good idea."

She hurried down the hall. The Casey-Beavers lived in a one-story sprawling ranch, and—thank God—they wouldn't have to negotiate the horrors of a staircase. Stealthily making her way down the corridor, she spied the target.

A white door with *Oliver* painted in whimsical lettering.

Bingo!

She raised her arms, channeling an enthusiastic tour guide, and waved for Jordan to join her.

"Easy," she cautioned as he grew cocky and picked up a little too much steam for her liking.

Step by step, her big strong husband made his way toward her as little Ollie went on a raspberry bender. If she hadn't known that the man was holding a baby, it would have sounded as if he'd just departed a bean eating contest —and won—by a landslide or a bean slide.

She chuckled to herself.

"What's so funny?" Jordan asked, arriving with Ollie. "Wait, let me guess. Farting humor?"

She nodded as the boy released another rip-roaring raspberry, making her point.

She opened the door as Ollie shot off a few more. They stood in the doorway to the baby's room and assessed the dim space. With a rocking chair in the corner next to a wooden crib, the room most definitely belonged to the little raspberry machine. A small lamp cast a dim golden glow, highlighting a dresser equipped with a changing table and a precious mural of a mountain scene, complete with skiers peppering the slope.

"Why don't you sit in the chair, and I'll pass him over to

you," Jordan offered as Ollie continued to serenade them with fart chorale.

She entered the baby powder-scented room, placed the bottle on a side table, then settled herself in the rocking chair.

"Are you ready?" he whispered.

She flashed her husband two thumbs-up. "We are a go for bottle time."

So far, so good! They'd successfully moved the baby from point A to point B.

The next challenge: filling him up with formula.

With the ease of a man who's done a bazillion squats, Jordan lowered himself, inch by inch, positioning the baby into her arms.

"And three, two, one. We have infant touchdown," he said through a sweet smile.

Yep, they were NASA-level baby passers.

The boy wiggled in her arms, then smacked his lips. She took a breath as Jordan handed her the bottle.

Real baby. Real bottle.

"I'm going in," she said, then brushed the bottle's nipple across his lips.

"Easy," Jordan cautioned.

"And contact," she whispered as the baby stopped dropping raspberries and started sucking the hell out of his dinner.

"Wow, he's a total pro, and with all those raspberries, he probably could play the trumpet," Jordan offered, pulling over an ottoman and sitting down to watch Oliver down eight ounces of formula as if he'd just finished a baby Iron Man.

Shrouded in the dim light and surrounded by stuffed animals, she leaned down and smelled Ollie's head.

"He smells like spring rain."

Jordan rested his hand on her knee and rubbed gentle circles with his thumb. "I wouldn't know. All I've been able to smell for the last few months is pineapple from those dryer sheets," he teased.

She gazed down at the boy. "He's precious, isn't he?"

"Yeah, he sure is."

She pulled her gaze away from the child and met her husband's eye. "Do you have a preference?"

"For what?"

"For us. Do you think we'll have a boy or a girl?"

"I don't think of our baby like that," he said as the light played off his dark tangle of hair.

"I hate to break it to you, but babies don't come out gender-neutral like our Faby," she answered, but Jordan wasn't trying to be funny or evasive.

His expression grew pensive. "I don't mean it like that. I think of our baby more like a part of us. No matter if it's a boy or a girl, we'll be a family, and this baby will be our everything."

She blinked back tears.

"Are you all right? Are you hungry? Do you need to eat some pineapple? I've got five cans in the back of the car—in case of a pineapple emergency."

She sniffled, overcome with emotion. "No, it's not a pineapple emergency."

"Then what?" he whispered.

"That might be one of the sweetest things you've ever said. And when I met you, you were such an asshat," she answered on a teary exhale.

He cupped her face in his warm hand. "I love you, too, messy bun girl."

Ollie turned his head from side to side, and she pulled

the bottle back and handed it to Jordan. She rocked back and forth, inhaling the baby's sweet scent. He released a lazy sigh before closing his eyes—so trusting and so innocent. She stared at his little nose and his delicate eyelashes, resting on porcelain cheeks, and all her worries about her mother's reaction melted away. She'd been consumed with anxiety, wondering if she had what it took to be a mom, worrying she couldn't do it all.

She stopped rocking and watched the baby sleep in her arms.

"I know when I want to tell my mom and Howard about the pregnancy," she said, meeting Jordan's gaze.

"You do?"

She nodded. "After the Battle of the Births gender reveal. It's only a month away, and then, not only will we be telling them about the pregnancy, we'll know if we'll be welcoming a little miss or a little mister."

"What do you think we're having?" he asked, rubbing sweet, slow circles on her knee.

She relaxed into the rocker. For the first time in a long time, the twist of nerves in her chest loosened. Her breathing matched that of the peaceful, sleeping infant in her arms, and she exhaled a slow breath that seemed a long time coming.

An easy smile pulled at the corners of her lips as she gazed at the man, perched on a little blue ottoman, ready to give her and their baby the world. Perhaps, it was the cheesecake or the pineapple juice she drank before they'd left, but a slight flutter tickled in her belly.

"I don't know, but in a few weeks, we're going to find out."

Chapter Thirteen
Jordan

Jordan cracked open his eyes and glanced out the window. A silvery haze hung in the darkness, signaling first light was at least a few hours off. His best guess? It had to be somewhere between four and five in the morning—probably closer to four. He shifted his large frame and untangled his legs from the bedsheet.

He'd always been a morning person—a morning person whose day usually started closer to seven a.m. rather than four. Still, he wasn't complaining.

He rolled over and reached for his wife. But he wasn't surprised to find her side of the bed empty. He was about to pull up the covers and get in a few more z's when the clap of a cabinet, or maybe it was a door clicking shut, caught his attention.

Nesting.

That's what Maureen had called it when he'd asked her what had happened to his wife, who, up until about a month ago, enjoyed sleeping until at least eight in the morning.

Now, she rose before the ass crack of dawn to reorder

the spice rack, alphabetize their takeout menus, or empty out the linen closet, only to rewash and refold their sheets, blankets, and towels, then methodically place them back in their original resting spot. During another dawn nesting session, she'd doled out his protein powder, putting a perfectly measured scoop into forty reusable baggies so he wouldn't have to measure the mixture when he was making his morning energy shake.

It was damn kind of her.

She was an unstoppable organizing force of gestating nature. A few days ago, in a three-hour block of frenzied pregnancy persistence, he'd awoken to find that she'd assembled the baby's crib and had reread half of *Pride and Prejudice*—at the same time. She'd explained that the process of going back and forth, her mind nourished by Austen's prose, gave her the wherewithal to decipher the assembly instructions he would have sworn were crafted by a drunken toddler.

God help any piece of clutter, non-assembled furniture, or stray item that entered Georgiana Jensen-Marks' orbit.

But it wasn't only the nesting that signaled the progression of the pregnancy. Clocking in at twenty-three weeks, there was no hiding the little human residing in Georgie's belly. With her rounded abdomen and smelling of pineapple, she was beautiful and radiant—the picture of citrus-scented maternal bliss. Still, it also wasn't the nesting instinct that had ushered in the return of her easy smile and sparkling eyes.

After their night babysitting little Ollie, a weight had lifted from his wife's shoulders. He'd seen the distinct shift with his own eyes because he'd experienced it himself.

When it came to the question of fatherhood, he'd wrestled with his own demons. While other couples planned when they wanted to start trying to conceive, he and Georgie had landed right in the thick of it. And with the most stressful of times, he and his wife were prone to fall back on the things that served them the least.

For him, it was that itch to be the best.

The drive to push harder hadn't vanished. It would always be there. What he'd learned from his wild Georgie-Jensen-infused life was how and where to focus that energy.

Did he always get it right?

No.

Had he gone to the baby NFL website six thousand times and almost registered a non-existent child to join the tot league? Maybe. Fine, yes! But he knew better.

Their journey to the altar had taught him that while he wasn't about to change her and she wasn't about to change him, they could refocus and reframe any situation to make it work—and that happened by supporting one another.

That was their path. A continuum of learning and laughing and falling more in love with this woman with each twist and turn the universe threw their way.

He listened as Georgie's footsteps drew closer, reached beneath the bed, then swiped a bottle of an electrolyte-infused sports drink.

She may be eating for two, but he had to maintain his strength as well...for other activities.

While his wife enjoyed nesting on her own in the early morning hours, there was one particular activity where she sought his company.

Namely, doing the naughty—a lot.

If he had to name this portion of the pregnancy, he'd call it the Nesting and Naughtiness phase.

This little pregnancy perk wasn't something he'd been expecting.

They had a terrific sex life. Cars, couches, tents, more cars, offices, barns, beds, chairs, tables, in front of an alpaca —there was not a bad place to get down and dirty with his wife.

Scratch that. He didn't recommend having a member of the camel family intrude when knocking boots in the great outdoors—otherwise, he was always game.

All the same, when it came to pregnancy and sex, he'd figured there might be a lull or at least a drop in demand. She was, of course, growing a person. If it were him, or probably any other male on the planet tasked with being a walking incubator, he'd take the entire forty weeks off.

But holy hell! He'd misjudged that assumption by a mile.

A clickity-clack coming from outside their bedroom sent his pulse racing. He took a quick swig of his sports drink, then slid the bottle back into its hiding place under the bed as a heady jolt of excitement coursed through his body in anticipation.

Who would he meet this morning?

Georgie opened the door, and he gazed at her silhouette. Yesterday, she'd come in wearing boots and a cowgirl hat. They'd reenacted the naughty rancher's daughter scenario, which had become one of his favorites. They had to get more creative with their sexual positions, thanks to his wife's blossoming body, and that's where a well-loved book came into play. After consulting their worn copy of the *Kama Sutra*, his dirty cowgirl rode his hard length like the rodeo beauty queen temptress she was.

That was the best part of this nesting business. It usually ended with his wife organizing her old costumes, and then, modeling an outfit for him in the wee hours of the morning.

He narrowed his gaze in the dim light and took in the splendor of his wife. The hem of her costume caressed her upper thighs, revealing her smooth, toned legs. The bedroom door creaked open a few more inches and let in the light from the hallway. And anchors away, his blood supply headed south.

Standing in front of him was the sexiest sailor he'd ever set eyes on. In a short, pleated dress with a folded collar adorned with shiny gold stars and a red bow resting below her ample breasts, his wife had him giving her a morning salute.

"What do you think?" she asked.

But before he could answer, the clickity-clack was back as Georgie busted out a four a.m. tap routine—all with Faby in her arms.

"I think you've sold yourself short on the skill set you developed when you were a teenager on the pageant circuit," he said as his wife tapped out a rhythm, then set the fake baby on the bedside table with a pizazz not often exhibited at the crack of dawn.

"Oh yeah?" she replied, doing a shimmy twirl that revealed her bare ass hidden beneath the pleated layers.

He should take another gulp of his sports drink, but that would mean taking his eyes off his sexy sailor wife. Nope, that one sip would have to sustain him, no matter what sexual acrobatics his wife demanded.

He propped himself up and took in the full splendor of this morning's randy role-play costume. The snug white sequined sailor dress accentuated her baby bump as well as her heaving breasts, which had him at full mast. And while the costume designer of this gem probably never would have predicted that this garment would be worn for a session of early morning hanky-panky, he sent a quick thank you out into the universe for seamstresses everywhere.

But he forgot all about costume design when he watched Georgie tap dance her way to the other side of the room. With her back to him, she leaned over and pressed her palms to the top of their dresser. The pleats of the sailor suit skimmed her legs, exposing the taut globes of her ass, and he flexed his fingers—his digits aching to grip the supple flesh.

Georgie glanced over her shoulder. "The captain says we've got rough seas ahead, and I need a strong deckhand to get me through the storm."

She'd gotten damn good at the role-play dirty talk. But two could play at that, and he was always up for sharpening his skill set.

Naked as the day he was born, he maneuvered his large frame out of bed and sauntered over to his wife. These days, it made things easier to go to bed naked. And he was rewarded for the gesture when Georgie's gaze dropped to his hard length, and a mischievous smile pulled at the corners of her mouth.

This sexy sailor didn't mind his lack of sleeping attire one bit.

He came up behind her and met her gaze in the mirror that hung on the wall above the dresser.

"Sounds like you're in need of a seaman."

God's honest truth? Seaman is a funny-ass word—except when your wife is dressed in a sequined sailor suit, bent over in front of a mirror and beckoning for a deckhand. Then, the word sounds as naughty as hell.

"Do you think you're up for the task? It could get dangerous, Seaman Marks," she purred—and again, there was nothing silly about seamen.

He pressed his rock-hard cock against her ass, then ran his hands up the sides of her body. His wife arched into him as he massaged her breasts, barely contained in the costume's bodice. He kissed the delicate skin below her earlobe and watched in the mirror, like a predator assessing his prey, as she parted her lips and gasped.

"I can handle dangerous," he whispered against the shell of her ear.

"And wet. It's going to get very, very wet," she rasped on a heated exhale.

If she ever tired of blogging, she'd be an ace at scripting NC-17 flicks.

He reached between her thighs and caressed her most sensitive place. "You weren't kidding. You're soaked," he growled, then rocked his palm against her tight bundle of nerves as he teased her slick entrance with his fingertip.

But his wife was greedy. A click and a clack cut through her lusty moans as she spread her legs, granting him complete access. He worked her in perfect rhythmic circles, rubbing her sweet bud and driving her toward wanton release.

"Hold on to your hat, sailor girl. It's about to get rough," he said, reveling in the quickening of her sultry, audible breaths.

"I don't have to hold on to my hat. I have mad bobby pin skills. A tsunami couldn't knock this sucker off," she whispered, then gasped for breath.

He slid his hand from her breasts to her neck, then angled her head back, capturing her mouth in a fiery kiss. With the passion of an angry, roiling sea, he thrust his hard length past her delicate folds. She tightened around him, taking each hard, thick inch of him. He released her mouth and inhaled a sharp breath. The sensation of plunging deep inside his wife never dulled. It never ceased to send an electric charge racing through his body. He glanced into the mirror and locked onto her gaze.

"Jordan," she whispered, her eyes hungry with need, her bottom lip trembling with desire.

The costumes and the dirty talk made it fun, but this moment, in these precious seconds when he saw forever in her eyes, this was when he lost any inhibition and gave in to desire.

Lost in her blue-green gaze, he set a deliciously frenzied pace, bringing her right to the edge before pulling back. But the measured thrust of their lovemaking quickly transformed into an impassioned raging storm—their sweat-slick bodies moving together in wave after furious wave.

Georgie cried out, and carnal victory tore through him as she reached back and gripped his muscled forearm, riding the rough seas into orgasmic oblivion. Her heated center, slippery with desire, tightened around his hard length and sent him overboard into the churning sea of sweet release. They rode each crashing wave, winding down slowly, and soon, her lithe frame rested, warm and pliable, in his arms.

He pressed a kiss to her shoulder and inhaled her sweet scent when a gentle pulse fluttered against his palm, pressed to her abdomen.

"Is that the baby?" he asked, scared to move or even breathe.

Still wearing the sailor hat, his wife nodded.

"Is it kicking?" he whispered.

He hated referring to their alien peanut blueberry turned mini pineapple turned little mango as an *it*. But they still didn't know their child's gender. While they'd had the ultrasound to determine the sex, the results had been sent to

Lenny and Stu for the big Battle of the Births reveal, happening later today.

Her expression softened. "Yes, that's the baby."

He met Georgie's gaze in the mirror and gasped when the flutter-pulse happened again.

Gently, he rubbed the spot where his wife's belly inhabitant had kicked. "What does it feel like for you?"

"Strangely awesome. Does that make sense?" she answered.

"Yeah, it does." He waited for the subtle sensation to return, but the place once pulsing with life went still.

"It looks like we're all early risers," she said.

And then it hit him.

They'd had sex—like, really good naughty sailor sex—and the baby was awake for it.

He carefully pulled out, stepped back, then stumbled to sit on the edge of the bed.

"What's wrong?" she asked, plucking a tissue to do a little post-sex cleanup.

He wasn't an idiot. He understood anatomy. The baby didn't know what they were doing or that his cock had been inserted into the baby escape route. Still, it was surreal.

He blew out a breath. "I just realized we had sex."

"You just realized that?" she asked with a playful twist to her lips, then clickity-clacked it over to the bed and sat beside him.

He chuckled and took her hand into his. "Believe me. I know we had sex. It's..."

"What?" she asked softly.

"That was the first time I felt the baby move, and we'd..."

"Did the naughty while pretending to be sailors lost at sea?" she supplied.

"It's a big moment, and you're dressed as a sexy sailor, and I'm buck naked."

"The doctor said sex is completely safe for us, and the baby's fine." She threaded their fingers and gave his hand a squeeze. "Now, I don't think our predawn sexcapades is something we'll want to add to the baby book."

He stared into the eyes of the woman who could quell his fears with one snarky comment. "Best to keep this aspect of the pregnancy between the two of us."

"Would you like to see something else that we should keep between the two of us?" she asked, going all sly sailor.

That was a no brainer.

"Hell yes!" he exclaimed.

"Would you like to see my pageant act?"

His eyes went wide.

She giggled. "It's nothing naughty, Seaman Marks. Just listen," she instructed, then clicked her heels and started tapping out the tune to "Row, Row, Row, Your Boat."

He reared back, damn impressed and about to tell her so when a sharp ping cut through the *merrily, merrily* part.

He glanced around the room. "What is that? Did you turn on the oven, or is that the kitchen timer?"

She shook her head. "No, this morning, I stuck to organizing my historical romances by period. I don't know what that noise is."

"Commence Hospital Practice Run. Commence Hospital Practice Run," came the same creepy robotic voice he'd heard during their VR grocery store nightmare.

They turned as the eerie robotic voice continued repeating the phrase, and he damn near fell off the bed when he figured out where it was coming from.

"Faby?" he cried, staring at the fake baby, whose head glowed red—its baby eyes flashing like a beacon to hell.

"The timer has started. Commence Hospital Practice Run," the possessed Faby commanded.

Of all the times for this challenge to happen—this had to be the worst!

"Georgie, we have to get to the hospital!"

Lenny and Stu had mentioned they'd need to complete a hospital practice run. But what they'd failed to disclose was that the command would be sent by their infant care simulation doll.

They must have activated Faby while he and Georgie were getting crapped on by the VR baby.

Georgie sprang to her feet and scooped up the glowing fake baby. "Have you always been able to talk, Faby? Can you hear me?"

"We have to get moving. This is for the Battle of the Births," he said, pulling on a pair of jeans and a T-shirt.

"I have to change," she cried, looking around the room.

"Fifteen minutes remaining," Faby instructed.

Fifteen minutes!

"Babe, there's no time. This is the drill. We have to make it to the hospital in—"

"Fourteen minutes," Faby answered.

He broke out into a cold sweat, then forced himself to take a breath. Georgie's bag was packed. The car was gassed up. They had a plan.

"I'll keep Faby with me and make sure Mr. Tuesday is safe in his crate," Georgie offered.

He nodded. "And I'll get the bag and pull up the car."

"Thirteen minutes," Faby announced.

"Go, go, go!" he cried, the competitive part of him, pumped and ready to crush this challenge.

The hospital was nine minutes away. They could do this.

He grabbed Georgie's suitcase and the baby carrier. He'd installed the infant car seat unit last week, per Lenny and Stu's instructions. He'd thought it was a little early to worry about that, but their hospital dry run must have been the reason why.

He slowed his breathing, going into focused trainer mode as his mind methodically fixated on the task at hand.

Bag. Baby carrier. Car keys. Wallet.

He was a man on a mission with—

"Twelve minutes remaining," came Faby's super-creepy robot voice, counting down from somewhere in the house.

He gathered the essential items and flew out the door. The adrenaline in his bloodstream centered him, driving him to move with the agility of a cheetah—the stealth of a jaguar, the concentration of a hawk.

He clicked the car seat into place and set the hospital bag beside it. Before he could blink, he was in the driver's seat and poised behind the wheel.

A man on a mission.

And Denver, we have ignition.

The email regarding the Battle of the Births hospital practice run had conveyed that Stu and Lenny would be at the hospital, waiting to do a debrief, and assigning points to those couples who successfully made it to the hospital in the allotted time.

However, there was nothing about a Faby creepy voice countdown. He'd figured the challenge would come via text. But he was ready. He gripped the steering wheel and narrowed his gaze. Grand Prix drivers had nothing on him as he sped down the street this fine, crisp morning until a faint sound caught his attention.

"Hey, Emperor of Asshattery! Stop!"

His heart jumped into his throat.

Only one person called him by that name.

With a piercing squeal, he slammed on the brakes as the BMW came to a screeching halt, and the scent of burning rubber infiltrated his nostrils. His gaze swept to the passenger seat—the empty passenger seat—and he knew he was toast.

He glanced in the rearview mirror to find his pregnant wife, running down the middle of the road, carrying a demon-glowing doll, and wearing a cardigan over a sequined sailor costume.

Christ! Of all the things to forget!

He threw the car into park and busted out of the vehicle.

"I'm sorry, Georgie!" he cried, sprinting toward her as the clickity-clack of her tap shoes grew louder.

"What were you thinking?" she gasped, holding her belly as they met in the middle of the road.

"I was focused on my tasks. You know, bag, baby carrier, car keys, wallet."

"And wife!" she yelled as she headed for the car with him a step behind.

"Yes, you're right! Bag, baby carrier, car keys, wallet, and *wife*," he repeated, helping her into the vehicle when the *whoop, whoop* of a police car siren cut through the air and the flash of blue and red reflected off the car's window.

Perfect. Their early morning antics had attracted the Denver PD.

The police car pulled up behind their BMW, and the officer exited the vehicle.

"Everything all right, sir?"

"Nine minutes," came the robotic voice of their demon fake baby.

He mustered up what he'd hoped looked like the

expression of a decent, law-abiding citizen because he was! Unfortunately, this early morning *pregnant-lady-chasing-a-car* ruckus probably appeared otherwise.

"I'm sure this looks strange, but we've got everything under control, Officer."

The man frowned, unconvinced. "I was passing by and noticed a pregnant woman running down the street, chasing after your car."

Yup, exactly what he was worried about.

"I can imagine you don't see that every day," he replied, doing his best to play it cool and keep it light.

The officer gave him the once-over. "Yes, this is a new one for me. And you're not wearing any shoes, sir."

Jordan stared down at his bare feet and shook his head. "Bag, baby carrier, car keys, wallet, wife, *shoes*," he mumbled. He needed to write this down.

"What was that, sir?" the officer asked, his frown deepening.

"Sorry, I was reciting a list."

"Sir, have you been drinking?"

"It's barely six in the morning," he fired back.

The officer crossed his arms. "That's not an answer, sir."

The minutes—the precious minutes—were ticking away!

How the hell would he explain this?

Sorry, Officer. No, I haven't been drinking. Our demon-talking doll told us that we needed to get into the car and drive like maniacs to do a hospital practice-run that will earn us badly needed points in the Battle of the Births. Except, I forgot my wife, so that's why she's yelling and chasing after the car.

No! Even in his shoeless, addled state, he knew that would not help get them on their way. In fact, that monologue sounded like the perfect way to initiate a psych hold.

Georgie exited their SUV and pulled the cardigan closed, but it was no use. The sun glinted off the sequins as if she were a pregnant disco ball.

"Hello, there! Sorry for the commotion, Officer. Can we wrap this up? We're in a bit of a hurry."

Jordan ran his hands down his face. This wasn't good. He should have gone with the demon-talking doll story.

The officer stared at his wife and cocked his head to the side. "Are you headed to a costume party?"

"No, the hospital," she answered.

He had to give it to her. For someone wearing a sparkly sailor suit and tap shoes, she carried herself with exquisite poise.

"Are you in labor?" the officer asked.

Georgie pursed her lips. "No, it's a challenge event for the Battle of the Births."

The officer took a step back, his gaze swinging between them, then landed back on his wife.

Twenty-four-hour psych hold, here they come!

The officer whipped off his mirrored sunglasses. "Wait a second. Your Georgie Jensen, aren't you?"

Georgie's jaw dropped. "How did you know that?"

"You're the Own the Eights lady!" the man replied, now grinning ear to ear—which was better than whipping out his handcuffs or calling in for backup.

"Can I get a picture with you?" he continued, pulling a cell phone from his pocket.

Georgie met his gaze, and all he could do was shrug and give her husband eyes for *just do it!*

"Okay," she answered.

"Thank you! My wife's sister is a CityBeat blogger in

Wisconsin, and she told my wife about your blog. She's a huge fan. That's how we got together! I'm her solid, reliable eight."

Georgie pressed her hand to her chest. "That's wonderful! I'm so happy for you."

"Not to mention, my wife's pregnant, too! She'll get such a kick out of knowing you're also expecting," the cop exclaimed, then handed him his phone. "Would you mind taking the picture?"

"Sure," he answered, lining up the photo of an officer of the law standing next to his wife, who sported wild sex hair with a sailor cap securely pinned to the crown of her head while glinting in the early morning sun.

You know, what they called Thursday morning.

"Smile," he said, hardly able to believe this was happening. Then again, it was better than getting arrested. He'd gunned the engine back there and was probably speeding.

Still, he should ask Georgie to pinch him once this police encounter ended, just to make sure this wasn't some expectant father pregnancy delusion. While they'd gotten themselves in plenty of bizarre situations over the course of their relationship, this one has to rank in the top five—no, probably three.

He returned the phone to the officer, and he and Georgie waved as the man got back into his cruiser and started down the street.

Georgie rested her head against his chest. "Jordan, what a mess! All I want to do is crawl back into bed and sleep until our little pineapple surprise is done baking."

"No, Georgie! We can't go home and sleep. We can salvage this. There's got to be some time left to get to the hospital. Where's Faby?"

"In the car," she answered wearily, then gasped and nearly jumped out of her skin.

"Georgiana, what is it?" he asked, scanning the road for another cop car.

"We left Faby unattended in the car! That's got to be like one of the worst things you can do!" she said, then sprinted the few steps to the SUV and swung open the car door.

Beep, beep, beep, beep!

Faby glared at them. Maybe it was him, but the fake doll looked pissed off.

"Do you think it's about to explode?" he asked as the devil baby continued to beep.

"I don't—" Georgie began as his phone rang.

He pulled his cell from his pocket. "It's Lenny."

"Answer it! Put him on speaker," Georgie directed.

He accepted the call. "Hello."

"Hey, it's Lenny and Stu. Where are you guys? You were supposed to be at the hospital eight minutes ago. Didn't your infant simulation doll alert go off?"

"It went off," he answered as Faby stopped beeping.

"Then, where are you? Are you close?" Lenny pressed.

Jordan stared down the block and could still see their bungalow. "No, we're on our street."

"You haven't left yet?" came Stu's concerned voice.

"We tried to leave, but Jordan forgot something," Georgie answered, crossing her arms—one very perturbed sexy sailor.

"What did he forget?" Stu asked.

She let out an exhausted sigh. "Me."

"I see," Lenny replied as a pregnant pause hung heavy in the air.

"And we got stopped by the cops," Georgie added, followed by a yawn.

"The police!" the men exclaimed.

He stared down at his bare feet. "We're fine. Everything's good. Can you reset Faby, and we can start over? Georgie and I are ready."

He glanced at his exhausted wife. Usually, after a few hours of nesting, followed by an imaginative costume-inspired sexytimes session, she'd zonk out until eight or nine in the morning.

"I'm sorry, but Lenny and I can't stay at the hospital," Stu replied.

"We can be there in nine minutes," he shot back as Georgie blinked her eyes, looking as if she might fall asleep while standing.

"We've got too much to do. It's a big day for us and for you as well," Stu answered.

"We do?" he replied. After all the excitement this morning, he could barely remember his name, let alone an appointment.

"Did you forget?" Lenny asked.

Jordan yawned, ready to crawl into bed alongside his wife. "We've had a very eventful morning already. Can you remind us?"

"You'll need to bring your A game today. There are only a few hours until the Battle of the Births Gender Reveal challenge. The email of the location will go out in a few minutes."

Jordan glanced at his punch-drunk pregnant wife, rocking side to side, half-asleep. "We'll see you there," he answered and ended the call.

Their A game?

He rubbed his bleary eyes. This challenge wasn't going to be pretty. After the antics this morning, they'd be lucky to bring their X, Y, or even Z game.

Chapter Fourteen
Georgie

"Georgie, you'll never believe where I think we're headed!"

She nodded but kept her eyes closed, hovering in that comfortably cozy place between being asleep and waking up.

After the botched hospital dry run followed by the lovely, yet ill-timed run-in with an officer of the law, all she'd wanted was to go back to bed. Her weary body ached to slide back under the covers. Then, after at least a solid two-hour nap, she'd wanted to wake to the scent of pineapple muffins warming in the oven. Jordan made them for her every morning before he assembled his protein shake.

Warm in bed, she'd lie there, savoring the warmth. The pregnancy was progressing without any problems. Their alien blueberry peanut was chugging along with no complications. And a few weeks ago, they'd succeeded at keeping baby Ollie alive. In fact, they'd done better. They'd enjoyed their time with the cherub-cheeked five-month-old.

She even felt like a million bucks on the Lorraine

Vanderdinkle-front. They had a plan on how they would break the baby news to her mother and Howard that didn't leave her wanting to crawl into a hole and disappear.

And on top of all that, she'd become a master organizer. She'd acquired ninja skills in the folding department. And there was no stopping her when it came to pantry prioritizing. In the wee, predawn hours this morning, she'd checked the use-by date on every canned good in the house, then fired up her laptop and knocked out an expiration date database. This feat of organizing excellence had earned a thumbs-up from her trifecta's resident detail-oriented, fictional know-it-all witch, Hermione Granger.

Georgiana Jensen-Marks, organizer extraordinaire.

Did she have a nesting chip on her shoulder?

Possibly.

But feng shui had nothing on her!

She'd spark joy alphabetizing her bookshelf, then slip into something sparkly or frilly from back in the day and make sparks with her sexy bed-headed husband. Who would have thought that the pageant costumes she'd despised as a teenager would turn out to be so useful in the dirty girl department?

She inhaled, wondering if she'd entered a *farting-without-knowing-it* phase of her pregnancy. But all she smelled was crap—like, actual manure.

Could that be right?

She didn't have a second to consider the smell when the gentle hum that had lulled her to sleep was replaced with a violent shake.

An earthquake?

Did they get earthquakes in Denver?

She jolted upright. "I'm awake! We have to get out of here!"

"Georgie, it's just a gravel road," her husband said with a reassuring pat to her leg.

She collapsed into the seat. "For a second, I forgot we were in the car."

"You've been out like a light for most of the drive."

She nodded and smoothed her dress. Thankfully, they'd had enough time to race home and grab a shower before leaving for the Battle of the Births event.

"Look, messy bun girl! Check out where the gender reveal challenge is being held," Jordan said as they continued up the bumpy road, and her jaw dropped—like, *catch-all-the-flies* dropped.

"The baby goat yoga farm?" she said, hardly able to believe her eyes.

"Yeah, crazy, right?"

She rested her hands on her baby bump. "Thank goodness I was able to cure you of your goat phobia. Who knows what kind of scene you would have made today?"

Jordan chuckled. "I'm a lucky guy," he said and rested his hand on top of hers.

"A lucky guy who's no longer afraid of baby farm animals, but alpacas—"

"Hey," he shot back, cutting her off playfully. "We agreed. Alpacas can be real assholes when they want to be."

"Very true," she said, shaking off the heebie-jeebies from the memory of being spit on by one serious asshole alpaca, as they continued down the country road toward a sea of cars.

For both her sake and her husband, hopefully, this place was still alpaca-free.

Jordan parked their SUV between two sedans, then gazed at all the cars in the makeshift dirt lot.

"It's pretty full. They must have another event going on."

Last time they were here, it was just the two of them, and, for a short while, the brother and sister blogger team turned convicted felons they'd competed against in the Battle of the Blogs. But today, there had to be more than twenty cars packed into the dusty lot.

"What do you think we'll have to do for this challenge?" he asked, cutting the ignition.

"I'm not sure how goat yoga could be a Battle of the Births challenge. Goat yoga isn't a challenge unless you're afraid of things that go baa in the night," she replied, biting back a grin as her trifecta nodded in appreciation at her clever wordplay.

Jordan unbuckled his seatbelt, then leaned over the console. She met him in the middle.

"When did you get so funny?" he asked on one heck of a sexy rasp.

Her prego-libido revved. "I've always been this funny."

He closed the distance and pressed the sweetest kiss to her lips.

"What do you say, messy bun girl? Whatever this challenge is, I think we're golden. We know this place. We're ready for whatever they throw at us."

"What's the score?" she asked.

Jordan pulled out his phone. "Eleven couples competing."

"And?" she asked, trying not to cringe.

After the simulation from a diarrhea-infused hell and their no-show at the hospital this morning, it couldn't be good.

"We're number ten," he reported.

"Okay, not dead last."

A muscle ticked in her husband's jaw. Oh, her competitive asshat!

"I have an idea," she said in her best dirty girl voice.

"What's that?" he asked, lowering his as the twitch disappeared.

"After we rock this challenge and jump to the head of the pack, we should go by that barn we passed last time we were here. You know, the one where..." she trailed off as a blush heated her cheeks, her prego-libido raring to go.

A cocky grin stretched across Jordan's face. "Where I *rocked* your world."

She lifted her chin. "No, no, it's where I rocked *your world*."

A whole lot of naughtiness glimmered in his eyes.

Look at that! She was a bona fide cocky, competitive asshat calmer.

A *BCCAC*.

She chuckled.

"What's so funny?" he asked.

She pressed her hand to her mouth to hold in a bout of giggles. "I'm just amusing myself."

She was ready for him to toss back a feisty reply. But his expression softened as his gaze slid to her exposed wrist and settled on her charm bracelet—the bracelet he'd given her on their wedding day.

"You wore it," he said with that boyish grin she loved.

She glanced at the charms, taking in the silver ten and eight, the computer mouse, the tiny barbell, the mini sandal, and the trowel before tapping the cookie charm.

"For so long, even thinking of vegan cookies made me want to hurl. But when I caught a glimpse of my bracelet in my jewelry box, I didn't feel like losing my breakfast. And for some strange reason, it seemed right to wear it today."

"Our good luck charms?" he teased.

"I think so," she answered, jangling the silver charms.

"We need to add another."

"For the baby?"

"I was thinking a pineapple," he said with a wink.

"That would actually work for the baby, and I could totally pound a pineapple juice right about now," she said, then sighed longingly.

"Would you now?" he asked with a sly expression, then popped open the glove box to reveal a tiny, lunchbox-sized can of her drink du jour.

She plucked the can from its resting place, popped the top, and downed the liquid like a frat boy pounding a Natty Light.

"God help anyone who gets between you and a pineapple. And by the way, that's the last one. We'll have to stop at the store on the way home after the challenge and stock up," he said, clapping the glove box closed.

She set the drained can on the dashboard, sweetly sated by the drink. "Noted. We're pineapple or bust after the challenge ends."

He tapped his hands on the steering wheel. "All right, messy bun girl. We've got you properly juiced-up. Let's go kick ass in this challenge. I'll help you and Faby out."

She lifted Faby from the floorboard, then gazed into its, thankfully, not demon-red face. "I think we're okay to get out of a car on our own," she said, opening the car door and immediately wishing she hadn't.

Sweet cow patties! The smell!

"That's awful! What do you think that is? A buffalo?"

"Um...Georgie," Jordan said as a couple, looking like they'd walked straight out of the caveman exhibit at the

Museum of Natural History, got out of the car parked next to them.

"That's the smell of an environmentally-friendly pregnancy. We're a part of Nadine's natural birth group. We're here for a prenatal goat yoga session," the hairy pregnant woman barked.

Cornelia was not kidding. Nadine's birthing group was hardcore. And Georgie couldn't fault the woman for being in a bad mood. Walking around like a pregnant Oscar the Grouch couldn't be fun.

"That sounds lovely. It's a perfect day for goat yoga," she answered like a ventriloquist, keeping her lips pressed together and wishing she could clamp her nostrils shut.

She plastered on a closed-mouth smile as the couple headed toward a group of other pregnant cave people, and Jordan came to her side.

"I think you're smelling the cows, babe," he said, then pointed over to a pasture beyond a row of cars where a trio of hay munching moo machines grazed.

"I didn't know they had cows! Were there cows here last time?" she asked, taking his arm.

"I wouldn't know. I was more focused on the goats."

"Where do you think we should go?" she asked just as she spied Barry near the barn, blessedly, not anywhere close to Nadine's group.

The CityBeat producer waved them over.

"We missed you this morning!" he called, filming them as they walked up.

"We had a little mishap with the law," she answered, then looked up at her now rose-cheeked husband.

Barry nodded. "I know. I saw the—"

"Georgie! Jordan!" Lenny interrupted, standing next to

the barn door. "You're the last couple to arrive. You better hurry. We're about to begin."

"We'll talk later," she said to Barry, patting the man's arm as they hurried inside.

"We'll let you get to work," Jordan said to the man over his shoulder as they entered the giant structure.

Last time they were here, they hadn't ventured inside the weathered enclosure. She blinked, allowing her eyes to adjust to the dim interior. Thin slivers of light carved their way through large wooden beams crisscrossing the top of the barn. Stalls with a few horses lined the sides, but still allowed for a great open space in the center where a circle had been made using hay bales.

Jordan leaned down and lowered his voice. "It's too bad you left your cowgirl boots at home."

She inhaled a sharp breath. *Vroom, vroom!* Who knew pregnant women walked around like roly-poly sexpots?

"I have an idea," she whispered back.

"What?"

"The naughty milkmaid and the ripped farmer."

"They do say milk does a body good," he replied when Lenny stopped and turned to face them.

"What was that, Jordan?" he asked with a crinkle to his brow.

Jordan's blush returned. "I was wondering if they produced their own milk at the farm—from the cows because if Georgie was dressed as a milkmaid, she could milk a cow."

She nodded as if her husband made perfect sense and hadn't replied with a comment best described as vitamin D enriched nonsense.

"I'm not sure. We're not here to do any farm work or

milking," the man answered, then pointed to a spot on the ground between two couples. "You can settle in right here."

Straw had been scattered over the barn floor, and Georgie glanced at the other couples to get the lay of the land. The non-pregnant partner took a seat on the ground and leaned against the bale of hay while the pregnant partner scooted in between the non-prego person's legs and relaxed into their embrace.

It was very maternity ward meets *Little House on the Prairie*.

"You're going to get me into trouble, messy bun girl," he teased, getting into the non-pregnant position.

"Save it for the lake, farmer boy," she parried back, handing him Faby while she maneuvered to the ground.

She nestled into her ripped farmer's embrace as a guitar strum cut through the couples' murmuring.

"Let's start with a singalong everyone knows," Stu said, tambourine in hand.

"How about, 'You Are My Sunshine,'" Lenny called, strumming the refrain.

This might be weird had their first encounter with these two not started with singing. This whole sitting-on-the-floor thing had an odd summer camp vibe to it. At least they weren't doing goat yoga with the angry hairy pregnant people. The song ended, and Lenny and Stu took a bow as everyone clapped.

"We are so excited for the Battle of the Births gender reveal challenge," Lenny said, addressing the group as a trio of CityBeat cameramen spread out along the periphery of the circle, filming the event from all angles.

Stu took a step forward. "Let's recap. Everyone did a great job on the Virtual Reality simulator challenge," he announced, when Lenny whispered something into his ear.

"*Almost* everyone did a great job on the simulator," the man said, amending his statement.

"We would have been fine if that VR baby hadn't been a diarrhea volcano," Jordan said under his breath.

"And all but one couple made it to the hospital on time for the practice-run challenge," Lenny chimed.

Jordan tensed, and she craned her neck to whisper in his ear.

"Don't worry, Emperor. Even with a boatload of diarrhea, we're still not in last place."

"Unfortunately, we had to say goodbye to one of our couples. They moved overseas and had to pull out of the competition," Stu added.

Welp, they were dead last. But that was about to change.

More than that—today, they'd know if they had a little miss or a little mister on the way!

They could debate names and go back and forth over what color to paint the baby's room.

Then, a wave of relief settled over her. This was also the day she was going to contact Howard's office, and all the weeks of worrying and wondering how her mother would react would be over.

Would the woman go full-on socialite or insist on a spiritual in utero chanting session? Either was possible. But they'd be okay. Their time with Ollie proved they were up for the parenting task.

"I'd like to ask the non-pregnant partner to take out their cell phone and open the Battle of the Births app. Then, click on the heart icon," Lenny instructed.

Jordan slipped his phone from his pocket and opened the app.

"Thanks to the hospital practice-run challenge, you all

know that your infant simulation doll is a technological feat. And guess what? This doll has another surprise. Now, we'd like the pregnant partner to place the doll in your lap, then grip your baby's left arm," Lenny instructed.

"Here we go, Faby," she said, following directions.

Jordan held his phone so she could see the screen. "Georgie, I think Faby can act as a heart rate monitor."

"What?"

"Like the handlebars on the treadmills at my gym. It looks like the information is sent to the app," he explained.

"Look at you, Faby. You're not just a beeping demon-baby," she said, then instantly felt like an idiot when the pregnant woman next to her gasped at her demon-baby description.

"I'm being silly," she said as the woman gave her a curt, *we're-done-here* nod.

"Play nice," Jordan teased.

"Is the app doing anything?" she asked.

"Yeah, it's tracking your heart rate. You're clocking in at a respectable eighty-two," he answered, showing her the heart icon blinking with an eight and a two next to it.

"Is that good?"

He nodded. "A resting heart rate should be between sixty and one hundred. You're doing great."

She nestled into him. "We've got this challenge in the bag."

Lenny strummed his guitar to get everyone's attention.

"We've got every contestants' heart rate readouts on our laptop," Lenny said as Stu held up the device.

"This challenge is about meditation and staying calm under pressure," Stu explained, then gestured to a woman who looked like she came straight out of a yoga apparel advertisement.

"Dawn is a meditation specialist," the man continued. "She's here to lead you in some breathing exercises you can utilize during your child's birth."

Lenny held up several white envelopes. "Here's the catch. We're going to hand you the envelope with your baby's gender information inside. It would be easy to get excited and send your heart rate through the roof. We know that you're all eager to learn if you're having a boy or a girl."

"The challenge is to maintain a resting heart rate for the entire forty-minute meditation. Then, we'll head outdoors—after Nadine's group is safely off the premises—and open our envelopes as a group."

She felt her husband shift behind her as he raised his hand.

"Yes, Jordan," Lenny said, calling on him.

"How do we know who wins?"

Georgie tried not to cringe.

No, no, no, no!

He was not about to go all asshat competitive—not when this challenge was about being chill. She dug her elbow into his belly, but he didn't flinch. The man had rock-hard abs. Something she usually reveled in, but not today.

"All you have to do is get through the meditation, and everyone wins," Stu answered.

Jordan raised his hand again.

"Yes, Jordan," Lenny replied.

"That's great about everyone winning, but what if one wanted to earn some extra points? Would there be an opportunity for some extra credit? Like if Georgie went all Zen-master meditator, could that help our rank?"

And hello, Emperor of Asshattery! So nice of you to show up—not!

"There's no extra credit, but there is one more challenge

—a secret challenge we're keeping close to the vest," Stu added.

She sighed with relief when her husband's hand didn't rocket back up for another question.

"Without further ado, we'll let Dawn start the meditation practice," Lenny said with another strum as the cameramen continued rolling.

Miss Yoga USA pressed her hands into a prayer position. "We usually like to do our meditations outdoors with our animal friends. But we're double-booked today, so we're bringing a few of our goats in here to join us in the barn," she said as a farmhand opened one of the stall doors and a troop of baby goats bleated and pranced toward the group.

"It's baby goat meditation, Jordan," she whispered.

"We've totally got this, babe," he replied as Stu handed her the envelope with their baby's gender.

She pressed the paper to her heart. "This is it. We'll know if we've got a Georgie junior or a Jordan junior on the way," she said as a curious baby goat sniffed her shoes.

"Babe, take a breath. Your heart rate jumped into the nineties," he replied, gaze on the phone.

"Aren't you excited?" she pressed.

He kissed the crown of her head. "Let's just say that if I were holding Faby's heart rate monitor arm, it would be off the charts. And not because I'm scared of the goats, but because I can't wait to be a father. Boy or girl, this is going to be one special kid."

This man! One minute, he's a competitive douche canoe, the next, he's melting her heart.

"Couples, I have a few announcements before we begin. As you can see, we're in a barn, and barns have their share of creepy-crawly friends," the woman said, causing the breath to catch in Georgie's throat.

Creepy-crawly things were definitely not anyone's friend.

"If you don't bother them, they won't bother you," the meditation guru added.

"Georgie, take a breath," Jordan coaxed as Lenny and Stu glanced over their iPad at her.

Let's get real. Spiders weren't just creepy and crawly—which was bad enough. No, they were eight-legged harbingers of hell.

She shifted her body, scanning the hay for the little buggers as the yogi instructed the group to close their eyes.

"What's wrong?" Jordan whispered.

She swallowed hard. "I'm not a fan of spiders."

"I can tell. Your heart rate shot up."

She squeezed her eyes shut. "I checked the hay. I didn't see any. I should be okay."

Should be—but she couldn't make any promises.

Jordan moved from side to side.

"I don't see anything. We're in the clear. But..."

"But what? Did you see a spider?" she whisper-shouted.

"But...you have a ridiculous phobia," he said, and she could hear the cocky grin in his voice.

"It's not silly," she hissed when someone in the room hushed her.

The nerve!

"There's nothing on the ground but hay," he said gently.

She nodded, then worked to slow her breathing.

Only hay. No spiders.

This would be her mantra.

She closed her eyes, listening as the baby goats padded around as the yogi instructed the participants to picture a serene place.

That was easier said than done.

All she could conjure up were rows of people seated in a darkened ballroom as bright lights cast her in an unearthly glow. She stood there, shoulder to shoulder, with the other teen pageant contestants, smiling into the void like animated Barbie dolls until the tiny beast descended from its hair-thin silk rope.

A spider, going about its spider life, crashed the Miss Drumstick Pageant.

She hadn't wanted to compete in a Thanksgiving-themed pageant, but her mother had signed her up, nevertheless. And there she was, smiling so hard she thought her lips would snap while a spider hung, suspended a breath away from her nose.

Legs wiggling, she'd hope the pageant-crasher would continue its creepy descent without touching her. And it might have. But at the very moment the spider stilled, the contestant next to her flipped her hair, sending a whoosh of air strong enough to carry Mr. Spider right onto her cheek.

If ever she could sympathize with Miss Muffet, it was that moment.

And that's when it happened. At this exact moment, in this very barn, she sensed a bevy of tiny arachnid eyeballs staring at her.

"Georgie, are you okay? Your heart rate is through the roof," Stu said from somewhere in the barn.

Slowly, she opened her eyes and...

There it was.

Suspended in the air and lit by a shard of light, a spider descended from above.

And he was headed straight for Faby!

Oh, hell no!

She lunged forward, slicing at the eight-legged micro-monster with the envelope. Back and forth, she wielded the rectangular paper like a pregnant Lancelot brandishing a sword, intent on fending off an evil attacker—or multi-legged bug.

But her actions were in vain. She sliced through the thread of silk, and the spider landed right on Faby's leg. She shot to her feet, dropping the envelope and swinging the fake baby like a tiny sack of potatoes.

"You will not touch my Faby!" she called as the spider seemed to hang on for dear life.

"Georgie!" Jordan cried, but she had to get that damned creature off of her fake baby.

She dragged Faby's legs across the floor, praying the friction would knock the wicked arachnid off. After making a few circles in the hay, she lifted the doll, checked its fake baby body, then blew out a relieved breath. The spider was nowhere to be found, but Faby was covered in slivers of golden hay.

She gently dusted off the doll, then glanced around the barn. Shock and dismay graced every expression as the cameras recorded what must have looked like an insane outburst from an unstable pregnant woman. Even her trusty trifecta was left speechless.

She parted her lips to say...

Say what?

Sorry for that freak-out, but spiders are real asshats.

She wracked her brain, searching for the appropriate thing to say after a near homicidal outburst, when the smack and chomp of a goat chewing caught her attention. She glanced at the animal to find the last bit of their reveal envelope dangling from its mouth.

The room remained dead quiet, with only the thumps of the goats padding around and munching on her child's gender. She hugged Faby to her chest, then felt a warm hand press against her back.

Without even looking, she knew it was Jordan. But she couldn't look at him. She couldn't look at anyone. She'd hung all her hopes on this day. For weeks, she'd thought of it as not only the day she'd learn her child's gender but also the day when she could come clean to her mother.

Why was this difficult? What was she frightened of? People got pregnant every day.

People announced their pregnancies in a myriad of ways.

Why was she making this so hard?

Her eyes burned as angry, humiliated tears threatened to spill.

"Georgie, babe," Jordan said as if he were addressing a wounded bird.

She handed the fake baby to her husband, tried not to see the worry in his eyes, then ran out of the barn like a pregnant bat out of hell.

Because, as much as she teased her husband about his competitive streak and always wanting to win, she was the one who needed a win today.

And she'd needed it badly.

Instead, just like with the VR simulator challenge, they'd failed.

Again.

Chapter Fifteen
Jordan

Jordan stood in the center of the pregnancy meditation circle turned spider-freak-out crime scene as the clap of Georgie's footsteps, booking it out of the barn, echoed through the cavernous space.

Not counting the baby goats, who hadn't been bothered by the crazy lady dragging a doll in circles across the creaky hay-covered planks of wood, the room remained stock still. Lenny and Stu stood with their heads cocked to the side while the meditation specialist's eyes looked ready to pop out of her skull. He glanced around the room as the three CityBeat cameramen pointed their cameras straight at him. Even Barry, who'd been with them through the majority of their bizarro moments, stared slack-jawed at the goat eating the envelope containing their baby's gender.

He did one last scan of the stunned group, then tucked Faby in the crook of his arm.

"That was something, wasn't it, folks?" he said, going for breezy-casual, but, from the gaping silence, he'd only managed to appear run-of-the-mill cuckoo.

He sucked in a tight breath through his teeth. "It looks

like Georgie and I are cutting this one short. Enjoy the rest of your day. Namaste and all that bullshit," he finished, giving the yogi a quick bow before following in his wife's footsteps and hightailing it out of the barn.

Was this one of their best moments?

Oh, for Christ's sake, no!

But was it one of the worst?

He let that sink in.

Yeah, maybe it was.

A non-spider phobic person might have simply brushed the creepy-crawly away and left it at that. But that is not how it went down today. And to add insult to injury, the cameras had caught Georgie losing her ever-loving mind over an arachnid, then dragging her infant simulation doll across the ground. An activity he would bet every dollar he had was a big no-no with a real infant.

Out of the barn and away from the gaping mouths and bugged-out eyes, he patted Faby's head.

"You're okay, aren't you, Faby?"

The fake baby stared up at him. Streaks of dirt ran down its plastic cheeks.

He rubbed out a smudge with his thumb. "You look okay to me. Do you want to guess who's not doing okay?"

He glanced around the half-empty parking area and spied his wife pulling on the locked passenger side door handle like a common pregnant car thief.

He jogged across the lot and came to her side. "It's easier when you have these," he said, pulling his keys from his pocket, then pressed the fob as the click of the locks disengaging cut through the air.

He rubbed her shoulder. "Do you want to take a minute and then go back into the barn?"

She rested her forehead against the car. "Is Faby all right?"

He looked at the lifeless doll. "Never better. Don't forget, Faby survived being kidnapped by wild dogs. Faby is a badass fake baby."

"It wasn't wild dogs. It was a dog," she replied against the car window, her breath making little puffs of condensation.

"A pack of wild dogs sounds better," he countered.

She sighed, then met his gaze. "I can't go back in there, Jordan."

He nodded. "Then, we'll leave."

"You're not upset about the Battle of the Births score? We're probably still dead last."

"They said there was another secret challenge. We'll aim for a Hail Mary finish," he replied.

Did it stink to lose?

Yeah.

But he wasn't about to make his wife feel bad about her spider phobia.

As far as he was concerned, after alpacas, spiders were the next asshole creatures on the asshole creatures list.

He opened the passenger side door and helped her in. He wanted to keep this light. But the slump of Georgie's shoulders and the tremble of her bottom lip spoke volumes. This was more than a failed challenge. It was even more than an unfortunate interaction with an arachnid.

He got in the car, handed Faby to his wife, and started the engine.

"Where to, Spider-man?"

"Oh, stop!" she huffed, staring out the window.

"You never mentioned that you had an irrational phobia," he teased.

"Let's just say, I totally understand why Little Miss Muffet took off when the spider intruded on her tuffet," she replied, but there wasn't any sass or sarcasm in his wife's reply.

He watched her out of the corner of his eye. From her pinched expression, he knew not to take it any further.

She shook her head as if trying to push something from her mind. "Let's hit the grocery store first and then head home. I'm warning you now. We're buying every can of pineapple juice, every pineapple fritter, every pineapple yogurt, and I may even throw in a few Hawaiian pizzas."

Holy pineapple bender! This was not good.

"You may be blowing this up in your head, babe. It didn't look as bad as you probably think it did," he said as they started down the gravel drive back toward the interstate.

She turned in her seat and pinned him with her gaze. "Did it look like a screaming pregnant woman attacking a bug the size of a nickel followed by said pregnant woman dragging an infant simulation doll across a dusty, hay-covered floor?"

She had him there.

"Technically, yes."

She sank into the seat and pressed her fingertips to her eyelids. "It's a sign."

"What's a sign?"

"All of it. All the relief I felt after we picked the gender reveal as the date to tell my mom about the baby. It was a facade, hiding what we both know is true."

He frowned. She was being damned hard on herself.

"What are you talking about, Georgie? What do we know is true?"

She waved him off. "And we don't even know the baby's gender."

That was an easy fix.

"We can call Dr. Beaver's office," he replied.

"And say what?" she asked, her voice going up an octave. "They know this was supposed to be the big reveal for the Battle of the Births. We signed a waiver saying the office could share the information with Lenny and Stu. How do we tell them that I obliterated a spider to defend a fake baby and dropped the envelope with the gender information only to have it get eaten by an asshole goat! Do things like this happen to other people? Is there something wrong with us?"

"There's nothing wrong with us. We can pull over and call the doctor's office now. We'll know the gender of our pineapple surprise in minutes," he said, doing his best to ease her anguish.

"No, this is the universe telling us something. We're not supposed to know the baby's gender. I don't even know if we're supposed to be parents," she added, back to shaking her head.

"Georgiana, you're upset, and you're low on pineapple. That's all. In a day or two, we'll probably be laughing about this."

He swallowed hard, feeling her gaze bore into him.

Yep, probably not a good time to throw out the whole *laugh-about-it-later* comment.

"We don't know the gender, so we can't tell my mom," she said, biting out the words.

"We don't have to know the gender to tell your mom," he countered, trying to make sense of what was going on with his wife and the crushing anxiety around telling her mother.

Georgie threw up her hands. "Then why did I want to wait? What am I supposed to say now? In my head, it made sense. We waited to tell them because then, not only were we telling them that a baby was on the way, we were also sharing the exciting news of it being a boy or a girl. And now, we're not supposed to know the gender. A goat and a spider made sure of that. It's like the asshat version of *Charlotte's Web*, except the spider is a psychopath, and the pig was replaced by an envelope gobbling goat."

He signaled, then maneuvered the car off the highway and onto the exit ramp, headed toward the market.

"That's not how I remember that book, babe," he said gently.

She lifted her chin. "You know what I mean!"

He didn't. He really didn't. But he wasn't about to dissect the plot and character arcs of *Charlotte's Web* with his upset pregnant wife when he wasn't armed with at least three pineapple products.

Georgie stared out the window as they weaved their way through the city and toward the market. He pulled into the parking lot, then glanced at his wife. His heart broke at the sight of her in such pain.

There was nothing he wouldn't do to make her smile—to make her see how any kid would be lucky to have her as a mother.

"Why'd you pick this location?" she asked.

He glanced out the window. They lived within a few miles of several organic grocery stores, but it had been ages since they'd visited this one—which happened to be the location of their first Battle of the Blogs challenge back when they could barely stand each other.

He stared at the entrance. "I don't know. I was driving on autopilot."

"This is where I watched you pick up that woman using honey as a prop," she said with the faintest hint of a smile.

"And where you ruined cucumbers for poor Save the Whales Steve," he replied, taking her hand.

Yep, they'd been challenged to use their former blog's dating philosophies to meet a possible significant other at the grocery store. This was also the location of—

"We had our first kiss here," Georgie said, reading his mind.

"You were neglecting the science of physical attraction. I had to prove you wrong."

"And now look where we are," she said, teary-eyed as she stared down at her baby bump.

He rested his hand on her belly. "Amazing, huh?" he answered.

"Don't get used to me saying this, but it's pretty obvious that you were right on the chemistry and attraction hubbub," she said with a sly twist to her lips.

There she was. There was the snarky bookshop owner who'd stolen his heart.

"Oh, Jordan," she said on a wistful sigh.

"What is it, babe?"

"After my outburst at the farm, who would trust me with a real baby?" she said, about to sink into the seat again when a sharp knock ricocheted through the car.

"I need you to take my baby!"

Their gazes shot to the passenger side window. Standing only inches away was Brice's sister Briana with Ollie in her arms, her expression awash with anxiety.

He jumped out of the car and came to her side as Georgie exited the SUV.

"Are you guys okay? Are you hurt?" he asked.

The woman shook her head. "No, we're fine. But I just

got a call from the hospital. A patient I operated on yesterday is experiencing complications, and I need to go in. But no one is available to watch Ollie. Thad's still not back. My family is attending a big pest control expo in Boulder. My mom is on her way here, but it'll take her at least half an hour. And I don't have that kind of time."

Little Ollie reached for Georgie, and Briana passed the boy over.

"We're happy to watch Ollie for you," Georgie said, patting the boy's back.

Briana pressed her hand to her heart. "Thank you! It's like the universe put you right in my path."

"Do we need your car seat?" he asked.

"No, my mom has one in her car, but would you mind doing something for me?"

"Anything," Georgie answered.

"I'm forever waiting until the last minute to buy formula. Could you pick some up for me? And, of course, I'd pay you back."

He waved her off. "No need. We're happy to do it, Briana."

"You two are lifesavers. Here," she said, handing him Ollie's diaper bag. "I'll call my mom on the way to the hospital and let her know to meet you here."

"Good luck! We hope everything goes well with your patient," he said.

The woman nodded, kissed her son's cheek, then jogged back to her car.

They watched as Dr. Briana Casey-Beaver sped out of the parking lot and disappeared into the city. Unmoving, they stood there for a beat before his wife broke their dazed bout of silence.

"Did someone just trust us to take their baby grocery

shopping?" Georgie asked with a bewildered bend to the words.

He glanced at the smiling Ollie as an image of the VR diarrhea baby flashed through his mind.

But this was not virtual reality. This was a flesh and blood baby, who needed formula.

"Yeah, I think that's exactly what happened," he answered, the weight of this moment sinking in.

Georgie's expression grew pensive. "We know the brand of the formula. We saw the can at their house. I assume we just buy the same thing."

"Yeah," he answered, still a little dumbstruck.

"Would you like my cart?" a man said, pushing an empty one toward the outdoor cart corral.

"Sure," Georgie answered.

The man grinned as his gaze slid to Ollie. "Mine are nine and thirteen now. Enjoy them while they're little. It goes by in the blink of an eye."

"Okay," Georgie replied, sounding stunned as the man turned and headed for his car.

"Should we put him in it?" he asked, angling the offered cart toward his wife.

Georgie shook her head. "Not yet. Grab the disinfectant wipes from the back of the car. We need to get it sanitized. And get Faby. We're all going in together."

"Right!" he said, remembering the wipe stand in the simulation, then sprang into action as hope and anticipation fluttered in his chest.

This was their chance. Their shopping with a baby re-do.

Lucky for them, Ollie looked wholly incapable of shooting an endless stream of baby poo. Thank Christ, they had biology on their side—or at least basic volume.

He wiped down the cart, then buckled little Ollie into the seat. Georgie set Faby next to him, and the delighted six-month-old giggled and cooed, tapping and touching his plastic seatmate.

"Look at that. Faby made a friend," Georgie said, pushing the cart toward the entrance.

And that's when he discovered he'd developed dad eyes.

Yep, dad eyes—the ones that see danger lurking around every corner.

All of a sudden, every crack in the pavement, every bird, every car, every person near them became possible threats.

"We'll want to go in with a plan," he said, eyeing a pair of teenagers carrying skateboards.

"I agree. Let's get the formula first, then do the pineapple grab."

"Roger that, MBG," he parried back.

The market's automatic doors slid open, but Georgie stopped in her tracks.

"Who's MBG?"

He held her gaze. "You are. Messy bun girl. *MBG.*"

"You're not playing around?" she replied, that playful twinkle back in her blue-green eyes.

"That's an affirmative, MBG."

They were taking this to combat-level serious with code-names and everything.

She grinned up at him. Her real smile. Her Georgie smile. "Let's do this, *PTA.*"

He frowned. "PTA? Like the parents who run the bake sale at elementary schools?"

"No, perfect ten asshat," she replied, looking damn pleased with herself.

PTA didn't have the badass quality of MBG, but if it made his wife smile, he was totally good with it.

"PTA, MBG, the F-A-B-Y, and the real O-L-L-I-E are good to go," he said, holding her gaze for a fraction of a second before they moved in on the target aka the grocery store.

They sailed down the aisles and even maneuvered past one of those little caution wet floor warning cones with ease. They picked up the formula. They plundered the pineapple yogurts. They pillaged the juice display. They filled the cart with pineapple delights and were headed for the check-out when a smell akin to roadkill wafted up from little Ollie.

They stared at the boy, who'd nixed the giggles for a pensive pout.

"You don't think Faby made that smell, do you?" he asked.

Georgie shook her head. "Diaper bag. Family restroom. This mission is taking a detour."

"Jesus, babe!"

"What?" she asked.

"It's pretty hot when you go *GI Georgie*."

And boom! They'd added another sexy role-play scenario option to the naughty-times' portfolio. As much as he would have liked to take a minute or twelve to think about a commando-clad Georgie, they had a bomb to defuse —a stink bomb.

A fart, smelling as if it came from a water buffalo, cut their sexytime talk short. They changed course, slicing and dicing past shoppers, cutting corners, and nearly taking out a pallet of sparkling water before making it to the family restroom.

The vacant sign above the door handle signaled they were good to go.

Georgie plucked Ollie from the cart, and the three, well, four counting Faby, of them entered the market lavatory.

And...

"Wow, it's nice in here!" Georgie said, glancing around the spacious room.

"There's even a chair," he remarked, setting the baby bag on it.

"Okay, I need you to clean the changing table with a disinfectant wipe. I'll get the diaper and the baby wipes."

In action movies, there's often a scene accompanied by an intense techno soundtrack where the characters operate in sync. Hacking the FBI—the real one. Fortifying a stronghold. Whatever the high-stakes scenario, that serious *shit-is-getting-done* music starts to play, and you know it's that part of the film where the real nitty-gritty gets done.

In that quasi-luxurious family restroom, he and Georgie fell into that very scene. Except, the store didn't have hardcore techno playing. No, the piped-in background music was...

He could barely believe it!

"Michael Bolton," Georgie whispered as a lovely instrumental version of "How Am I Supposed to Live Without You" played over the market's sound system.

He caught Georgie's eye, and she nodded. A tiny move that would have gone unrecognized by most, but not him.

This song had been with them from the beginning. It couldn't be a coincidence that it was playing now.

Table down.

Wipes deployed.

Jordan Marks was a man on a disinfecting mission. He raised his hands, then stepped back and allowed Georgie to move in.

Gently, she laid the baby on the changing table, then

proceeded to remove his little baby shoes and his little baby jeans, which were, honestly, damn cute.

"Mr. Ollie, that is quite a smell," Georgie said, adding a *pee-ew* sound that had the boy laughing a toothless baby giggle that was also cute as hell.

But the smell!

"You want me to do it?" he asked, eyeing the bulging diaper.

"No, I'm going in. Baby wipe," she said, holding out her hand like a surgeon requesting a scalpel.

Wipe in hand, she removed the diaper, and, while the VR simulation wasn't completely accurate, it was still freaky how much poop a tiny person could produce in real life. Still, at least this stuff wasn't erupting out of him like Mount Saint Diarrhea.

It took a good ten or eleven wipes, but together—no, mostly Georgie with him earning a solid assist—they'd cleaned up the boy, disposed of the diaper, and had those baby jeans and shoes on before that Michael Bolton song even ended.

Things moved quickly after their diaper change win.

They'd washed their hands, left the bathroom oasis, and paid for their items.

And just like that, they'd mastered the real grocery store challenge.

He carried the groceries and Faby while Georgie lifted the boy out of the cart.

"Let's wait on the bench," she said with a mischievous grin.

"Ah, the very bench where you cracked open a tube of—"

"Don't say it. We will not be speaking the name of my former favorite snack," she replied, giving him a warning glance. "It's one thing for me to be able to wear my bracelet with the cookie charm. It's another tube of cookie dough to bring it up in conversation."

He chuckled, remembering the moment he happened upon her on this very bench, squeezing the raw vegan cookie dough straight into her mouth like a modern-day female cookie monster.

"Hello, there! You must be Georgie and Jordan," a woman said, waving as she walked toward them.

Ollie clapped his hands and reached for the woman.

"You must be Brice and Briana's mom," Georgie said, handing the boy over.

"I'm Louise Casey. It's so nice to meet you both. Thank you for taking care of our little Ollie. You two were in the right place at the right time when Ollie and Briana needed you."

Georgie parted her lips to speak, but nothing came out.

"We're glad we could help," he said, handing Louise the diaper bag, then wrapping his arm around his wife.

"Here's Ollie's formula," Georgie said, finding her voice as she removed the can from their grocery bag and slid it into Ollie's diaper bag.

"Say goodbye to the nice people, Oliver," the woman said to her grandson.

The child made a raspberry sound as Louise turned and headed toward a sedan parked a few rows over.

"That was amazing," Georgie said with tears in her eyes.

"It appears that we're not half-bad at caring for real babies," he replied, then glanced down at Faby, sitting on top of one of the grocery bags. "No offense, little buddy," he added.

His wife sank onto the bench. "Had that spider not

freaked me out and tried to kill Faby, we would probably still be at the farm."

"You're right," he answered, taking a seat beside her.

"Briana said she was grateful that the universe put us in her path," Georgie continued.

His wife wasn't wrong. They were supposed to be at that grocery store at that exact time.

Georgie reached into her pocket and pulled out her phone.

"What are you doing?" he asked.

She held the phone to her ear and met his gaze. "Listening to the universe."

He watched the worry and stress caused by the spider melee melt from his wife's expression.

With one hand on her belly and the other holding the phone, she grinned at him.

"Hello, this is Georgiana Jensen-Marks, Howard Vanderdinkle's stepdaughter. I need to get a message to him and my mother."

Chapter Sixteen
Georgie

"It's Georgiana Jensen-Marks, again. I'm calling to leave another message for my stepfather, Howard Vanderdinkle."

Georgie paced the length of the kitchen, then caught a glimpse of the calendar tacked to the wall with a giant thirty-one written in today's date box.

She'd been cooking a baby for thirty-one weeks, and holy Goodyear Blimp, could anyone within a five-mile radius tell. Her alien peanut blueberry turned mini pineapple turned mango, now felt like one of those giant prize-winning watermelons that took several brawny men to lug around from town fair to town fair.

Being thirty-one weeks pregnant also meant she'd spent the last several weeks trying to contact her mother and Howard.

"Mrs. Jensen-Marks, Mr. Vanderdinkle left word six weeks ago that he and your mother were entering a critical phase in their spiritual journey and would be completely off the grid until—"

"Until they discover their *Sankalpa*. I know. The last

person I spoke with told me the same thing," Georgie said, hating to interrupt but totally floored that Howard seemed to have jumped onto the psychic energist bandwagon with her mother.

She assumed he was there to placate her mom and figured he would have left the retreat to see to his businesses in the region months ago. But no. From what she'd gleaned from his bevy of assistants, he'd left strict orders not to be disturbed.

"Is there anything else I can do for you?" the woman asked.

Georgie drummed her fingers on the kitchen island. "Do you know what their *Sankalpa* is?"

"A *Sankalpa* is one's innermost intention," the woman answered with the hint of irritation in her voice, which may be warranted.

She had called the office on a Friday, one minute before five o'clock.

She stopped drumming her fingers and eyed a slice of pineapple upside-down cake. "Yeah, the last person told me that, too. Do you know how long that takes to find?"

"The *Sankalpa?*"

"Yeah."

"No, ma'am, I don't."

"So, there's no estimated arrival time for a *Sankalpa?*" she asked, tearing off a piece of the cake and popping it into her mouth.

"Not that I'm aware of, Mrs. Jensen-Marks. Is there anything else you need?"

Georgie swallowed the bite and sighed.

She needed to talk to her mother. The day she and Jordan had rocked their shopping trip with baby Ollie had sent a palpable zing of excitement through her body. She'd been sure that all signs had pointed for her to contact her mother, right then and there.

Why else would the events of that day have gone down the way they did? At the time, it was like her destiny was written in the stars.

But all that excitement had fizzled.

When she'd called from the grocery store, she'd told the receptionist that she needed to speak with her stepfather, and the assistant had simply taken her message. But after hearing nothing for two days, she'd called again, and this time, a different secretary delivered the *Sankalpa* line.

She stared at the cake and decided against breaking off another piece.

"I guess that's it. Please pass along my messages as soon as you're *Sankalpa-capable,*" she said, then cringed.

Who made cheesy wordplay jokes like that?

Clearly, she did. And they weren't even that amusing.

"All righty, then," the umpteenth person to answer Howard's office line said before the call ended.

"No dice?" Jordan called from their bedroom.

She shook her head. "Howard has a zillion assistants and secretaries. I'm not even sure who I'm talking to from one week to the next. But they've all been telling me the same thing."

"The whole *Sankalpa* response?"

"Yep," she said, then changed her mind and broke off another bite of the cake.

"Just cut a piece of cake and eat it, Georgie," her husband called.

She looked around the kitchen. Her only company was a snoozing Mr. Tuesday and Faby, who had no qualms with her scarfing down a cake, piece by broken-off piece.

"How do you know I'm eating the pineapple upside-down cake?" she called.

"Are you?" he shot back, and she could hear the cocky smile in his voice.

She wiped the crumbs from her lips. "No," she answered with the giant bite still in her mouth.

"The email said they're going to serve dinner and dessert tonight. You don't want to ruin your appetite," he chided playfully.

"When in the last month has eating before a meal ruined my appetite?" she tossed back about to break off another hunk of cake when a sexy hunk of a cowboy entered the kitchen. And all thoughts of pineapple-sweet-ened carbohydrates evaporated.

"Speaking of appetites," Jordan said and moseyed across the room.

And hello, hotness!

She tried to speak, but she couldn't exactly form words other than a sultry, "Oh."

"Have I rendered you speechless, Miss Rancher's Daughter?"

"It's just that when we do our morning sexcapades, I'm the one in costume," she replied, finding her voice—but just barely. This man could have been plastered on the cover of every Western romance novel in her bookshop.

"Not tonight, little lady," he said with the tip of his cowboy hat. "It's a Western-themed gala, so we're both dressing up."

"Yeah, but you look like cowboy sex on a stick, and I look like I swallowed the cast of *Little House on the Prairie*."

He chuckled and shook his head.

She gestured toward his body. "Do you mind if I take a second? I'd pictured this way back when we'd found out we were going to have a baby. I just didn't expect it would exceed my fantasy."

"Are you asking if you can ogle me, MBG?"

"That's exactly what I'm asking," she said, not messing around with her ogling.

More than that. Any ranch he'd work on would be a mess. How the heck could any rancher's daughter get even a lick of work done with a man like this walking around.

And there was more.

Standing in front of her, in full cowboy regalia, Jordan Marks had donned not only the signature cowboy hat, plaid shirt, and jeans. He had chaps.

Let's repeat that.

Jordan Marks was wearing leather chaps.

Black leather cowboy chaps.

In her kitchen.

Right this very moment.

"Are you doing okay there, messy bun girl?" he asked when her phone pinged.

"Yup," she replied, her eyes still glued to her husband's strong, chap-wearing legs.

"Should you check that?" he pressed with a devilish grin.

The man knew exactly what he did to her.

She glanced down at her phone. "It's a text from Irene."

"More baby pics?" he asked.

Why was he talking? He knew she was mid-ogle!

"What?" she asked, finding it hard to concentrate on anything other than...chaps.

"You know, your best friend who had a baby two weeks ago in Iceland. Did she text more baby pictures?" he asked.

Georgie glanced at her phone again and saw a sweet-faced baby bundled in blue.

"Yes," she answered, damn proud of herself. Juggling chaps ogling and cell phone use was quite an accomplishment.

"Can you show them to me?"

She shook her head, her gaze trained on cowboy heaven. "No."

"No?" he replied.

She shook her head, working to have a thought that didn't involve peeling those sexy chaps off.

"I mean, yes. I'll show you later," she answered.

"Okay," he said with a self-satisfied twist to his lips.

"Why didn't you mention you'd ordered chaps with your costume?" she asked, in full-force ogle mode, unable to pull her gaze from the cowboy clothing.

Their gala outfits had arrived this morning. The best they could do to accommodate her blooming midsection was to send a white dress with a plaid shirt that matched Jordan's. She'd tied it above her giant bump—because there was no way in hell that thing could be buttoned up with the pineapple surprise she was packing. Even with her cowgirl boots and hat, she looked less like a naughty milkmaid and more like a dairy cow.

He crossed his arms, which only made him sexier—like a brooding cowboy.

"The costume store called yesterday and asked if I wanted to add them in."

"I'm glad you did," she answered as the temperature in the kitchen went up ten thousand degrees.

She was used to her husband looking good in his workout clothes. Thanks to owning and working at a gym, that's what he wore ninety percent of the time. He'd pull out his khakis and button-ups from time to time. But not in her wildest dreams—and they'd gotten pretty wild with her pregnancy—did she imagine how hot her husband would look as a real cowboy.

"You should call the costume shop."

He frowned. "Why?"

"Because you'll need to inform them that you're never returning that costume," she replied, then licked her lips.

Pregnancy horny had no shame.

"I'm not?" he asked, his boots slapping the wood floor as he moved toward her.

She closed her eyes and inhaled. "They smell all leathery-good, too."

"Do you know what else smells good?" he asked.

"What?" she replied, her eyes still closed. She could feel the heat of her husband standing only inches away, and her skin tingled in anticipation of his touch.

"You," he said, removing her cowgirl hat before pressing his lips to hers in a whisper-soft kiss.

If she hadn't done her makeup, she might have allowed herself to melt into a pool of swoon.

But one thing was for sure. Locking lips with this man never got old.

"How much time do we have before the car arrives?" she asked between kisses that grew more impassioned by the second.

Since they were hosting the hoity-toity Denver Literacy Gala for her mother and Howard, the event staff had informed them that a car would be picking them up.

Tonight, they'd rub elbows with Denver's elite movers and shakers while presenting the auction portion of the evening. And while she wasn't a huge fan of the city's socialite scene, this fundraiser was for a good cause close to her heart.

Raising loads of cash to purchase books for kids. Who can argue with that?

Jordan pulled back a fraction, and his gaze flicked to the clock. "We've got about ten minutes."

She gave those chaps another glance. "What do you think we can do in ten minutes?"

A naughty glint sparked in his eyes. "A lot."

"Define a lot?" she pressed on a breathy exhale.

He ran his hands down the length of her body and lowered his voice. "Turn around. Now."

The breath caught in her throat as her body tingled, awash in his growly tone. She liked this bossy cowboy!

"Hold on to the counter," he commanded.

A delicious shiver danced down her spine and settled between her thighs as her cowboy pressed a kiss to her neck, then slipped his hand beneath her dress.

Jordan slid his hand inside her panties and stroked her tight bundle of nerves. Just the right amount of rough from gripping barbells and thick cords of rope at the gym, he worked her in agonizingly slow, sensual circles. She bucked against his hand, wanting more, craving sweet release as her core clenched in anticipation.

"Do you like that, cowgirl?" he purred with a low, gravelly rasp.

She hummed a wicked moan. "You know I do."

His carnal cowboy control over her body continued as he stroked between her thighs and assaulted her neck with his teeth and tongue, licking and nipping her sensitive skin. She teetered on the edge, hovering between the desire for release and the sweet anguish of knowing the rush of her orgasm was only a breath away.

She closed her eyes and focused on her husband's magical fingers, stroking her in perfect, rhythmic circles.

She rocked against his hand, pure animal instinct taking over, then reached back and held onto the band of his jeans.

Her nails dug into the smooth, cool leather chaps. "Do these come off?" she pleaded.

"They do. But this is all for you," he answered, inserting a finger inside of her, then cupped her sex as he worked her slick center.

Jordan coaxed her to give in to the intense sensations, whispering in her ear, telling her all the dirty things he was going to do to her in these chaps when they got home tonight. But she couldn't reply. She could barely think. All she could do was ride his hand, bucking and thrusting like a wickedly wanton cowgirl, drawing out every ounce of pleasure.

And then, she was there. Flying, falling, spiraling. Her body tingling, head to toe.

His warm breath came in scorching puffs against the shell of her ear as she collided with her frenzied release in an explosion of passion.

"Don't stop," she bit out, riding an exquisite wave of insurmountable carnal gratification.

And bless this man, he did not slow down. Instead, he doubled his efforts, lengthening each tantalizing swell of her release until her body returned to her, leaving her warm and delectably relaxed.

She blinked open her eyes, feeling delightfully sated and peaceful, to find herself face-to-face with Faby.

"This is strange," she said on a dreamy sigh.

Jordan pressed a kiss to her temple. "I don't think Faby minds."

"I mind," she said, turning the doll to stare at the wall.

Jordan stilled. "Georgie, the baby!"

"I know, we've probably scarred Faby for life."

"No, the real baby. It kicked," he said, placing his hands on her belly.

She rested her hand on top of his. "It's freaky how this baby seems to know when I..."

"Get off?" he teased.

She pursed her lips. "Can we call it attaining sweet oblivion? It has a more poetic ring to it compared to—"

"Getting off in the kitchen?" he interrupted again with a wicked grin.

She shrugged. "I can't even think of a pithy response when you're looking all cowboy hot."

"I'm definitely keeping this costume," he said as his phone pinged.

"Time to go?" she asked, adjusting the tie on her cowgirl shirt.

"Yep, the car's here."

She checked her appearance in the reflection of the metal tea kettle and sighed at her doughnut-shaped midsection. "This is as good as it gets. At least, I've certainly got some color on my cheeks now."

He cupped her face in his hand, then brushed his thumb over her kiss-swollen lips. "You're always beautiful to me. And now I'll have the satisfaction of knowing, while we're mixing with the upper-crust of Denver at this ritzy Western shindig, that I made the naughtiest cowgirl there come hard in my hand."

Hello, dirty talk cowboy!

She opened the freezer and waved the cold air onto her face. "You get Faby. I need to get my preggo-libido under control."

"Don't freeze it all. Remember, I've got lots of ideas for what we can do with these chaps when we get home."

She swallowed hard, then started waving the cold air

with both hands when a knock at the door ended her hormone cooling session.

"It's the driver," he said, closing the freezer, then passed her a can of pineapple juice.

"One for the road?" she asked, actually quite thirsty after their sexy kitchen caper.

Jordan retrieved Faby while she inched her way down to say goodbye to Mr. Tuesday.

"Be a good boy. We love you," she said, scratching between the dog's ears.

"Georgie, we need to go," her husband called.

"Remember, Mr. Tuesday, you'll always be my first baby," she added, then kissed his nose.

In true Mr. Tuesday fashion, the pup cocked his head to the side with a big doggy grin.

She hurried out of the kitchen and met Jordan on the doorstep. They followed the driver and settled themselves in the luxurious town car as her phone pinged. She pulled it from her clutch and grinned when she saw Irene's name and picture flash on the screen.

"Hey, Irene! You're on speaker with me and Jordan and..." She tapped the driver. "What's your name, sir?"

"Um...Frank," the man replied, looking perplexed.

"You're on with me, Jordan, and Frank," she continued, greeting her friend.

"Hello, Jordan, and hey, Frank," Irene said, her voice ringing out with the soft murmurs of a baby cooing in the background.

"How's the little guy?" Jordan asked.

"Nathaniel is an absolute dream when he's sucking me dry. I've become a milk machine. Get ready, Georgie! You don't have long now."

Georgie glanced down at her ample C-cups, hardly able

to believe that she'd be feeding a baby with those things soon.

"Pregnancy is like a sci-fi movie," she said.

"And post-pregnancy is half horror flick, half comedy, but it's all worth it, isn't it, sweet Nathaniel," Irene added, her voice going gooey enamored.

Jordan pointed to his wristwatch, and she nodded.

"Irene, we don't have long to chat. We're on our way to host that fundraiser for my mom and Howard."

"What did they say when you told them about the baby? I figured they would have hopped the next private jet home."

Georgie shared a troubled glance with Jordan. "They don't know about the pregnancy yet."

The line went quiet.

"Last time we talked, you said that you'd called Howard's office," Irene replied with a puzzled edge.

Georgie released a frustrated sigh. "According to fifteen of Howard's assistants, he and my mother have gone off the grid to find their innermost desire. I've left messages, but I don't think they've gotten any of them."

"Georgie, I'm sorry. I know what a big deal it was for you to make that call," her friend replied, then yawned, and it sounded like a bear had taken over her BFF's body. "You know what my innermost desire is?"

"What?" Georgie asked.

"Eight solid hours of sleep," Irene answered on a dreamy exhale.

"Any chance of that happening in the near future?" Jordan asked.

Irene chuckled. "Nope, the milk machine is open twenty-four seven. But, Georgie?"

"Yeah?"

"Have you tried contacting your mom's assistant or the energy lady in Boulder, who hooked your mom up with this spiritual retreat?"

"No, but I think that's our next step," she answered as Jordan nodded.

"Okay, I'll let you two go back to playing socialites. Drink all the champagne for me, Jordan, and try not to annihilate any tropical fruit displays, Georgie," Irene said with a weary chuckle.

"Will do, Irene. Take care," Jordan said as she ended the call.

She reclined into the seat. "Tomorrow, we can reach out to Nicolette and the Boulder psychic lady. I don't know why I didn't think to do it sooner."

Jordan took her hand and gave it a gentle squeeze. "I agree. We'll get through tonight, then tackle all the calls tomorrow."

She nodded, ready for a nap. Sexytimes, while gestating, really took it out of a gal.

But it was showtime.

She stared up at the hotel hosting the gala as the car slowed and pulled up to the grand entrance.

"We're here," the driver said, rolling up to the Ritz-Carlton.

"The Ritz. My mom's old stomping ground," she said, tucking her pineapple juice into her purse. She could chug it in the restroom like the heathen, anti-socialite she was.

Jordan took Faby, then helped her out of the car as clapping erupted, and Hector and Bobby descended on them.

"As I live and breathe, you are as big as a house," Hector crooned with a set of air kisses.

Dressed like a fashionable hipster cowboy, his signature style screamed, look at me.

She shook her head and chuckled. "I'm not sure what a girl says in response to that, but it's nice to see you, too."

"How are you feeling?" the soft-spoken Bobby asked with a tip of his cowboy hat as Hector moved on to say hello to Jordan.

"A lot like what Hector said, honestly," she replied and patted her belly.

"And your mother?" Bobby asked quietly. "We noticed she and Howard weren't on the guest list, and your mom never misses a costume gala."

Of course, she didn't.

Georgie lowered her voice. "We haven't gotten ahold of them yet."

"Georgie! You haven't told them!" Bobby whisper-shouted.

"It's not for lack of trying. They're in seclusion, searching for their *Sankalpa*."

The man weighed her response as he dropped his shocked expression and nodded. "That makes sense. It took me years to figure out mine."

"Years?" she parroted back.

"I didn't run off to a retreat in India, but I'd thought about it for many years."

She leaned in. "And...what is it?"

Bobby went all Zen cowboy. "I am present in every moment."

She frowned. "After years of contemplation, that's it? I mean, by virtue of existing, isn't every person on the planet present in every moment?"

"It's more about relinquishing control and accepting the world for what it is and ourselves for who we are. It's about witnessing the gift of life as our true self."

"Wow," she said, hating that, at this very moment when

she should feel profoundly inspired, all she wanted to do was crack open the mini can of pineapple juice hidden away in her purse.

"Georgie," Jordan called. "Do we need to give Hector and Bobby any instructions for caring for Faby?"

"Let's chat more about the *Sankalpa* business later," she said to Bobby before they joined Hector and Jordan near the entrance.

"Here you go," Jordan said, passing their fake baby to Bobby. "You two are on Battle of the Births Faby-sitting duty."

"Here are the basics, boys. Don't lose the fake baby, and don't allow dogs or spiders anywhere near it," she added.

Hector cringed. "How's the challenge going?"

"Your face says you know exactly how it's going," she teased.

"We've gotten a few updates, here and there, from Barry, but we've been so busy creating another CityBeat offshoot," Bobby replied.

"For what?" she asked.

"Foodies. We're calling it CityBeat Eat. We've been working with several of our most popular food bloggers," the man added.

"Catchy name," Jordan replied as they entered the hotel.

"Our early beta testing is promising—especially with the breakfast food bloggers," Bobby continued as they headed toward the ballroom.

"Lucky for you, you're hosting the event and not on the auction block like you were at the last literacy fundraiser we attended," Hector added with a wink.

Sweet relief washed over her. During the Battle of the Blogs, Hector and Bobby threw a twist into the last gala they'd attended by making a book discussion session with her an auction item. And Jordan wasn't at all pleased when another guy started bidding.

"We've come a long way since then," her husband said, wrapping his arm around her.

"Agreed! You've come a long way since yesterday. Bobby and I saw a picture of Georgie taken not too long ago. And let me tell you, it *does not* do you any justice, sweetie. Even if you were going for nautical glam," Hector said with a chuckle.

What did he mean by *nautical glam?*

She was about to ask when a woman in red glittery Western-wear teetered toward them on sky-high heels.

"Georgiana and Jordan! I'm so glad you're here. I'm Muffy Bradford. Remember, we chatted over email a few months back. Come with me. We need to get you all squared away. There's been a slight change in the order of events, and we've decided to jump right into the auction."

Georgie shared a glance with her husband. "Okay. We're ready to go."

"We'll catch up with you after the auction," Jordan said to the CityBeat founders.

"And take good care of our fake baby," she added as Hector, Bobby, and Faby entered the ballroom.

The middle-aged glitter cowgirl waved for them to follow her down a hallway that ran adjacent to the ballroom.

"How are your mother and Howard?" the woman asked from over her shoulder with a flip of her glossy hair.

Georgie swallowed past the lump in her throat. "I think they're doing well."

Muffy opened a door and ushered them up a few steps to the area behind the stage.

"Do you expect them back soon?" she asked with another hair swish.

The lump in Georgie's throat doubled in size.

"We're not sure."

"I see," the woman replied with a crafty twist of her lips, then gestured toward the thick blue velvet curtains. "Wait here. They'll introduce you, and then you'll walk out on stage. And take this," she said, swiping a folder off a nearby table. "It contains all the auction items."

"So, we just read from it?" Jordan asked, accepting the folder, then glancing inside.

"Yes, and ad-lib a bit. All the ladies at the country club are enamored with you, Jordan. I'm sure you'll be a big hit with the crowd. They love your blog."

Georgie held the red sparkler's gaze. "Jordan and I work together on the More Than Just a Number blog. It's not only his blog. It's our blog."

She was not feeling this glossy crow, one bit.

A slight crease formed on Muffy's Botox-smooth forehead.

"I guess I never noticed you, dear," the woman said, then gobbled up her husband with one last thirsty look.

Georgie gave the woman a pinched grin. This Muffy character was one to be watched.

"She seems like a nice lady," Jordan said offhand as the woman's heels clickity-clacked down the hall.

Georgie crossed her arms. "That's debatable."

"Are you ready for this?" he asked, tapping the auction folder.

She glanced around the empty backstage area. Hopefully, someone running the show would check in with them.

"Do you think I have time to drink my juice?" she asked, sounding like a kindergartener, but not caring.

Shit got real when she ran low on pineapple.

Jordan bent down and pressed a sweet kiss to her lips. "You probably do. You drink, and I'll read over the auction items. We can't have you running on empty while we're on stage."

He wasn't wrong. The other day, she hadn't hit her pineapple quota and had flipped out when he'd unloaded the groceries and placed the yogurt in the crisper drawer.

Who does that, right? Still, he didn't deserve the pineapple-depleted epic tongue lashing she'd doled out.

She listened to the buzz of voices on the other side of the curtain making chitchat, then opened her purse and spied her can of salvation. She popped the top and grinned down at the liquid that used to make her hurl. The first sip never disappointed, but she didn't have time to savor the pineapple goodness. She needed to pound those six ounces like nobody's business.

Tipping the can, she channeled her inner frat boy and started gulping. She was nearly done when a gust of air and the whooshing slap of fabric, followed by blinding bright lights, left her frozen in place. With her head tilted back and the can pressed to her lips, she must have looked like a pregnant pineapple pinup girl.

Specks of dust and bits of lint hovered in the thick beam of light as she lowered the can and shielded her eyes. A shiver spider-crawled down her spine, accompanied by the crushing suspicion that something was off when a woman's shriek caught her attention and proved her premonition was correct.

"I knew it! I knew it, Howard!" came the voice she'd recognize anywhere.

Chapter Seventeen
Georgie

C lang! *Clang-clang-clang!*

Out of shock or some strange pregnant spasm, Georgie dropped the empty can of pineapple juice. And, as if swallowed by silence, everyone in the room watched the little cylinder roll to a stop at the edge of the stage.

Jordan lowered his voice. "Georgie, I think it's—"

"I know," she whispered back, feeling the color drain from her cheeks.

Her mother was here. Had the messages made it to her? Perhaps, this was a surprise?

Georgie took a few steps forward, trying to find a way to see into the ballroom without frying her retinas.

"Mom, is that you?"

"Of course, it's me," came the moneyed huff of a woman who did not sound like she was there for a pleasant surprise.

The glare of the spotlight dialed back a bit, and Georgie blinked once, then twice as she took in the scene. Hector and Bobby sat at the center table, slack-jawed and eyes as wide as saucers with Faby seated on the table.

Her gaze slid from the men and landed on her mother, standing in the center of the room.

Georgie did a double take, hardly able to believe her eyes.

There was one thing about Lorraine Vanderdinkle that remained the same no matter if she were shopping the couture racks at Chanel or reading the psychic energy of a piece of toast.

The woman was always put together. Be it jewelry from Tiffany's or crystals from some high-end hipster spiritual shop in Boulder; the woman never looked less than perfect in her chosen persona du jour.

But that wasn't who glared up at her. No, this woman sported a wild mane of hair with glints of gray—like her natural hair color gray—which hadn't been seen since the beauty disaster of 2012 when her stylist came down with the flu, and she had to wait a whole week before getting her roots done. One would have thought the world was about to implode. To ease the pain, she'd checked herself into the Ritz and gone into hiding between room service and spa treatments.

But there was more!

Her mother's usually chemically smooth face wrinkled —like, muscles actually moved—as she frowned without even the hint of makeup. And her outfit, a dull pale green tunic and flowing pants, was crumpled and—God forbid— probably not dry-clean only.

Georgie pressed her hand to her rounded belly and did her best to compose herself as the ballroom, filled to the gills with rich people in Western garb, sat stupefied.

"You look different, Mom," she stammered, then realized, a second too late, that spectacularly inarticulate utterance was probably the worst thing she could have said under the circumstances.

A few better choices...

How was your trip?

Did you nail down that *Sankalpa?*

If you haven't noticed, I'm super pregnant.

Any of these would have sufficed as a more appropriate greeting when coming face-to-face with an angry socialite who needed to have her roots done ASAP.

Her mother lifted her chin and tucked a mostly blond and partly gray strand of hair behind her ear. "This, Georgiana, is what one looks like after flying commercial for twenty-three hours straight in..." she paused, taking a moment. "Coach," she finished with a pained twist to her lips.

The ballroom flooded with gasps as women fanned themselves, and men shook their Stetson-clad heads.

Georgie glanced at her husband in an attempt to flash *oh-shit* eyes, only to find the man flashing the same expression when a bearded gentleman in a white flowing robe walked through the ballroom and stopped next to her mother.

"Namaste, Georgie and Jordan," he said with a deep bow.

"Howard?" Jordan asked, squinting into the dim ballroom.

Now, Georgie was the one gasping. Her venture capitalist, all-about-the-numbers, worth-a-boatload-of-money, pragmatic stepfather looked like a cross between a monk and a shaman. For all the years she'd known him, the clean-shaven, pressed businessman only deviated from tailored suits to don tennis whites at the country club. She figured the guy slept in some version of a business outfit.

"I go by Wandering River now. But, yes, Howard Vanderdinkle is my former, unenlightened name."

Georgie turned to her mother. "What happened to him?"

Lorraine raised her hand and waved away the kindly shaman, aka, her husband. "I cannot even get into that right now," she huffed.

It was jarring to see such depth of emotion on her mother's face. Botox had kept her Stepford-smooth for the last decade.

"Okay," Georgie uttered, stranded between shock and unmitigated awe at the sight of these two.

"Would you like to know why I've spent the last multitude of hours in a chair labeled twenty-six C?" her mother asked, throwing it out to the audience as a shockwave—presumably from the idea that Lorraine Vanderdinkle had been seated at the rear of a plane—rippled through the ballroom with another round of gasps and profound astonishment.

"Because my daughter is pregnant, and she didn't even think to inform her mother," she said amid a sea of shaking heads as a bevy of disapproving eyeballs ping-ponged from her mother to the stage.

Georgie stepped forward. "I'm sorry you didn't hear it from me, but Jordan and I have been trying to get in touch with you. I called Howard's office, and they said you were in a—"

"Critical phase of spiritual transformation," the woman supplied.

"Yes."

Her mother had to know how hard it was to get a message to them.

"You didn't think to mention that you were pregnant?"

her mother threw back. But the slight shake in her voice revealed more grief than anger.

Georgie took another step forward. "We were ready to go all out tomorrow, doing whatever we had to do to get in touch with you. Nicolette was going to be my first call."

Her mother released a frustrated sigh. "That would have done no good."

"Why?"

"She chartered a private flight—on our account—and has been living large at our bungalow in Fiji. That was another fun surprise we learned today."

"That's terrible!"

"That's a Libra!" her mother shot back.

Georgie shared a glance with Jordan. "How did you even know I was pregnant?"

Her mother crossed her arms. "A Belgian duchess."

This debacle was turning into a soap opera.

"Where did you find a Belgian duchess at a spiritual retreat in India?" she asked.

"She joined our party a few days ago and had smuggled in a cell phone. She was there to appease her daughter and wasn't at all interested in finding her *Sankalpa*. She and I bonded instantly, thanks to my knowledge of fashion and time spent on the French Riviera," her mother added, throwing that tidbit to their audience, who nodded approvingly.

"Mom, that still doesn't answer how a Belgian duchess knew I was pregnant!"

Her mother lifted her chin. "Yes, that part. Well, she and I would look through her pictures from her shopping trips in Milan as well as her favorite food blog images."

"Wait...weren't you supposed to be discovering your

innermost desire and honing your chi?" Georgie threw back.

"Your mother veered slightly from the enlightened path," Howard, Wandering River, whoever chimed.

Lorraine ran her hands through her disheveled hair. "You can only chant and look inside yourself for so long before all you want is Gustavo, delivering a dry martini after a day of shopping and three sets on the tennis court."

"The path is long and winds near the deer and the caterpillar," her stepfather offered with a sage nod.

"Is he okay?" Jordan asked, but her mother waved him off.

"Yes, I mean, the sex with Wandering River is out of this world, but that's not important now. We're not discussing Howard—"

"Wandering River," the man corrected.

"Wandering River's innermost desire," Lorraine finished.

"My innermost desire is being present in the moment, like I am right now. I am presently here, as are you," the man replied, clasping his hands behind his back.

"That's mine, too," Bobby called with a wide grin only to have her mother raise a hand and silence the man like a stern headmistress.

Georgie glanced around the ballroom to find a flurry of attendees holding up their phones and recording this train wreck of a mother-daughter reunion. These people were getting a heck of a lot more out of this night than just an auction and some square dancing.

"What is important," her mother continued, "is that the Belgian duchess follows a Belgian waffle blogger, who posts her pictures on the CityBeat site."

Georgie's jaw dropped as it all came together in a perfect blog-a-licious cluster.

"Does the duchess follow the Belgian Waffle Princess blog?" she asked.

"She does. And she's not even a real princess. She's from Sheboygan, Wisconsin, of all places. But she can knock out an amazing waffle montage. I'll give her that. But there's more. She posted a picture sent to her by her sister, who lives in Denver," her mother finished, confirming what Georgie had feared.

The policeman's wife's sister was a breakfast blogger from Sheboygan.

The Belgian Waffle Princess must have posted that picture she'd taken with the police officer.

Her mother's frown deepened. "What were you doing in your sailor suit that day? Did you enter a pregnancy beauty pageant? If so, I would have insisted on altering the costume to something more flattering. But your work pinning the hat was spot-on."

Outed by a waffle blogger and on display as Denver's worst pregnant daughter, Georgie shook her head as the room went topsy-turvy. This insanity is why she hadn't wanted to share the news with her mother. She stared out at the sea of sparkly cowgirls and leather-vested cowboys, then met her husband's gaze.

"Is this happening, or are we trapped in a pregnancy delusion?"

Before he could answer, her mother cut in.

"This is no delusion, Georgiana. This is a mother confronting an ungrateful daughter."

Jordan took a step forward and hardened his features. "Go easy, Lorraine. We understand that you're upset, but I will not stand here and allow anyone to accuse my wife of being ungrateful. Georgie has been trying to get ahold of you for weeks."

Howard pressed his hands into a prayer position. "Well done, harnessing the tiger within, Jordan."

This was too damn much!

Georgie stared up at the ceiling, shaking her head before meeting her mother's eye. "This is why I didn't know how or when to tell you."

"It's not that hard, pumpkin. Three words. I am pregnant."

"It's not that easy. Not with you, Mom," she bit back.

"Georgie," her husband whispered.

"I'm fine. If she wants to do this here and now, we do it." She lifted her chin, mirroring her mother. "I didn't know how to tell you about the baby because I was afraid that you'd go overboard."

Her mother scoffed. "Overboard like what? Fly in a couture baby's clothing designer from Paris to create a complete line of signature baby outfits? Rent out the botanic gardens and invite every spiritual energist in the state to commune with nature, then chart your baby's astrological life course?"

Georgie released a humorless bark of a laugh. "Yes, that's exactly what I was worried about!"

"Georgiana, worry is an emotion as helpful as the dew on a blade of grass," Howard replied.

"Is this how he talks all the time?" she asked as her mother huffed her frustration.

"Ignore him. Now, who here is a grandparent?" her mother asked, again turning to the audience like a talk show host.

Hands shot up throughout the ballroom.

"And how did you find out you were going to become a grandparent?" her mother pressed.

"My daughter told me over brunch at the country club," a voice called from the back of the room.

"My son and daughter-in-law broke the news by putting a message in a specially made fortune cookie," offered another woman.

"A fortune cookie, Georgiana!" her mother repeated theatrically.

Somebody needed to get this drama llama a microphone.

"And my daughter and son-in-law invited the whole family to Hawaii and told us at a pineapple farm," a man offered.

"Pineapple," her mother repeated, then gasped and stared at the can that had come to rest near the edge of the stage. "The day that I snuck away to call you—the day I felt the need to see my baby's face. That wasn't urine in the glass that you drank. It was pineapple juice. You can't stand the stuff. I watched you projectile vomit an entire pineapple fruit cup onto a row of pageant judges."

Georgie looked on, her heart in her throat, as a bitter realization swept over her mother.

"It's a pregnancy craving," she offered, but her mother shook her head.

"On the day that we arrived in India. We called to find you in the bathroom. That box in your hand, it was..." she trailed off as it all came together.

"A pregnancy test," Georgie finished, but she didn't have to. The betrayed look in her mother's eyes said it all.

"You knew that day and didn't say anything?" her mother asked, losing the talk show host vibe and now just looked like...a mom. A crestfallen mom.

Georgie's chest tightened as she felt a tiny shift in her abdomen—her baby—and stared at her mother. She didn't know what to say or where to start as the complicated dance she and her mom had been doing for so long played out in her mind.

Why hadn't she explicitly left the message that she was pregnant?

Did she want to break the news in person, or was there something deep within her that didn't want to tell—didn't want to open the *mother-daughter-crazy-train* floodgates?

She parted her lips to say, say what? I'm sorry, or even, when you caught me on the toilet, I was too freaked out at the moment to manage your reaction as well as my own? But her husband's hand clasped around hers, and the man cleared his throat before she could work out what to say.

"Ladies and gentlemen," he said, then gave her hand a reassuring squeeze. "We're taking this family discussion out of the spotlight. I'm sure my friends and CityBeat founders, Bobby Chen and Hector Garcia, wouldn't mind taking over our auction duties."

"We'd be happy to," Bobby replied as he and Hector hurried toward the stairs leading up to the stage.

Jordan led her away from the spotlight, and they met the men halfway.

"Good luck, honey," Hector said with a wince, then handed Faby over.

"We'll take it from here," Bobby added as Jordan gave him the folder.

"And you two," Lorraine called, pointing an unmanicured finger at the CityBeat duo.

"Yes, Lorraine," Hector answered, jolting upright like a soldier addressing a general.

"You own the internet! I cannot believe you didn't send

a flying robot to my location to tell me that my daughter was pregnant."

"It doesn't work like that," Bobby murmured, but her mother seemed to have passed rational thought and moseyed on into full-fledged gala spectacle.

"And last but not least, Muffy Bradford," she called out in socialite meltdown mode. "I know you're here because you made the awful choice of serving spiced meatballs and goat cheese croquettes at the gala last year. And I see that, despite my firm warning, you've made the same perilous choice again this time around."

A shimmer of red sequins skulked toward the back of the room.

"And, Muffy Bradford, if I hear you've been trying to get Gustavo to give you our table at the club, we will have words!" she roared, then stomped out of the ballroom.

Decked in head to toe Gucci or a retreat-issue tunic, this Denver socialite was back, and she wasn't messing around. And she was hurting. Georgie had seen the flash of wounded vulnerability in her eyes. A look her mother had never given her. Even after all the pageant fights and the back-and-forth over her choice to own a bookstore and make her way on her own, her mother had never looked so brokenhearted.

Howard raised his hands as if he were readying himself to broadcast a message from the great beyond. "My cowboy friends, the road is long, but the journey is short. Meditate on that and skip the meatballs. Namaste," he said, then turned to follow her mother.

Georgie clutched their fake baby as she and Jordan weaved their way through the packed ballroom, now buzzing with whispers and hushed conversations. But she didn't give a damn about what any of these people thought.

"I need to get to my mom before she leaves. I need to talk to her without every jet setter in Denver watching," she said, emotion welling in her chest.

Jordan threw open the ballroom doors, and she ran into the hotel's main vestibule. Her mother stood, dabbing at her cheeks with a handkerchief, but returned the item to her pocket when they spied each other from across the cavernous space.

"I was going to tell you, Mom. I was," she pleaded.

"Georgiana, you could never understand," her mother answered.

"Lorraine?" came a man's voice in a thick French accent.

Everyone turned toward a spindly gentleman dressed to the nines, wearing a Ritz-Carlton name tag with Jean-Philippe written in gold lettering.

As if a switch flipped, the thread of vulnerability she'd seen in her mother disappeared.

"Dear, dear, Jean-Philippe! Aren't you a sight for sore eyes!" she purred as the two exchanged air kisses as if nothing life-shattering had occurred.

The man frowned with concern etched on his expression. "It has been several months. The staff and I have missed your visits."

Her mother smoothed her tunic. "As you can see, I'm in bad shape, JP. You're the best concierge in Denver. I'll need the full spa package, and I need it now. Can you make it happen?"

"Mom, can't we talk?" Georgie sputtered as Jean-Philippe clapped his hands, and a woman, materializing from nowhere, sailed over and handed her mother a glass of champagne.

"Mr. and Mrs. Vanderdinkle are checking in. Ready the

spa. Call her stylist. Let Chanel know we have a wardrobe emergency."

"Thank you, darling," her mother said, squeezing the concierge's hand.

"And I promise you full discretion. We will never talk of this dark, dark day," JP added, touching the fabric of her mother's tunic, then cringing.

Georgie's mouth hung open in astonishment. Was that it? Was everything okay?

"And your daughter? Will she be joining you at the spa?" Jean-Philippe asked.

Lorraine Vanderdinkle met her gaze, and Georgie felt an icy chill trickle down her spine. That uncharacteristic flash of vulnerability she'd seen in her mother's eyes was gone, and flippant indifference had taken its place.

"No, JP, she won't be joining me. I'm far too much to handle and such a burden," her mother said in a teasing tone, but she wasn't joking. The hard glint in her mother's gaze conveyed that much.

"Mom—" Georgie tried, but her mother waved her off.

"No, no, no!" the woman said, then flashed a plastic smile. "There you go, pumpkin. You don't want me involved —so I'm not! It's done. I'll be no more trouble for you."

Georgie ran her hands down her face. "I don't want it to be like this," she said, barely able to get the words out.

Lorraine Vanderdinkle's socialite smile wavered a fraction, but the woman was able to get her emotions in check.

"But you do, Georgiana, you do. Your actions or, more like your inaction, proved it," she finished.

"This way, Mr. and Mrs. Vanderdinkle, your suite is ready," the concierge said and gestured toward a bank of elevators.

"That's it?" Georgie asked, her voice cracking as her mother and Howard started for the elevator.

Her mother stopped, then turned to face her. Georgie rested her hands on her belly, and her mother's gaze landed there as well. For a split-second, she'd thought all had been forgiven until her mother's expression hardened. A plastic smile stretched across the woman's lips as she donned her socialite armor.

"Yes, pumpkin. That's it."

Chapter Eighteen
Jordan

"You should try calling your mom," Jordan said, then took a sip of his chocolate-flavored protein shake as Georgie entered the kitchen.

He took the pineapple muffins out of the oven, then poured her a glass of pineapple juice as she headed for the table.

She blew out a weary breath. "That was quite a feat."

"What was?" he asked, returning the juice to the fridge.

"Crossing the room," she deadpanned.

He met her at their compact kitchen table, then pulled out a chair for her. She sank into it, her charm bracelet jangling as she settled in, then kicked her bare feet up onto an adjacent chair. With the morning sun streaming in through the kitchen window, the rays highlighted the copper and chestnut in the tendrils that fell from her messy bun. He stared at this remarkable woman. Clocking in at thirty-eight weeks pregnant, she couldn't have been more beautiful. That pregnancy glow was the real deal. With her hair piled on top of her head and her hands resting on her belly, he could make a sport out of admiring his wife.

The soon-to-be mother of his child.

He'd understood the biology of having a baby, but bearing witness to the changes in his wife's body had made him sure of one thing.

Women were a hell of a lot stronger than men.

By a mile.

Probably more.

Sure, he could flip a six-hundred-pound tractor tire. But that lasted seconds. Georgie was saddled with the weight of making a baby twenty-four seven. That took balls—no, not balls—a damn powerful uterus. If, in some far-off dimension, a pair of balls challenged a uterus to a fight, his money would be on the uterus, hands down.

Jesus! People always say it's the pregnant women who have strange, vivid dreams, but he was living proof fathers-to-be could have some whack-a-do observations of their own.

On the baby front, after the gender reveal debacle, they'd stuck to their—well, mostly Georgie's choice—and decided not to learn the baby's gender.

Yeah, he was good with it.

Okay, maybe good was a misleading characterization.

Now, mere days before he was due to become a father, he understood the plight of the men he'd met in the noisy part of the waiting room at the obstetrician's office.

In a strange daze a few nights ago, he'd crept out of the bedroom, after Georgie had fallen asleep, and worked a little obsessive pre-parent baby magic on the computer.

Had he broken down and possibly added their unborn child to the wait-list for the Denver baby NFL?

Yes, yes, he did.

Had he also gone down another strange rabbit hole after

a few clicks and descended upon the world of toddler trombone lessons?

Was their child on the wait-list for that, as well?

Yes, but only because he had to list a gender on the baby NFL registration page. He'd ticked the boy box and then felt like an absolute asshat because, of course, a baby girl should have an equal shot at the baby NFL. What kind of father wouldn't want the same for his daughter? So, he'd switched the baby NFL to girl, and then chose boy for the trombone classes.

It was completely illogical, but it gave him a strange sense of security.

Very strange.

At least he was doing something—even if this *something* could be considered a prerequisite for admittance into a psychiatric facility.

If Georgie freaked out and put the kibosh on the idea, they'd only be out the deposits. And even though he knew Thad and Briana, two doctors he trusted, weren't on board with all the baby-this and baby-that classes, a drive inside him implored him to do more. Here, Georgie was carrying the baby and working and blogging and doing a damn good job pretending like she wasn't upset about the fallout with her mom. Sure, he'd taken over doing the laundry, cooking, and cleaning, but that seemed a far cry from the full-time job of growing a human.

Georgie stared at the muffin and the glass of pineapple juice he'd set in front of her and sighed.

"My mother knows how to get in touch with me. I'm sure she's got a new Nicolette by now, who could unlock her phone for her," she answered, but there was more hurt in her voice than bite as she stared at the meal she'd been eating for breakfast, day in and day out, through her pregnancy and frowned.

"You're not hungry?" he asked, watching her closely. She'd been a pineapple consuming machine for months. She usually drained a glass in seconds. You'd think she'd just rolled in from a stint on the Sahara.

"I'm not feeling so much like pineapple today," she said as her gaze slid to the chocolate protein drink in his hand.

He held out the shake. "Do you want this?"

"Yeah? Is that weird?" she asked, taking his protein drink, then chugging down half of it in under ten seconds.

"Protein is a good energy source and great for the baby," he replied to the spirit of the frat boy who decided to invade his wife's body.

"Perfect! I was thinking of knocking out a quick 10K run this morning," she teased, wiping away her chocolate mustache.

"You are one pregnant badass. I'll give you that, MBG. But, at your race pace, I think the baby would be born before you made it one kilometer."

She took another sip, then gave him a healthy dose of side-eye. "You better watch it, mister. All these hormones might make me supersonic fast or Superwoman strong."

He glanced at his phone. "Well, Ms. Supersonic, we don't have a whole lot of time before we need to head over to the bookshop for—" he paused.

"The baby shower," she supplied flatly, her gaze trained on a spot on the wall.

Yeah, today might be a tough one.

They'd decided not to follow convention—imagine that —and settled on having a joint baby shower, men included, with their close friends and family. Becca, citing the fact that she was unable to throw her sister a proper shower, had designated herself, and Brice, as the lead party planners.

What could possibly go wrong with those two in charge?

Still, it was the least of his concerns.

"Did your mom even RSVP? I know Becca invited her," he asked, treading lightly.

The last thing he wanted to do was upset his wife. But it was a coin toss when it came to her reaction regarding her mom. Sometimes, she wanted her mom to show up to the shower, and then she'd change her mind and say that she wanted her to stay away. Other times, she wanted her mom to *want* to show up, and then not show up—but then decide to show up anyway.

This mother-daughter business was thorny stuff.

He and his father had been estranged for many years after his mother passed. But all it took to get them back on track was Georgie, charming the pants off his dad, and a Michael Bolton ballad.

"Oh yes, Lorraine Vanderdinkle is always one to RSVP," she answered, injecting a thread of mock-haughtiness into her reply.

"And?"

Georgie made a flippant flick of her wrist. "And she's unable to attend due to a brunch commitment."

He frowned. She couldn't be serious.

"A brunch commitment?" he pressed.

"At the country club, of course. She wouldn't want to disrupt the delicate balance of the Denver elite brunch dynamic now that she's back. I'm sure Gustavo has her table all ready," she said, back to mock-haughty. But even her terrific impression of a deranged socialite couldn't hide the disappointment he saw as plain as day in her eyes.

It had been a rough last couple of weeks. Being pregnant has its emotional ups and downs. Being pregnant and balancing a damaged mother-daughter dynamic had taken a toll on his wife. He'd reached out to Howard, aka Wandering River, to try to orchestrate a reunion, but the man was still in full-on yogi mode and spoke entirely in metaphors for their entire conversation.

He'd said that Lorraine was a rock, wanting to roll but stuck in the moss.

Like mother, like daughter.

"I told Howard about the shower," he said, coming to sit with her at the table.

"When?"

"A couple of days ago."

"What did he say?"

"He wished us every blessing and suggested the next time it rains, we dance naked under the storm clouds and pay homage to the showers that nourish the planet."

She pressed her fingertips to her eyelids. "Do we have the strangest life ever?"

He rubbed her arm, then touched the charm bracelet, gazing at the little shit shovel.

"Yes, we're probably in contention for the couple living the strangest life ever. What do you think, Faby?" he said, turning to the baby doll seated in the center of the table.

They may have failed every Battle of the Births challenge, but they'd done a damn good job keeping track of that fake baby.

Georgie opened her eyes and chuckled. "We should probably add a Faby charm," she said, brushing her fingers over the bracelet. "And thank God you got me a bracelet and not an anklet. Look at my ankles! Wait, I can't even see them," she added, trying to get a glimpse over her belly.

What she didn't know was that he'd already ordered not one but two surprise charms.

He took her feet into his lap and massaged her arches. "Your ankles look all right to me."

"Good, because last time I could see them, it wasn't pretty," she replied, then blew out a tight breath. "How about we walk to the bookshop?"

He wasn't expecting that.

"Are you up for it?"

"I think it would do me good," she replied, then sucked in a tight breath.

"Are you having another Stevie Nicks?" he asked, feeling his heart rate kick up.

"Braxton Hicks, you giant asshat," she replied, half laughing half trying to breathe through what joyless Joyce had explained were practice contractions that Georgie needed to "put on her big girl panties and tough out."

Ah, Joyce! The answer to the question, name something that doesn't grow sweeter over time.

"I think it's over," she said, relaxing into the chair.

"Are you sure you want to walk to the shop today?"

She nodded. "It's not that far, and I'd like some air."

"All right, team! We're walking!" he announced to their dog and fake baby.

He helped his wife to her feet, corralled and leashed the dog who had started running insane loops around his legs at the mention of a walk, then scooped up their baby doll.

Perhaps Georgie was right. They really were a bunch of freaks.

"Oh, Birkenstocks! You've never failed me," she said on a dreamy exhale as she slid on her sandals, and they headed out the door.

He took her hand as they strolled at a pregnant snail's pace down the street toward the shop.

"Do you remember chasing Mr. Tuesday when he snagged Faby and made a break for it?" he asked.

"Do I remember? That was the fastest I've ever run. And I was eight weeks pregnant at the time."

He glanced at her. "Back then, it seemed like we had all this time before we were going to become parents, and now, here we are."

"Here we are," she repeated with a pat to her belly.

They turned the corner, and Georgie hummed a sweet sound.

"What?"

"The park," she answered.

The location of their not-so-cute meet-cute when he was all about being a perfect ten asshat.

"I can picture you in that awful cardigan, chasing Mr. Tuesday and calling after him like a lunatic," he said, egging her on a touch.

"Oh, come on. You know that's when you fell in love with me," she teased, but she wasn't far off the mark.

From the moment this sassy woman anointed him the Emperor of Asshattery, he was a goner.

"I think that's when *you* fell in love with *me*," he said, making sure to sound as asshattish as possible.

She barked out a laugh.

"Maybe not at that exact moment," he conceded.

She glanced up and caught his eye. "But it wasn't too long after."

He gave her hand a gentle squeeze as they continued down the street in silence, Mr. Tuesday padding along beside them. The memories of their relationship flashed through his mind like one of those old slide projectors.

Click.

First image: Georgie staring him down with those flashing, blue-green eyes, demanding he help her catch her dog.

Click.

Georgie standing in the produce aisle, ruining cucumbers for Save the Whales Steve.

Click.

Georgie staying by his side, smiling up at him as he overcame his baby goat phobia.

Click.

Georgie in her wedding dress.

Click.

Georgie rocking baby Ollie to sleep.

Click.

Georgie with sex hair, pressing her hands to his chest and riding his hard length as their souls intertwined.

"Hey? Earth to Jordan. Come in, Jordan?" she said, gazing up at him with a creased brow.

"Slide projector sex hair," he blurted, for what reason, he didn't know. He was pretty damn sure slide projector sex hair never was, nor would it ever be, the response to any reasonable question.

She gestured with her chin. "We're here."

He blinked a few times and focused on the bookshop entrance.

"Were you having a man-pregnancy delusion?" she asked.

"More like a man-pregnancy delusion oasis filled with a bunch of hot Georgies."

"That's a new one! I was thinking about you in your cowboy chaps," she confessed with a devious grin.

"At least we're on the same creepy wavelength for thoughts one has before a baby shower."

He opened the door to the shop, smelling the familiar sweet scent of hardback books and freshly baked muffins, then spied Talya and Simon at the register, making googly eyes at each other.

Despite being head over heels and *epically* into one another, they were hardworking kids, and Georgie had hired them on for the summer.

"How are sales?" he asked as the teens blushed and straightened up.

"Epic sales," Talya answered as Mr. Tuesday ran behind the counter to curl up in his dog bed.

Simon nodded. "Totally epic! This is the first lull we've had all morning."

Talya pointed toward the children's area. "Becca said to send you back when you got here. We can keep Mr. Tuesday with us."

"But first, we had something made for the baby," Simon added.

"You didn't have to get us anything," Georgie said, but Simon's grin only got bigger.

"We wanted to, and it's also from my grandma. She actually came up with the idea."

"Here," Talya said, passing a small gift bag across the counter.

"We hope you think it's epic," Simon added, sharing a look with Talya, as Georgie pulled a tiny baby onesie from the bag, then pressed the small garment to her heart.

"Epic, right?" Simon said, almost laughing.

Okay, he'd gotten used to the *epic* talk, but today they seemed to be pouring on the epic sauce a little heavier than usual. Simon was still his best high school student, knocking out daily early morning workouts at his gym. From all the time he'd spent with him, he knew the kid could come up with at least a few other adjectives.

"Totally epic! You two are so thoughtful," Georgie answered, flipping the shirt so he could see it, then pointed to the letters *E-P-I-C* embroidered across the front.

Now he was the one pressing his hand to his heart. Dammit, he was a brick house of a guy. Brick houses did not cry over sentimental gifts.

He sniffled but pulled it together. "It's an epically thoughtful gift. Thank you."

Georgie brushed a tear from her cheek. "And please, tell your grandmother we love it," she said when Talya gasped.

"What is it?" Georgie asked.

"Becca said not to make you cry. She wants that to be her job," Talya replied, worry marring the poor kid's features.

Georgie laughed. "It sounds like her."

"They're all set up in the children's story time area," Simon said.

"There aren't any toddlers in there, are there?" Jordan asked.

Talya chuckled. "No, not today. We promise."

He mimed wiping his brow. "Thanks for holding down the fort during the shower and keeping an eye on Mr. Tuesday."

"Have fun," Talya called as Georgie took his hand, and they wove their way to the children's story time area.

She held up the little shirt and admired it as they walked. "I did not expect to be so emotional today."

"Just remember to cry for Becca," he teased as the story time room came into view and...

"Wow!" Georgie said, taking the words right out of his mouth.

"It's something else in here, isn't it?" Barry called from the far side of the room with his camera trained on them.

That's right! They'd agreed to provide baby shower footage for the Battle of the Births. But the man wasn't wrong about the décor.

The children's area had been transformed into a baby wonderland.

Braided streamers in cream, a soft shade of yellow and light green crisscrossed the ceiling while matching crisp tablecloths lined a buffet table dotted with delicate flower arrangements made of tulips and other flowers. He didn't know the names of the other flowers because he was a dude. But it looked fantastic.

Becca groaned. "I know! It's awful. I'd planned a whole creepy baby doll theme to pay homage to Faby, but the party store sent the wrong stuff. By the time I got back here to check on the setup, they were done. I hope you don't mind."

He glanced around the space, and while anything sounded better than a creepy fake baby shower, this looked like a baby shower right out of a magazine.

"I'm sure your idea would have been...fun, but this is very nice," Georgie said, glancing around the room and doing her best not to look too pleased when Brice joined them.

"I told Becca I could run out and buy a bunch of dolls, and we could pop off their heads for decorations."

"But there was no time," Becca lamented with an irritated harrumph.

Thank the universe for that!

"Yeah, too bad. A creepy baby shower would have been unique," he added, sharing a relieved glance with Georgie.

"My goodness! It's lovely back here!" Marjory Gilbert

said as she and the blue-haired knitting brigade made their way into the room with Gene close behind.

"This may be the most gender-neutral I've ever felt," Hector added as he and Bobby trailed in behind the octogenarians.

Becca stood in the center of the room, and Barry maneuvered to get everyone in view.

"Hello, everyone and our CityBeat friends at home," Becca began, glancing over at Barry. "Welcome to Georgie and Jordan's baby shower. Please, get something to eat! It's a complete pineapple spread in honor of Georgie. Pineapple dream cake, pineapple crisps, pineapple cheesecake from that little shop she loves. And pineapple mimosas—but not for you, Ms. Preggo," Becca added. "I've got a pineapple sherbet seltzer concoction for our soon-to-be new mom and those unable to partake in alcohol," Becca finished, then directed the group toward a table lined with treats.

"Do you want me to make you a plate?" he asked, but Georgie shook her head.

"I'm not hungry."

"You're not hungry?" he asked, eyeing her carefully when a thunderous pounding boomed through the shop.

"Jordan! Jordan! We have a gift for you and Georgie," Mia and Mya, Maureen's girls, called, charging into the room like twin bulls.

He handed Faby to his wife as the girls wrapped their arms around his waist, nearly knocking him over.

He looked up to see his father and Maureen enter the room. They waved, then beamed at each other—the lovebirds.

It was like the roles were reversed. Here he was, married and about to become a father. And there was his dad, making goo-goo eyes with his girlfriend. Still, it did his heart good to see his father and Maureen so happy. If two people deserved it, it was the two of them.

"Here's the present," Mya said, giggling, as she and Mia exchanged a knowing glance.

"Something is up with you two. Is this a trick present? Will confetti explode into my face when I open it?" he joked, taking the slim rectangular package.

But his teasing expression disappeared when he'd read what they'd written on the gift card.

To our brother and sister-in-law

Georgie glanced at it. "Are you sure this gift is for us, girls?"

"You're married to Jordan, right?" Mia said, like the cat who ate the canary.

"Yes," Georgie answered with a dubious lilt.

"Girls, you know I love you like a brother, but I'm not officially your brother," he said, trying to work this out without hurting their feelings.

Maureen raised her left hand, revealing quite a sparkler on her ring finger. "You'll be their brother soon," she said, grinning as the room broke out in applause and congratulations for the newly engaged couple.

"Barry, are you getting this?" Hector called to the City-Beat producer.

"Every last bit," the man replied.

Jordan had almost forgotten they were recording. But what a great thing to capture!

"When did this happen?" he asked, shaking his father's hand as Georgie hugged Maureen, Mya, and Mia.

The twins bolted over to his dad, and the man wrapped an arm around each girl.

"Well—" he began, but the twins were faster.

"Denny took us all to the botanic gardens last night," Mia began.

Mya hopped from foot to foot. "You know, where you and Georgie got married."

He barely had time to nod in agreement before Mia took over.

"And then, he told me and Mya that he loved our mom and wanted to marry her, but only if it was okay with us," Mia continued, their twin-speak shifting into warp speed.

"Yeah, and then we said yes and asked if that meant you would be our brother."

"We always wanted a brother."

"And now we have one."

"Plus, with Denny's garage, he says that when we can drive, he'll make our cars go super-fast, right?"

Jordan could barely keep up with the back-and-forth between the tweens.

His father chuckled and gazed lovingly at the girls. "Right to everything but the super-fast cars. That one we'll have to run by your mother."

Mya rolled her eyes as only a newly minted twelve-year-old can. "Anyway, Denny got down on one knee and said some super sweet stuff to Mom. Then, Talya and Simon picked us up and babysat us for the rest of the night because Mom and Denny said they were going to go do boring adult stuff."

"Boring adult stuff, huh?" he repeated, eyeing his father and Maureen as the woman who'd been like a mother to him for the past decade blushed.

"Open the present, Jordan! Open it! Your dad was so excited to get it for your baby," the girls chimed, pointing to the gift.

He tore the wrapping carefully, then tears blurred his vision.

"Your mother used to read that book to you all the time when you were little," his father said, growing misty-eyed as well.

Jordan nodded, his throat tightening as he stared at a copy of *The Tale of Peter Rabbit* by Beatrix Potter. "Yeah, I remember."

"Do you like it?" Mia pressed.

"I do. Thank you," he said, emotion coating the words as he held his father's gaze.

"Can we go talk to Simon and Talya now?" Mia asked, injecting a bout of tween humor into the wave of emotion that nearly overtook him.

Maureen nodded. "You may. First, tell Georgie and Jordan congratulations."

"Congratulations, bro!" the girls chimed, then skipped out of the room toward the front of the shop.

"I know your mother is looking down on you from heaven. She'd be so proud and so happy for you and Georgie," his father said, blinking back tears.

Jordan looked between his father and Maureen. "I think Mom would be happy for the both of us," he replied.

He passed the book and Faby to his wife, then embraced his father—so grateful to have the man back in his life. He was beyond excited his dad had proposed to Maureen. If anyone deserved to be loved and cherished, it was her. And he knew his father was the one for the job. All he had to do was watch his dad for a second to see the absolute devotion in his eyes when the big guy caught a glimpse of her.

"You're familiar with this book, aren't you? It's about a mischievous bunny who'd disregarded his mother's warning to steer clear of Mr. McGregor's farm, only to go straight there, and barely escape by the skin of his teeth."

"I—" she began when Gene and Marjory handed her a slim rectangular box.

"We should have checked with Denny and Maureen first," Gene said with a chuckle.

"Go on and open it, Georgie," Marjory offered.

Georgie handed him the picture book and their fake baby as she unwrapped the gift, revealing another copy of *The Tale of Peter Rabbit*.

"This book was also one of Georgie's favorites as a girl," Gene announced to the group.

She nodded. "My dad introduced me to it."

"No, he didn't, dear," Marjory countered, then shared a look with Gene.

Georgie cocked her head to the side. "Sure, he did. My dad was all about the books—even when I was little."

Gene shook his head. "No, sweetheart, open it. We added an old photograph to the title page."

Gently, Georgie lifted the cover to reveal an image of a woman, who looked like the mirror image of his wife, holding a baby in one arm and a book, none other than *The Tale of Peter Rabbit*, in the other.

Georgie stared at the image. "I had no idea."

"It was almost a running joke with your mom and dad," Marjory added.

"How so?" Georgie asked.

The man chuckled, then waved them all over to sit as Barry hung back, capturing the moment.

Gene settled into a chair, then met Georgie's gaze. "Peter Rabbit was all your mother, Georgiana. Your father wasn't crazy about that book at all. He hated that Peter was such a naughty rabbit and almost got himself caught by not listening to his bunny mother and avoiding the dangerous farm. But not your mom. That's not how she saw it."

Georgie's hand went to her belly. "What did she think?"

"She saw Peter's day of dodging the farmer and barely making it out alive as a grand adventure. Naughty Peter might not have gotten the reward of eating bread and berries like his siblings did when he finally returned home, but he had something they didn't."

"What did she think Peter Rabbit had gotten?" Georgie asked, her voice barely a whisper.

"Experiences. Your mother argued that, thanks to his wild day, Peter had encountered the world. And that was worth the risk to her," Marjory explained.

"I would venture to say all those pageants she'd entered you in was a way to give you a taste of the world—a way to gain new experiences and learn about different places," Gene added, then paused. "And, if I remember correctly, she was also avoiding carbohydrates, so a dinner of bread sounded ghastly to her."

Georgie released a teary chuckle. "It does sound like her."

Jordan reached over and took his wife's hand. "Are you okay?"

Georgie sucked in a tight breath, then leaned forward, and squeezed his hand.

"Stevie Nicks?" he asked, then shook his head. "Paxton Dicks?"

That wasn't it either!

Dammit! How could he not remember the name of the practice contractions?

"Oh! I've got it! Braxton Hicks!" he called out.

She nodded, giving him a thumbs-up, then exhaled as her body relaxed. "Just a little one, but..." she trailed off.

"Do you want some water?" he offered.

"Or a pineapple sherbet seltzer?" Becca chimed, holding up a pitcher of a godforsaken lumpy mixture.

Georgie stared out at their friends and family, then her gaze landed on him.

Her bottom lip trembled. "What if our child wants to enter beauty pageants? There will be so many things out of our control, Jordan. Maybe keeping the pregnancy from my mom was my attempt to hold on to some semblance of control? And more than that, is our child going to think we don't have his or her best interest at heart? What kind of mother will I be? Will I be a total control freak and not allow them to figure out who they want to be? Am I strong enough to let them reject everything I stand for to allow them to find their way?"

Sweet self-help soliloquy! This got deep quickly.

The room erupted into a flurry of reassuring comments when he said the only thing that he thought could ease her mind—or at least distract her from her worries.

"I signed up a dual sex baby for toddler trombone lessons and the baby NFL."

The chatter stopped.

"You did what?" Georgie asked as Barry took a step toward him, camera in hand.

This guy was going to hit the baby shower bizarro moments mother lode.

"What's a dual sex baby?" Hector asked, sharing a look with Bobby, who shrugged.

Jordan looked out at the group of people, all staring at him as if he had ten heads.

"It's a baby with a penis and a vagina," came one of the blue-haired brigade members, holding up her smartphone.

"Georgie's baby has a penis and a vagina?" asked another.

"This is what the phone says."

Becca frowned and crossed her arms. "I didn't think you learned the sex! That could have helped me with planning the games and added a whole new dimension to this party. The only interesting baby game I could find on the internet was when you melt a bunch of different chocolate bars into diapers to make it look like poop. Then, everyone gets a taste of each baby candy poop diaper, and they have to guess which candy bar it is," Becca said, her pout still in place.

Brice winced. "Oh no! I ate them all. I didn't think you needed those for the shower."

Jordan raised his hands to get the group's attention. While he was grateful they wouldn't have to sample chocolate baby poop, he needed to clarify the dual sex baby comment.

"What I meant was that I made up a boy and a girl baby profile and put our child on two waiting lists."

"I thought we agreed not to do that?" Georgie said with a pinched expression, which could either mean she was pissed or having another Stevie Nicks practice contraction.

"We did," he conceded.

"Then why did you do it?"

He held her gaze. It was the moment of truth.

"Maybe for the same reason you didn't tell your mom— wanting some control over the unknown."

Her lips twisted into the hint of a grin. "You really are the Emperor of Asshattery."

He grinned right back at her. How he loved this woman!

"We can't have you being the only one freaking out

about losing control," he said, leaning over to press a kiss to her temple.

"I think you guys are missing the point," Brice said, through a bite of a pineapple scone.

"And what's that?" Georgie asked.

"Control is an illusion. Things always change, Georgie," Brice said, tossing the final bite into his mouth, then reaching for another flaky pastry.

Georgie leaned forward and stared at the man. "Did you call me *Georgie?*"

The guy grinned through the bite. "Yeah, that's your name."

"I'm amazed you remembered. You've called me Virginia and Georgia for so long, it almost sounds odd to hear you get it right."

"You can thank Becca for that. She said that if I got your name right at the baby shower, she'd get down on her knees and—"

Becca's cheeks bloomed scarlet as she clapped her hand over Brice's mouth. "This is not an appropriate place to discuss our Georgie arrangement."

"You called it the Georgie arrangement?" Georgie balked.

Yeah, he had to side with his wife. Having your name equal a BJ was pretty gross.

Becca threw up her hands. "What did you want me to call it? The Virginia arrangement? That would have only confused him more!"

"Did you say the baby has a vagina?" another blue-haired brigade lady called.

Sweet Jesus! The nice knitting ladies hadn't moved on from the dual sex fiasco—and it would all be captured on film.

"Not vagina! He said, Virginia, like the state," Becca answered, raising her voice and speaking slowly.

"Can I explain my thoughts about change?" Brice asked, his voice muffled by Becca's hand.

"Do your thoughts involve whipped cream or handcuffs?" Becca queried as everyone's eyebrows shot to their foreheads.

"Becca!" he and Georgie cried in unison—with a searing parental bend to the word.

Becca was like a little sister to him and to Georgie! Sure, she was a grown woman—but still!

"What do you do with the whipped cream?" a blue-haired briagader asked.

At least they'd moved on from vaginas.

"Ask the phone?" another offered.

Becca shook her head and removed her hand from Brice's mouth.

"Keep it clean," she warned.

"Got it. Now, Georgie," Brice said, then glanced at Becca as if to make sure she was keeping track of all the correct uses of *Georgie*. "Control is an illusion. Like I was telling Becca the other day when I was here for a pest inspection. I can't get all the spiders out of the bookshop. There will always be some I miss. All I can do is try my best, and the rest you've got to leave to the universe."

"Are there spiders in my shop?" Georgie asked, her gaze rocketing to the ceiling where, thankfully, there wasn't a spider about to pull a Little Miss Muffet caper.

"No," Becca replied as Brice nodded yes.

"You see, Virginia," the man continued, two for three on the Georgie front. "All you can do is sit back and love the people around you. Also..."

"Yes, Brice?"

"Good hair never hurts," the man added, running his hand through his exceptionally good hair.

Becca shrugged, then grinned at her boyfriend. "He's not totally wrong."

Georgie stood up. "No, he's not wrong at all. We're not in control. Not one little bit. I've lost my father. Jordan, you've lost your mother." She gazed around the room. "All we can do is love the people we have in our lives."

"Are you all right?" he asked his wife as she nestled Faby into the crux of her arm, looking decidedly like a woman with a mission.

She nodded. "Yes, I'm good. I know what I need to do before this baby is born."

"And what's that?" he asked as a determined spark gleamed in her eyes.

"I'm taking Faby, and we're getting out of here."

"You're leaving?" Becca cried.

Georgie nodded resolutely.

"Yes, but it's for a good cause. It's something I have to do."

He cupped her face in his hand. "Is it something with the baby? Do you need the doctor?"

She shook her head. "No."

He held her gaze. "Then what?"

She schooled her features—going full-on hardcore MBG. "I need you to be the Clyde to my Bonnie."

That was a new request, but one he had no trouble answering.

He met her badass expression with one of his own. "Call me Clyde. What do you have up your sleeve, Bonnie?"

Her blue-green eyes flashed unwavering determination.

"We're about to go country-club-gangster and crash brunch."

Chapter Nineteen
Georgie

"Land ho!" Georgie cried, pointing at the street sign for Country Club Drive as her trifecta bristled at her attempt at pirate-speak.

Jordan cranked the wheel, and the van shrieked and heaved as they took the corner. She didn't need to supply directions. Her husband knew the way to the posh playground for Denver's elite families, but the urgency coursing through her body had given her the fortitude of a dogged sea captain, trapped in roiling waters and hellbent on making it to shore. Besides batten down the hatches, land ho was the only pirate phrase she could think of, and lucky for her, it suited the situation.

Thanks to Brice Casey—yep, the once douche canoe whose asshattery had sparked the Own the Eights blog and tipped the first domino that had led her to this very moment —she'd had an epiphany. She also needed to find another pest control company to dispose of the spiders Brice had missed—but that was a task for another day.

Here's what hit her like a wrecking ball. It was the same

thought she had when she saw the first positive pregnancy test—but with a twist.

Life is a roller coaster. She wasn't wrong about that.

But, unlike the day she learned she was pregnant, reeling from how she'd manage to do it all, Brice's words led her to see that she didn't have to.

She and Jordan weren't going to be perfect parents.

They would be loving parents.

Love couldn't be measured by a score or a competition. Love was beyond that—infinite and abundant.

He'd said that all you can do is hold on to the ones you love—and he was right.

She and Jordan had each lost a parent. They'd battled their own demons and insecurities, but one thing remained true.

Love.

It was their foundation, and thanks to the wacky ups and downs the universe had thrown at them, love was all around them. Bobby and Hector, Gene and Marjory, Denny and Maureen, Irene and Will, even Becca and Brice. But two people were missing.

Her mother and Howard.

But with love comes risks. And just like Peter Rabbit, she was ready to put it all on the line.

Had she momentarily lost her gangster edge and bawled her eyes out, then hugged everyone at the shower before they left?

Yes.

Did she then steal Brice's car keys off the counter and tell Talya and Simon to let the guy know that they'd hijacked his van?

Yep, at that point, she'd regained her Bonnie and Clyde

vibe and went with it. Plus, everyone else who'd arrived at the party had walked, so their choices were limited when it came to securing a vehicle.

"What's the plan?" Jordan said, starting up the long drive leading to the country club.

She chewed her lip—a very un-sea captainy behavior, but she had a lot going on. Hormones, adrenaline, that boost from Jordan's shake. It all came together like a pregnancy pick-me-up that sent a zing through her body until another Braxton Hicks contraction knocked her down a peg. Truth be told, even with the practice contractions giving her a run for the money today, she was so amped up, she could probably power the city with the stimulants in her bloodstream.

"We're pulling a Peter Rabbit," she answered as her trifecta donned leather jackets to add to the badass, break-the-rules vibe.

"You want us to enter a dangerous place and barely make it out in one piece?" he questioned.

She nodded. "I don't know about you, but that's exactly how I describe brunch at the country club."

He glanced over. "And once we crash the place?"

"I'm going to confront my mother. There's no more hiding behind late RSVPs and unanswered emails. If she wants nothing to do with me, she'll have to tell it to my big, fat, pregnant ankles. I'm going to apologize, and like it or not, she'll have to listen."

There, that was a plan.

"There's nothing wrong with your ankles, MBG," her husband replied.

"Fine. My big, fat, pregnant face!" she amended as the van sputtered and came to a standstill.

Jordan tapped the gages on the dashboard, and she craned her neck to see what he was doing.

"What's wrong?"

He leaned back. "We're out of gas. We were low, to begin with. But I thought we'd make it."

She blew out a frustrated breath, then gathered her resolve. Her date with destiny was just up the road. A little car trouble was not about to stand in her way.

She snagged Faby, then swung open the door. "It's not too far. We can walk."

Jordan jogged up alongside her and shielded his eyes, staring down the treelined drive. "This might be a longer walk than you think. I should call up and have them send a golf cart."

She shook her head. "Oh no! I am not losing the element of surprise. This is the last place in the entire world my mother would expect to find me."

"Why is that?" he asked, offering his arm, which she gladly took.

"Because after she made me compete in the country club's debutant pageant here when I was seventeen, I explicitly told her I'd never set foot in this place again."

She froze and gripped her husband's forearm as a lightning bolt of a contraction tore through her.

Jordan stroked her cheek. "Georgie, let's call the doctor."

She shook her head. "No, not yet. The contractions are still pretty random. Dr. Beaver said to wait to call until they were five minutes apart. Something just like this happened the other day. I had a bunch of contractions, and then they stopped. I need to see my mom. I need to have some kind of resolution. And I need it today."

"Why today?" he pressed as they continued up the drive.

She stared down at her belly. "Call it pregnancy intuition. Call it indigestion. Call it never wanting to see another pineapple for as long as I live. I just know that I have to do this."

His jaw dropped. "Are you serious about the pineapple?"

"Yeah, in fact, whatever happens inside this godforsaken place, afterward, we're calling for a car and having it take us to get a giant tube of vegan chocolate chip cookie dough."

"Wow! I never thought that I'd hear you say that again. Pregnancy cravings and anti-cravings come out of nowhere," he replied.

"I know. It was like a switch flipped," she answered, rubbing her belly.

They continued up the drive as luxury cars whipped past them. Maybe Jordan was right? What she thought would be a two- or three-minute walk was taking much longer. Then again, she'd never walked it. After a few more steps, she was ready to give in and let Jordan call for a golf cart when they rounded the bend, and the pristine country club building emerged. Shrouded in emerald green fairways and manicured hedges, the June sun glinted off a sea of luxury cars parked in the circle drive.

"We made it!" she cried, walking up the steps as two men opened a set of grand double doors for them to enter.

Jordan lowered his voice. "We'll play this cool, right?"

"Right, I don't want to make a scene. What happened at the gala cannot happen again," she replied, then spied the man she needed.

Gustavo.

The Country Club General Manager.

And Denver upper-crust insider.

"Hello, Gustavo!" she said as the man did a double take.

"It's been ages, Georgiana," the man said, dipping down for a set of air kisses. "Your mother and Wandering River didn't mention you and your husband were joining them for brunch."

She had to bite back a grin. Howard, still calling himself Wandering River, had to have raised some eyebrows. Then again, this was Colorado, and he was loaded.

"I'm dropping in unannounced, and I'd like to keep it that way," she answered.

"I see," the stately gentleman replied with a weary nod.

A nervous grin stretched across her face. "No funny business. I just need to see my mom."

"I've seen your video," the man parried back.

She shared a perplexed look with her husband. "Which video? Jordan and I make lots of them for our More Than Just a Number blog."

"This one was from a benefit," the man added, raising an eyebrow.

Oh no! Gustavo could not think she was a rabble-rouser! He'd never let her into brunch!

She cringed.

"Shall I let your mother know you're here?" the man offered.

Oh, hell no! He was trying to brunch block her!

Gustavo had over thirty years handling Denver's social elite, but she was armed with something that gave her the license to do whatever the hell she wanted.

She was mega-pregnant, carrying a baby doll, and packing a giant belly.

She lifted her chin. "No, you shall not let my mother know we're here."

"Georgie," her husband said under his breath, but she'd decided not to take his warning.

"Like it or not, Gustavo, we're crashing brunch," she said like a mob boss.

"Hi, there, I'm Jordan Marks," her husband said, cutting in and shaking the man's hand.

"Could we at least find a jacket for your husband—club dress code policy, you know—and then I could escort you in," the manager offered, but she could sense a crack in his brunch defense facade.

She waved him down. "Look at me, Gustavo! I'm as big as a whale and could blow at any minute. We don't have time to play dress up. Do you have kids?"

"Yes, they're grown now," he answered with a distinct look of terror in his eyes.

"Do you remember what it was like when your wife was pregnant? The cravings, the hormones, the yo-yo emotions? I'm going into brunch, Gustavo. And you don't want to get in my way today," she continued.

"I'd listen to her, man," Jordan cautioned.

Gustavo swallowed hard. "I think we can waive the jacket requirement due to your delicate condition."

She patted the manager's arm. "You're good people, Gustavo," she said, then grabbed her husband's hand and entered the sanctuary of chef-prepared omelets and a pastry table the size of Cleveland.

"I see them. They're in the center, close to the windows," Jordan said, pointing past a swath of club members.

Georgie nodded. With not a strand of gray hair on her head, her mother was back to looking socialite fabulous.

This was it!

They wove their way through the dining room when her nerves started to get the best of her. Her stomach—or the baby—did a flip-flop as another contraction took her breath away.

"Georgie, are you okay?" Jordan asked.

She leaned over, gazing down at the white marble floor, and breathed through the pain.

"Georgiana, what are you doing here?" came her mother's surprised voice.

Georgie blew out a tight breath, rode out the last spasm of the contraction, then met her mother's gaze.

"I'm here because we need to talk."

"As you can see, we're in the middle of brunch," Lorraine Vanderdinkle replied with a demure wave of her hand toward Howard, who'd donned a sport jacket over his flowing robes.

Georgie glanced around, trying to figure out where to start, her brain temporarily scrambled from the searing contractions that seemed to be growing stronger.

"It looks like you were able to keep your table," she threw out, then wanted to jam a tube of vegan cookie dough into her mouth to keep the idiotic comments from flying out.

"Of course, we were able to keep our table. Do you think I'd allow Muffy Bradford to steal it out from under me?" her mother replied, gesturing toward the back of the room where a miffed Muffy pretended not to notice.

"Mom, I need a minute with you and Howard."

"It's Wandering River, and you've got quite an aura, Georgie. Lots of energy. Something psychedelically powerful is about to happen to you," Howard or whatever the hell he went by said with his hands in a prayer position.

"Thanks for that," she replied, still floored that this guy was her formerly pragmatic, anti-yogi stepfather.

Lorraine folded her hands on the table. "Perhaps, I have

an opening after brunch. You'll have to check with my assistant."

Georgie's jaw dropped. "Another Nicolette?"

"No, her name is Colette. I'm moving on."

"Mom, what I have to say to you is bigger than brunch at the club," she replied as the room went silent.

"Bigger than brunch?" her mother repeated in horror as if anything could top brunch at the club.

"Yes."

Lorraine glanced at her watch. "Shouldn't you be at your baby shower?"

"I left it to come here."

Her mother gasped. "You didn't like it? Were the colors off? I specifically asked for spring green—not pale green. Now, I'll have to fire Colette. You have no idea the amount of effort it takes to manage an assistant."

"That was you?" Jordan asked. "You changed the theme?"

Her mother smoothed an already smooth lock of hair. "I know every party planner in the city. I couldn't let the news get out that my daughter had a headless doll-themed baby shower."

But it was more than that. She could see it in her mother's eyes.

The emotion the woman was working so hard to hide was love.

"The tablecloths had great energy. I could feel it when we picked them out," Howard added.

Georgie stared at her mother, who was trying to play it cool. She thought back to the picture the Gilberts had taped into the book. While her father had given her the gift of experiencing life through literature, her mother had given her the gift of rebellion—of saying my path isn't your path. The gift of knowing her choices were her own.

All those pageants had cemented who she wanted to be. Without them, her passion to own a bookshop may have never ignited.

The strange yin and yang push and pull that made her who she was today was, in part, thanks to her mother.

"Mom," she said gently. "We're here because I wanted to apologize. I should have told you about the baby."

"Well, pumpkin, you didn't, and that's that," she replied sharply, dabbing at the corners of her mouth with her napkin.

"No, there's more. I need to say this."

Her mother schooled her features. "Say what?"

Georgie held the woman's gaze. "I'm glad you're my mom."

That got her attention. Her mother stood, and not even the Botox could mask her shock.

"You are?"

"Yes," she answered, tears coming to her eyes. "Don't get me wrong, you can be a lot. But so can I. You see, I thought that if I didn't tell you about the pregnancy, it gave me control over the uncontrollable. But I was wrong. Life is a roller coaster—an adventure like in *The Tale of Peter Rabbit*. The Gilberts gave me that book and told me you used to read it to me when I was little."

A sentimental smile pulled at the corners of her mother's lips. "Your father hated that book. He'd say, 'what if she wants to be like Peter,' and I'd answer back, 'then we should let her.'"

Georgie took a step toward her mom. "You and dad gave me everything I needed to become who I am today. With the books dad left me, I created an imaginary world with my favorite literary characters."

"Lizzy, Jane, and that poor girl with the unfortunate name that starts with an *H*," her mother interjected as Hermione balked.

"You know her name," Georgie chided.

Lorraine sighed. "Yes, I do. It's Hermione. I'd hear you talking to them in your room."

"Do you want to know what you did for me, Mom?" Georgie asked.

"I'm not sure," her mother replied. "Do I?"

Georgie swallowed past the lump in her throat. "You helped me learn who I am—and who I want to be. All the pageants let me see that I wanted something that was mine and not yours. It gave strength to my convictions."

Her mother's twist of a grin was back. "A little rebellion goes a long way. But I do have to say..."

"Yes?"

"I'm still disappointed you weren't crowned Miss Cherry Pie. That sailor costume was perfect, and your tap skills were top-notch."

"They still are," Jordan said under his breath, biting back a dirty grin.

"You're practicing your tap, pumpkin? I'm so pleased!" Lorraine replied with a little clap.

Georgie shared a look with her very naughty husband.

"Something like that," she answered when her mother's expression grew pensive.

"I don't say this enough, but I'm proud of you, Georgiana. Even though I'd like for you to incorporate more designer pieces into your wardrobe—"

"Mom..." she warned.

"But you've made your way in the world, and you've done it on your own terms. I don't say this often because sentimental talk often leads to tears and tears lead to streaked mascara. But I love you very much," her mother finished, eyes shining.

Georgie leaned in, and mother and daughter embraced in an overdue hug. And despite her mother's mascara warning, tears trailed down the woman's cheeks.

The room exploded into applause, and she looked up at her husband. "We're making another scene, aren't we?"

"It wouldn't be us if we didn't," he replied, then gestured behind her.

She turned to find that everyone from the shower had come to the country club.

Barry, Becca, Brice, Denny, Maureen, Hector, Bobby, Marjory, Gene, and even the blue-haired knitting brigade had filed into the country club.

"You all came!" she exclaimed, emotion or another contraction welling in her belly.

"We had to see how it turned out," Gene said, giving her a hug and then turning to embrace her mother.

"Thank you for suggesting we give Georgie *The Tale of Peter Rabbit*," Marjory said to her mother.

Georgie's jaw nearly hit the floor. "You suggested it?"

Lorraine Vanderdinkle smoothed that same blond lock of hair that never required smoothing. "I can be sentimental from time to time, can't I, Howard?"

"She can, especially for the spa. It's her *Sankalpa*."

"The spa is your *Sankalpa*?" Bobby asked.

Her mother lifted her chin. "It would probably come out sooner or later, but yes, after my time spent enhancing my spiritual skills, my *Sankalpa* came to me in a dream."

"And," Hector pressed.

"My innermost desire is to spend the day in the lap of luxury, and that's when I knew."

"Knew what?" Jordan asked.

Her mother glanced over her shoulder at Howard, then leaned in. "That this psychic energist business was for the birds," she whispered as the group chuckled.

"But it wasn't just the spa, was it?" Howard asked with a knowing twist to his lips.

Her mother's expression softened. "I wasn't alone in my Sankalpa vision. In my dream, you were with me at the spa. I'd suggested you choose a pink polish for your manicure. But you dismissed my comment and chose a rose shade instead."

Georgie brushed a tear from her cheek. "That sounds like us."

Her mother chuckled. "It does indeed."

"I know what makes me happy. Thanks to you, Mom, I know how to fight for what I want," she said, her voice thick with emotion.

Her mother nodded. "You certainly do."

Despite the country club crowd hanging on every word of their brunch bonding session, a profound sense of certainty held them cocooned inside this moment where the connection between mother and daughter, no matter how strained, could never be broken.

"We're so glad to see you and Georgie getting along so well," Maureen said, popping the bubble and bringing them back from that place only mothers and daughters reside.

"We sure are," Denny agreed.

Georgie glanced around. They'd become a giant spectacle.

"Mom, do you think we should leave? I didn't mean to bring an entourage on my brunch crashing."

Teary-eyed, Lorraine shook her head, then waved over the country club manager. "Gustavo, we'll need the gazebo set up immediately. I've got an impromptu baby shower to host for my daughter—which is where it should have been to begin with, but..."

"Mom..." Georgie began, but her mother kept going.

"But...I'm grateful everyone's here now," she added, dropping the socialite pretenses.

Howard jumped up, whipped off his sport coat, and made little okay signs with his fingers.

"Should we chant?"

"No!" she and her mother replied at the same time.

"Georgie, could you look this way? This is great stuff!" Barry called, still rolling.

She turned to Jordan as her mother went about throwing together part two of the baby shower.

"Why didn't you say anything and let me know everyone was here?" she asked.

Jordan gave her that cocky pantie-melter of a grin. "And ruin the moment? Only an asshat would do that."

"Then, we're lucky that you're not just any asshat but the emperor of them all," she replied.

She started to push up onto her tiptoes, not an easy thing to do when carrying a watermelon in your belly, to press a kiss to his cheek. But just before she could pucker up, a splash of liquid hit the marble floor and stopped her mid-lift.

Jordan's eyes went wide as he held onto her forearms, keeping her upright.

The breath caught in her throat as another contraction hit.

They were coming faster now.

"Did someone spill a glass of water?" she asked on a tight exhale, once the pain subsided.

He shook his head, wide-eyed as his gaze bobbed between her face and the floor.

"No, that was all you," he replied, looking shell-shocked.

She stared at the liquid pooling on the pristine marble tiles.

"Messy bun girl," he said, his voice full of wonder.

She held his gaze. "Yeah?"

"Your water broke in the middle of brunch."

Chapter Twenty
Jordan

"The baby's coming! This is it, Georgie!"

His wife stared at him, looking as bewildered as he felt.

"What do you mean this is it? We have to have brunch first. We're going to have the shower here. Aren't we supposed to eat chocolate baby poop? And we haven't picked up any cookie dough, and we don't even have my hospital bag," she rambled, the moment hitting her like a ton of bricks.

"Eat what?" Lorraine exclaimed.

"Remember, Virginia, I ate all the candy bars," Brice called.

Two for four—poor bastard.

"Okay, so no chocolate baby poop," Georgie repeated. "But, what about my bag? We don't have it. And what about Mr. Tuesday? He's at the shop."

"I'll call the store and let Talya and Simon know that they're on dog duty. They'll make sure he's taken care of," Becca said, pulling out her cell.

"Mia and Mya are with them at the shop. Tell them to

take Mr. Tuesday to my house when they bring the girls home," Maureen added.

A flurry of activity buzzed around them as a life-altering event materialized before them.

He cupped Georgie's face in his hand. "See, we're all good."

"What about Faby? We didn't even make a plan for our fake baby."

"I'll take care of your fake baby," Brice called.

Georgie leaned forward as another contraction hit. "Can we trust him with Faby?" she bit out.

This was not the birth plan they'd been practicing, that was for damn sure!

"I think so." He handed the doll over. "Just don't pop Faby's head off."

Brice cradled the fake baby in his arms. "That's what Briana says to me when I babysit Ollie, and he's still in one piece."

Jordan nodded, not one hundred percent reassured, but it was better than nothing.

"We have to get to the hospital. Lorraine, can we take your car? The one we came in is out of gas," he called.

"You'll never make it," she answered with a Botox version of worry written all over her face.

"What do you mean? The hospital is only fifteen or twenty minutes away from here."

"If Georgiana is anything like me, my mother, my grandmother, my great-grandmother, my great-great-grandmother, or my great-great-great-grandmother, this baby will be here in minutes."

"Minutes?" he and Georgie echoed.

"Yes, the women on my side of the family have exceptionally short labor on account of our exceedingly flawless cervixes," Lorraine explained.

Dr. Beaver must have been serious when he'd complimented Georgie's lady parts.

"I can't believe it!" Georgie replied, then gripped his wrist as another contraction hit.

But he believed it. They had to act—and fast.

"Help Georgie over here, so she can lie down," his father called, removing the throw pillows from one of those fancy half-couch half-bed-looking things.

"Yes, let's get you to the chaise lounge," Lorraine agreed.

"So I can deliver a baby inside of a country club next to an ice sculpture?" Georgie threw back, glancing around wildly.

He rubbed between her shoulder blades. While there were worse places to deliver a child, he could certainly understand her trepidation. She wasn't wrong. How many women gave birth in the same room as an ice sculpture?

"It's that or the backseat of a Prius, pumpkin," her mother said gently but firmly.

Georgie cried out as another contraction hit. Without thinking, he lifted her into his arms and carried her over to the couch.

"Is this actually happening, or is it a pregnancy delusion? Please, say it's a delusion," she added, blowing out tight punctuated breaths.

"This is happening," he answered, resting her on the cushions.

She closed her eyes and squeezed his hand, going back to pregnant labor panting.

She gasped. "The contractions are coming fast. They feel like they're right on top of each other."

He was thinking the same thing. Unfortunately, he didn't know the first thing about delivering a baby. But he was the city's top trainer. He knew how to take control and get shit done.

He glanced up and assessed the scene.

"Hector, call for an ambulance. Let them know Georgie's gone into labor," he said, then barked out more orders, directing his friends and family to find towels, blankets, and even hot water because that's what they called for in all the historical romance movies Georgie loved to watch. And it didn't seem like a bad thing to have around. Hell, they had an ice sculpture. Why not a bucket of hot water, too?

"Another contraction's coming," she rasped, then released a piercing screech.

He turned to the brunch crowd. "My wife is in labor. We need a doctor. Can anyone help us until the ambulance gets here?"

Dozens of hands shot up.

"This is great," he said, sharing a look with Georgie's mom.

Lorraine shook her head. "No, most of them are plastic surgeons. Unless Georgie wants vaginal rejuvenation surgery, which is a great idea after the baby comes, these people will be of no help," she answered.

"I'm a psychiatrist," called a Freudian-looking guy.

Jordan hardened his features. "Nope, dude, I need somebody who knows what they're doing."

"I'm an obstetrician," came a familiar voice.

And then a familiar face.

"Dr. Beaver," Jordan exclaimed.

Georgie sat forward and took in the man, rocking tennis whites.

"Which Beaver are you? There are two of you. One of you is my baby doc—the other works on brains. I need the Beaver twin that knows my beaver!" she exclaimed.

Clearly, his wife had hit the part of the labor process where shit gets crazy, and she can say whatever the hell she wants without any threat of repercussions.

"I'm your Beaver, Georgie," Dr. Beaver said, dropping his tennis racquet and rushing over.

"The one who complimented my cervix?" Georgie pressed, then leaned forward and groaned as another contraction hit.

"You better be the right Beaver, man," he said, holding the guy's gaze.

"Yes, that's me! You're Joyce's favorite patient, Georgie. She talks about you all the time. I promise. I'm the right Beaver."

"I'm Joyce's favorite?" Georgie said, falling back onto the pillows in dreamy exhaustion.

"Jordan, can you believe it? Joyce likes us."

He couldn't believe it, but he honestly didn't give a damn either.

"What is all this Beaver talk?" his dad asked, looking downright mortified.

"I'm the Beaver. Chad Beaver," the doctor replied, flashing his toothpaste commercial smile.

"Georgie's lady doctor is named—"

"Dad!" he said, cutting him off. The Beaver talk needed to end.

"Let's go wait for the ambulance, hun," Maureen offered, taking his father's arm.

The pair headed for the entrance as Dr. Beaver moved to the end of the chaise lounge and got down on his knees.

"I'm going to check you, Georgie. Keep breathing."

Everything seemed to be moving a mile a minute—as if the universe hit the triple fast-forward button.

Lorraine draped a tablecloth over Georgie's lower half to give her a little privacy. Because, one, they were still smack-dab in the middle of brunch, and two, they'd garnered quite a crowd, and three, Barry was there, capturing footage.

You know, your run-of-the-mill birth for CityBeat's sweethearts.

"Gustavo assured me that the tablecloths were laundered this morning and are of the highest thread count," Lorraine said, adjusting the pristine linen.

"Got it. Clean sheet. High thread count," he replied, kneeling down to be eye to eye with his wife.

"Doctor, do you need anything?" Lorraine asked.

"No, my husband's gone to the car to get my medical bag. But this baby is coming, and it's coming fast."

Georgie's mom paced back-and-forth. "Can we give my daughter anything for the pain? This is a country club. It's crawling in valium."

Dr. Beaver shook his head. "That's not a safe choice for Georgie. She's having this baby the old-fashioned way."

"Jordan," his wife said, eyes wide with fear as she tightened her grip on his hand.

He rested his hand on her belly. "Hey, messy bun girl. You're doing great. Just think, we're about to meet our alien peanut pineapple surprise," he added, trying to make her smile.

"I don't know if I can do this," she said, her voice shaking.

Dr. Beaver looked up and held his wife's gaze. "The baby's head is right here. A few good pushes are all you'll need. I'll tell you when."

"Mom," Georgie said, glancing up at Lorraine.

The woman held up a pool towel. "You're doing a terrific job, pumpkin. I've got this gorgeous Hermes pool towel. The best quality towel available, and it'll be perfect for swaddling the baby. Oh, and Gustavo said your baby can be a member for life. This is the first country club birth. You're quite a trendsetter," she finished as Howard twisted his body into a pretzel shape and chanted a bunch of gibberish in a language he couldn't recognize.

Georgie turned to him. "I'm still not totally sure this is real."

"I promise you; it is. You can do this. I'm right here with you," he answered.

"What if something happens and the baby needs medical care? I can't imagine there's a neonatal unit, let alone a scale in this place," she blurted out, her nerves kicking in.

"We've got a scale!" Gustavo called, holding up one of those scales you see in the grocery store.

She glanced around. "How many people are watching me have a baby?"

He looked up. A shit ton of people—but he wasn't about to say that.

She needed a distraction.

"I want to show you something," he said, then pulled a small envelope from his pocket.

"What is it?"

"An addition to your bracelet."

She gave him the hint of a grin. "Let me guess. It's a pineapple."

"One of them is. The other is this," he replied and held out a delicate infinity charm. "Because we're more than just a number."

"Infinity isn't a number. It's a concept," she said, still able to take him to task, even in labor.

He hooked the charms onto the bracelet. "You're right. It's the quantity larger than any number, and that's how much I love you and how much I'm going to love this baby. Our baby."

He leaned in, and Georgie rested her forehead against his.

"Thank you for being my messy bun girl and for making me a better man. You're my whole life, Georgiana. You are the sassy eight to my asshat ten, and together, there's nothing we can't do."

"I needed that," she said, relaxing a fraction.

He listened as she took two deep breaths as if her body were preparing for the final push. As a trainer, he'd worked his body to the max and could sense Georgie's body responding as instinct and biology prepared to take over, ready for the endgame.

The all-or-nothing moment—where nothing wasn't an option.

He lifted her chin. "Look at me and focus on my voice."

She held his gaze.

"Today, when we walked to the shop, I couldn't stop thinking about you and our life."

"Goats and alpacas and spiders, oh my," she bit out through another contraction.

She was even funny in labor.

"I never dreamed of finding someone like you, Georgiana Jensen."

"That's because you were following your flawed Marks Perfect Ten Asshat Mindset," she replied on a tight breath.

He brushed a sweat-soaked lock of hair from her forehead. "All I know is that the minute you came into my life, I knew I would never be the same. Do you know how tough you are? Do you know what a hard-ass you were when we first met?"

"I was actually a nice person until I met you," she teased through tight breaths.

He gave her a cocky smirk. "I bring out the best in people."

She blew out a ragged breath. "Jordan, I'm scared."

He was, too. But, right now, it was his job to be her rock. He held her gaze. "You can do this, Georgie."

She shook her head. "I don't know if I can."

"You're the strongest person I know, MBG. And don't forget."

She blew out a breath. "Forget what?"

"There's nothing we can't conquer together—nothing we can't get through. Well, maybe not a virtual reality baby simulation. But besides that, we've got this. The baby, you, and me. We've got this."

Dr. Beaver patted Georgie's leg. "All right, Georgie, we're going to countdown from ten, and then I want you to give me a big push."

"Can we count from eight?" she asked.

"Um...sure. The number is arbitrary," the doctor replied, a little confused.

"It's not arbitrary to me and Jordan, is it?" she answered, turning to him.

He pressed a kiss to her temple. "Georgiana Jensen, owning the eights even while giving birth."

"Okay, here we go. Start counting. After this contraction, you're going to push," Dr. Beaver instructed.

Jordan held his wife's gaze.

Eight.

Seven.

Six.

Five.

Four.

Three.

Two.

One.

"Big push, Georgie!"

Georgie squeezed his hand, bearing down. He watched his wife in utter amazement as the image of a little girl flashed in his mind. Bubbling with sunshine, skinned knees, and a *read-one-more-chapter-daddy* smile, this mini Georgie gazed up at him with blue-green eyes.

He blinked, then focused on his wife as she gritted her teeth.

Dr. Beaver glanced up. "Keep going, Georgie. The head's out. One more push, and you'll get to meet your baby."

Georgie fell back, breathless. "Next time, we're doing this at a hospital, and I'm getting all the drugs."

He brushed a lock of hair from her cheek. "Deal—all the drugs. But you can do this, babe. Think of it as the final mile of a 5K where we get to meet our little girl at the finish line."

She stared at him. "You think it's a girl?"

He nodded with tears in his eyes, overcome with emotion. "I do."

"Now, Georgie! This is it. Push!" the doctor called.

He held his wife's hand as the fast-forward mode switched to slow-mo.

People clambered around them as he caught a flurry of movement in his peripheral vision. He could hear the wheels of the stretcher coming. But all that was white noise —a blurry background bringing this moment with Georgie into sharp focus when the piercing cries of a baby cut through the air, and tears streamed down his cheeks.

"It's a girl. A healthy baby girl."

Jordan glanced down and saw two EMTs crouched beside the doctor and couldn't even remember when they'd arrived. All he saw was his wife—his strong, beautiful, warrior of a wife.

"Can I hold her?" Georgie asked.

Dr. Beaver looked up and waved him over. "After Dad cuts the cord."

Jordan glanced over his shoulder and found his teary-eyed father.

"Not me, son. The doc means you."

The weight of who he would be to this tiny person sank in.

Daddy. Dad. Father.

He kissed the crown of Georgie's head, then joined the doctor and the EMTs.

Partially wrapped in a designer country club pool towel, his daughter stared up at him with her mother's blue-green eyes. And for the second time in a year, love at first sight struck again.

Now he was the one blowing out a nervous breath as the doctor instructed him on how to cut the umbilical cord.

And with a snip and a few quick movements by the doctor, the EMT swaddled his baby and placed her in his arms. This tiny, beautiful baby was their daughter.

Carefully, he brought the baby to Georgie.

"You're going to be smart and sassy like your mom, aren't you, Lizzy?" he said softly.

"Lizzy, like my Lizzy Bennet?" Georgie asked with a sweet, weary smile.

"It suits her," he said, running his knuckle over the baby's cheek.

"Lizzy Lorraine?" Georgie asked, glancing up at her mother.

He wrapped his arms around his wife and child. "Welcome to the world, Lizzy Lorraine, we can't wait to watch you grow."

"Can we get a quick weight?" an EMT asked, swooping in.

The woman took the baby and set her on Gustavo's scale.

"Eight pounds and ten ounces."

"Eight pounds, ten ounces," Georgie repeated, wonder coating the words as the EMT passed the baby back to them.

He gazed down at his daughter. "With numbers like that, Lizzy Lorraine, the sky's the limit."

Epilogue: Part One
Georgie

"Good morning, messy bun girl," came the voice that made Georgiana Jensen-Marks' toes curl.

Georgie arched into the wall of hard muscle pressing against her back.

"Hey, yourself," she said, then gasped when she reached for her husband and found him wearing...

Chaps.

Sweet dirty cowboy!

"Remember these?" he purred, sliding up her night-gown before trailing his warm hand between her thighs.

She sucked in a titillating breath and instantly grew hot and wet.

"Oh, yes! The naughty rancher's daughter remembers. Where did you find them?"

"I was up early with the baby and found them in a box when I was looking for my jump rope."

"I need to thank that jump rope," she replied, then released a low moan.

He kissed the back of her neck. "I'm surprised they fit."

She wasn't. The man looked as good today as he did the

first time she saw her Emperor of Asshattery run past her bookshop.

Georgie hummed her pleasure as her husband's hard length rubbed against her ass. The smooth slide of the leather chaps against the back of her legs sent sparks through her body.

"Are you kidding?" she said, turning to face him.

She ran her fingers down his ripped abdomen and licked a trail to where the chaps revealed her husband's perfect hard length.

She'd never tell him, but yeah, he definitely had the Marks Perfect Ten cock.

She wrapped her lips around him and took in every inch.

"Georgiana," he growled as his fingers tangled in her hair.

Her body ached to have him inside of her, pumping and filling her to the hilt. But he'd gone to such lengths to brighten her morning with a chaps-wearing surprise that the naughty rancher's daughter felt compelled to show her cowboy a little dirty girl love.

His grip tightened as deep, dirty moans emanated from her fitness god. She increased her pace, taking him faster while grazing her teeth on his velvety smooth cock, using just the right amount of bite to bring her cowboy to the edge. He bucked his hips and twisted his hand in her hair. The delicious pull on her scalp sent tingles to her most sensitive place.

She might get off just listening to her husband.

He pumped, once then twice before pulling her back. His rock-hard cock stood at attention. This man was not done yet.

Not even close.

She licked her lips. "Why'd you have me stop?"

He met her gaze as his eyes positively devoured her. "We don't want this to end yet, do we?"

"We don't?" she replied, playing coy.

He gave her a cocky grin, and God help her, she still couldn't resist it.

"Doesn't the naughty rancher's daughter want a ride?" he said, his grin growing positively carnal.

If she were wearing panties, they would have melted off her body.

They had taken the dirty talk role-play to the next level —which took steadfast dedication and was no small accomplishment for busy parents.

She ran her hands up his powerful, leather-clad legs and inhaled her husband's earthy, sensual scent. He gripped her waist and sat up to take her tight nipple into his mouth as the tip of his cock teased her entrance.

"I'm ready for my riding lesson," she purred, her lips parting as Jordan licked and caressed her breasts.

"How do you want it, cowgirl?" he growled like a rough and ready ranch hand.

She rocked into him. "This naughty rancher's daughter wants it hard and fast."

"Jesus, Georgiana," he bit out, thrusting his cock inside of her.

The searing connection between them hadn't dampened. Each time his hard length entered her body, the sweet sting of him filling her completely made her bite her lip as she reveled in wanton pleasure.

He rolled his hips as she rode his cock. Arching her back, she ran her fingers through her sex hair as he gripped her ass—his strong hands guiding her up and down in heated strokes. Their bodies grew slick with sweat as she rode him, true to her word, hard and fast. The slap of skin, coupled with the sweet grind of his pelvis against her tight bundle of nerves, had this naughty cowgirl teetering on the edge of oblivion before you could shout yeehaw.

"Georgiana, you're so damned beautiful," he said, his voice low and husky and exactly what she needed to hear to let go.

She collapsed into him. Her world shrank into one tiny ball of light before exploding into a spray of heated, frenzied energy as they met their earth-shattering orgasm. Their lips crashed together as he swallowed her lusty cries. Her greedy body writhed with his, drawing out every ounce of gratification.

"You should keep the chaps in the bedroom," she said on a winded breath.

"You were the one who said they were never going back to the costume store."

She maneuvered her body off of his, and they turned to face each other, lying side by side. She traced her finger down his jawline and stared at his handsome face, unable to imagine a life without this man. Together—and often with the world watching—they'd crafted a life that was uniquely theirs.

The eight and the ten who became more than just a number.

"Look at all the things I've been right about," she teased, reaching down to see if her randy ranch hand was up for round two when the door to the bedroom swung open.

"Look, Mommy! Daddy's dressed like a cowboy who lost his underwear!"

Epilogue: Part Two
Jordan

"**C**owboy Daddy! Mommy! Come quick! You have to see what Janey did!"

Jordan pulled the bed covers up to his chin and plastered on an *oh-shit* grin.

No parenting manual teaches about the *oh-shit* grin. This is the face you make when your kid busts in on you while doing the naughty, and you try to appear as *unnaughty* as possible—which is harder than you'd think, especially in assless chaps with your dick hanging out.

"What is it, Lizzy? Is everybody okay?" He glanced at the clock. It was barely eight in the morning on a Saturday, but that didn't mean anything to kids.

His precocious six-year-old daughter cocked her head to the side, looking like an exasperated version of her mother.

Yep, Elizabeth Lorraine Marks, who'd come into the world on a chaise lounge at the Denver country club, was six years old.

Another whopper?

He'd become a girl dad—three beautiful times over.

"Lizzy, sweetheart, give Daddy and me a minute, and

335

we'll be right there," Georgie said, modifying her *oh-shit* grin to the slightly nuanced, *I-may-look-like-I'm-composed-but-I'm-in-bed-with-a-man-wearing-assless-chaps* face.

Another thing they don't teach in VR simulations.

Lizzy pursed her lips. "You better hurry. They're in Mimi's room, and Janey's got the markers out."

He frowned. Oh, shit—his real *oh-shit* face.

He shared a look with his wife, who was rocking some amazing sex hair—something he'd love to mess up, even more, but...kids.

"Wrap the sheet around your body. You don't have time to take the chaps off!" Georgie cried, springing from the bed and throwing on her robe.

Why didn't he wear a robe?

A question for another time when his four-year-old daughter wasn't armed with a Sharpie. He took his wife's advice, yanked the sheet off the bed, and wrapped it around his body like a toga-wearing cowboy. It would have to do.

After Janey, named after Jane Eyre, was born, they'd outgrown the bungalow and had moved to a larger home in the same neighborhood. Now, all three girls had their own room—which they destroyed daily...or hourly. It was a crapshoot.

He followed Georgie out of their room, and Mr. Tuesday met them in the hall. With a touch of gray around his nose, he'd become the keeper of the girls, completely devoted to their happiness.

But something was different.

"Is Mr. Tuesday wearing lipstick?" Georgie asked.

"It's marker makeup, Mommy," Lizzy called with her head peeking out of Mimi's room.

He shared a look with his wife, and they bolted down the hall, then skidded to a stop.

"Whatever we find in there, there's got to be some substance that can clean it or paint over it," he said, more to himself than to his wife.

Georgie sighed. "Okay. We tackle this on three."

"One," he began.

"Two," she said with a chuckle.

"Three!"

They entered the bedroom, prepared for complete Sharpie devastation, only to find the cream-colored walls marker-free.

"Hi, Daddy! I'm a pretty, pretty princess, and so is Mimi," Janey, his flirt, said, marker in hand and flashing a fire engine red smile with one of Georgie's old pageant crowns sitting cockeyed on her head.

"Okay, we can wash that off, I think," Georgie said, kneeling to get a better look at the four-year-old's face.

His gaze went to the crib where, at thirteen months, Hermione or Mimi, who'd gotten the nickname because Janey couldn't quite pronounce the vowel-laden moniker, stood in her crib with her back to them and Faby in her arms.

Good old Faby was still with them and had turned out to be their ticket to winning the Battle of the Births. The Hail Mary he'd been hoping for actually happened. It turned out that they were the only couple that kept their infant simulation doll with them night and day. Thanks to Faby's high-tech tracking abilities, which had since been turned off, they'd learned that the other participants only took the poor fake baby out of its bag for the challenges. And boom! Their attentive care of that sweet hunk of plastic had put them over the top and made them the winners.

He took a step forward and focused on the doll.

"Mimi, is Faby wearing lipstick?" he asked, and then it happened.

Mimi, the beefcake baby after his own heart with energy for days, did a one-eighty jump—an advanced skill she'd picked up in the baby NFL.

Yep, that's right! The baby NFL.

Georgie might have nixed the toddler trombone lessons, but she'd caved on the NFL classes, which weren't much more than music and movement activities. Still, he already saw his Hermione rocking those ninja courses. She gravitated toward the tractor tire in his gym and could fart like a grown man.

A tomboy in the making until...

"Holy, circus act! Janey, what did you do to Mimi's face?"

Looking like a tiny drunk clown, Mimi stomped around her crib, dragging poor Faby like a caveman.

"She's a pretty, pretty princess for the pictures, too!" his daughter replied as pleased as punch.

"Pictures?" he repeated.

Georgie gasped. "Everyone is coming early this morning for that CityBeat photo shoot. You know, the one with everyone who's been with us from the beginning. I told the girls about it last night!"

That's the other thing. Besides bringing their own trifecta into the world, they'd managed to become a worldwide brand, endorsing items from toys to gym equipment to books. They blogged for CityBeat, CityBeat Rattle, and were frequent guest bloggers on the Belgian Waffle Princess's page.

Today, their closest friends and family were scheduled to come over for a group photo shoot. Hector and Bobby had the idea of doing an origin piece on them. And, of course, because that was their life, it just happened to be the day when two of his three daughters looked as if they were ready to run off with the circus.

Not to mention, with the outfit he was sporting, he looked ready to join an X-rated rodeo.

He shook his head and stared at the ceiling.

As if on cue, the doorbell rang, and then the door opened.

"Knock, knock! It's Grandma Lorraine and Grandpa River, and we've got Uncle Gene and Aunt Marjory with us."

Georgie glanced at the clock. "My mom and Wandering River are here with the Gilberts, and they're early!"

Yep, Howard had kept the moniker and the spiritual yogi vibe, which didn't bother Lorraine all that much. In fact, she'd even dropped a few pegs on the mega socialite meter. So, all that great sex she'd mentioned—not that he ever wanted to imagine his in-laws doing the dirty—must have paid off.

"Girls, Uncle Hector, Uncle Bobby, and Uncle Barry are here, too, and we have presents."

"Who all is coming?" he asked his wife, then licked his finger and rubbed it on Mimi's face, trying to remove the marker.

"Daddy, that's gross!" Lizzy said, completely aghast.

"You're right! Why did I do that?" he answered, staring at his finger covered in spit and red marker.

"It must be a parenting instinct," Georgie said, kneeling next to Janey and staring down at her spit-covered red fingertip.

"Son? Georgie?" called his dad, which meant Maureen, Mia, and Mya had arrived.

The doorbell rang, and one of the bajillion people who'd let themselves into their home answered it.

"Talya! Simon! Look at you, two! We were thrilled to get the invitation to your wedding! Come in!" Maureen exclaimed.

Yep, the epic duo was still epically in love.

Jordan held his wife's gaze. "How many people are in the house?"

Georgie stared at her fingers, then started to answer when Becca called up to them.

"Hey, blogosphere superstar family! Come say, hello. The party is starting without you."

"And I saw a few spiders in your yard, so we should talk about spraying," Brice added.

"I think Becca and Brice make fourteen?" Georgie said, giving up on her fingers when the doorbell rang again, followed by footsteps charging up the stairs.

Irene and Will's son, Nathaniel, peeked in the room, saw the girls, then ran away screaming.

Jordan clapped his hands. "Getting the old band together. Good times!"

Georgie shook her head. "Just look at us."

His gaze slid from his oldest daughter to his beautiful marked-up babies to his best friend, his business partner, and the love of his life.

"Is this where you thought you'd be when the first pink lines appeared?" Georgie teased, her blue-green eyes twinkling.

He plucked Mimi from her crib and sat down on the floor next to his wife. Mr. Tuesday nuzzled in next to him, and he scratched the old boy's head as Lizzy and Janey joined them. Together, they listened to the chatter and laughter of the people they loved the most float up from downstairs.

He took Georgie's hand and pressed a kiss to her knuckles. "Georgiana Jensen-Marks, my messy bun girl, not in a million years could I have imagined a life as perfect as this."

"It's eight ten, Marks family! The photographer will be here in five minutes!" Lorraine called from the bottom of the stairs.

He held Georgie's gaze and knew they were thinking the same thing.

"It appears this family is about to own the eights yet again," she said, flashing him the same smile he'd fallen in love with back when he was an asshat of a ten, and she was his perfect eight.

The Inside Scoop

When I was finishing up writing the Bergen Brothers Series, I went for a long run. The song "The Winner Is" from the movie *Little Miss Sunshine* came on. It's a jaunty, charming little tune, and instantly, two characters popped into my head: a gal who shunned all things perfect and a guy whose life revolved around the pursuit of perfection

Now, throw in a contest that pits these two against each other while also forcing them to work together—and boom! There's going to be some conflict—and some sexytimes.

It's a romance novel, for Pete's sake. Of course, there's going to be some heat!

I mentioned this couple to my cover designer, Marisa-rose Wesley, owner of Cover Me Darling. She came back to me with the first cover. It was absolutely perfect. It embodied the sexy whimsy I was aiming for, and the series was born.

In Own the Eights Maybe Baby, I was able to pull from my experiences with my two pregnancies and the experiences and stories my friends shared.

When I went into labor with my youngest son, the

doctor on-call from the practice just happened to be the one doctor I'd never met.

The man had a beard, so he came in looking more like an astronaut than an obstetrician with this crazy head covering. And, by the time he arrived, I'd realized that the epidural didn't work. My first baby was a nine-pounds giant, that, thankfully, I was able to deliver with an epidural. My youngest was estimated to be even bigger— and I wasn't about to be a hero with the second.

Well, an epidural that didn't work plus an astronaut sauntering in to deliver my baby threw me over the edge.

I yelled at everyone in the room and told them there was no way in hell that I was delivering this baby without pain medication.

My husband will tell you that I used more colorful language.

Here's the thing, when a baby is coming, the baby is coming. My son was ready to meet the world, and that's what happened less than ten minutes later.

In the Own the Eights Series, I pulled from these life events then added a rom-com twist.

I'm going to miss these two.

I hope you enjoyed Georgie and Jordan's journey.

Books by Krista Sandor

The Starrycard Creek Bachelors Series

A small town rom-com series set in the mountains

Book One: The Business Card Boyfriend

Book Two: The Birthday Card Boyfriend

Book Three: The Baseball Card Boyfriend

The Nanny Love Match Series

A nanny/boss romantic comedy series

Book One: The Nanny and the Nerd

Book Two: The Nanny and the Hothead

Book Three: The Nanny and the Beefcake

Book Four: The Nanny and the Heartthrob

Love Match Legacy Books

Nanny Love Match Series Spin-off Books

Mistletoe Love Match

The Sebastian Guarantee

The Oscar Escape

The Bergen Brothers Series

A steamy billionaire brothers romantic comedy series

Book One: Man Fast

Book Two: Man Feast

Book Three: Man Find

Bergen Brothers: The Complete Series+Bonus Short Story

The Farm to Mabel Duet

A brother's best friend romance set in a small-town

Book One: Farm to Mabel

Book Two: Horn of Plenty

Farm to Mabel: The Complete Duet

The Langley Park Series

A suspenseful, sexy second-chance at love series

Book One: The Road Home

Book Two: The Sound of Home

Book Three: The Beginning of Home

Book Four: The Measure of Home

Book Five: The Story of Home

Box Set (Books 1-5 + Bonus Scene)

Own the Eights Series

A delightfully sexy enemies-to-lovers series

Book One: Own the Eights

Book Two: Own the Eights Gets Married

Book Three: Own the Eights Maybe Baby

Box Set (Books 1-3)

STANDALONES

The Kiss Keeper

A toe-curlingly hot opposites attract romance

Not Your Average Vixen

An enemies-to-lovers super-steamy holiday romance

Sign up for Krista's newsletter to get all the up-to-date Krista Sandor romance news!

Learn more at www.KristaSandor.com

Acknowledgments

Writing the last book in a series always makes me think back to the beginning. My editing masterminds Tera and Marla have been with me since the Langley Park Series. I'm beyond grateful to have these talented women in my life.

The romance community has become my home. I couldn't imagine a day that didn't include interacting with readers, authors, and bloggers. The support in this group is awe-inspiring.

And to my husband. David, you have always been in my corner. No matter how crazy the idea, you were right there cheering me on.

About the Author

 If there's one thing Krista Sandor knows for sure, it's that romance saved her sanity. After she was diagnosed with Multiple Sclerosis in 2015, her world turned upside down. During those difficult first days, her dear friend sent her a romance novel. That kind gesture provided the escape she needed and ignited her love of the genre. Inspired by strong heroines and happily ever afters, Krista decided to write her own romance series. Today, she is an MS warrior, living life to the fullest. When she's not writing, you can find her running 5Ks with her husband and chasing after their growing boys in Denver, Colorado.

Never miss a release, contest, or author event! Visit Krista's website and sign up to receive her monthly update.

www.ingramcontent.com/pod-product-compliance
Lightning Source LLC
Chambersburg PA
CBHW020242200626
46816CB00001BA/95